THE STAGE WAS SET

In the silence Jeb reached out and, before she could wonder what he might do, drew her into the warm fold of his embrace, his beautiful gray eyes shadowed, his beautiful mouth grim.

Susannah stared at him, certain she'd never experienced a more powerful, or baffling, moment. He pushed both his hands into her hair and lowered his mouth to hers. She felt her limbs weaken, something she'd thought only happened in stories. She'd gotten more than she bargained for. In front of two thousand people, in the glare of the lone spotlight, he kissed her.

———

By Leigh Riker

Morning Rain
Unforgettable
Tears of Jade
Just One of Those Things
Oh, Susannah

Available from
HarperPaperbacks

OH,
SUSANNAH

Leigh Riker

HarperPaperbacks
A Division of HarperCollinsPublishers

HarperPaperbacks *A Division of* HarperCollins*Publishers*
10 East 53rd Street, New York, N.Y. 10022

Cover illustration by Jeff Cornell

First printing: January 1995

Printed in the United States of America

HarperPaperbacks, HarperMonogram, and colophon are trademarks of HarperCollins*Publishers*

❖ 10 9 8 7 6 5 4 3 2 1

With friendship and thanks
to Karen O'Keefe
for finding that perfect house,
then pointing out that I now
live near the heart of country music
and "wouldn't it be fun to write about?"
It certainly was.

And with love for my sons,
Scott, a devoted music listener,
and Hal, who plays a mean drum,
for my brother Gary, another country fan,
and my brothers-in-law, Muns and Wayne,
both fine musicians.

1

Help him.

The two-word message had been left on her answering machine three days ago. Susannah had ignored it then, though she guessed immediately to whom it referred, just as she recognized the caller's unusually breathy tone. If she'd only known what that tone had meant. . . .

Now it was too late. She couldn't bring Clary back.

And she couldn't get the message out of her mind.

Turning away from the projection television in her father's den, she shut out the disturbing image on its screen, which she also wanted to avoid. Hugging herself, she stared through the long windows that looked onto the vast side lawn of the Greenwich, Connecticut, estate; stared at the snow, which fell faster, harder, with each passing moment.

Susannah, who spent most of her time in California and seldom saw snow, welcomed the worsening weather even more for the distraction it provided. From the television she heard a song kick in, its tempo upbeat, "a foot stomper," Clary would have said, its lyrics—rendered in a husky, intimate baritone—about a simple man with a complicated marriage, bent upon retrieving his wife. Susannah might have snickered, not being a country music fan and certainly not a fan of the singer's, but she felt emotionally numb.

A week ago Clary, her closest friend, had been alive.

Susannah lightly touched the underside of her left breast through her black wool dress, but the habitual gesture didn't comfort. She wished her father would turn off the television and let silence, like the falling snow outside the windows, settle over the dimly lit room. He wouldn't, she knew. Drake Whittaker wanted to watch the image on the screen, to blame it for Clary's death.

Resigned, she faced the screen again and the news update in progress. Considering the circumstances, the scrap of song, a cheerful sound byte, struck her as particularly offensive. Like the singer himself.

Jeb Stuart Cody.

She took a harsh breath. On the immense screen he appeared nearly life-size: slightly over six feet tall, she knew from Clary, with dark hair, which Susannah assessed now for herself, too long and caught back at the nape of his neck, and arresting gray eyes the color of the pearly light outside the windows. He had a sensual mouth and a broad-shouldered, lean-hipped, long-legged body that women screamed for at his concerts. In the clip being shown he wore a biceps-revealing T-shirt littered with sayings that, except for the bigger word *Kentucky* were impossible to read, and a pair of tight jeans with ragged but strategic cutouts that showed a hint of knee and thigh. As a silver hoop flashed in one ear, Susannah fought a wave of disgust.

"I can never believe that he and Clary were related," her father murmured from a corner of the hunter green and burgundy print sofa, his legs crossed, a filtered cigarette dangling from one long-boned hand.

Susannah didn't want to talk about Clary's oh-so-public brother.

She leaned over the sofa from behind, taking Drake Whittaker's lit cigarette. "I can never believe you're still smoking." She stubbed it out in a Limoges ashtray. "After the government warnings, and your being a—"

"We surgeons can fix anything. Cut and staple." It was his standard answer, and untrue, but she let it pass. "Besides," he said, "there's no history in our family."

"You're pushing your luck."

"So are you." He looked back over his shoulder without a smile. His hair shone silver under the overhead light like the hoop in Jeb Stuart Cody's left ear. "I just remembered all over again why I divorced your mother."

Susannah let that pass too. Earlier that day they'd buried Clary—his second, and much younger wife—and she supposed he needed his illusions. But then, so did she. Needing to be safe from the horror of the past three days, the loss, and her own sense of helplessness, she wound her arms around his neck.

As she knew he would, he ducked away, pointing toward the television as the concert clip snapped in mid-phrase, and Jeb Stuart Cody appeared in close-up outside his New York hotel.

"Look at that. It's not enough the station showed a concert clip with that disgusting honky-tonk ballad—he has to give an interview, business as usual . . ."

Drake trailed off and Susannah stayed behind the sofa, hands at her sides, her throat working. Only last week, by phone, Clary had seemed so excited about her latest project, a biography of her famous brother, and the press conference to announce it. Susannah didn't normally allow herself to cry, and she hadn't thought she had any tears left, but—Oh, Clary . . .

His dark hair sprinkled with snowflakes, the man onscreen looked unfazed by tragedy, almost blasé. Fans shouted in the background, and one poked a hand into camera range as Cody—Clary's name for him—spoke briefly about his sister, a flat-toned few sentences that to Susannah's astonishment merely segued back into his money-making world. Responding to the reporter's question, Cody said that the coming concert at the convention center had been standing room only since the first half hour tickets went on sale.

The woman shoved the microphone closer. "The National Weather Service tells us an advisory has gone into effect, that people should stay off the roads. Do you expect anyone to come?"

"Some will, even if they shouldn't." His intense gaze met the camera eye. His faint drawl could have melted the snow. "But whoever comes, I won't disappoint those good people, even if, as I hear tell, this may be the worst blizzard of the century. If y'all can walk to the center, then come on down."

Susannah couldn't take any more. She fumbled for the remote control on the sofa cushion, aimed it at the screen, and the set crackled into blessed silence.

"I can't believe he ever cared about Clary." She clenched her hands into fists. "Three days, without a word from him."

"What would you expect?"

"More," she said. "Much more."

Cody's brother and four of his remaining five sisters had all come to Greenwich. The fifth was in a hospital where she'd just delivered a baby, and she had sent flowers. Only Cody had stayed away.

Even in Susannah's own family, in which people rarely said, "I love you," or hugged each other, no matter how at thirty-one she still craved that, no one would have ignored death. Even her mother had attended the funeral that morning, if not the reception afterward, and had managed to convey her condolences without quarreling with Drake, her ex-husband.

That was the least Susannah had expected, or yearned for. Glancing down, she noticed the stack of newspapers at Drake's side, the maudlin, screaming headlines:

Prominent Surgeon's Wife Killed By Gunman
Central Park Tragedy Ends Socialite's Life
Police Search for Mugger Continues
Jeb Stuart Cody Mourns Loss of "Kid Sister"

Publicity even there, Susannah thought. "Kid Sister" was the top-selling single from Cody's first album. His only album thus far, and, she fervently hoped, his last.

"He's trash," Drake said, following her gaze to the papers. "A flash in the pan."

"So the critics say." Her voice dropped low. "But Clary loved him."

Why? she wondered. What kind of man turned his back on his own flesh and blood? Despite their long-time rift, there had once been love between Clary and her brother. Susannah had heard the stories in endless late-night talks. Of course she'd also heard the bad side. Now Clary was gone, leaving a hollow ache inside her.

Why not in Clary's brother?

Susannah was an only child, which she'd rued all her

life. Clary had been her college roommate, her closest friend . . . her surrogate sister.

With a last brush of her hand over her father's well-styled silvery hair, she walked to the window again. Snow swirled in thick, gusting sheets like laundry flapping on a line. It covered the lawns and hedges and the now barren, spring-flowering azaleas and rhododendrons; it hung like tinsel garlands from tree branches; it carpeted the garden sidewalks and the side veranda of the sprawling white brick mansion. Soon even its dark green shutters would turn white. Darkness would fall and the late March air would be still, soundless, like Clary's grave.

Give a concert, would he? With smoke and mirrors and noise? The twang of guitars and the roar of applause? Fans spilling from their seats and rushing the stage, women prostrate with ecstasy at his voice, their arms outstretched, tossing flowers and bras?

Like hell, Susannah thought.

She turned from the window, for the first time noticing the overpowering scents of roses, daffodils, chrysanthemums, freesias—and other, more typical bouquets. Studded with cards of condolence, they adorned every surface in the house, mingling with the smells of furniture polish and smoke.

"Where are you going?" Drake held the folded program from that morning's service with the white lily on the cover.

"To another funeral."

"Susannah—"

"I didn't mean to sound flippant. But I'll have his explanation—tonight."

She stalked out into the hall, her black heels clicking on the marble tiles. The funeral, his lack of caring was one thing. Her own conviction that Clary's death had been anything but accidental was another. About that, it had seemed, she could do little. The police said only that the investigation remained open; that they were still following clues. She could track down Jeb Stuart Cody herself, though. Thanks to the dubious miracle of television, she even knew where he was staying.

He didn't need her help; but Clary needed his.

"Susannah." Drake had followed her into the hall.

She kept going, up the stairs to her room. She'd need warmer clothes. Thank God she was no longer the child she'd once been, coming home to an empty house, or even worse.

"He owes us," she said over her shoulder. "He owes her."

She'd heard too many stories about Clary's family and believed in her brothers and sisters, in parents sticking together though she'd tried to stop believing in her own, in Drake and Leslie.

"Come back here, Susannah."

"I'm going. You can't stop me."

"How well I know," he said. "That willful streak—"

"I've had to be." She'd been looking out for herself all her life.

"All right, then." As if giving permission, he stood at the foot of the stairs. "I'll call the garage. I don't want you driving yourself in this storm, and the limo will make better time to New York."

"The trains must be running. The car can drop me at the station in Greenwich."

At his Manhattan hotel off Central Park, Jeb Stuart Cody sprawled in a low-slung chair, his hands laced across his stomach, his eyes closed. In both ears state-of-the-art headphones played a Brahms cello sonata, among Jeb's favorite music when he wasn't working. At the moment he was trying to shut out his thoughts—and a world he normally chased after when it didn't come to him.

He didn't hear the bedroom door open—one of the suite's six bedrooms along the nearby hallway, didn't open his eyes until the music abruptly stopped. Then he looked up at the woman who stood by the stereo controls, at her long sweep of white-blond hair, the familiar deepset dark blue eyes, the voluptuous body in a scarlet satin blouse and black satin pants.

"Breeze, you know better than to interrupt Yo-Yo Ma."

She surveyed him from loosened tie to dark pants. Her soft drawl matched his. "You have a sound check at the convention center. The streets are a mess. The buses stopped running half an hour ago by executive order from the mayor's office. If the limo's going to get through, you'd better shower and start moving."

"It damn well better get through."

"We could give rain checks." His manager forced a smile, her full lips painted red. "Your schedule's open a few days in May. If the center agrees, we could come back then."

Jeb yanked the headphones from his ears. "I'm giving my show. Tonight." Coming to his feet, he pushed past her. "If there's only one teenage girl in that audience, who saved her baby-sitting money for months to buy a ticket, she's gonna hear me sing."

Her smile faltered. "Jeb, maybe you shouldn't. Maybe—"

"What?" He turned on her. Seeing the brightness in her eyes, the insight, he wanted to smash something. "Did you watch the news? That clip they've been showing? The reporter who nailed me outside the hotel—thank you very much for running interference?"

"Yes."

"What did you see? What did you hear?"

She hesitated, not normally cowed by anyone's moods, even Jeb's rare ones, usually knowing what they covered. But she'd never seen this one. Breeze Maynard hadn't been around the last time. She didn't know Clary. Thirteen years ago she'd been riding high herself, the queen of country music. She walked closer.

"They . . . showed the Phoenix concert. Showed you singing 'Lou'siana Lady.'"

"Right," he said.

"I thought it was tasteless. I told the network so."

"You know damn well they picked it on purpose."

"But today, because of Clary? Jeb—"

"Clary's death is old news already. You know that too. So I said what I had to say on the air. They want hooting and hollering, they want to hear the voice breaks on that song. They want applause." He lowered his tone. "They want ratings."

"Jeb."

He turned his back. "That's what everybody wants. That's what they're gonna get."

He strode from the suite's immense living room, snapping off the elaborate stereo that filled most of one wall on his way past, and down the long hall to the end bedroom. It wasn't the largest, but it felt more comfortable to him. More like home, as if he had a home these days. By the end of his first national tour in July he would have worked two hundred forty concert dates in a year, and he'd given up even his apartment rental in Nashville before it began.

"I think we should cancel," Breeze said, which at any

other time would have amazed him. If anything, she had more regard for his career than his agents or the promoters—hell, more than he did.

She dogged his steps, past her bedroom and then the one his grandfather had used for a few days. Jeb missed him already. It was hard enough convincing an old country doctor to leave his dwindling practice now and then, to follow his favorite grandson on tour, especially to the big cities, but . . .

"I feel the need to go home," John Eustace had said earlier, only minutes after the small service he and Jeb had held for Clary, and minutes after that, as Jeb might have predicted, his grandfather had been on the way to the airport.

He'd left him with the usual memories of watery blue eyes and a shock of white hair that would put Kentucky's Colonel Sanders to shame and of the hard look when he said the word "home."

"I can't go back, PawPaw," Jeb always told him. "Maybe someday but not now."

"It's a circus here, boy. Not the real world."

But it was the only world Jeb had now, and he meant to give it everything. He reached his room but didn't close the door before Breeze stepped inside with him. She pulled him slowly around.

"Jeb."

"I'm gonna do this, Maynard."

She held his gaze. Breeze was six years older than Jeb and had been one of his idols, singing her heart out for the fans who adored her. She'd given her last press conference just weeks after most of her band, guys she'd played with for years, had been killed in the crash of their tour bus on a highway going home to Nashville.

"Sometimes," she said, "you have to stay off that stage and let yourself heal."

"I got nothing to heal."

Jeb clenched his jaw as Breeze touched his cheek, tracing the small scar on his upper lip with one finger. She'd quit the business. Quit it cold. She hadn't been on a stage since, except in her capacity as his manager and mentor, and the world, he knew, because she still got tons of letters, missed the sweetness of Breeze Maynard, her voice and her songs. And Breeze herself.

"Big tough cowboy," she said. "You ought to be a Hat Act like Strait or Brooks."

Ordinarily he might have smiled. Like the other new, young country superstars, he preferred traditional music, but he hadn't bought himself a big Stetson yet.

"I'll do it my way," Jeb told her. "I'll do it better."

He steered her from his room, avoiding Breeze's blue gaze, and after shutting the door flopped down on his bed across the Indian star-patterned quilt he carried with him on the road. He stared at the ceiling until the swirls of white plaster blurred into shapes, and he remembered that, long ago, he and Clary had lain on their backs in the grass near the creek, finding dragons and castles and—on Jeb's part—guitars in the clouds.

Years ago, he thought. Before he lost her. The first time.

Now the only thing that mattered was his music.

Breeze couldn't understand that, but Jeb Stuart Cody wouldn't make the same mistake. He reached across the wide, empty bed and picked up his guitar.

Susannah shifted from one foot to the other, eyeing the floor indicator as the elegant Central Park South hotel's private elevator glided upward. Holding her one suitcase, she shivered, not only from the bone-chilling cold. On the train from Greenwich she'd had plenty of time to remember Clary's harsh words about her brother. He'd married young, but his wife had been even younger, "hardly old enough for *that*," Clary had said, and Susannah's fertile imagination easily supplied the rest. Clary and Cody had grown up in poverty, in a large, backwoods family. He might have been eager to escape in the most obvious fashion. As the train had plowed along the snowy track toward New York, she envisioned his early courtship, the careless breeding—the term that leapt to mind—with a girl who might have been no older than thirteen. Wasn't that common practice in the hills? And that wasn't the worst of it.

Susannah's skin felt even colder, and she tried to push away the memory of Clary's bad stories about her unfeeling brother. She didn't have to recall the details. The bare facts fueled her existing anger.

The train had been delayed an hour en route while the tracks were cleared of snow, and then of course she hadn't seen a single roving taxicab on Forty-second Street, Vanderbilt, or Madison. It was as if they had melted like sugar cubes in the continuing hard snowfall. If she'd been in a different frame of mind, Susannah would have enjoyed the city's slowed pace, its deserted, fairy-tale quality, but she had Jeb Stuart Cody on the brain. And giving him a piece of that mind. Six, seven, eight . . . she watched the numbers rise. Lucky for her that she'd been able to breach hotel security.

Luck? She was a Whittaker. Before she'd started kindergarten—at the most exclusive private school Greenwich had to offer—the duties and rights of privilege had been drilled into her. Her mother's doing, at the time Leslie's chief role in life. Susannah had learned her lessons well, not that she liked them. But a dash of bravado could stiffen her spine, and an unnaturally haughty tone could work wonders. That, and a bit of charm, had gotten her past the waiting crush of Jeb Stuart Cody's fans at the hotel entrance, straight into the manager's office.

Susannah knew the man. Several years ago she and her mother had cochaired a Christmas debutante cotillion at the hotel, and he remembered her, too. She'd easily convinced him that, as a relative of Clary's by marriage, she had every right to pay her respects to Cody without an appointment.

She glared at the floor display. Twenty-eight,-nine, thirty. The manager himself had ushered her into the private elevator, bypassing its security and standing guard as the gleaming mahogany doors closed her in. So why was her heart racing, her mouth dry?

She stamped a booted foot.

It didn't hurry things but restored some circulation to her frozen toes. After standing in the snow-heaped street for nearly a quarter hour, she'd commandeered a ride from some passing motorist near Grand Central. She'd been grateful but couldn't make herself understood. The driver didn't speak English, and the rusted black sedan, years past its prime and smelling of some unfamiliar spice, its heater not working, had creaked and rattled its way uptown. Her fingers still felt stiff and cold.

Or was that nerves? Not many people knew how thin her haughty veneer could be. She'd see Cody, then hop the first plane to the coast, back to San Francisco and the house she loved, her favorite charities, the man she was expected to marry. Back to her safe, predictable life.

The car stopped at the penthouse floor, and the elevator doors slid open, onto the beige-and-gold foyer of a large suite.

A blond woman in royal blue satin appeared on Susannah's left, in the middle of a long hallway, then strode toward her, dark blue eyes rimmed in kohl blazing. She looked familiar in a vague way that Susannah couldn't place.

"How did you get up here?" She reached for a phone on an ebony hallway stand. "What do you want?"

"I need to see Cody." Susannah set her suitcase down. She'd never met Cody, but Clary's name for him didn't feel strange on her tongue. She hadn't wanted to meet him . . . until today. "My name is Susannah Whittaker."

Before the name registered, another door opened at the end of the hall.

A man started toward them, his walk slow and easy-rolling, athletic, as she imagined a rodeo rider might walk. Susannah didn't need the introduction. Even if she hadn't seen him on television, she would have recognized him from Clary's description and the photograph of a much younger Jeb Stuart Cody that had always graced her nightstand.

She expected to see a three-day stubble of beard. The silver earring. Tattered blue jeans. A charming, aw-shucks smile as he shuffled his feet, looking at his shoes.

Jeb Stuart Cody didn't shuffle. He ambled down the hall, wearing a crisp white dress shirt that looked soft and sleek, handsewn in Susannah's practiced opinion, two buttons open at his throat; a gray-and-black tie, obviously silk, loosely knotted below the shirt's opening; a black suit, custom-fitted to every impressive plane and angle, every discreet muscle of the long, lean body that inspired his fans to make fools of themselves.

"Oh." Stopping a foot from her, he flicked a disinterested glance over her, then looked away. "Susannah."

The blond stepped between them. "She came up in the elevator. No one called. I'll get Security—"

"No, let her come in."

He walked left into the suite's cavernous living room, leaving her to follow if she would. The woman in blue satin obviously thought better of joining them. With a disapproving look at Susannah, she marched back down the hall, hips swaying.

Susannah went into the room.

"My manager." He waved his hand in the direction the woman had disappeared. "Do you mind takin' off your boots?" He nodded at the thick taupe carpet under her feet. "A lot of bands, rock and country, trash these hotel suites and I'm not sure the hotel even minds, 'cause they get to redecorate on a regular basis—but I mind. My mama always made me leave my shoes at the door and right now this is my house."

Susannah made a small sound, whether of agreement or objection she couldn't have said. He stood at the windows, his back to her, his hair shorter, without the ponytail she'd seen before. She'd anticipated a country-boy twang to his speech but heard only a soft drawl that unnerved her even more, like a small shock, as if she'd stuck a curious finger, which she'd done once, into an empty socket in a string of Christmas tree lights.

She tugged off her knee-high boots and wiggled her icy toes. Then she padded across the wide room to the windows that overlooked Central Park and Fifth Avenue. She could barely hear the hum of traffic from below, muted by glass and snow.

"You recognized me," she said.

He turned, giving her that slow, careless once-over that made the room seem suddenly too hot. From the naturally curly, untameable chin-length hair that was the bane of Susannah's grooming life, to her hazel eyes, spaced too far apart, she'd always thought, to her mouth with its cupid's bow upper lip, its bee-stung lower one. An embarrassing mouth at which men always stared. But before he'd completed the appraisal, his gaze shuttered. "Sure, I recognized you."

His lowered lashes hid his eyes, but she could feel him looking further at her open, down-filled trench coat, showing its fox fur lining, her ivory wool suit, which she'd layered for more warmth with a black turtleneck cashmere sweater under a cinnamon-colored V-neck. His gaze wandered to her usually slim but now nonexistent waist, her well-padded hips. The heavy clothes seemed to add ten pounds. When his gaze dropped to Susannah's dark brown tights and saffron leg warmers, she felt like a stuffed sausage in front of a man who was watching his fat and cholesterol.

"I thought you were thinner," he said. "Clary sent me pictures from school once."

"I've changed."

His gaze lifted, fixing on her mouth. "Not that much."

"Mr. Cody—"

He turned away, looking out again, not at the traffic, but up at the sky, dark now but lightened to silvery gray by the reflected glow of city lights, and thick and cottony with falling snow. "What do you want from me?"

"I came about Clary."

"It's late for that, isn't it?"

"It's late for your apology too, but I'd like to have it." She drew herself up, making the most of her five feet seven inches without shoes. "Neither my father nor I heard a word from you, you weren't at the funeral this morning—"

"I held my own memorial service." He spun around, his gaze intense. "A private one. Right here in this room. My grandfather, a few friends, my manager. Do you have any idea what kind of sideshow there would have been if I had shown up in Greenwich? At your daddy's fancy estate? At the Episcopal church? Or the gravesite?"

"No," she admitted.

"Well, let me tell you. More than one night—or rather, morning—my granddaddy has opened his door at three o'clock to a barrage of press cameras. He's seventy-eight years old, and not in the best health. Every time it happens he nearly has a coronary. If he hadn't been with me when my sister . . . when we got the news, there'd have been press camped on his doorstep again. Now I realize Drake's younger than my grandfather is—by a few years," he added dryly, raising an eyebrow, "but would you have him deal with all those reporters, with flashes and microphones? At a time like this?"

"No," she said. "I hadn't thought of that."

"If you lived the public life I'm livin' right now, and the people close to me, it would be the first thing you thought about." Then he said, "What about Clary?"

He said it blandly, as if they'd never shared any closeness.

Susannah studied an arrangement of low, taupe sofas and chairs, one of several seating groups strewn with black, cinnamon, and off-white pillows in the huge room, then at the filmy white wool draperies. And nearly smiled. Her clothes all but matched the room's colors, as if she belonged there, in his world. Nothing could have been farther from reality.

"You might have called, Cody." Using Clary's name

for him, she touched his forearm. "You could have at least left a message, as other people did, people with less connection to my father, to her."

"And what good would that have done?"

The words rendered her speechless.

"What did you want, Miss Susannah?" he drawled. "A bunch of flowers on a stand, with an 'All my abiding love, your brother Jeb' card sticking out for everyone to read as they passed by the coffin? That's not my way. It wasn't Clary's either—which shows how well you really knew her."

"She wanted you in her life again."

He freed his arm. "Is that why she held a press conference with some publisher a few days before she died, and announced she was writing my biography?" He shook his head. "Maybe she wanted peace between us, maybe not. We'll never know, will we?"

"I'm wasting my time."

She took two steps before he stopped her. Susannah wished she'd left her boots on. He seemed to loom over her, but she'd been right in one expectation. The silver earring winked in the light.

"Hell, did you want her to marry Drake? You got more than you bargained for when you showed her the rich life, didn't you?"

"Clary was bright, she needed more than some small Kentucky town. She said she felt stifled there."

"Stifled? She never knew the word until she went away to school and met you."

"Is that what bothers you? Or that she fell in love with my father? I watched it happen. I learned to live with that. So why couldn't you?"

"Clary may have liked what you and Drake gave her," he said. "But we have a saying in the hills back home. She got above her raisin'."

Susannah didn't flinch. They stood closer still and she saw that he had a hairline scar on his upper lip, a flaw that humanized his male perfection. His gray eyes looked darker than she'd first thought; his hair not merely brown but layered with rich chestnut and tawny gold, the kind of layering women like her, as he might have said, paid hundreds for in a good salon. She didn't like him but couldn't deny his appeal. And she didn't think his words, his reasoning, rang true.

"What about you? Jeb Stuart Cody with his hottest-selling first album, his half-dozen hit singles, and his brand-new Grammy? What about your 'raisin'?' Or doesn't it count when you're a man from Elvira, Kentucky, with women throwing their panties at you onstage?"

She saw the twitch of his lips before he flattened them.

"They only throw clean ones."

"Oh, you are disgusting!" She shoved past him, returning to the windows that overlooked the darkened park. "Your sister died not two blocks from here. How can you even stand at these windows and look out toward those trees, that path, and that park bench and not do anything to help find her killer."

"They're not going to find her killer." He joined Susannah at the windows. "She was mugged, plain and simple. Not pretty, not right, but she's gone."

"She was murdered!"

"Premeditated?" He frowned. "Now if we were settin' on my granddaddy's porch in Elvira, and Clary had turned up in a ditch somewhere I'd give that theory credence. I'd think maybe someone she knew put that gun to her chest. But we're here"—he looked through the dark glass—"in New York City where people get mugged every day, and some of 'em get killed in the process."

"I don't believe that."

"Whether you do or not, nothing will help Clary now." He rubbed the back of his neck, then murmured almost too softly for Susannah to hear: "'Lay her i' the earth/And from her fair and unpolluted flesh/May violets spring . . .'"

"Shakespeare?"

"*Hamlet.* I haven't seen my sister in thirteen years. Not since I was seventeen years old. That's a lot of living gone by. You think I turned my back on her, abandoned her then? I guess that's what Clary would say. It's a matter of opinion." His voice hardened. "I'd say it was quite the reverse—she betrayed me. How, is none of your business. When she tried to pretty things up with letters from school, pictures of her friend, I didn't answer back, as I'm sure you know. My choice. So if there's anything to be done now, I'd suggest you talk to your father."

"He's tried. He's not a celebrity, not in the same way you are." She'd always hated that Drake's work kept him from her, that neurosurgical patients around the country, however needy, could demand his presence. Now she could find it easy to hate Jeb Stuart Cody—by orders of magnitude.

"There's nothing I can do," he said, sounding weary. "That's what I was tryin' to tell you with that quote."

"You could pressure the police. Hire private detectives. You could hold a press conference and tell the media you think she was murdered."

"Next thing, you'll be saying I'm the killer."

Shock ran through her. She hadn't thought anything of the kind. Seeing him shake his head, she threw up both hands. "I should have known you wouldn't take me seriously. I should have trusted my instincts about you."

"Maybe you should." He watched her cross the room,

watched her pull on one dripping boot. "But where I come from, we get to know a person before we pass judgment."

"I did that years ago. I know you from Clary." The bad stories, she thought; remember those. He'd married young, made an even younger girl pregnant. Something had happened to his wife and newborn child. Shuddering at the memory, Susannah tugged on her other boot. He'd buried them in the backyard, Clary said. No surprise.

When she hefted her suitcase and headed for the door, he lifted his gaze, as dark as unpolished pewter, and she saw not the alternately charming, brooding sex symbol of his album cover and magazine photographs, not Clary's callous brother. But a man for whom Susannah could think only one word: *bewildered*.

"Goin' somewhere?" he said.

"To find a cab—"

"In this blizzard?"

"Then to find the answers myself. You stay right here in your flashy little world, Cody, and write another hit song to record—which I assure you, I won't buy."

"I'll bet you've never heard one of my songs."

Surprised again, she stood frozen in the entryway of the spacious suite, in the hotel whose lobby couldn't contain the fans who had waited hours, hoping for a glimpse of him.

"No," she admitted, "except snatches, on television or radio."

"Then, city girl, it's time you did."

He came toward her. He plunked her suitcase down, took Susannah's arm, ignoring her soggy boots, and hauled her after him down the hall to the bedroom at the end. He flung the door wide, gesturing her inside.

The same taupe carpet cushioned the floor, and the walls were painted the same off-white. The oak dressers were similar to the living room's stereo equipment shelving. But an ivory quilt, worked in a beautiful Indian star pattern of burnt orange and black and taupe, covered the king-size bed. On top lay an abandoned acoustic guitar.

"Whether you or some of the critics look down your nose at me, my music is who I am. Every song I write, I try to go one better than the last. But you have a point: I'm not having much luck tonight." A knock sounded at the door just before it opened. "What is it, Breeze?"

"The limo's here." She glanced at Susannah, then at his black suit. "You'll have to change at the convention center. I'm sorry, Miss Whittaker, but—"

"She's comin' with us."

Susannah stared at him.

"Listen," he said, "then judge me for yourself."

"Jeb, I don't think—" Breeze began.

"Then don't think, sugar." He looked more intently at Susannah, who tried not to notice the heat racing along her nerve ends. "Are you goin', or what?"

"I'm coming," she said as much to irritate his manager, who clearly didn't like her, as to satisfy her own curiosity, not only about his work but about him.

Susannah still couldn't believe a man could blithely give a concert on such a night. And she didn't mean the blizzard.

2

Breeze Maynard hated snow. She was a country girl from a small farm town in Alabama, and until she'd come north for her first concert date at twenty-one, she'd rarely seen snow.

In the rear seat of the limousine she gazed out at the swirling white clouds all around, at the snarled traffic. If she closed her eyes, though, she didn't hear the blaring horns, the shouted curses that penetrated the car's heavy frame and bullet-proof glass. She heard the soft bawling of cattle in the pasture near her childhood home, the sigh of wind through the willow trees that swept the ground, the gentle sound of her mother's voice, singing her to sleep.

Breeze wasn't escaping just the snow. When they entered the limo at the hotel, she'd tried to take the center of the wide rear seat, but Jeb had gestured her over to the far window, letting Susannah sit in the middle. Breeze hadn't missed the look in Jeb's eyes the

instant he saw Susannah. He'd quickly masked his feelings, as he often did, but Breeze wasn't blind. And if he
tried to lecture *her* again about her own love life, she
wouldn't miss the opportunity to speak her mind.

The only reason she hadn't done so already was
because of Clary. Jeb was holding himself together too
tightly, and she only hoped his control lasted until after
the concert. If it lasted longer than that, she'd tell him
that Susannah Whittaker couldn't be more wrong for
him, even as a one-night stand.

Breeze stared openly at her. Slim hands encased in tis-
sue-weight brown leather gloves folded in her lap. That
trench coat lined in fur. The expensive suit and cashmere
sweaters. The surprisingly casual blond, I've-just-run-
my-hands-through-my hair style. The color, she decided,
didn't come from a bottle. Her classically boned face
made Breeze think of Michelle Pfeiffer, but Jeb's obvious attraction to her couldn't be more than physical, the
appeal of the exotic to a boy from the Kentucky hills.

The attraction wouldn't last. Like the snow, it would
blow and drift then melt away. Jeb never lingered long,
even if the heat was mutual—which, in Susannah
Whittaker's case, Breeze sensed it wasn't.

Susannah hadn't looked at him once since climbing—
gracefully—into the car. Her assessment of him at the
hotel, while Breeze looked on, had been as heated as
Jeb's, but more the heat of anger. Susannah Whittaker
didn't like Jeb, and like most men he didn't take sexual
rejection well.

With any luck, the Yankee princess would evaporate
after the concert. If she didn't . . .

Jeb had been spoiling for a fight for weeks, long
before Clary's death drove him inside himself, in fact as
soon as Breeze started seeing Mack Norton, and after so

many years together she knew how to give Jeb what he wanted. So she was screwing his guitarist/band leader? If he had no right to criticize her current relationship, she had no right to judge Susannah Whittaker. Which wouldn't stop either of them.

She smiled slightly. Early in his career and at the end of hers, she and Jeb had been lovers for a time. They knew how to draw blood. She settled back in her seat and resumed staring at the falling snow. With a shiver for the frigid temperature outside, a last comforting thought of home and willow trees, and a final glance at Susannah, she told herself spilled blood wouldn't prove necessary.

Susannah had been riding in limousines for most of her life, though she still wasn't certain she should be riding in this one. She'd expected Jeb Stuart Cody's limousine to be as white as the swirling blizzard that coated the windows, coming down so fast now that the wipers barely cleared it. She'd imagined a gaudy interior. Instead, she sat stiffly on the gray rear seat of the black stretch Mercedes with her suitcase stowed in its trunk, appearing to contemplate the plush carpeting, the built-in stereo/television unit that softly played a guitar piece by Carlos Montoya, the shiny burled walnut bar from which Jeb had taken a small bottle of sparkling water and a few squares of dill bread topped with brie.

She eased an inch to her left. Jeb hadn't actually touched her, but his very presence beside her made her head swim. When he moved again, as he'd done in counterpoint to each of her own moves during the downtown drive, his arm brushed hers, and her body grew warm.

Susannah didn't have much experience with men like Jeb Stuart Cody. In fact, her on-again, off-again relationship in San Francisco involved little touching and not much heat. When she sat next to Michael Alsop, she didn't feel in imminent danger of burning her skin against his overcoat sleeve. Even when they shared a bed, she couldn't term the experience more than pleasant.

Her whole life lately seemed to be only that . . . pleasant.

It consisted of her volunteer charity work, her golf and tennis lessons, lunches with other society friends, occasional dates with Michael—when his work permitted—or dinners with her mother, who was still "trying to find herself." The sixties term drove Susannah crazy and the litany of her own interests sounded drab.

She looked at Breeze Maynard in her blue satin blouse and short, tight skirt, her knee-high navy-and-silver cowboy boots. Her blue-and-silver cape couldn't possibly keep out the cold, but Breeze didn't seem to care about comfort. She was sitting on her own long blond hair, which Susannah had noted came to just under her rear, cupping it in a provocative way.

Jeb's apparent fondness for classical guitar music came as another surprise. The choice hadn't been Breeze's; she'd wrinkled her nose at the album's first piece and turned away to the window. Now she was humming a standard country ballad that even Susannah recognized as one of Breeze's own.

It had taken Susannah some time to realize why she looked familiar. Other than the face and the name, she knew little except that the once-famous singer no longer sang, at least not in public. In a rich contralto Breeze negotiated a complex bridge between the verse and the song's chorus, and Jeb leaned forward to look past Susannah.

"Cut it out, Maynard."

"You know I can't stand flamenco."

"Too bad."

The limo skated around a last corner and into the parking garage at the convention center. The streets nearby looked as empty as a country club's first golf tee at cocktail time, making Susannah smile as she wondered how she'd survive two hours of a country music concert. Maybe no one would come tonight to hear the illustrious Jeb Stuart Cody sing and play guitar. Maybe he thought so too, because he tensed beside her.

"Our boy always gets nervous before a show," Breeze announced, pulling a walkie-talkie from her bag. "Sometimes he gets sick backstage."

"Once. In Washington, D.C.," he told Susannah, his gray eyes cool on Breeze. "Before I sang for the president. I'll bet you did, too, Maynard. Puke, I mean."

"Charming," Susannah murmured.

The limo stopped at an underground entrance, and Jeb opened the door before the chauffeur came around. Breeze stepped out on the other side, the walkie-talkie already in hand. "Feeling queasy?"

"No, you've been bitching about the sound check. And I'm running late."

The five-minute ride from the hotel had taken nearly an hour.

"Come on," he said, helping Susannah from the car.

Inside he marched her into an elevator to the concert arena where a group of technicians coiled cables and tested lights, where another group of five men in blue jeans and T-shirts fussed with musical equipment, tuning up guitars, blaring amplifiers, pounding keyboards, thumping drums. Among themselves, they laughed and called insults.

"My band," Jeb said, then disappeared.

From the wings Susannah watched the activity. Banks of lights were also being tested one by one, but she could barely see the empty seats in the still-darkened arena beyond the footlights that ringed the stage. At its center front a silver microphone waited. At the rear of the stage a huge backdrop showed a sequence of Jeb's face in close-ups, his upper lip beaded with sweat, his eyes bright, his hair wet from the effort of some previous concert.

The sound check didn't take long. Jeb made sure the mike worked properly, then stormed through a few bars of an upbeat song, the one she'd heard on television earlier and been repelled by, then a few more bars of a mellow ballad, his tone soft and sultry, enough to curl toes—if she'd been susceptible.

Jamming the mike back onto its stand, he nodded at some technician she couldn't see for the lights, then came into the wings and took her by the hand.

"Jeb." The sound man and Breeze spoke at once.

"No more time." He didn't miss a stride despite Susannah's resistance.

Breeze raised her voice. "Get back here. Those levels aren't—"

"You work it out." He grinned at Susannah. "Let's get dressed."

His dressing room on the lower level didn't impress her any more than his brief singing, which had been simply that, without any of the histrionics for which he was known in concert. And the room wasn't really his. He hadn't picked the thick white carpet or the comfortable peach sofa and chair. He hadn't stocked the makeup table with dozens of bottles and spray cans, with hair dryers and curling irons. Or chosen the knock-off

Impressionist-style prints framed in copper on the beige grass-cloth walls. She wondered whether he'd hung the poster of himself, though—bare-chested and glistening, his muscles obviously pumped.

Jeb followed her gaze. "Management's idea of making me feel at home." He draped his suit coat over the makeup chair. "Sure wish I had time to exercise and shower." He motioned for her to sit. "But we're gonna open at eight o'clock if I have to stalk on that stage buck naked."

Susannah sat on the peach-colored sofa. Her face felt hot.

"What if no one shows up?"

He smiled, rummaging in a drawer of the wall-length dressing table. "Then Breeze and I go head-to-head a few rounds and I give back all that ticket money."

"Assuming you win."

"I always do," he said, holding a thick terrycloth towel. "I'm payin' her salary."

"And why is that?" She averted her head when he stripped off his shirt and reached for the zipper at his fly.

"Hell if I know."

Susannah blinked. He'd changed from the cool, indifferent man she'd first seen at the hotel to the good ol' boy his fans must expect. When she looked again, he had his shoes off, his pants undone. She saw a swathe of bare abdomen, an arrow of dark silky-looking hair before she glanced away.

"Even you must read the headlines on the scandal sheets," he said. "But to refresh your memory—considering that country music celebrities can't be your favorite topic and that maybe you don't stand in line to buy your own groceries—Breeze was at the top of all

the charts, at a point when real country was mostly out
of favor, when her band got killed. All of 'em at once."
He frowned. "Some drunk with no idea where the center line might be, drivin' a semi with bad brakes."

"How terrible." She hadn't remembered the story.

"It was a tragedy all right." He headed barefoot for
the door to an adjoining room. "She was the best damn
female singer in the business, a damn fine songwriter
too. But as much as I hate what happened to those boys
of hers, I hate even more that she gave up."

"You seem like a persuasive man. Maybe you could
lure her back again."

"I've tried. You heard the only singing she does these
days. That's another tragedy." Jeb opened the door to a
cream-and-peach marble bathroom, the towel slung
around his bare neck. It drew Susannah's unwilling
attention to that now-covered but vulnerable spot
between his neatly trimmed hairline and his impressive
shoulders. "You'll be relieved to know my mama raised a
polite southern boy." He ducked into the bathroom,
then gave her a wink around the corner of the doorframe. "I'll do my changin' in private, not to offend your
rich-girl sensibilities"—he paused—"or to turn your
cheeks the color of the prize watermelons in my granddaddy's garden."

"I never blush," but the door closed on the words.

When it opened minutes later, Susannah blinked
again.

Not the man in black, not the good ol' boy, but Something Else stood there. Jeb Stuart Cody himself. She
tried not to look, then couldn't help herself and immediately wished she hadn't.

In tan cowboy boots, tight jeans, and a blue chambray
shirt unbuttoned halfway to his navel, he both drew and

offended Susannah. This, finally, was what she'd expected: an earthy, physical, virile slap in the face to Clarice Cody Whittaker. The hoop in his left ear—a gold one this time—caught the light like another wink at Susannah from the bathroom doorway.

"Your sister is barely cold," she said, rising to her feet. "I thought I could overlook your insensitivity to her long enough to find out what all the fuss is about—long enough to see for myself how a man like you could get up on a stage tonight and desecrate her memory. But I can't."

She walked toward the door.

Jeb caught her, turning her around, the lazy smile and the warmth in his eyes gone. They looked the color of lead, and just as deadly.

"You're here and you'll stay."

"Don't manhandle me."

He steered her into the hall. "You'll hear me," he said. "And you'll sure as hellfire find out what the damn fuss is all about."

Streamers and sparklers, like arching showers of fire, rained down from the ceiling. Smoke rose, billowing from the floor in dense, colored clouds: red, white, and smoky blue. Spotlights played over and under, giving the stage an even more unreal aura, as if to herald the arrival of some otherworldly prince. A prince of darkness, of desire.

From her front row seat, still feeling like a prisoner chained there, Susannah watched the spectacle. She heard slow, deep drumbeats next, joined by the haunting clarity of a guitar. But the stage remained empty.

A fresh shower of sparks dripped onto its wooden

boards, skittering, dancing. A new cloud gently enveloped the stage like segments of a huge parachute, puffed up from nowhere, and the footlights died for a moment. A hush settled first over the audience, then a lone spotlight penetrated the pillowed cloud and the chant went up: "Jeb, Jeb, Jeb."

No more than two thousand people of the twenty-some thousand who had purchased tickets had shown up for the concert, but they made the most of what they had. Their voices lifted, echoing his name. Susannah held her breath. The white spot turned rose, then blue, a harsh, electric, drilling blue. The five-piece band exploded like a rocket of sound. Jeb Stuart Cody appeared out of the blue mist onstage, as if conjured up by Merlin himself, and the crowd went wild.

Susannah's heartbeat skipped, then picked up speed and she could feel the drumbeat in her pulse, the sound of stamping feet vibrating through her skin.

The lights changed, sweeping over Jeb's enormous image on the multipaneled backdrop, then shifted again, turning from blue to natural, a pinpoint spot homing in first on his legs, covered by mist to the knees, then up his long, well-built frame to those shoulders, and at last, to his face.

He was grinning as he picked up the song's beat, tapping one foot. From nowhere it seemed, from the darkness offstage, a guitar came flying through the air, its rich wood and metal accents striking fire as it reached the range of light. Jeb caught it neatly, holding it aloft, and the crowd cheered.

"How y'all doin'?" he called out, and two thousand voices answered.

"We're doin' fine!"

"All right, then," Jeb said, and launched into the first

verse of a song called "Country Justice." His rich baritone soared and dipped, capturing his audience. He invited those who knew the lyrics to join in, and within seconds those two thousand voices threatened to bring the roof down. Outrageous, she thought, as the din assaulted her ears and increased her heartbeat even more. Sacrilege. Pure selfishness and greed. And yet, despite her own resentment of Jeb Stuart Cody's performance so soon after his sister's death, she had to fight the urge not to sing along herself.

When the song ended and the roar of applause died away, Jeb waited a beat. The lights mellowed again and the last wisps of smoke faded, leaving him alone on the clean stage, his band shadowed in the background. He plucked the microphone from its stand and holding it close let his voice drop low, into the subtler, sultrier sound of a love ballad.

A far cry, she thought, from her usual classical concert or ballet.

By the end of the second song, Susannah had nearly forgotten her resentment. In a spellbinding sequence, Jeb went from the ballad into a playful rhyme song perfectly suited to children, then shifted into high again for "Huntsville Prison," a protest song about fair treatment, then crooned again through two verses and the chorus of "Mama's Songs."

It was Jeb's most recent hit single, she learned, blowing the tops off all the charts. At the end of two hours he stood, visibly breathing, dripping wet. Applause reverberated through the arena. Roses pelted the stage, and women rushed forward, throwing their underwear.

"What do you want?" he asked the audience, which demanded an encore.

"'Country Justice.'"

"Not again?" He made a face, and even Susannah smiled.

"'Country Justice!'"

"I feel a lynchin' mood in the air." He snapped the mike back onto its stand. "So all right."

Wild cheers. Whistles and shouts.

"Jeb, Jeb!"

Varicolored lights played randomly among the audience, swung in dizzying arcs over the stage, and homed in on the strings of Jeb's gleaming acoustic guitar.

This time Susannah knew the words. She wanted to keep her bottom solidly on the seat, her hands in her lap. She wanted to think about going back to San Francisco and never seeing Jeb Stuart Cody again. But she shot to her feet with the rest of them, applauding, singing, forcing Jeb into a repeat of the last chorus, her heart wildly pounding in exhilaration.

She felt as close to hysteria as the teenage girl next to her, who was jumping up and down, tears running down her cheeks, a look of adoration on her face.

"Isn't he wonderful?" she asked Susannah.

"For two hours, he is."

The screams continued, and Jeb held up a hand for silence. Waiting for the crowd to quiet, he wiped an arm across his forehead. "Come on now. Settle down." He was smiling, but more softly, without the exuberance she had seen for much of the night.

As if sensing his change of mood, the crowd quieted. Jeb looked out over the darkened arena, and Susannah imagined him looking straight at her.

"Y'all know that my sister died the other day," he said, as if Clary had gone to the corner store for a loaf of bread. "This is a song I wrote for her a few years back. I thought you might like to hear it tonight."

The stage went dark except for the lone spot, gentled by some gauzy filter, and the world seemed black and white, just the one light and Jeb's dark clothes, his boots.

"Kid Sister," a tender ballad, spoke of love and regret, ending with the words, "Kid sister, I should have taken better care of you."

With the last, sweet chords from the guitar Jeb bowed his head.

When he lifted it again, he acknowledged the rainlike splatter of restrained applause. "Thanks. That's always been a favorite of mine."

"Amen," someone called softly.

Jeb's smile lifted only one corner of his mouth. "I see we have some good Baptists in the audience tonight. When my sister Clary and I were just kids in the hills of Kentucky, our mama sang in the church choir on Sundays. She had the purest, most beautiful voice—and I thank her for giving me some small part of that." He gazed out over the arena. "All week long Clary and I might raise hell, but on Sunday mornings we sat on those hard church pews and didn't move a muscle while Mama sang."

He seemed to look at Susannah again. Then at his signal, the lights softened even more, giving the big arena an almost reverent air, and he stood in the hazy white light at the front edge of the stage, alone.

"This was Clary's favorite then," he murmured. "I think it still might be."

And without accompaniment, without even the sweet strains of his guitar, he sang "Amazing Grace," his voice breaking perfectly on the notes.

When the final, pure notes died away in the resounding silence, leaving her with gooseflesh all over, Susannah didn't think there was a dry eye in the house. She gazed up at Jeb, alone onstage. So alone. Then he spoke.

"In the audience tonight is Clary's closest friend. Come up here, Susannah, and remember her for us in your own way."

She sat for a moment, feeling the curious gaze of the audience as the spotlight hit her, before she rose and made her way on shaky legs to the stage. Jeb helped her up the last steps and to the microphone.

When she spoke, shrieks of sound radiated into the darkness.

"Feedback," he whispered, clamping a hand over the mike. "Hold it down a little, not so close."

Her heart pounded. Susannah had given speeches before, at ladies' luncheons, to the Junior League, to the alumni associations of her various schools, but she hated it. She'd been the kind of girl who hid behind her desk, praying to be last for oral book reports. Wishing her mother or father could be there—just once—to see her win the school spelling bee.

She cleared her throat.

"I met Clary when we were both eighteen, our first day at college. By the luck of the draw, we had gotten the same room—and would share it for the next four years." Susannah felt her nerves begin to ease. She took a firmer grip on the microphone, the faint scent of Jeb rising from it. "We came from very different backgrounds, but we shared a very special friendship."

He made a sound, and she turned slightly toward him.

"I know she loved her brother, too." She held his gaze. "I admired Clary's loving spirit, her brilliant mind, her loyalties . . . and, yes, her amazing grace. She was a wonderful girl. She became a truly wonderful woman." Her gaze told Jeb she was sorry he'd missed seeing that. "I'm glad I knew her and—and I'll miss her. Always. God bless you, Clary."

Susannah handed the mike to Jeb, whose hand felt as warm and damp as hers. He put the microphone on its stand in silence. No one clapped. No one shouted.

It was no way, she sensed, to end a concert, not even tonight. But Jeb didn't play to the moment, didn't raise an arm to signal his band for an upbeat number, and he didn't move. He simply stood, watching Susannah, his gaze blurred with the tears he had suppressed all evening. She saw that now. He wasn't as cold, as unfeeling as she'd thought. As Clary had implied.

In the silence Jeb reached out and, before she could wonder what he might do, drew her into the warm fold of his embrace, his beautiful gray eyes shadowed, his beautiful mouth grim.

Susannah stared at him, certain she'd never experienced a more powerful, or baffling, moment. He pushed both hands into her hair and lowered his mouth to hers. She felt his beard against her skin, felt her limbs weaken, something she'd always thought happened only in stories. She'd come to see the fuss and gotten more than she bargained for. In front of two thousand people, in the glare of the lone spotlight, he kissed her.

A scattering of confused applause, a sprinkle of soft hoots and hollers went up, and so did the house lights. To her embarrassment Jeb's band struck up the ballad he'd sung earlier, about a man loving a woman all night, someone else's woman, and the crowd came to its feet, at last applauding in force, cheering and shouting, gathering programs, souvenirs and heavy coats, and heading for the exits.

With his arm around her, Jeb leaned toward the mike, sounding as shaken as Susannah felt. "Thanks for honoring my sister with us. Thank y'all for comin' tonight," he called into the mike, his honeyed voice sapping the rest of her strength. "I appreciate it. They tell me it's still snowin' out there. Get home safe now."

He stepped back, then grabbed the mike again. "There'll be hot coffee and cocoa in the rear entrance hall downstairs. And free posters with an autograph for any of you who want to stay."

"Are you out of your mind?"

Breeze Maynard followed Susannah and Jeb down the lower level hall.

"They came to see me. Risked their lives in this blizzard. The least I can do is sign my name a few times."

"A few thousand. And stay up all night to do it. Do you realize we're supposed to be in Memphis by five o'clock tomorrow? On stage by eight?"

"If it's possible to get there, I will."

"You're damned right. Jeb—"

"Stop jawin' at me. Go unpack a bunch of those posters—the ones like the backdrop for the show—and find me a couple of pens."

"I'm off duty." Still carrying her walkie-talkie, she swung him around in the hallway, nearly ramming Jeb into Susannah beside him. "Maybe your new friend would like to help out."

"Get 'em," Jeb said in a hard tone. "Then, when you've stacked them up nice and neat on a table over there"— he gestured near the back door—"you can meet the man and go on home . . . to his place."

"Why don't you just say it?"

"Say what?"

"What's been on your mind for weeks. Just so you'll know, who I date is my own business."

"Date?" he said. "Is that what you call seein' a married

man?" He turned a shoulder toward Susannah, as if to shut her out of the private conversation, but she had nowhere to go. The long hall stretched forever, and she didn't remember where his dressing room was, or the door to the parking garage. "Hell, Breeze, what about his wife and kids? It's not like you to—"

"His marriage stinks."

Jeb snorted. "You mean, his wife doesn't understand him? Peggy's a good woman, a good wife and a fine mother. You really want to break that up?"

"They're already separated, as you well know. You're not concerned about your guitarist, Jeb. Or about me."

"What am I concerned about then?" His tone was hushed.

"Your own ass," she said.

"If you mean, do I want you breakin' up my band—a bunch of guys I've played with for ten years—you're damn right. It's a too common thing, and you know it." He studied her coolly. "Why don't you get your priorities straight? You know what I mean, too."

Breeze's eyes frosted over.

"We'll talk about this some more. Tomorrow," she said, shooting a hard look at Susannah. "We'll talk about this and other things. Count on it. Right now Mack's waiting for me."

"Damn. Goddamn."

Breeze Maynard's hips swayed beneath her blue satin skirt, and the heels of her cowboy boots tapped, echoing, on the tile. When she swung through a door near the far end and off to the left, Susannah realized that must be the way to the parking garage.

She cleared her throat.

"I should go," she murmured, certain that "other things" included her. Breeze's dislike seemed clear enough. "If your driver could drop me at Grand Central or Penn Station, I could probably get a cab." Sooner or later, she added silently.

"There's not a taxi on the streets now. Or any other sane driver either. Where are you plannin' to go anyway?"

"To a hotel. By tomorrow morning the airport should be open. I'll get a flight back to San Francisco."

"San Francisco?" He looked blank.

"It's where I live."

"But I thought—"

"Jeb." A wiry man in jeans and a plaid shirt whom Susannah recognized as Jeb's keyboard man appeared from a room along the hall. A dressing room, she supposed. "People are lining up outside in the snow. You really gonna give 'em coffee and freebies?"

"Sure am." Jeb looped an arm over her shoulder. "How about you find me those posters? They should be in boxes stacked in the corner of my dressing room. The second door on the right. Tear 'em open and we'll drag a table out in the hall." He hurried back the way they'd come. "I need to find somebody with a coffee urn and some hot chocolate mix. Damn Breeze," he added. "I told her to get me some pens." In the center of the hall, he whirled around. "Hey, Susannah. Forget that notion about the hotel. They're all overflowing by now, and I've got a suite with six bedrooms. Take your pick, but you're stayin' with me tonight."

3

Jeb smiled at the girl in front of him, his mind on Susannah Whittaker. He'd been standing behind the table strewn with eleven-by-fourteen full-color posters of himself for two hours, signing his name and bantering with fans like this one. He let his gaze slide over her from red-striped stocking cap and bright blue eyes to her worshipful smile and mittened hands.

"Hey, darlin'. What's your name?" He poised a ballpoint pen above the poster that Susannah dutifully handed him. Their arms brushed and he felt a trickle of heat run down his body.

"Oh, Jeb." Squealing his name, the girl gazed at him, batting her eyes. "I can't believe I'm meeting you!"

"Mr. Cody needs a name," Susannah murmured.

"Oh. Gee. Sure." She mumbled it so that Jeb had to ask her again. Blushing, she showed off her prize to the others still waiting in line, sipping now-tepid coffee and bland hot chocolate that had cooled in the cups. Midway down the hall to the exit, she whirled around. "I love you, Jeb!" she said and ran for the door, giggling with her girlfriends.

"My God." Susannah shifted from one foot to the other. Her sleeve stroked his, creating another small brushfire along his spine.

"Hi, how y'doin'?" he said to the next woman in line.

His fans were overwhelmingly women, at least in concert, but he remained most aware at the moment of the woman beside him. In his peripheral vision Jeb saw her thrust both hands through her already-tangled blond hair and remembered the feel of it onstage when he'd held her, kissed her; remembered his first sight of her in the hotel suite entryway. "Thanks for comin'. How do I sign this?"

Damn. He always felt high after a show, but Susannah made it worse.

As he scrawled his name, she stifled a yawn.

"Bored?" He kept his tone low, his smile on the fan whose poster he was autographing. "Either that, or you're exhausted." He glanced along the hallway at the line. "There's only another fifty or so. Do we have enough posters?"

"Yes."

"Then why don't you leave 'em and wait for me in the car? There's a lap robe in the drawer under the jump seat, but I'll have the driver turn up the heater for you too."

"I'm all right."

The girl in front of him nearly curtsied in excitement, which Jeb felt too at his fans' devotion, his own new fame. "Thanks, Jeb. I love your songs." She giggled. "Maybe you'll write one for me someday."

"Maybe I just might. You take care gettin' home in this blizzard, hear?"

In an obvious burst of bravery, she said, "I'd like to take you home with me!"

Susannah made a strangled sound.

The girl turned away, clutching her poster to her skinny chest, but when he looked at the next person in line, Jeb groaned. Wild, streaky brown hair. Three holes in each ear. A mouth slashed with bright orange lipstick. Skintight pants and an off-the-shoulder sweater. And Jeb knew, he just knew, what was coming.

"Susannah, why don't you go on now and wait—"

She slapped a poster in his hand. "I'm not tired."

"It'd be hard to feel tired around Jeb Stuart Cody." The streaky brunette grinned at him. "I've been crazy about you since that first song."

Jeb returned the grin but his stomach clutched. "What do I sign?"

"You mean where." The orange mouth seemed to flash at him like a neon sign outside some cheap motel. The kind of place he knew well enough from his early days touring the tristate area around Elvira, but one that Susannah had probably never even seen. The girl eased her large sweater down over one shoulder, exposing the top of a breast, obviously unbound. "And you *know* where, baby."

She leaned over the table, letting him have a good look down the sweater, and Jeb obediently braced one hand on her bare shoulder to scrawl his name with the other across the jiggling swell of her breast.

She sighed. "I'm never gonna wash again."

Then, to his greater discomfort, she grabbed him around the back of the neck and pulled his head down for a slack-mouthed kiss. She was going back for more when his fingers closed around hers, prying them from his skin. "Only one to a customer, sugar. Listen to my next album. I'll be singin' for you."

Susannah watched the girl walk away. "I don't believe you did that."

"I don't believe she did that," Jeb murmured. Not that it hadn't happened before. But Susannah Whittaker already seemed to think he was a lowlife. Minute by minute her conviction must have been growing. Like her certainty that someone had murdered his sister.

She yawned again.

"That's it," he said. "You're outta here." He raised a hand for one of the gofers who trailed him like bloodhounds. "Find my driver, will you? And while I finish here, will you see Miss Whittaker to the car?"

He and Susannah exchanged looks. Jeb heard "Amazing Grace" in his mind, the hush of the crowd afterward, imagined again the look on Susannah's face when their eyes met across the footlights. He remembered her shaken breathing when he kissed her. His own swift reaction.

"Wait for me," he said. "I won't be long."

The purr of the limousine's engine nearly lulled Susannah to sleep. It grew warm in the car, but she didn't shake off the gray cashmere blanket. She lounged on the rear seat, her boots off, her coat open, rubbing the lap robe's silvery satin facing against her cheek. It felt windburned from standing outside Grand Central earlier. Or was it from the rasp of Jeb's late-day beard stubble when they kissed?

He'd only meant to comfort, she told herself, to make some civilized connection between them; or maybe he'd intended it as apology for their quarrel about Clary. A natural enough gesture in private.

More tired than she cared to admit, moved by the

surprising end of Jeb's concert and his embrace, she felt her eyelids droop.

When she got back to San Francisco, she'd sleep for a week and wouldn't cry again for years. She'd forget today, this evening. She'd forget Jeb Stuart Cody before he got any deeper under her skin.

Susannah glanced at the digital clock, part of the stereo equipment. She'd been sitting in the limo another hour and it was now after one thirty in the morning. Didn't musicians ever sleep? She rarely stayed up so late, even when Michael Alsop dragged her to the Bar Association's annual Christmas dance. She yawned then long before midnight.

Alone in the Mercedes, she had to fight off a natural inclination to feel grateful for Jeb's kindness. Southern charm, she thought. Clary had been a true steel magnolia, and at times her charm had worn thin. She didn't think it would take long to see through Jeb's, which, though powerful, had to be less genuine.

A metal door creaked open but Susannah didn't move. Several men spilled through from the hallway into the darkened parking garage, heading for their cars. She saw Jeb's driver start toward the limousine, then Jeb himself, calling a last good-night to a fan.

The chauffeur opened the rear door and Jeb slid onto the seat beside her. The doors closed and the car moved through the nearly empty garage and out onto the street.

"Will you look at that?" Jeb leaned across her. "Winter wonderland."

His scent, pure male, drifted into her nostrils like fine perfume, creating a small riot in Susannah's senses. She'd never felt this way before and didn't quite welcome it. She pressed a surreptitious hand to the underside of her left breast, a long-standing habit when she felt threatened or unsure.

"Isn't that beautiful?" he asked.

At first, startled, she thought he meant her breast. Dropping her hand, Susannah gazed at the still-falling snow. The cityscape looked white and soft and virginal, unmarked now by the passage of tires or booted feet. Looking up into the lights, at the steady drift of giant flakes, swirling and blowing, she felt giddy, as if she were the snow swirling through the dark air above them.

"In San Francisco I only see snow when I go to the mountains. It's been a while since I came back to Greenwich in winter."

"You don't come home for Christmas?"

She shook her head at the memory of the enormous tree in the foyer, two stories high and decked with lights, all white, with gold balls. The perfect presents underneath. The ritual order of opening each one, the ritual coffee and pastries on Christmas morning. She'd never thought of Greenwich as home, in the same way she imagined Jeb or Clary might Elvira.

"After my parents divorced and my father married your sister, I felt . . . superfluous. They seemed so happy, caught up in each other. I decided to be a grown-up and stay in California."

"If you and Clary were such great friends—"

"Last December they went to Cancún."

There. She could feel her muscles loosen, her heartbeat slow. She could handle Jeb's physical presence, but his emotional intensity . . . that kiss on stage. No. She was glad he'd retreated to his own side of the rear seat. For the first time, she sensed a lack of tension between them in the enforced intimacy of the limousine.

Susannah smiled faintly. "What happened to your hair tonight?"

"My hair?"

"No ponytail," she said. "I saw it on the news today. Tonight, it's gone."

"Oh, that." He grimaced. "Jericho, my label—the record company—and my producer thought my first album should lean toward rock, but when we put it together, only two cuts could be called country rock. The rest are pure country, or leaning toward mainstream. Which is where the action is." He dropped his head back on the seat. "That was an old concert clip. I had my hair cut a bit. I guess I'm still playin'—we are—with my ultimate image. Which, in my mind, is more classic, traditional."

He fought a yawn and she said, "You must be worn out."

"From the concert? A few autographs?"

"A few?" He'd stood there for hours, talking, signing . . . bosoms, too.

"I've stayed till four in the morning more than once."

"Why?" she said. "Once the tickets are paid for and they've seen the show—"

"My fans put me where I am. Breeze nags at me, but I can't turn my back on them. And on a night like this, every one of those two thousand or so people—she could tell you the exact number—deserve at least a few minutes of my time." He rolled his head on the seat back to look at her with lazy eyes. "I figure those few minutes sell my next album and the one after that. One fan tells another . . . it's like a daisy chain."

Susannah smiled slightly at the image.

Without looking away from her, he tapped a button on a console, and the sunroof's opaque cover slid open. Snow immediately began to accumulate on the glass overhead. Susannah tipped her head back, mimicking Jeb's.

"I'd like to catch the snowflakes on my tongue," she murmured, surprising herself.

Except for the engine's hum, sounding far removed, and the calls of several children out playing, the air grew completely quiet. Except for Jeb's breathing.

"You want to get out and take a walk? My driver'll wait. We could have a snowball fight."

"I don't have the energy." She looked back at him. "How can you?"

"I'm always up for a concert. Before, during and after. I have trouble sleepin'."

She shook her head. "Cody . . ."

"What?" His gaze drifted over her.

"Why did you kiss me tonight?"

His voice dropped. "You gonna slap me after the fact?"

"No, but I wondered."

"If I embarrassed you in front of all those people, I apologize."

"I think they understood."

"But you don't." It wasn't a question.

"Do you?" Susannah asked.

"Hell, no." He smiled. "Or maybe. A little." Closing his eyes, he smiled more broadly at the snow-laden sunroof above them. "A lot." He looked at her again. "Is there anyone waiting for you in San Francisco?"

"I'm seeing a man."

"Special?"

"We're good friends," she said and watched his smile fade.

She was still studying his face when he moved, sliding across the seat and under the lap robe, lifting the edge, then letting it fall so that the satin lining caressed Susannah's chin, making her shiver.

"What are you doing?"

"Getting ready to kiss you again."

He touched her mouth, his fingers tracing the lower lip and then the upper one, teasing at the corners. She inched away, wondering whether he thought she owed him this for getting her a front row seat at his concert, as he felt he owed his fans autographs and posters.

"I hardly know you."

"I thought you knew all about me." He paused, looking into her eyes. "I knew you the minute you walked into my hotel suite. Except it has nothing to do with Clary."

The heated car, the cashmere lap robe, the touch of Jeb's hand on her mouth, brushing back and forth, his gaze idly following the motion, all played havoc with her mistrust of him. She shouldn't have removed her boots; perhaps she'd given him a wrong message that she was easily available. Lonely. But watching him through drowsy eyes, feeling almost drugged by the long, sorrowful day, by his close observation of her, by the very scent of him, suddenly she didn't want to fend off his advances in this dark, luxurious setting—which confused her more.

"Cody . . ."

Her lips half parted, and he covered them with his. There was no stage now, no watching audience, no band. Not even the sharp memory of Clary's death to guard her. Just their two mouths, together.

Jeb's tongue stroked along her lips, opening them as if he had a key. He was a stranger, she told herself, a celebrity, a man to whom women's favors after a concert must be routine. A favor he felt entitled to. Susannah nearly groaned.

"Does performing arouse you?"

"Um-hmm. Some—Breeze used to say so—think it's better than sex."

She squirmed but Jeb only moved closer, fitting himself to her, lowering her into the dark corner of the dark car with the dark city all around them, safe from any prying eyes.

The car slipped around a corner, its back end slewing in the packed, icy snow, and her equilibrium spun. Jeb pulled her closer, tighter, dropping his mouth to her throat, to the few inches of skin exposed above her clothing. When he lightly bit her neck, the merest scrape of his teeth on her skin, she actually quivered. She didn't push him off, didn't move. She threaded her fingers in his hair, tugging his head back for another kiss.

"I could tell backstage, you were remembering the kiss too, and then you said it, and I knew neither of us had stopped thinking of it . . . wanting more." Jeb's voice trembled in her ear.

He found her breast, gently kneading it through two layers of cashmere, moaning deep in his throat when the nipple beaded in his fingers. She felt him growing harder against the juncture of her thighs—and panicked.

Susannah struggled beneath him. She thrashed her legs, pushed against his chest with straightened arms, turned her head away from his kiss.

"Cody!"

He sat up, his chest moving, his mouth open as if he'd run the annual San Francisco Bay to Breakers race in record time instead of, as the event intended, having fun. Flinging off the lap robe, he retreated to the other side of the rear seat and stared at her.

"Miss Susannah."

She couldn't read his expression. Looking away, she pulled the blanket around her, busily rearranging her skirt and smoothing her tights. Her sweaters. Somehow, in the last few moments, her fox-lined trench coat had come off and lay in a lush pool on the gray carpet. Though little had actually happened, to Susannah the car smelled of lovemaking.

She couldn't meet Jeb's gaze. "I've never—ever—done anything like that before."

"Had sex?" He was still fighting for breath.

"You're a country singer. Don't even try to be a comedian."

"You found my performance funny?" He looked at the seat between them. "We didn't even come close to the fireworks at the end of the show."

She jammed a fist against the door handle, but it was locked. And all she saw beyond the window was a wall of white. His matter-of-fact tone made her crazy.

"You wanted me. I wanted you. What's the crime here?"

"We defiled Clary's memory."

"We did no such thing. Maybe this happened too soon, but this wasn't a normal day, a normal week." Looking back at her, he caught Susannah's gaze. "You ever seen a southern funeral? A real country one, I mean?" She shook her head. "People sing. And celebrate that person's life, the way I celebrated Clary's tonight at the convention center."

"Until the last."

"'Amazing Grace'? And bringin' you up on stage? That was for you as much as Clary. Your world," he said. "A little bit of each. But down home my daddy—if he was around—would have laughed and told stories, and my mama would have remembered the funny things Clary did when she was small. That's my way too."

"And this?" she said bitterly.

"You felt it, I know you did."

"You're making excuses."

"You'll notice I didn't try to force you. When you said stop, I stopped."

The limousine slowed, then stopped, and the driver's voice came through the intercom. "Sir? There's an accident here on Fifth at Forty-ninth. We'll be a few minutes until they clear the intersection. You folks warm enough back there?"

Jeb frowned. "Oh, we're warm."

He wedged himself deeper into the corner, while Susannah studied the stalled traffic around them. No one car seemed to be in the same lane—or what had been lanes only that morning before the storm hit. What were her chances of spending the night anywhere but with him? Even if she walked uptown. . . .

"I've never been snowbound before," he finally said. "With anyone quite like you."

It didn't sound like a compliment. "Should I say thanks?"

"No, ma'am." Jeb looked at her. "Say amen."

Susannah wasn't much of a churchgoer, and she'd never attended regularly. She couldn't call Drake religious, or Leslie. Her mother had never found adhering to a schedule easy, or to any belief system in conflict with her own, very private one. So Susannah didn't give thanks or say amen, not even when Jeb spoke again.

"Be thankful for the things in this world that feel good."

Nevertheless, the rest of the way to his hotel she prayed the snow would end and the airports reopen. She didn't relish the hours until morning with a thwarted male who might or might not be sulking, who might or might not try to retaliate. He seemed sensible enough, even decent, yet hadn't Clary implied more than once that he'd hurt not only her feelings? She'd never said exactly how, but . . .

With an impatient punch at several buttons, Jeb tuned the car's television to an update by a female newsperson about the worsening blizzard.

"On this wintry Friday night thousands of stranded workers are scrambling for shelter, people bunking down on the floors at Grand Central and Penn Station—at all airports, which are closed. No trains or buses are running. Abandoned cars litter every roadway. Midtown Manhattan, for the most part, is a wasteland—except for more vehicles. The city looks like a giant parking lot."

"What about area hotels?" the coanchor asked.

"Overbooked. So are the YMCA, YWCA, and all shelters. We understand the mayor is trying now to get the schools opened and some hot food for all those tired and hungry travelers."

The wind howled down the concrete corridors of the city, whistling a mournful, keening tune. The limousine alternately slid and plowed through the deepening snow, taking an eternity to cover a single block, and she wondered whether they'd make it to the hotel. But she felt certain of one thing: Jeb had turned on the newscast to prove she had no other choice but to stay with him.

The update signed off with "one of tonight's few entertainments and certainly the liveliest, Jeb Stuart Cody's performance. . . ."

"Shit," Jeb said. "I don't think I'm going to like the publicity." He sank down in his seat. "Breeze'll have my butt. She thought we should cancel. Now I suppose I'm about to be taken to task for makin' my fans come out in the storm."

"Those who came, wanted to come."

But his frown only intensified, as if he didn't welcome her defense.

"If one person didn't get home, it's my fault."

Susannah thought that was nonsense—especially when the news program rolled tape, panning the concert's small audience of eager, shouting fans.

"He sure knows how to give a show. And so soon after his sister's tragic death." The anchorwoman looked into the camera, her eyes bright. "Our sympathies are with you, Jeb."

Hitting the Off button, he sat stiff and silent. At the hotel he rode up with her in the elevator, not touching, not speaking. He seemed to have drawn into himself, whether sulking or grieving, and Susannah didn't even consider intruding. Tired herself, she could think of nothing but sleep. And forgetfulness.

"Where should I . . .?" she began, removing her boots in the suite's entry hall.

"Anywhere you want." Without looking at her, Jeb walked down the hall to his own room at its end and softly shut the door, leaving her five other bedrooms from which to choose.

"Good night," Susannah whispered to the silence.

She awoke to the sound of music. Twisting in a warm tangle of sheets and blankets, she peered at the bedside alarm. Four A.M. She couldn't have been asleep more than an hour. She heard the soft strumming of chords on a guitar and a song melody she didn't recognize.

No surprise. Susannah's knowledge of country music

at best could be called sketchy, but the poignant melody drew her in. It was Jeb's voice she heard, Jeb's guitar. Getting out of bed, wearing a satin night shift, she padded on bare feet into the hall. She'd chosen the farthest room from his and locked the door. A needless precaution, it seemed.

In the suite's huge living room she discovered she'd been hearing a tape. Various red lights flashed on the stereo unit, and a steady bass thump issued from the large speakers. Snatches of melody alternated with rephrasings of lyric, with changes of chord.

She leaned in the doorway from the entry hall, her arms folded against the nighttime chill in the room. "Are you writing a new song?"

At her voice Jeb turned his head. Wearing only a pair of worn blue jeans and holding a plain dark guitar across his right thigh, he sat on an oversized taupe-colored hassock that matched the room's sofas and chairs. Except for the stereo lights, the room was dark, and his bare shoulders glowed bronze in the low light. "Tryin'," he said.

"The same one you worked on before I came?"

He hesitated, as if not certain he wanted company or conversation. "We laid down a few tracks the other day at the studio, but nothing came out right." He got up to switch off the tape, then sat down again. "Did I wake you up?"

"Yes."

"I'm sorry. I told you I have trouble sleepin' after I work."

Susannah crossed the room. "I rarely have trouble falling asleep or getting enough rest. But then, I don't work," she added. "So I never get that tired, or that wired."

"That's a shame." Jeb strummed a few chords, his lean fingers fluid on the strings. "Wired?" he said. "You're not into drugs, are you? Runnin' with the jet set like you do?"

"Of course not." She'd long ago promised herself to avoid excess, of any kind, which made her think of her mother. But from what she'd heard of musicians . . .

He glanced at her. "In case you're wonderin', I don't allow any of that stuff, not at home or on the road. No coke, no pot. And my band drinks beer, nothin' harder."

He held a tortoiseshell pick in his right hand, plucking it across the strings while his left hand worked higher on them, along the—Susannah didn't know what else to call it—the guitar's handle. The most beautiful, hauntingly simple notes came out. She stood closer, intending to change the subject.

"That's lovely."

"So," he said, tilting his head to listen to the notes, then adjusting the guitar strings, "what about San Francisco?"

She wasn't quite sure what he meant but wondered if it was his turn to judge her. "I spent my summers there when I was young. With my mother's mother. I inherited my grandmother's house when she died a few years ago. It seemed the right time to leave Connecticut."

"You felt superfluous in your own family." He echoed her earlier words. "What do you do there, besides clean house?"

She strained to hear ridicule in his tone. "I don't clean house. I have a housekeeper five days a week."

"Does she cook too?"

"If I ask, yes."

Jeb raised his eyebrows. "My mama could have used a housekeeper, for sure. What do you do with all that free time?"

"I have my charities," she said, sensing how that must sound to Jeb. According to Clary, they'd never had much, growing up in a family of eight children. But why look down his nose at her now? "I do some fund-raising for the Arts Commission, I was cochair last season for Healthy Heart, a San Francisco public awareness program." She paused, wondering if she sounded useless. "A few other groups ask for my time. And I volunteer one day a week at a privately sponsored animal shelter."

He stopped playing and turned on the hassock to face her, his eyes dark, his mouth not quite smiling. "You know what we're like, Miss Susannah, you and me?"

"No," she said.

"We're like the guy and girl in Garth Brooks's version of the song, 'Friends in Low Places.' You ever heard that one?"

"No."

"It's a good one. I'll play it for you."

She thought he'd sing, but instead Jeb walked over to the stereo and slipped a CD into the player. He punched a button, and a clear, strong voice, but not as clear or strong to Susannah as Jeb's had sounded in concert, came on, singing about a man who drank beer but ruined a woman's—his ex-lover's—champagne party.

When Brooks launched into the chorus and his voice became gritty, even raunchy, Jeb laughed from his place on the hassock. "Damn, I love that. He sure can sell a song. You see what I mean, sugar? About us bein' different?"

"What's your point?"

"That is my point." He set the guitar aside with tenderness, as if it were a sleeping child, then looked up at her. "You ever give a tired, wired man a back rub?"

"No."

Laughter warmed his eyes. "You mean, not even out there in San Francisco? With that friend of yours?"

"No," she said, her pulse drumming.

"Then—again—it's time you did. Call this a night of firsts."

He turned his back to her, fully expecting Susannah to comply. As he'd expected her to in the limousine. She stepped backward.

"Listen, Cody—"

"My name's Jeb." He spun around, his handsome face all shadows and angles in the darkness. "Don't start up again about Clary or about before, in the car. It's the middle of the night. Just you and me. And I already feel as if someone's buried a hatchet between my shoulder blades." He rubbed the back of his neck. "Come here, will you, and work out the knot in my muscles. I'd do it myself but I can't reach."

Shifting on the hassock, Jeb showed her the full splendor of his naked back, his shoulders and that vulnerable nape of the neck. His dark hair feathered there, not quite straightly cut.

"I don't know how," she said.

She lifted her hands and held them an inch above his skin, feeling the heat radiate from it as she had during his concert, when they stood together onstage, when they kissed; as it had in the limousine when he'd bent over her, their foreplay another surprise. Susannah touched him once, tentatively, snatched her hands back from his sleek, fiery flesh, then let them settle again over the corded muscles.

"They're really tight," she said.

"My whole body's that way by the time I finish singing. I always tell myself I'm not nervous, but I always am."

Her fingers seemed to know the cure. Without training,

without conscious intent, they began manipulating, soothing, easing the taut ropes of muscle in Jeb's shoulders,
upper arms, back, and neck, until, with a soft groan, he let
his head drop low.

"God, that feels good."

Garth Brooks sang on, his "No Fences" album piecing
words and music together like the intricate star design
quilt she'd seen on Jeb's bed.

The last song, the poignant "Wolves," ended but
Susannah's uncertain, soothing touch went on, the only
sounds in the room the soft whir of the stereo and Jeb's
occasional low moans, his few words of encouragement
or direction. "Ah, that's great. Right there. No, a bit
lower." When at last he turned and took her hands in
his, she felt strong and somehow . . . destined.

"All my bones are gone," he whispered, his eyes even
darker, his smile flashing white in the black room. She
could see his intent—in his eyes, in his smile, in the
gleaming flesh of his bare chest, in the snug fit of his
jeans. "Come down here so I can thank you. Properly."

Susannah pulled free. She didn't owe him sexual
favors, or explanations of her life, for that matter; yet
her sense of purpose suddenly matched his. Frightened
of the feeling, sensing she was already lost, Susannah
shook her head.

"No. I can't."

He didn't argue. Slowly, with his gaze holding hers,
he stood and held out a hand.

Susannah hesitated, her heart thumping. Alarm and
desire battled in her veins. She'd locked her door
against him, then willingly come out. She glanced
toward the windows and the steadily falling, silent snow.
She'd never known a man like Jeb Stuart Cody, but he
might be right. They hadn't come close to the finish.

The night—this one, shut-away-from-the-world night, snowbound together—belonged to them. Her gaze didn't waver from his. Reaching out, she took the hand he offered and walked with him along the hall, lit only by the soft overhead light Jeb flicked on, to the room at its end—to the wide bed covered by an Indian star-patterned quilt.

4

"*Last chance,*" Jeb said, and Susannah fought back a moan.

When she didn't speak or get up off the bed, he followed her down onto the soft mattress. Somehow, in the brief time and space from the living room to the bedroom, between lush kisses and Jeb's whispered promises of pleasure, he had half opened his jeans and drawn off her chemise, tossing it to the floor. Somehow, between their argument over Clary and now, she had moved with him from awareness to passion. Not all of that, certainly, came from Jeb. The very quickness of her own response to him made Susannah dizzy. She knew she wasn't going anywhere.

Jeb must have sensed her acceptance.

He had left the door ajar and the hall light on, and in its reflected glow lowered his head, briefly nuzzling the side of her neck, burrowing his nose under her hair before he brought his mouth, soft and hot, back to hers.

The kiss started out slow and light, but quickly intensified, becoming dark and deep. His hand skimmed over her body, warm against her breast and belly and, soon, between her legs.

Making a sound, Susannah ran both hands down his bare back, touching heated, silky skin over hard muscle. Over his shoulder she watched the snow, still falling outside the windows opposite the bed. She felt the star quilt's pattern beneath her spine, felt her legs part at his touch, but when she would have come to her senses again and closed them, Jeb held her, his thumb caressing the soft skin of her inner thighs.

"Not this time," he whispered, taking her mouth again.

His tongue sought hers, and Susannah moaned. His upper lip tasted faintly salty, his mouth tasted of coffee and a hint of the brandy he must have been drinking before she woke. Without acknowledging her own intent, she reached out, finding the undone snap on his jeans, the half-opened zipper. She rasped it down the rest of the way, hearing him take in a harsh breath.

"God."

He was kissing her still, at the same time tangling his fingers with hers, working off the tight denim. When they'd shed his jeans, she pushed them to the foot of the bed, and saw him. Naked, fully aroused. Beautiful. Her eyes widened, and to her surprise, Jeb's cheekbones stained a dull red.

"Are you tryin' to make me wilt?"

Susannah smiled. "Do you think that's possible?"

His gaze darkened. "Not just now."

When she reached for him, he caught her hand. He kissed her fingertips, her palm, the inner surface of her wrist and the pulse beating there in a slim blue vein. Susannah tried to keep her eyes on his but couldn't.

Because, oh, to look at the rest of him . . . lean, hard, magnificent and so obviously wanting her, to really look her fill . . .

She'd never wanted to look at Michael this way. Or the first man she'd made love with either. In wonderment she shook her head.

"Thinkin' you can get away again?"

"No," she said, and then, "But Cody . . ."

"What?" He dipped his head, kissing her mouth, as if unwilling to be distracted. He seemed to sense her misgivings. "Your friend in Frisco let you down?"

"Maybe I let him down." She swallowed. "Maybe—" she trailed one finger down his bare chest, around a concave brown nipple and watched it tighten, "maybe I'll disappoint you too."

"I doubt it."

When he touched her, low and sweet, his fingers came away wet, and Susannah's fears seemed foolish. She cried out, arching into his hand, arching her back, bringing her breast to his mouth.

Jeb bathed it with his tongue, first one breast, then the other. His mouth damp from their kisses, he drew it lightly back and forth before taking a hardened nipple to gently suck and teethe. He played her with all the tender skill she'd seen him use on the guitar, his fingers, their callused tips like another instrument of pleasure, flicking over her too, dancing, plucking, heightening her response until she had no will left, no resentment of him—and no longer an awareness of her grief for Clary.

"I don't think you'll disappoint me," he whispered. "And I sure don't plan to disappoint you."

Susannah moaned, alive in Jeb's arms, so powerfully alive. And so was Jeb when her fingers found him, hard and throbbing.

"'Passion, I see, is catching,'" he added, his mouth pressed to her throat.

"Shakespeare?" Susannah could hardly breathe the word.

"Julius Caesar." He groaned.

One instant he was there, surrounding her, making her feel more than she had ever dreamed of feeling, despite their differences, and in the next, he had left her. He scrambled to the end of the bed.

"Cody."

"Be right there. Where's the damn—?" Susannah heard the nightstand drawer open, then slam shut, and the sound of foil tearing. Jeb came back to her, lobbing the packet at a wastebasket into which it dropped, neatly. "Safe sex and spontaneity," he said, as he rolled on the condom, "sure don't go together."

She wanted to really feel him, close and bare, but knew he was right; that he was being sensible, even honorable as well as responsible.

Jeb moved over her, braced on one arm, his muscles tight and quivering but strongly defined in the low light that streamed from the hall. In his right hand, he took Susannah's, her shaken breathing an echo of his own, her gaze locked with his.

"Help me." He guided her, guiding him inside, slow and smooth and silky.

Susannah whimpered after all. The new heat, the well-known rhythm, the ancient dance. She couldn't get enough of it, of him. Clary's message had sent her to Jeb for a different reason, but maybe these few hours—this—was the only help he needed from her; all they needed from each other. She raised her hips, feeling wide and full and open to each slow thrust and withdrawal and thrust again, until the tempo built, the urgency, and she let her head fall back and the words rush out anyway, as if they could be true.

"Love me, love me!"

"All night," he murmured, "I've been tryin'." With a groan Jeb dropped his head into the hollow of her neck, his open mouth pressed to her skin, his breath hot, his hands holding her hips. She heard him urge her on and on to that split second, that eternity when she called out, called his name, and let go as she never had before. When he followed a second later, as if he'd been holding back just for her, she felt pure warmth. And welcomed it. Welcomed him.

He never slept, she decided. After the first time, Jeb had wanted more. Susannah tried to tell herself she didn't, that the first time had been a mistaken indulgence, that she craved nothing but sleep. Then Jeb's mouth sought hers, his hands streaked across her still damp skin, and she had only wanted what he did.

A dangerous notion.

"You lyin' there plotting revenge, or what?" he asked.

The room had cooled during the last hours of the night, and as the first fingers of dawn stroked the gray sky, she shivered. Jeb pulled her closer, tucking the star quilt around them.

"Revenge?" she said.

"I suppose you've never done anything like this before"—he quoted her from the limousine—"and your bein' a woman, I suppose that's all my fault."

"As I said before, you can be persuasive."

"A man never gets anywhere, unless he sets his mind to it."

Susannah let his lazy tone lull her. She snuggled

deeper into the covers, relishing the faint scents of warm skin and Jeb. "And where do you plan on going next?"

She thought he might tease her about lovemaking, but he didn't.

"In my career?" He jerked a thumb at the ceiling. "Straight up. To the top. And when I get there, they won't even remember Dwight Yoakam or Travis Tritt."

Susannah fingered the small gold hoop in his ear. "I like your name better."

"Well, that's something."

"What is?"

"That you like at least one thing about me."

"I never said I didn't."

Jeb squeezed her shoulder. "You never said you did either." He laughed a little. "And, Miss Susannah, when you look at a man you don't much care for, that look could fry his skin."

"Are you saying I'm—"

"Snooty?" He laughed again. "Hell, no. Why would I think a thing like that? Of course there are some men who can see right through that getup you had on last night, who can see past this aristocratic little nose." He tweaked it, then kissed the spot.

"See what?"

He shook his head. "I save my best notions for my songs."

"*Jeb Stuart Cody.*"

He rocked her in his arms. "That's what my mama used to say whenever I was bad. She'd stand on the porch, her arms folded over her chest, and that's all she had to say. I'd come runnin'."

"Did you misbehave often?"

He grinned. "Every chance I got."

"In my family, that—or the perception of it—is known as a willful streak. Did your mother believe in spanking?"

"She did not." Under the covers Jeb dragged a hand across her bottom. His tone warmed, as it did when he sang a sexy ballad. "But I believe I might." His hand paused, hovering over one bare, rounded cheek. "Have you done anything tonight that deserves a spankin', Miss Susannah?"

She flushed. "Why do you call me that?"

"Because that's what decent women are called where I come from. Miss Breeze. Miss Clary." Before either name registered, his hand glided over her backside again. "You done anything wrong?"

Arousal flared in her once more. Feeling breathless, Susannah buried her nose in the hollow of his shoulder, moving it back and forth as a negative reply.

"Think now. Anything you're sorry for?" His breath hitched too, but he sounded uncertain, as if he expected her to say yes; that she shouldn't have stayed with him, shouldn't have made love to a man like him.

"No," she finally said.

"Good."

Jeb lowered his head, nuzzling her neck. A chain of warm, openmouthed kisses formed a necklace there and down Susannah's sternum to her breast. So fast, she thought. He only had to touch her now, and she wanted him. Even if that was all they had.

"Cody," she whispered, half afraid, tugging at him until he raised his head. She tracked the faint scar on his lip. "Where did you get this?"

He stiffened. "In a fight." Then ducked his head, returning his attention to her breasts, kissing one, then the other, as seemed to be his habit, before he froze again.

"What's this?"

Her left side faced the windows, and the rising sun illuminated her skin, the curved underside of her breast. In the dark last night he must not have seen it. Susannah wriggled under his hands, which bracketed her ribs, holding her still for his examination.

"A tattoo," she admitted, her cheeks heated now.

Half-smiling, he tilted his head and peered closer. "A heart?"

"A small one."

"I thought there was no one special in San Francisco."

"It's not what you think."

Jeb gave her a jaundiced look.

"College," she murmured. "Clary and I had a few beers one night and she dared me to go first. After I did, she lost her nerve." Susannah avoided his gaze. Clary had goaded her, laughed at Susannah's anger. "I'd just broken up with someone, my first serious someone, or so I thought at the time." She hesitated. "I guess I picked the heart for another reason too," she said, trying to sound light though the memory still hurt. "I had a horse then, for three-day eventing. I had hopes of an Olympic spot, but she took a fence wrong, broke her leg, and my father had to put her down." She paused again. "He and my mother said they'd buy me another horse, a better one." She shrugged. "I didn't want another, though. Her name was Heart's Desire. So I guess the heart was partly for her."

Jeb's head dipped lower, and she felt his lips against her skin, against the small red heart. "Oh, Miss Susannah. You keep throwin' me curves." He blew gently on her, then stroked the spot with his tongue. "And I purely love this one."

Sliding higher, he put a finger to her chin, lifting it for his kiss.

She didn't need sleep either, Susannah decided as she pushed closer to Jeb under the star quilt, under the pearly light of morning. She could sleep the rest of her life, back in San Francisco. Right now, Jeb Stuart Cody was lying over her once more, as thousands of women wished he would with them, looking down into her eyes and smiling, a wicked smile that made her want to join him in doing naughty things. Susannah had never been disciplined, even in mock fashion, with love. She'd never had a famous man all to herself. A shockingly tender man. She felt his hard length nudge between her thighs, and lifted herself to greet him while she could.

"I know another thing you like," he whispered in her ear.

"How'd you like to do something really exciting?"

Jeb stood at the windows of the suite's living room, looking out over a mostly white Manhattan. The sight, if not Susannah's enticing presence, soothed him. The park looked to him this afternoon like the hills and hollow beyond his family's house during a winter storm. Not a car crawled along the street far below, and from the hotel's top story, he couldn't see any footprints in the fresh snow.

The blizzard had lasted through Friday night, and on Saturday the airports were still closed and Susannah, in the Kentucky T-shirt he'd given her that morning to wear at breakfast, was still with him. Maybe too much, he thought, but smiled at the sight of her, Miss Susannah Whittaker, blue blood and all, her breasts pushing out the crooked letters of the shirt's humorous list below its header: You Know You're From Kentucky When . . .

"Like what?" she asked.

Jeb's favorite saying, nearly last on that list, referred to attending family reunions as a way to meet girls. He was glad he'd met Susannah, but talk about being far from home. Maybe he should send her away now, as he usually did occasional women on the road.

"That snowball fight you turned down last night," he heard himself say. "And whatever else we can get into."

She laughed, a clear, musical laugh he'd only heard a few times. Susannah Whittaker needed more laughter in her life. He just didn't know why—except for those few references to her wealthy family.

"I've never had a snowball fight," she admitted. "I don't have any brothers or sisters. Drake's house—my father's—is off by itself on thirty acres, behind stone walls. Neither he nor my mother could be called athletic."

Jeb turned from the windows, amazed. "I guess they're not very playful either." He frowned. "Which doesn't surprise me, the little I know about Drake." He looked at her. "Didn't you have friends?"

"Enough. A few."

None, he heard in her tone and decided he could sort his own feelings later.

"Central Park is one big snowball." He pushed down the thought that Clary had died there, in a spot he wouldn't recognize. "Let's find you some jeans and a sweater." She'd brought a suitcase from San Francisco with clothes for the funeral but nothing casual. "Breeze must have something in her room," he said. "Then let's get going. I want to see what kind of an arm you have."

Susannah said she had expected Breeze's sweater to be sequin-studded, her jeans made of satin, but her own fox-lined trench coat and knee-high leather boots made quite an outfit of the standard blue chambray shirt and jeans underneath. In his own jeans and sheepskin jacket, Jeb led her out a side entrance of the hotel, for once avoiding the fans who still ringed the main doors. In the park, after wolfing down hot dogs with sauerkraut from a sidewalk vendor, they spent two hours firing icy grenades, ducking behind snow-laden bushes, tackling . . . and of course, kissing.

Susannah had been slow to join in the play but seemed to get the hang of it. When Jeb suggested they return to the hotel, she didn't jump at the notion of getting in out of the cold. As darkness fell and other Manhattanites took their skates and sleds home, Jeb drew her close for another warming kiss. She smiled against his mouth.

"I haven't had this much fun in years. At your concert, and . . . just now." She sounded wistful.

"Then how'd you like to have some more?"

Jeb stuck a hand in the air to hail a rare taxi. Within minutes, as the sky overhead darkened and the stars came up, it halted in front of a red-canopied building on the trendy West Side, on the other edge of the park. The canopy read Boots and Spurs.

Several private limousines waited at the curb, their engines running. As Jeb and Susannah got out of the cab, another stretch Cadillac pulled up, and a man and woman stepped out, the man wearing a Stetson, the woman a fur coat and elaborately tooled western boots.

"Cowboys?" Susannah said.

"Just their pricey clothes. Wait'll you see inside."

The bouncer at the door admitted the first couple but gave Jeb and Susannah's plain jeans, wet to the knees from playing in the snow, a thorough once-over.

"Sorry. Reservations only."

"Make an exception." Jeb met the man's gaze and waited, counting. The time gap between sight and recognition was growing shorter these days, and he only reached three before the bouncer's expression lightened.

"Mr. Cody." He swept the door wide, affecting a poor Texas accent. "Go right in and have yourselves a stompin' good time."

The minute they walked through the door, the loud, upbeat music proved infectious, as he'd hoped it would. There'd be time later to assess his own reactions to Susannah, to wonder whether he'd made a mistake, except in bed. Now, he simply wanted to show her some fun on the dance floor.

He watched her gaze in wonder at the crowd, uniformly dressed to the teeth in New York's version of Texas high style, the large room grandly decorated with longhorns and saddles, even a mechanical bull, which Jeb thought more a relic of country music's brief urban cowboy phase in the early eighties. The scents of smoke and mingled perfumes filled the air. The floor vibrated with the sounds of fancy footwork as the crowd en masse executed an intricate line dance.

"It's all the rage right now," he said, steering Susannah first to a side table with ponyskin-upholstered chairs. Leading her onto the dance floor, he looked at her knee-high English-style riding boots, his own worn cowboy boots. "We'll just have to make do without the hats." He put his arm around her waist and, as if they'd never left the line, seamlessly joined the high-spirited Boots and Spurs imitation of the achy breaky.

By the time they'd danced every dance until midnight and consumed several drinks, by the time Jeb had signed autographs and sung a few numbers, Susannah's face was flushed, her eyes shining.

"I caught on quickly, didn't I?"

"You have a natural sense of rhythm." Whistling for another cab outside the club, he pulled her close, not only to shield her from the frigid wind. "On the dance floor too."

But Susannah still didn't want to go back to the hotel. Jeb paid the driver, who dropped them half a dozen blocks downtown, and they began walking, arms around each other, laughing and talking, especially Susannah.

"Could you believe that man with his wife? They must have been eighty."

"They could dance with the best of 'em."

She leaned her head on his shoulder. "It's wonderful to see that," she said, "to know that people can grow old together and have love. It's foolish, I know, but I still wish my parents—" She broke off, clutching his sleeve. "Look. That poor woman."

Jeb saw the bent figure sidling along the deserted street, coatless, her head uncovered, her hands bare, dragging a metal shopping cart behind her. Every few steps the cart caught in the snow, and she had to pull it free. Mumbling to herself, the woman, one of the city's street people, neared them, then passed by, her gaze downcast.

"She reminds me of too many I've seen in San Francisco. It's so sad. You'd think the authorities would find shelter—for everyone," Susannah said.

"There's not enough room. Last time I played New York City, I saw men sleeping on the subway grates, and one living in a cardboard box on Madison Avenue, right across from a five-star restaurant. Limos lined up out front two deep." The old woman glanced back at them, her eyes rheumy, her nose runny. "He was eating beans from a can. With his fingers."

Susannah looked especially stricken by this woman. "Can we give her something? I left my wallet at the hotel but I'll pay you back." She was already hurrying after the woman. "Wait!"

Jeb reached into his rear pocket, then stopped. His boots slipping on the icy sidewalk, he caught up with them. The woman had stopped but looked wary, as if they might be plainclothes officers about to hassle her. Jeb touched Susannah's arm. "I won't just give her money," he said.

She looked at him accusingly.

"We'll give her the help she needs right now." Bending, he met the woman's gaze and felt shock run through him. She couldn't be more than thirty-five or forty. "Ma'am," he said, "my friend and I would like to buy you a hot meal and coffee. It's a mighty cold night out here. Wouldn't you keep us company for a while, somewhere warm?"

After first refusing, the woman changed her mind, having satisfied her pride, he supposed. She looked on the verge of freezing. Susannah suggested a restaurant advertising quiche and crepes, but Jeb shook his head, taking them another block south to a burger joint, which seemed a safer choice. Plain, wholesome American food.

Once their orders arrived, the woman wrapped her grimy sweater tightly around herself and dug in to her burger platter with fries. For Susannah's sake, he wanted the conversation to go well, but it didn't go at all. Though well-spoken, the woman, who wouldn't give her name, obviously didn't wish to share her life story, and Jeb couldn't blame her. He'd been poor enough himself and knew that the time came when pride was all a person had.

Susannah watched every lift of the woman's fork, each swallow of coffee. Jeb nursed his own, as Susannah did, and when at last the woman set aside her plate and began to gather her belongings, he reached for his wallet.

Giving their guest a handful of twenties, he satisfied Susannah's need to be charitable but not his own. Three blocks after they'd left the woman with a full stomach, her mumbled thanks still echoed in his mind, and Susannah was apparently still trying to make sense of the event.

"I can understand buying her dinner," she said, "but did you have to give her your sheepskin jacket? My gloves?"

"'The living need charity more than the dead.'"

"Shakespeare?"

"George Arnold. *The Jolly Old Pedagogue*." Jeb shivered against the wind that smacked into him as they turned a corner, half-running back uptown toward the park and his hotel. "How do you define charity?"

Her breath came in white gusts. "You think—to me—it just means writing a check?"

"What else could it mean?"

She reminded him of her volunteer work. "And I give all my outdated clothing away. . . ." She paused. "That sounds . . . shallow, doesn't it? I suppose you're right. At first I think I wanted to press money into that woman's hands, as I have with others, add a look of pity, then send her on her way. I wanted to feel good that I'd done something." She looked at Jeb. "But I wouldn't have, would I? Being thanked isn't the point, or taking a tax deduction . . . or even being willing to listen to someone's sad story."

"No," Jeb said.

"Or feeling safe myself that I needn't live like that." Susannah glanced down at her expensive boots as if seeing them for the first time. "I've always considered myself a soft touch. The groups I work with, the animal shelter where I cuddle abandoned puppies for a few hours . . ." When she met his gaze, hers looked shamed. "It's not about any of that, is it? Or giving away money I don't need?"

"It's about a laying on of hands, Susannah. As my mama used to say."

"Preserving dignity."

"Yeah." Shivering, he put an arm around her shoulders and hurried her uptown to the warmth and light of his hotel suite, knowing all over again how far apart they were.

In the suite's kitchen, fighting his own guilt that he hadn't done more for the homeless woman, Jeb searched the cabinets. He could have given her a room for the night, but Breeze warned him to be careful; that he could no longer trust such impulses. The press siege around his grandfather and the souvenir hunters at his family's house nearly convinced him. Feeling chilled clean through after the icy walk, but not only by the weather, he wanted hot chocolate, preferably laced with brandy. He took out Breeze's carton of milk and a can of chocolate syrup that he'd bought for making sundaes.

"Why don't we call room service?" Susannah asked.

"Money. Housekeepers." He frowned. "Don't you do anything for yourself?"

"I take care of me," she said. "Maybe that's all I can handle."

It was an honest answer, but he didn't look at her face. Carrying a tray into the living room by the fire, which he'd laid before they went to the park, he thought maybe Breeze had a point. She'd come home that morning, walked into the suite to find Jeb and Susannah sharing breakfast in the same spot, and sworn at him. There'd been no time for the discussion they'd promised. She'd grabbed fresh clothes from her room, informed him that the Memphis concert had been canceled, and slipped back into the elevator before he was on his feet. Back to Mack Norton, he supposed.

Another unlikely combination. Why blame Susannah? She'd tried to help tonight in the only way she understood, but it wasn't the way he knew. One more gap between them.

As if she'd read his thoughts, she hovered in the doorway. "When do you suppose the airports will open?"

"You in a hurry, sugar?" He gestured for her to sit by the fire. When she sank onto a cushion beside him, without touching, she took the cookie he offered, a chocolate chip from Breeze's stash, then made things worse—without half-trying.

"Cody, what was it like growing up in a big family?"

"A poor one, you mean?" He hesitated. "Clary must have told you."

"I'm asking you."

"Crowded," Jeb said and she echoed his laugh, as if to ease the tension between them. "No, I'm serious. I never had a room of my own until I moved to Nashville. I always slept with my baby brother. Our house only had three bedrooms. Three girls in one room, three in another. My folks converted the dining room for themselves, but they didn't have a door." He wouldn't look up; wouldn't see the shock in her eyes. "I suppose that's hard for you to imagine."

"Maybe. But I think I'd like to have shared a room with a sister or two. To lie awake nights and not be afraid of the shadows on the ceiling or the monsters under the bed. To giggle and make wishes on the stars. To dream about tomorrow." She met Jeb's gaze, and he felt something melt inside, as it had when he'd seen the small heart tattoo. "I never came close to that until I met Clary. I'm so glad we roomed together at school those four years . . . that I didn't turn away from her when she married Drake."

Jeb got to his feet. He poked at the fire.

He'd enjoyed Susannah's company these past two days. He'd liked getting to know her, and catching glimpses of the warmer woman—the vulnerable woman—beneath the snooty mask. He'd sure as hell liked making love to her. But he wasn't sure even that was a good idea. And if she succeeded in getting him to talk about Clary, he knew she'd reopen the airport her-self, single-handed, to get away from him. He knew enough about Susannah to know she'd already made up her mind about that issue.

He set the poker back in its stand and turned around. As a shower of sparks erupted in the fireplace, he slid a CD into the player. George Strait began singing "Amarillo by Morning," and Jeb turned the lights low. He gave Susannah the deliberately dark, intense look that made his female fans scream and throw underwear. They might as well do what they did best, together. Let the rest lie. Until morning.

"Come here," he said.

She looked at him a moment, then set down her mug of hot chocolate and scrambled to her feet, into his arms. Not quite smiling, she showed her reservations too.

"This could get to be a habit."

"Sure could."

"If I let it," Susannah said. Then she kissed him.

Which Jeb had figured was safer than talking about their backgrounds and beliefs, about Clary. But then, he'd figured wrong before.

When Sunday morning dawned, bright blue and dazzling, Susannah was still lying on the carpet near the still-warm embers in the fireplace, in Jeb's arms, satisfied again and sleepy. She closed her eyes and let contentment reign as he stroked her back, the length of one arm. She supposed his change of mood shouldn't have surprised her last night. To him she must seem self-centered. And she couldn't argue. Taking care of her own needs was a lifetime habit, and she had a tendency to believe that other people could do the same.

After her faux pas with that homeless woman—dear God, she couldn't have been much older than Susannah but looked so worn, so hopeless—she'd stick to safer topics. As long as they could.

"Cody," she said, "how did you get your name?" She moved enough to see his face. "Did you pick it for the stage? Jeb Stuart Cody's not your real name, is it?"

"No." He smiled, the effect devastating. "And yes," he added.

Susannah raised up on an elbow but he drew her down again.

"My mama had a fancy for family names. She put stock in history, and she had a powerful lot of it in her family. It's said that her granddaddy—I don't know how many 'greats' removed—served under the cavalry general J.E.B. Stuart himself during the War Between the States, but I'm not sure of that. Mama liked to tell a good story."

"So do you, apparently."

"Nevertheless, she named me, all six and a half pounds of newborn baby boy, before—so she always said—PawPaw, my grandfather, cut the cord."

"Named you what?"

His drawl grew stronger, and she had the unshakable feeling that he was putting her on. "John Eustace Beauregard—"

"You can't be serious." John was simple enough, though it didn't suit him, but the next and, "*Beauregard?*"

"J.E.B." He laughed too. "John Eustace is my grandfather's name. His whole name, and everybody uses both. The next that so amuses you"—he leaned closer, kissing the corner of her mouth—"is for my daddy's maternal grandfather, supposedly a southern colonel. The Stuart comes from Mama's side again, and the Cody of course is obvious."

"No wonder Clary used it."

"But you're gonna quit now, aren't you?" Jeb drew back. At dawn, after he'd made love to her again, she had pulled on the Kentucky T-shirt he told her to keep and Jeb had tugged on his jeans, but they were still unfastened. "My last name's about as far away from me as you can get," he said, holding her gaze. "Is that what you want, Miss Susannah?"

"I'm not sure."

"Neither am I."

At his harder tone, she sat up, pulling the oversized T-shirt down, sensing that time had run out.

"I see. Maybe we should have kept to the subject then," she said, "to Clary."

"Susannah."

"I know you don't want to talk about her. You don't want to feel anything for her, but you do." She stretched the cotton fabric over her knees. "How can you not want to help find the person who killed her?"

"I've already told you . . ."

"You're a highly visible person. You could—"

Jeb sat up too. "I've told them what I know. You think they didn't haul me in the night she died? Question me? And everyone else she knew in New York, including Drake? I told them I was with Breeze, which I was, and they let me go." He paused. "Not that I'm sure they wanted to. They'd love having someone to hang her death on, to close the case."

"They haven't even found the murder weapon."

"They haven't termed it murder, Susannah."

"The gun wasn't that common." She could see immediately that he didn't know about that. "My father doesn't feel it would have been used by a junkie, a mugger."

"What kind of gun?" he asked with obvious reluctance.

"A .357 Dan Wesson with a short barrel."

"Two and a half inches," Jeb said, frowning. "How do you know about that?"

She might have asked the same question of him. "From the ballistics findings. And Drake saw the autopsy report."

"The police know it too. If you came here hoping I could crack the case for you, like some amateur detective, just because Clary was my sister—" He broke off, getting to his feet. "Why *did* you come here? It wasn't just to tan my hide for not comin' to her funeral, and when you learned I didn't think it was murder but an accident—Why in hell did you come?"

Stay, he meant. Susannah looked away as she stood up. Two days ago she wouldn't have mentioned Clary's message on her machine, but in short phrases, she told him about it now, hoping it might sway him to her theory. "I think Clary knew she was being stalked," she finished, "that someone might harm her. If that happened, she wanted me to . . . ease your pain, I guess."

Jeb's gaze darkened. "More charity?"

"I didn't say I could do it." She gave him her best haughty look, straight down her nose. "Or that I considered helping you. I came here for the reasons I stated—and it's obviously time I left. If the airport's not open, I'll wait like everybody else." Shaken, she crossed the room to the hall, intent upon finding her clothes.

He spun her around. "Had about enough time in my company, have you? In my bed? Rubbed shoulders—and just about everything else—long enough with poor white trash? With some backward southern cracker and his five names, four of 'em last names?"

"I never called you trash."

Putting a hand under her chin, he forced her to look at him. "I can see it in your eyes. I could tell by the way you held yourself when you walked in my door, all stiff-backed and straight-legged." His gaze dropped to the thigh-length hemline of the Kentucky T-shirt. "They're damn fine legs, I have to admit. But I can't say as I like the rest of you that much after all."

"Listen—"

"No, you listen." He gestured at the shirt. "I'm a helluva long way from those Kentucky hills, but unlike Clary, they'll always be with me, in my music. And I've met your kind before. Even in Nashville before I signed my contract with Jericho. Sure as hell since I've come north." His grip on her chin tightened. "You think I don't know what's going through your mind? I'll tell you." He leaned toward her. "'He may be stayin' in a five-thousand-dollar-a-night hotel suite with six bedrooms, five baths, a swimming pool, and helicopter pad on the roof, with a private limousine and driver thrown in for good measure. He may be filling seats all over this country with screaming fans and getting interviewed on *Good Morning America*. But by God, he's still nothing but a damn hillbilly!"

"You said it. I didn't."

When she tugged free of his grip, he caught her shoulder.

"I know what else you're thinking. Nothing that hasn't been thought or wondered before." He swung her back to face him. "'What in hell was he doin' in the back end of nowhere all those growin' up years?'"

She stiffened her spine. "I don't care to hear about your insecurities, Jeb."

It was the first time she'd used his first name, which he ignored.

"Well, hear 'em anyway. What was I doing besides pickin' at a busted guitar? Wishin' my daddy would stay out of jail? What else, but the same things people like you always say about poor country boys? That I must have been abusin' dogs and sheep or any other four-legged animal that'd hold still long enough." He grasped her shoulders as Susannah's eyes widened with shock. "Sleepin' with my own—"

Just behind them, the elevator chimed and the doors opened. Breeze Maynard swept into the penthouse foyer, a stack of newspapers flapping in her arms. The sun had fully risen and she had no trouble seeing Susannah in the T-shirt, braless and barefoot; Jeb, his chest naked and his jeans undone.

"Zip up," Breeze said from the living room doorway. "The party's over." She stalked into the room. "I'm afraid you'll have to excuse us, Miss Whittaker, but we have a plane to catch. The airport will open in another hour, I'm told, and I already have our tickets on the first flight to Savannah. So I hope you'll understand that Jeb doesn't have time to satisfy you further."

"Breeze," he said in a warning tone, his heated gaze still on Susannah.

Breeze whirled around. "I have enough damage control to deal with—"

"What the hell are you talkin' about?"

She slapped the latest scandal sheets into his hands as Susannah tried to cover herself more. She tried not to look at the tabloids, then saw the pictures.

Her, with Jeb. Dancing at Boots and Spurs. Coming out of the park in the snow. Their arms around each other, her face raised to his, close enough to kiss.

"The bad news. Headlines," Breeze said. "Read 'em and weep."

Hunk Cody Goes High Society
Country Star and Socialite?
After Sister's Death, Monkey Business—What's Next for Jeb Stuart Cody?

Jeb flung the papers onto a chair. "You know better than to believe that shit."

"I don't have to believe it. Some fans will, though. You can count on that." She gave him a scathing glance. "How do you think it looks, you and her?" She pointed at him. "You have a humble, everyman image to project—classic country, new traditional—and now I have that image to protect. It's not a job I relish so I'm not in the best mood."

"Clint Black married an actress," he murmured.

"That's entertainment," she said, looking at Susannah, "of a different sort."

"What's the matter, Maynard? Mack run out on you, back to his wife and kids?"

She stepped closer. "I work hard, too damn hard, for you. I've got you where you wanted to go. Don't throw it in my face!" She jabbed his chest. "If you know what's good for you, you'll show Miss Social Register here to the door—" she glanced down, "then keep that thing in your pants where it belongs and go pack!"

"Breeze, dammit."

"I mean it. Do it now."

Jeb's voice grew soft. "Which one?"

She launched herself at him, blond hair flying, blue eyes flashing. "If you want to stay where you are, Jeb Stuart Cody—"

He caught her wrists. "You know I do!"

Breeze went very still. "You must have heard, then."

"What?"

"The good news." She paused dramatically. "The album just went double platinum. And 'Country Justice' is at a million and a half. Number two on the Billboard chart."

Susannah watched his eyes change. The darkness became light, the insecurities faded, and a half smile touched his mouth. Breeze Maynard had saved the best for last. Lowering her gaze, Susannah stepped around them. She hadn't wanted to be more to him, she told herself. Forget his feeling about Clary. Against Jeb's career she didn't stand a chance anyway. She'd seen that look in her father's eyes when his service called with an emergency, in Michael's when he talked about a day in court.

Susannah opened her mouth, but Jeb spoke first, making her humiliation complete.

"I think you'd better leave."

"I think I'd better leave," she said.

5

Jeb had always loved performing. Even as a kid, when he and Clary, the closest in age of their siblings at just ten months apart, had put on musical entertainments for their mother, he liked being center stage. Even then Jeb's pure, clear voice in boyish soprano could override anyone else's, including that of his slightly older sister. As he grew and his voice cracked, then deepened into a true, middle-range baritone, Clary had gladly stepped aside. By the time he began appearing in small clubs and honky-tonks around their hometown of Elvira, he'd already been hooked for years on the clamor of applause at the end of a song and the rush in his bloodstream when he came onto the stage.

It was beforehand that he hated.

Wishing he were alone in his dressing room, Jeb threw down the hand towel with which he'd just wiped his perspiring face. Tonight he not only had to deal with the insistent roll of nerves in his stomach but with the persistent journalist who sat across from him, a tape recorder by her side and her pen poised above a yellow pad. He couldn't miss the newspaper clippings about Clary, about Susannah Whittaker stacked on her lap either. She'd tried to show them to him repeatedly, especially the photos of him and Susannah at his New York concert, on stage, their gazes locked and intimate, and shoulder to shoulder afterward in the back hall, smiling at each other as she handed him posters to sign, but Jeb kept dancing away from the pointed questions. He could see the reporter becoming irritated but he didn't care.

Twenty-six thousand fans already filled the coliseum. The warmup band had just swung into its second number, and Jeb's stomach fluttered.

". . . not really your kid sister, was she?" the reporter was saying. "Yet you wrote and titled a hit song as if she were."

"Is that a crime? A lot of songs are just stories someone made up."

"Then there's no truth to the lyrics?"

"I didn't say that." In addition to "Country Justice," and just topping it, his single of "Kid Sister" had reached double platinum in the two weeks since he'd left New York after the blizzard and was still selling like tickets at a Billy Graham revival.

"But the last line says, 'I should have taken better care of you.' Any comment?"

Bile rose in the back of his throat and he swallowed hard.

"I had six sisters. I felt responsible for all of them."

She sent him a sympathetic look. False, he was sure. "As the eldest boy in the family, with your father often"— she paused, as if to be delicate—"away from home—"

"You mean in prison."

"And with your mother often out of work . . ."

"Mostly out of work." She'd had little training and few talents, except singing in the church choir, and Jeb could remember more than one missed meal as a boy. As a store clerk she'd never made enough to support them but that wasn't her fault. And PawPaw had helped. "She did what she could."

He turned his back. At the mirrored table he picked up a brush and ran it through his hair. His face looked pasty, and he wasn't sure he should have worn the same outfit as in New York. Damn, if he had to make a run for the john with her sitting right there . . .

"Let's get back to Clary," she said, making his stomach lurch again.

"My sister's death is a private matter. I won't talk about that."

"But the newspaper accounts"—she tapped a long fingernail against the stack on her lap, against the top picture not of Clary but of Susannah and Jeb—"have been contradictory. You must have an opinion. Do *you* think her death was accidental? Or that someone deliberately wanted to hurt you through her?"

Jeb swallowed again. He'd talked about Clary with only one other person, Susannah Whittaker, and she had her own opinion. After he'd virtually thrown her out of his hotel suite, he supposed her opinion on any issue would run counter to his. In the past two weeks he'd nearly convinced himself that she'd made love with him to set him up—to leave him before he could straighten out his feelings—because of Clary.

"I think that's absurd," Jeb said.

"Five minutes." With the words Breeze dashed into the room, hair flying, her walkie-talkie in hand. She wore black satin trimmed in white leather fringe, and Jeb frowned when he saw her. In two weeks they'd barely spoken a civil word to each other, which had begun to feel oddly normal if not comfortable. She looked at the reporter. "Mr. Cody is about to go on. I'll have to ask you to leave."

The reporter didn't move. "I just have a few more questions."

Jeb's stomach flipflopped. His mouth went dry and sweat beaded on his upper lip. His armpits felt wet. Goddamn. He took a breath, torn between bolting for the bathroom and shoving that stack of newspaper clippings down the woman's throat. Why in hell had Breeze booked the interview just before a show? So soon after Clary's death, when speculation hadn't settled down? When he hadn't forgotten Susannah Whittaker? Breeze had done it to get him back, Jeb answered himself. Then realized how paranoid that sounded.

In spite of himself, at the thought of Susannah, he felt his lower body tighten. He'd had more than one dream about those two nights and days with the haughty socialite in his hotel penthouse.

"Excuse me," he said, rising. "I've answered all I can for now." He turned on Breeze, his heart hammering. "About that opening number . . ."

She took one look at him and knew. He'd forgotten what the song was.

"'Do You Love Me?' What about it?"

At the merciful mention of the title, which should have been a duet about two lovers seeing other people, Jeb felt the blood drain from his head. He had wanted Breeze to record the song with him. They'd quarreled about that too.

"Tell the boys to tone down the tempo a little. Last

show it sounded more like a line dance than it did a ballad."

She would know he was on the edge. Breeze piled the journalist's papers, plunked the tape recorder on top, and steered her toward the door.

He flashed the woman a smile. Sickly, he supposed, but remembered his manners. He didn't need any more bad press.

"Thanks for coming by," he said.

"I'll be listening from the second row. Sing pretty."

If he could sing at all. Jeb cleared his throat, testing, as soon as the reporter disappeared. His throat felt scratchy, raw.

"All right now?" Breeze didn't expect an answer and she didn't meet his eyes, but as she straightened his collar, her hand lingered on his shirtfront. She turned away, heading for the door. "If you need a minute—"

He swallowed again. "I'm all right."

From the doorway she gave him an off-center smile. "Knock 'em dead, cowboy."

Like a mantra, Jeb repeated her words all the way down the hall to the backstage entrance. He loved performing. But he had to get there first.

With a glance over her shoulder, Susannah climbed the terraced steps to her front door. Her Victorian town house on the far fringe of Nob Hill perched on the long downhill slope—or uphill, depending on one's point of view—of California Street toward the Embarcadero and San Francisco's financial district. Several years ago, after moving from Greenwich, she'd had the three-story house with its wraparound porch and under-the-hill garage repainted from the original buff with brown shutters to its present gray-white with navy blue trim.

She looked back again, wondering for an instant whether she might be hallucinating. It had been a long afternoon—several hours at the animal shelter, then a talky meeting for the Arts Commission. But the same, thin child still stood on her front sidewalk, looking up at the house, at Susannah. The small face, the dark tangle of curls, the darker owlish eyes, touched her heart. She saw a short-sleeved T-shirt that looked stained and faded, a pair of too-short bluejeans with ripped knees, and a pair of battered sneakers. The child, no more than five or six years old, didn't seem dressed for even San Francisco's relatively mild April weather. There was still a strong bite in the air, a chill to the bay breeze.

"Hello," she finally called, but the little girl only stared up at her, and stuck a dirty finger in her mouth. Susannah felt a chill herself, though the child didn't appear distressed or lost. It was as if she were seeing herself but with darker hair, in different, more expensive clothes, years ago, loitering outside Drake's house because she didn't want to go in, didn't want to find her mother there. When the child didn't answer, she turned away.

The windows sparkled in the late afternoon sunlight as Susannah unlocked the front door. Or tried to. It swung open at the first light touch, before her key had even fit the lock. Susannah stepped inside, into the dim, cool interior of the front hallway.

She scooped letters and bills from the polished floor beneath the mail slot just inside, placing them on the mahogany Federal chest against one wall papered in off-white and beige muted vertical stripes. Turning away, she briefly met her own eyes in the gilt-edged eighteenth-century Federal tabernacle mirror above the chest. The house pleased Susannah. The shadows under her eyes and the fact that she obviously wasn't alone didn't.

"Leslie?" she called up the stairs.

No answer.

Susannah fought back a surge of alarm, which she still experienced upon coming home—to her own house now—whenever her mother was in residence. She glanced up at the globe of the Belgian hall lantern trimmed in brass. At the continued silence, she slipped off her salmon-colored pumps, then shrugged off her white wool suit jacket. In stockinged feet she padded through the entry hall past the simple dark Puritan bench under the stairs and into the living room flooded with sun.

To Susannah's relief her jeans-clad mother sat, one hand twined in her ash blond hair, bare feet curled beneath her, in one of Susannah's white-upholstered Sheraton armchairs. The balls of her feet, the pad of each toe, looked dirty and the room smelled faintly of moist earth.

"Feet down, Les. I know this isn't Greenwich but—"

Leslie didn't move and neither did the tall man sitting on the watered-silk celadon sofa, his dark brown hair sprinkled with premature gray at the temples. She had once considered him distinguished, but now he appeared pallid compared to her new memories of Jeb Stuart Cody.

"Michael," Susannah murmured. "I thought we had dinner reservations at eight." She looked pointedly at her watch, which read just after five.

He rose to his feet, lithe and brisk and looking crisply cool in a dark pin-striped suit. Slipping an arm around her shoulders, he kissed her on the cheek. "We've been waiting for you. I have good news."

"We need to celebrate," Leslie added.

Susannah didn't have to ask how or what. She knew. From the bright expression on her mother's high-boned face, the smile in her green eyes, that Michael's promised promotion had come through. Susannah had been dreading it.

She forced the smile. "You've made full partner. Congratulations."

"You didn't let me tell you," he said, pulling her down onto the sofa beside him. "I got the word at three o'clock and hurried over. Your mother didn't know where you were."

"I had a meeting."

"The Arts Commission?" Leslie asked. In Connecticut the arts had been a passion, but since she'd begun sporadically joining Susannah on the west coast, she'd given up her own role-model charities. Given up most everything, Susannah thought, though Leslie now seemed to take pride in Susannah's position as chairperson.

She pulled away from Michael's touch, the lazy circling of her shoulder with his thumb. They'd never enjoyed a particularly passionate relationship, but since Clary's death and the trip to New York, Susannah hadn't let him touch her. After two weeks he'd begun showing his annoyance and even Leslie had noticed.

"After last year and that inspired use of the Palace of Fine Arts for the annual banquet, the sublime music of Gershwin . . . no one else would do to spearhead this year's fund-raiser."

Susannah nearly winced at such praise. Once, she had craved it. Now, she wondered what Leslie wanted from her.

"What did you do today?" she asked.

"Worked in your garden." Leslie wiggled her feet,

which were still on the white cushions. "I've found I love digging my hands in the earth. If I'd done so years ago, when Drake and I first bought the house in Greenwich . . ."

"It would have changed nothing."

"Susie, you're becoming a cynic."

"No, a realist."

Increasingly, since New York, she added silently, and those two mesmerizing days with Jeb Stuart Cody. Days and nights. He'd given her a good waking up, just as Leslie used to do in a much different way. But she envied Jeb one thing, just as she'd always envied Clary: the closeness of family, even temporary, though she knew theirs had been dysfunctional in its own way.

". . . something to drink?" Michael was saying.

"Sorry. I'm being a poor hostess. I should have offered."

"Vodka with a twist of lime," he said, frowning.

She tried to focus on the butterscotch marble fireplace, on the chandelier, on the ebony grand piano in the far corner by the garden windows. She tried and failed. Her gaze skimmed past Leslie to the wall cabinet that housed the liquor supply. Michael knew better than to drink when Leslie was here.

Susannah stalked to the cabinet, unlocked it, flung open the doors, and pulled down three glasses. She opened the small refrigerator underneath the shelves and brought out the ice bucket, which her housekeeper had, as usual, filled before she left for the day. Susannah crammed cubes into the glasses, then reached for the bottles of icy sparkling water. Three of them. Filling the glasses to the brim, she located in the refrigerator a small bowl artistically layered with thin slices of lime. She added one to each glass, then passed them around.

Michael's hard blue gaze met Susannah's before he lifted his glass.

"A toast. To the Arts Commission's spring fund-raiser— its beautiful chairperson."

Susannah clicked glasses. "And to the finest law partner Wemberly, Dickens and Smythe has ever had. To you, Michael."

Leslie joined in, ruining the rest of Susannah's day.

"To you both. My dear children. And, I hope, to a summer wedding."

Michael managed a laugh. "Still plotting, Leslie? You should write a novel."

"I'd like a few grandchildren, you two. While I can still run after them."

She'd never run after a child in her life, as Susannah well knew. She glanced at the liquor cabinet again. Perhaps there really was nothing like a reformed sinner.

Excusing herself, Susannah went upstairs, still carrying her full glass of iced water. She drank it down in the privacy of her own rooms, with the door closed. Let Michael field the wedding plans. She'd take her time getting dressed for a dinner she no longer looked forward to, and pinch herself blue every time Jeb Stuart Cody entered her thoughts.

In her large dressing room, she plowed through the closets that lined the walls, coming up with a black pouf-skirted dress that ended above the knees. Wearing her black slip, feeling ready for another funeral, she pulled on black stockings, fastening them to black garters, then peered into her dressing table mirror and began applying makeup.

She was being unfair to Michael, petulant. Just because Leslie had taken over her home again didn't mean she should be rude to him. He'd had a triumph and wanted to share it with her. People had been pairing them for years, and since the newspaper accounts of her eulogy for Clary at the concert, since the photographs Breeze Maynard had first shown her, he'd even seemed vaguely jealous. Possessive.

But marriage?

Neither of them had wanted that. At least not to each other.

Susannah stared into the mirror. Maybe she was punishing Michael for Jeb's rejection of her in New York—which, she supposed, she richly deserved for becoming involved with him in the first place.

After putting on her makeup and dress, she smoothed out her skirt. She gave her image only a cursory inspection before starting for the hallway and stairs, intent upon rescuing Michael before her mother had named her fictional grandchildren and picked their boarding schools.

As she reached the top of the stairs, she could hear music from below. Loud and harshly strident, Janis Joplin blared from the stereo. It seemed Leslie was trying to recapture her youth; trying, in faded blue jeans and bare feet, to be young again. Lately she ran from one new interest to another. A midlife crisis, Susannah thought. Or was it an attempt to compete with Clary, who, though now dead, still retained Drake Whittaker's heart? A heart, Susannah knew, that her mother had never stopped wanting. In that, she supposed, they were alike.

"Les, please. Turn it down. You'll blow out my speakers."

She came into the living room, a sleek contrast in stylish blond curls and black silk to her mother's Haight Ashbury sixties' funk, and found Leslie dancing with Michael.

Susannah turned down the stereo.

She'd had no idea he knew how to dance, except for a tepid waltz at society balls. The two executed a few more fancy steps, reminding Susannah of dancing with Jeb at Boots and Spurs. Michael twirled Leslie under his arm and they subsided, laughing. Susannah couldn't help it. She shot another glance at the liquor cabinet, which she'd closed and automatically locked before going upstairs. The doors were still shut.

Michael grinned. "Ready to go?"

"Yes."

"Are you sure you won't join us, Leslie?" he asked. "We'll wait while you change."

She looked at Susannah. "I'll just stay in—and maybe give Drake a call later on."

"Leslie," Susannah said.

"He's grieving so. He cried last time on the phone. It worries me, his being alone in that big house. With all the memories."

She didn't mean Clary, Susannah thought. However much she still wished her parents would reconcile—the classic fantasy of children of divorce, apparently of any age—she wished even more that Leslie would find a new purpose in life before she got hurt again. Before she ended up in a bottle once more.

"Read a good book instead," Susannah advised, letting Michael usher her toward the door.

The evening stretched ahead. Even dinner at elegant, paisley-draped Fleur-de-Lys where Susannah as a first course ordered her favorite lobster soup with lemon grass didn't seem to help tonight, nor did running into mutual friends. Why had she agreed to the date? Out of habit, she supposed; a sense of obligation because she and Michael had been together, in other people's minds, for so long. Because they were friends, and sometime lovers, if not passionate ones. Susannah felt her cheeks warm. Because, she added to herself, like Leslie she had no real purpose in life.

Which had never mattered so much to Susannah before.

It was the world she knew, that all her friends knew. The world in which Michael lived, worked, succeeded. But the small fact nagged at her, and she realized she envied Jeb Stuart Cody something else: his commitment to his music. He had shown her another world, and as different as it had been, as unsuited to her, as rejecting as it had proved, she couldn't seem to forget it.

Late that night Susannah gazed out the car window. She'd been trying to forget all evening, but even through after-dinner drinks, thoughts of New York had played in her mind.

"You're very quiet tonight."

Michael's voice drew her thoughts back, and she started guiltily. "I'm not feeling well."

"You should have said something. We could have changed plans."

"I didn't want to dampen your celebration."

They'd met up with various well-wishers along the way, at Fleur-de-Lys and later at Top of the Mark, amid its magical mixture of glass, brass, and bronze overlooking the twinkling city lights. Michael's laughter had nearly brightened the night, but her continuing ennui remained Susannah's problem, like the low-down griping in her abdomen tonight, the familiar but increasing tenderness in her breasts.

"Would you rather I took you home?" He'd already stopped the car in front of his apartment building, a high rise that seemed to shoot straight to heaven, its penthouse floor appearing to graze the low-hanging fog over the city.

"No, I'll come up for a nightcap."

They rode the elevator in silence. Michael didn't touch her. When they'd danced he had kept a decorous distance, one hand lightly riding her spine, the other barely brushing her fingers.

When they reached Michael's duplex apartment, which tonight felt closed-in and overly scented with his herbal after shave, he mixed drinks and sat beside her on the gray leather sofa. The living room didn't appeal to Susannah. In gray and burgundy with chrome, it seemed masculine but somewhat sterile. The dramatic Georgia O'Keeffe paintings on the white walls and the one wall of windows bared to the San Francisco skyline and the sweep of the Golden Gate Bridge were its saving grace, in her opinion. She settled back against the cushions.

Michael sipped at his drink in silence for a moment. "Maybe your mother has an idea at that."

"What idea?" Leslie was full of them, most not very useful.

He toyed with the hair at the nape of Susannah's neck. "That we get married."

She turned to him in shock. "Is this a proposal?"

"Something like that. If you want it to be."

"Michael . . ." She laughed a little. "You've never been the reticent type. What on earth did Les say to you while I was dressing?"

"She waxed lyrical about marital bliss."

"As if she knows what she's talking about."

"Don't be so hard on her," he said. "I like your mother."

"So do I. In fact, I love her."

"But you treat her as if she were a five-year-old."

"Sometimes I feel as if I raised her instead." Susannah shifted away from his hand. She remembered her talk with Jeb about his family. "You don't know what it was like, growing up in Drake's house. Her house."

"Then tell me. You always change the subject when I ask."

Michael was the most normal man Susannah knew. He'd been raised in upper-middle-class stability by two parents who adored him. He had a younger brother and an older sister, and two living grandparents whom he called faithfully each weekend. He had no vices that she knew of, and he rarely swore. He didn't get angry easily or shout, and he treated her with unfailing courtesy and respect. Perhaps Leslie was right, she should marry him.

Then an unwanted image of Jeb crossed her mind again, a memory of throwing snowballs in Central Park and making hot chocolate; the memory of his hands on her body, his mouth on hers. The excitement when he walked onstage, catching his guitar in midair and saying, "How y'all doin' tonight?"

Maybe she couldn't help herself. Maybe, after growing up with Leslie, she actually gravitated to unsuitable men, not steady ones like Michael.

"Susannah?"

He had moved nearer and was bending his head, looking into her eyes. Susannah wished he'd take off his suit coat or loosen his tie. Something that might make him seem approachable, a little rakish, and perhaps dangerous.

"I don't want to talk about home."

More memories. Walking into the house, looking for Leslie, finding her. Hearing Drake's angry voice at night and sometimes the crash of glassware against a wall, the fireplace. The endless dance recitals and horse shows at which she'd searched the onlookers for either of her parents, seldom finding them.

"All right," he murmured. "But do you think Leslie has a point? About us, I mean."

Susannah laid a hand on his cheek. To her delight it felt faintly scratchy, imperfect. "Five o'clock shadow," she said. "It's late. I don't think we have to make a decision tonight."

"It's coming to that."

Her pulse sped up. "Michael, you're high on the partnership announcement and that new corner office. This isn't the time to plan the rest of your life. Or mine."

"Ours," he said. Then, "But you don't see any 'us' when you look at me, do you?"

"I—I haven't had a lot of practice with togetherness."

"I could teach you."

She stood, walked to the windows, and looked out at the brilliant lights of the city, at the wisps of fog drifting past. As, in New York, she'd looked at the snow.

"Or am I in competition since your last trip east?"

The word, the edge in his voice, made Susannah turn. "Competition?"

"Jeb Stuart Cody. I read the papers, Susie. I saw the pictures."

"That was publicity." She felt the color rise from her neck to her face.

"That's all? You went for Clary's funeral and ended up onstage at a redneck concert with that hillbilly singer. I'll grant you, he has a certain appeal—to some women, I suppose—but kissing him, Susannah? And hanging around afterward like some groupie? You never said where you were for the two days the airport shut down."

The word "hillbilly" made her wince. "I had a hotel room. At least I didn't have to sleep on a chair in some concourse." She hadn't quite lied, but the truth didn't seem to serve any purpose. Especially not when Michael was looking at her with such serious eyes and a down-turned mouth.

"The stories keep coming out," he said.

"Yes, I understand Cody and I are to be married in Las Vegas when he plays there next month."

"Not funny." He ran a hand through his hair. "I've been taking a lot of heat at the firm. You know, 'What's the matter, Alsop? Can't keep Miss Whittaker happy? Better watch out. If she buys a guitar, you're dead in the water.'"

"I'm not buying a guitar."

"The newspaper accounts aren't all flattering either. Some hint that this Cody knows more about his sister's death than he's telling," Michael said.

"Are you torturing yourself? Needlessly? Believe me, I heard enough stories from Clary about him. I didn't want to meet him in the first place. I wouldn't have if it hadn't been for his attitude about her funeral." She mentioned their quarrel about Clary and her message. "I went to give him a tongue-lashing, but he wasn't quite what I expected." Michael didn't look convinced. "He's charming at times, hostile at others." The word popped into her mind again. "Bewildered."

"By what? All those hit singles and a top-selling album? A bunch of screaming fans?"

Susannah nodded. "Yes, by sudden fame, I think. And Clary's death, though he wouldn't admit that. He probably doesn't know who to trust right now."

"My heart bleeds."

"Michael, you are jealous." She approached him, then leaned closer, giving him a kiss on the end of his nose, and to her surprise, he caught her close, burying his face in her hair.

"Stay with me. It's been months since we spent the night together. Stay and make the celebration complete."

"My staying won't convince you that there's nothing between me and Jeb Stuart Cody. Or convince either of us that we ought to set a wedding date."

"It might help."

She felt his muscles tense and eased from his embrace in the split second before it tightened. She loved Michael as a friend . . . but marriage? She wanted more than a lifetime of friendship and mediocre sex. Maybe, she thought, he was simply too normal for her.

"I'm really not feeling well." She crossed the room to retrieve her black evening coat. He helped her into it, his hands lingering on her shoulders.

"I can't change your mind?"

"I think I'm about to . . ." She gestured at her lower abdomen.

"Get your period?"

"My grandmother would have died at such frankness. I can almost hear her rolling in her grave at All Saints' Cemetery."

His voice turned husky. "I wouldn't mind . . . your being that way, I mean." His blue eyes pleaded with her, and Susannah almost changed her mind. "I really feel like making love tonight."

"I'm sorry." His expression fell, and she realized that, in trying to protect herself, she'd hurt him. "You needn't drive me, Michael. Your doorman can get me a cab."

"You're sure?" His eyes avoided hers.

"I'll take a raincheck if I may." She slipped into the hall, then gave him a last kiss good night. Michael kept his lips closed and his arms at his sides. "Congratulations again on the partnership. I'm very proud of you."

"Thanks." He closed the door before she stepped into the elevator.

Susannah chastised herself during the cab ride home. She should have stayed. But she did feel the cramps that normally heralded her period, and the tenderness in her breasts seemed worse than usual.

At the house, which was dark except for the Belgian hall lantern's glow, she let herself in and, leaving her shoes in the entry, went upstairs. Leslie must have gone to bed and Susannah hoped she'd done so without calling Drake. At her mother's room on the second floor, she paused in the doorway, hearing Leslie's soft breathing.

She remembered Michael's accusation that she treated Leslie like a child. He didn't know that their roles had often been reversed, and the old habit of checking on her died hard.

Satisfied that she was sleeping, Susannah climbed the last flight to her own rooms. Still feeling guilty that she'd refused to stay with Michael, she crawled into bed alone. She'd been sleeping only a few hours when the telephone woke her.

Struggling up on one elbow, she squinted at the bedside alarm. It wasn't quite five o'clock. Who could be calling this early?

"Sorry to wake you, Susie." She heard Drake Whittaker's deep voice on the line. In New York it would be eight o'clock, and he'd already have made his morning rounds, or be on his way to scrub for surgery. "I was half-afraid your mother would answer."

"Did she call you?"

"No," he said. "Thank God. I take it she was planning to."

"Then what—"

"I'm calling about Clary." His tone dropped lower. "Susannah, I've heard from the police."

She held her breath.

"A witness has come forward. A woman who saw . . . who saw Clary being mugged and then shot in the park. She says two men in dark clothes ran right past her, one with a gun still in his hand."

"Do the police believe her story?"

"She seems credible. They'll check her background of course, then have her undergo a lie detector test. She's apparently willing, even eager to take it. If everything checks out," he finished, "they'll have a description, someone to look for now." He sounded relieved. "At least we'll know it wasn't premeditated murder."

"You never thought it was." Jeb Stuart Cody hadn't either.

Remembering Clary's message, Susannah still wasn't that sure. Remembering Jeb's reaction to hearing about the gun's make and model, she suspected he had doubts now too, even though he'd probably deny them to his own dying day.

6

Late that afternoon Susannah's phone rang again. She was on her knees in front of the chair on which Leslie had curled her dirty feet the day before, and had to stretch to reach the extension on the end table. As she did, she set aside the dampened sponge she'd been about to use on the chair's stains.

Susannah instantly recognized Breeze Maynard's voice, but the ex-singer didn't bother to say hello. "Jeb wants to talk to you."

Before he came on the line, she heard a brief exchange, feminine then masculine, through an obviously muffled receiver.

"Hey. Susannah."

She fought the urge to hang up. "What do you want?" The mere sound of his husky drawl made her remember New York, his ultimate rejection, and her own seeming inability to block those days and nights from her memory.

"I know it's earlier where you are, but have you seen the papers?" he asked.

Susannah hadn't. But she'd talked to Drake.

"Don't tell me we've been married and are expecting our first child."

"Pardon?"

She pressed two fingers to the bridge of her nose. When she'd wanted to talk about his sister, Jeb had been unwilling, to say the least. "I assume the New York police have released the story about that witness who saw Clary's murder."

"They're still calling it a run-of-the-mill mugging—more officially now—only whoever killed her got surprised by someone—maybe that witness—and pulled the trigger." She heard the rustle of paper, then Jeb read her a few paragraphs from a newspaper account. "It's front page here too. I suppose because of Clary's youth, her beauty, the powerful man she married—" he paused, "and prob'ly because of me, I guess that makes headlines anywhere."

"Where are you?" she said, hoping she sounded merely polite, not interested. She picked up the damp sponge.

"This is from the New Orleans *Times-Picayune*. We're down here for a three-concert series, starting tonight."

He read her some more, and Susannah's stomach churned. The horror washed over her again, all the stronger for Jeb's restrained, impersonal tone. "How terrible it must have been to die that way. To know in a split second that everything was over."

"Turned sour," he said and she could almost hear the frown in his voice. "The police have said all along that nothing was missing from her purse. When they found it nearby, all her cash and credit cards, her ID, were still inside." Jeb paused again. "Hell, she probably had a gold chain hangin' from her neck, more chunks of gold at her ears. Drake spoiled her so."

Susannah saw through the words. He was trying to dismiss his doubts again, his feelings. Swiping the sponge across an earth-colored stain on her white-upholstered Sheraton chair, she said, "Drake loved her. He liked buying her beautiful things. Don't blame my father or Clary for what happened. A person should have a right to sit in the park in the sunshine, without fearing for, or losing, her life."

But it hadn't been a beautiful day. It had been March, damp, cold, gray, and starting to snow. The police had found Clary's handbag in a pile of snow-covered leaves a few days later.

Jeb corrected her about the weather, then added, "Why do you suppose she was there in the first place? Central Park's nowhere near Greenwich."

Except for his obvious recognition of the murder weapon's model and make, its barrel length, though he hadn't said as much, it was the first time he'd indicated interest in the case, challenged the official police reports. Susannah took heart.

"Clary's doctor has an office near the park. She might have gone there after an appointment, before the limousine drove her back to Connecticut." It was Drake's driver who had come looking for her, who had found her surrounded by onlookers. "She and Drake had been trying to have a baby and Clary was having tests."

"Did she have a doctor's appointment that day?"

"Her gynecologist said not, but what if Clary had seen another specialist? A new one? Her appointment book is missing."

"Then, for some reason of her own," Jeb said after a brief silence, "Clary probably sat down on that bench, wrapped up in a fur coat, clanking her gold jewelry, and when those guys demanded it, she wouldn't give it up. That would be Clary," he finished.

Susannah dabbed at the stain again, as if it were blood. "Are you saying she deserved what happened?"

"No, I'm saying she had a stubborn streak. And maybe it got her killed."

Killed, she thought. Her heart sank. Apparently, despite his interest, he could accept that without flinching, though Susannah couldn't. Hadn't Clary told her he knew violence? Death? He'd once shot a deer, she'd said; he'd gutted it, skinned it himself, and left its brown-eyed fawn an orphan. Susannah, who didn't know any men who hunted, supposed Jeb didn't even blink when he pulled the trigger. If he'd felt anything, he wouldn't have shown it. Just as he denied whatever feeling he had for Clary—except that one time, onstage.

"It's easier for you to dismiss her death as an accident—just as you dismissed her from your life—than it is to admit you care. I wonder who's really the stubborn one."

"I wonder," he said. "You still think she was murdered."

"The police don't think so. My father doesn't. You don't."

"But you do, Susannah. Why?"

"It's a gut feeling. Instinct." That *help him* message.

"Because she left you some cryptic phrase on the answerin' machine? Did you tell the police that?"

"Yes," she said. "They discounted it. I even played it for them, and they heard nothing in her voice, but they didn't know her."

"She was probably playin' games with you. Clary liked games. She liked putting people on edge."

"You're wrong. If you hadn't turned your back on her—"

"I had my reasons, dammit." He hesitated. "And she left home, not me."

"Not good enough, Cody. She was your *sister* and she never stopped missing you, loving you, but even now all you want is to push what happened to her away, to write it off, and keep going. Well, fine," she said, shaking. "Forget it. Forget her and forget me. I don't know why you called."

"You're still mad about New York. Aren't you?"

Susannah sat back, amazed all over again at the bewilderment in his tone.

She forced a cool tone herself. "It's not a matter of anger. We had a little fling—all very cozy and romantic, during the blizzard of the century—and it ended. You were right to tell me to leave." She took a breath, intent on saving her pride after the fact.

"You said you were leaving." He waited a heartbeat. "You mean you didn't hear me call after you?"

"Oh, come on."

"I stood in the hall, yellin'—but you'd already reached the elevator and the doors slid shut. I took the next car down, even with Breeze screamin' at me about the plane taking off without us, but your taxi was just pullin' away when I got outside . . . in my bare feet, I might add."

"I don't believe you."

"I wanted to offer you a ride in the limo with us. At the airport I had you paged, but you never answered."

"I didn't hear any page."

"If you had," he said, "would you have picked up?"

"Probably not." She'd have been tempted, though. "It's taken you two weeks to call me, to tell me this?"

"I've been thinkin' about you." His voice dropped lower, which made Susannah's senses more alert. It was a practiced maneuver, she thought. "Thinkin' about New York, the concert, the poster signing, the limousine . . ."

She said nothing. She gripped the receiver until her knuckles turned white.

"That little tattoo you have right under—"

"Don't!"

She could almost hear his retreat in the silence. When he spoke again, his voice sounded normal, though much of the drawl had disappeared.

"Well. I guess you're back in San Francisco, Miss Susannah, going to fancy parties and wearing your fox-lined trench coat to lunch with your society friends. I didn't mean to upset you about Clary."

"You couldn't upset me."

"Give it up, Susannah." Jeb's voice had gentled. "She's dead and nothing you—or I—can do will bring her back. That includes hunting down a cold-blooded murderer instead of two pathetic, doped-out guys who tried to rob her for a fix."

"You're wrong. All of you."

She was trembling. The dirt stain on the chair appeared to have spread and grown, and she didn't even think about trying again to rub it away. She should have left it for her housekeeper. She should have known she couldn't fix it.

"I'll leave you to do good works," Jeb said. "I shouldn't have called. But I didn't want you to learn the way I did. I had to read it in the papers myself."

"Drake called me this morning," she admitted.

"Well, I didn't expect to hear from him. But the police—they didn't call me either."

"They probably thought you wouldn't care."

*   *   *

Susannah abruptly hung up and Jeb slammed the phone down. They'd met under unusual circumstances, he told himself. As Susannah said, they'd made love under unusual circumstances. He figured, with a woman like her, he'd just run out of unusual circumstances. Susannah Whittaker was out of his league.

Jeb rocked back in his chair. Since New York, nothing seemed to be going right.

He'd spent the day before in Nashville, recording part of his second album. Still shy two or three songs, he was running out of time but couldn't find what he wanted. The label's A & R representative's submissions hadn't pleased him—or Breeze's, he admitted. And the session itself hadn't gone well.

Jeb was also fighting a faint hoarseness, though he wouldn't use that as an excuse. Last night, after dropping in at the Blue Bird, Nashville's famous club where performers often tried out new material, and singing a few songs for the mid-week audience, he'd blown a lyric. If it hadn't been for Breeze's quick prompting, he would have stood there with his mouth hanging open and people giving him funny looks, as if he'd deliberately ruined their evening, and their image of him.

Now he'd managed to turn Susannah off as well.

Hell. Why did he care?

And why had he called her in the first place? Because of the news about Clary or to hear her voice again? He already knew what she thought about his sister's death, could have guessed what she'd make of the witness. But if Jeb had growing doubts, especially after hearing about the gun, a model he knew well but which he'd always heard seemed popular with hired killers and the like, she was right; he wouldn't indulge them.

He propped both feet on the hotel suite's coffee table

and set about preparing himself for tonight's concert. Picking up his guitar, he strummed several chords and ran through some lyrics in his mind.

Minutes later, he slammed his right hand against the guitar strings, freezing a chord into silence. Since the release of his album, since it had gone platinum and then platinum again, since his tour had begun and people recognized him, he admitted he'd gone a little wild. Smiled a bit too often at a pretty girl. Taken more than a few to bed for a night or two. What was so different about Susannah Whittaker, other than her surprising vulnerability? Her obvious but touching lack of sexual sophistication?

He'd taken care of her. If he hadn't, he would have followed through on the foreplay in the limousine. He'd felt hot enough to overcome any resistance, he'd wanted her so badly. But no matter how appealing she looked with her fancy clothes askew, her lips so warm and soft, her eyes asking for something he wasn't sure he could supply, he'd pulled back. In large part because he couldn't protect her then. Jeb had fathered one child in his life and had promised himself he wouldn't make another woman pregnant. He'd done his duty by Susannah Whittaker. She'd have no worries from him and he'd have no surprises from her for the media to scramble over like free tickets to a sold-out concert. Setting the guitar down by the chair, he leaned his head back. So what more was there to think, or say?

"What did she have to say?" Breeze wandered into the living room, wearing yellow satin with copper trim and bronze-embossed boots. And an I-told-you-so expression.

"She thinks Clary was murdered. I think she wasn't."

"That's all?"

He fought off a sudden image of Susannah, her belly rounded with his child, her eyes soft with love for him. Jeb straightened in his chair. The image didn't send pain rushing through him, but need. Frustration.

"Isn't that enough? Susannah Whittaker and I are a complete mismatch, which you pointed out early on. I should have my head examined for spendin' time with her in New York. She sure as hell doesn't want to remember that blizzard . . . or being stuck in it together."

"Is that why you've been mooning around ever since?"

Jeb didn't answer. Seizing the guitar again by its neck, he settled it across his thigh, riffled off a complicated chord sequence, then the beginning bars of the song he'd been trying to write the day they met.

She listened for a moment. "That's a beautiful melody. We need it for the album."

"Maybe you ought to write some lyrics then. I don't have the words."

She crossed the room to him. "You're not pining for that woman, are you? So you spent a night or two together . . . so what?"

He strummed another chord. "You and I spent a night or two together."

"Past tense. And you sure aren't moonin' over me."

"My point exactly." He paused, wanting to change the subject. "As far as that's concerned I don't like a crowd in bed."

Breeze made a sound. "Don't you start on Mack. What's between us is ours, and nobody else's."

"Don't kid yourself." Unable to finish the melody line, Jeb put the guitar down, knowing he wouldn't pick it up again until he caught it in midair, on stage later. Or one of the dozen or so guitars he carried with him. Some of them had been handmade for him by fans and varied from sleek dark mahogany with simple brass tuning pegs to one made of rare black walnut inlaid with semiprecious stones.

"There are more people involved than you and Mack," he finally said. "And you know what I'm talkin' about so let's drop it. In another minute you're goin' to kick my mouth into high gear."

"I'd love to hear it."

Jeb grunted, ready to quarrel, but the suite's door opened, admitting Mack Norton, his tall, dark-haired, barrel-chested guitarist and band leader, Breeze's current love interest. If you could call it love, Jeb added silently. He glanced up, meeting Mack's dark gaze. Mack looked away, at Breeze, and his eyes warmed.

"You ready?"

She looked at Jeb. "More than ready."

"I'd like to talk to you, Mack." Jeb stood up, unwilling to give the other man the advantage of looking down at him. He glanced at Breeze, deliberately choosing his words to irritate her. "Go powder your nose, sugar."

"Go to hell. I'm staying right here."

Mack put an arm around her shoulders. "It seems Jeb and I have things to say. The car's out front. Meet me there in ten minutes."

"I won't be dismissed—"

"You already have been," Jeb said.

Breeze threw him a hateful look. "Pig." She stormed to the suite's exit, and the door slammed behind her.

"She'll be calling you names for a week," Mack said.

"I don't care what she calls me. I have her best interests at heart."

"Sounds good." Mack smiled faintly. "I don't suppose you mean me."

"No. And do I need to remind you who's payin' your salary? A pretty handsome one at that these days."

Mack's hands balled into fists at his sides. "Are you threatening me?"

Jeb walked over to the stereo cabinet. It wasn't as large or complete or first-rate as the one in New York had been, but he opened the CD changer and slipped in a disc. Trisha Yearwood's pure voice filled the room with the strains of a soft ballad.

"We've been around a long time, Mack. Playin' honky-tonks and dreamin' about the big time. Eating peanut butter and jelly sandwiches and drinking beer for break-fast." He smiled a little. "Remember that Christmas we both worked at Wal-Mart? You in Automotive, me in Toys?" He looked at Mack. "We're gettin' somewhere now. Don't blow it."

"You had your time with Breeze. It's over now."

"All the more reason why I care what happens to her."

"Are you warnin' me off?"

"I guess I am."

"And if neither of us listens to your advice?"

"Breeze is a great manager. You're a good musician, Mack, but I could pick up that phone"—Jeb waved a hand at the extension on the lamp table near the sofa— "and find a new guitarist before tonight's show. I don't want to but I will."

Mack's eyes darkened. "So fire me. If I go, Breeze goes with me."

"No, she won't."

"Don't bet on it. You think she's that loyal to you? Because you slept together when you were starting out? You're a fine-lookin' guy, Jeb, the hands-down winner in that department, but I seem to keep her happy enough these days."

Jeb's jaw tightened. "What about your family?"

Mack looked away. "You're right, we've come a long

way." He'd just bought a house near Nashville, a big white brick Colonial with formal gardens in back. His wife loved it, she'd told Jeb, and so did the children. "Peggy and I have our differences. It gets lonely on the road."

"I know that."

"Lonely for her at home too," Mack said. "She kicked me out for being gone so much, weeks before I took up with Breeze." He paused. "You've had your share. Women here, women there. In New York, Breeze tells me—"

"I'm not married any longer. I'm not hurtin' anybody."

He watched the lanky guitarist stride to the windows. "Hurtin'? When Breeze Maynard lost that band of hers, she lost her soul. Maybe I help her find pieces of it again."

Jeb ran a finger over the scar on his upper lip. The familiar anger for Breeze's lost chances swept over him. "She ought to be singin', not screwing you." He looked toward the stereo. "Yearwood's a great performer, a great stylist, but Breeze Maynard has the best voice I've ever heard—except for my mama's. The difference between them is, Breeze knows what to do with hers. Just like Yearwood and Reba McEntire. But she's not doin' it." He frowned. "She just tears me up."

"She doesn't want to sing." Mack turned from the windows. "Everybody's not cut out for stardom, like you. Or driven to it. We give each other what we can, so cut us some slack, will you?"

He tried not to hear the condemnation in Mack's words. If he was driven, he had reason, not just talent.

"Do you love her?"

"In my way." Mack looked at him. "Do you?"

Jeb ignored his tangled feelings for Breeze as he had

tried to block out what he felt for Susannah Whittaker. "Do you love Peggy? And the kids?"

"Sure I do." Mack studied him thoughtfully. "I think you're just jealous. And I think you better mind your own career, instead of telling me 'don't blow it.'" He swung around, heading for the door. "After you, Jeb Stuart Cody. You stank last night. And that's from Breeze too."

Late that night, Breeze slipped from bed, grabbing Mack's plaid cotton shirt from the bedpost and tiptoeing into the other room. His suite was smaller than Jeb's, like his talent, and she crossed to the compact armchair by the gauzy-curtained window in a few short steps. She sank down on it, drawing her bare legs up and hugging her knees.

She didn't deserve the small comfort, she thought.

Mack was married, the father of two small boys, and if her mother had lived to hear her daughter tell of the affair, she would have slapped Breeze silly. Never mind that the music business, country definitely included, was filled with such temptations.

It wasn't as if her work for Jeb left any time or energy, and tonight he'd gone flat on the last chorus of "Lou'siana Lady" in front of the hometown crowd. She had enough worries.

"What's wrong, honey?" Mack's deep voice startled her from the bedroom doorway. Breeze looked up at his sturdy frame, at his rumpled dark hair and sleepy eyes.

"The usual." The monsters hadn't come out of the closet yet tonight. She'd just been warming up.

Mack drew her from the chair and onto the nearby sofa. The love seat pushed them together, and she curled into his arms, one leg between his.

"What did Jeb say?" she asked after a moment. On the way to the coliseum and afterward, once they'd reached Mack's suite, neither of them had felt like talking.

"He was just flappin' his jaw."

"Did he threaten to let you go?"

"He won't fire me. We're like brothers." Mack smiled against her hair. "I've been with Jeb since his first gigs in Elvira when we were both eighteen."

"I know but—"

"We played every low-down, dirty bar in the tristate area . . . Covington, Cincy, Indianapolis, you name it. We were there." He hugged her. "He's just mad, that's all, 'cause he messed up a good thing with you and I got lucky."

Breeze felt his bare chest rise and fall. "He didn't mess things up with me. We just ran out of steam, Mack. Though I admit, it was pretty hot while it lasted." She tweaked some dark hair over his sternum. "I don't think he was much more than twenty then, though he seemed older. And his wife had died not that long before." She looked up at him, glad they could talk about something safer, if just as sad. "Sometimes I don't think he's over that yet. Do you know what really happened to her?"

Mack shifted, a hand skimming her spine. "Didn't he tell you?"

"He wouldn't talk about it. Neither will the rest of the band." It was one of the few secrets, she was certain, that Jeb had from her.

"It's been a while. He might not mind me telling you now. But hell, if he does, I'm mad enough at him myself tonight not to care." He took a breath, his soft Virginia accent soothing her. "Jeb and I talked about this only once—one night after a few drinks followin' a show. I think it was too fresh in his mind then, and he just hadn't skinned the hurt over yet." Mack paused before going on. "You know Jeb married real young. I think his wife was sixteen when they ran off. Her name was Rachel. He was seventeen. Jeb said his father was in jail for one thing or another at the time, but his granddaddy, John Eustace, was fit to be tied. Then he learned the girl was already pregnant and shut his mouth."

"So young," Breeze murmured.

"When she had the baby, there was some kind of medical problem, I forget what. But she died givin' birth to Jeb's son. They both died," he said softly.

Breeze pressed her cheek to his chest. "No wonder he and I turned to each other at the time."

Jeb had been new to Nashville, she recalled. He drove a delivery truck to pay his rent and hung around local bars at night, hoping for the chance to play and sing his songs. He was six years her junior, but it never seemed to matter. At the time, only a few months after her band's accident, after she'd quit singing herself and left behind an eight-year career, five of those years in the bigtime, nothing much had mattered.

She'd met Jeb over two cold beers. He'd recognized her instantly, even in the dark glasses and scarf she'd worn then to keep curious eyes away. She hadn't been able to keep away herself, though, from the music. The small dirt band playing that night hadn't offered much, and nothing new, but she'd tapped her foot anyway. The motion drew Jeb's gaze, just as she noticed his index finger keeping time against his sweaty beer glass. They'd gone home together that same night, not to make love, but to sit up all night, talking. The first time Breeze had heard Jeb play and sing, she'd known she didn't have a chance.

He'd pulled her in, out of herself and away from the tragedy she saw each night when she closed her eyes alone. For nearly a year he'd kept her demons at bay in bed too, and long after they'd stopped being lovers and settled for being friends, she'd kept her pledge to make him a star.

The pledge had taken ten years to fulfill, but Breeze didn't regret a moment, and she knew Mack didn't either. They'd hitched themselves to the comet's tail and were riding it straight over the moon.

"What's wrong with him now?" Mack asked.

"Clary, I suppose."

"He hasn't said much."

"Not even to himself, I'd bet. I thought you knew Jeb—enough to know that he hides what he feels strongest inside himself. Except onstage. I'm just hopin' he writes that song and gets it all out before he explodes."

"Perceptive woman," Mack murmured. He ran a hand through Breeze's blond hair. "You ought not to see through us strong, silent types quite so easily."

"Maybe I just recognize pain when I see it. Hidden or in plain sight."

"Jeb thinks you should start singin' again."

Her pulse jumped. She knew what Jeb thought. He hammered at her enough. Breeze untangled herself and rose from the sofa, remembering the fight they'd had when Jeb recorded his first album. He'd wanted her to turn "Do You Love Me?" into a duet but she'd refused.

"I know what he thinks." They'd sung duets before, perfect harmonies late at night, in bed together, or in the shower, their voices perfect complements. She didn't need this one about two former lovers seeing other people to hide what they felt for each other. Not even for the sheer pleasure of blending again with Jeb. "He's wrong. 'Do You Love Me's' climbing the charts as a single. Singin' again is the last thing I plan to do."

Mack's eyebrows drew together and his mouth turned sulky. She admired that lower lip, most of all when it was moving against her own, when his strong, callused hands were roving her body. "Come back to bed," she said, holding out a hand. Knowing that was all they shared.

Leading him back into the darkened bedroom, Breeze tried to push away her guilt. Whatever didn't work between his wife and Mack, his yen for her seemed a small enough consolation, at least to Breeze.

But when the loving ended and the room fell silent in the blackest hour before dawn, and Mack Norton snored gently again, she lay awake, her gaze fixed upon the dark ceiling.

She stared, unblinking, but she was in Atlanta once again, holding court in her hotel suite and waiting for the boys to arrive. She'd flown in early for an interview, the cover story of *People* magazine ("Country Music Still Alive with Breeze Maynard," it had said after the accident, just before she quit) and she'd missed the bus trip, missed the laughter and the griping and the growing anticipation before a big concert.

Then someone had knocked at her door.

Breeze answered, a big smile on her face. She'd been wearing her newest costume because the seamstress was there, marking the hem, and it trailed half up, half down, and full of pins as she opened the door. Her long hair in curling rags.

Not the sort of outfit for the news she received.

Dead. All of them. Chaney, Burt, Doc, Wilson . . . dead.

The bus had been smashed beyond recognition. Glass strewn over the road and through the grass. Blood and body parts, unrecognizable too.

She'd seen the pictures, visited the site herself. She hadn't been able to believe it until she saw. And she'd only seen what remained after the cleanup. Thank merciful God for that much.

Her heart pounded and her limbs felt weak. Breeze rolled against Mack's spine, pressing her cheek to his warm skin.

Never again. She'd keep them all alive this time. Keep them on top. Most of all, Jeb.

7

John Eustace flipped the catch on the front door and closed it behind him, hoping he'd set the new security system properly. Jeb had ordered it installed to prevent vandalism and the increasingly serious souvenir-hunting by his fans that threatened to strip the old house bare; but John Eustace hated the high-tech gadgetry he didn't understand. He shuffled across the narrow front porch and down the steps, feeling his bones rub together. He'd turned seventy-eight the week before Clary died, and he felt every year now, made worse by Kentucky's cool, humid late April weather. Even his stringy muscles seemed to creak.

Reaching the front walk, he stopped a moment to stare down at the sparse grass between the flagstones, trying to tell himself he didn't need the brief rest. Then he turned and looked back at the simple frame house. Its paint had begun to peel at one corner and along the porch railings, and he knew that, come summer, he'd have to hire someone to make repairs. He wanted everything to look right when Jeb came back.

Adjusting his battered straw hat, he took a few steps and found himself headed in the twilight across the side yard toward the slope down to the creek. In the years since Jeb had left home, he'd often come here, at first while his daughter, Jeb's mother, was still alive and looking so much like his own wife, and then because the younger children still lived at home and needed watching now and then. Jeb expected his occasional supervision, but John Eustace would have given it anyway. Family was all that mattered.

Ambling across the brown grass, he struck off down the hill, trying not to take exceptional care each time he planted a leg on the increasingly steep decline. His left hip began to ache but he ignored it. Time marches on, he thought, his steps hitching. Things change. John Eustace fought it as he could.

Halfway down the hill he snorted, carefully skirting a long narrow hummock of grass-covered earth that looked onto the creek below. Clary had had some notion that he and Jeb had buried their mistakes there, but the memory didn't make him laugh. She was gone now and the notion with her.

Clary's mother was dead too, the kindest, gentlest woman—other than his wife—he'd ever known. A twinge of guilt seemed to flash right through his hip. He'd wished often enough that his daughter and Clary could change places. Now, he supposed, though his daughter would have wanted Clary with her in the great beyond, Clary must instead feel warmer than an Elvira summer's day, down below.

So many gone, he thought. Good or bad. One trouble with growing ancient was that everyone else went before you. Even the young ones had drifted off, married or taken jobs in other, less economically depressed states, and the last two—at twenty and eighteen—were away at college. Jeb paid tuition for Ethan at the University of Kentucky and for Marilu at Ohio State.

Looking out over the creek, listening to it burble along in the early evening stillness, hearing the varied birdsong in the woods opposite, John Eustace rocked on his heels. He slipped his hands into his baggy brown pants pockets, and one closed around the latest check Jeb had sent.

"PawPaw, I'm makin' more money in a week now than you prob'ly made in the best year you practiced medicine in Elvira. Quit pissin' me off and spend it, will you?"

John Eustace's mouth curved a little, and the scenery before him seemed to blur. He ought to have his eyes checked again; probably those cataracts were growing and blocking off his vision. Jeb, thank the Lord, had his mother's sweetness, not his father's meanness. Clary had married well, he'd give her that much, that fancy surgeon old enough to be her father—and in his opinion that's what she'd been looking for—but she'd never offered John Eustace any unneeded money, never sent a dime to any of the younger children, and never helped her mama when she fell sick.

Jeb had paid the hospital bills even then, when he was still in Nashville, waiting for what he called his break. Every month he mailed John Eustace a similar check to the one in his pocket, and every month John Eustace added another to the uncashed stack in his bureau drawer.

Jeb might need that money some day. Just as he needed his grandfather, who wouldn't always be there.

Maybe he ought to give in more often while he still had time.

"You've worked all your life," Jeb kept saying. "It's time to slow down. Why don't you sell off your practice and come with me on the road? You could sleep late and eye the pretty girls, smell a few flowers, grow fat and lazy . . . keep me company."

"I belong in Elvira, boy." *And so do you,* but he rarely said that aloud. Jeb knew his position, which hadn't changed in the ten years Jeb had been gone. And when he said them, the words riled his grandson. Or worse, made him moody-sad.

So John Eustace always held out as long as he could, then temporarily farmed his few remaining patients out to that young upstart with the fancy new office in downtown Elvira and the fancy BMW, and joined Jeb on tour.

He hated every minute but he purely loved his namesake, John Eustace Beauregard Stuart Cody. Thinking of his last "visit," he stood for some time by the creek where long ago he and Jeb had fished and talked and worked out what life was all about, the same creek where Jeb and Clary had played. Where John Eustace had held his grandson right after Jeb lost his wife and child, and felt the boy's sobs soak right through his shirt.

John Eustace took his hands from his pockets and passed gnarled fingers over his eyes. That boy, no matter how big his talent or his paycheck, needed him, and Jeb gave John Eustace his reason to keep living. They were all each other really had. With the clear gurgle of the creek behind him and the birdsong dying down with evening, he started back up the hill in the near darkness, paying no attention to his wheezing breath or the burning in his hip.

"You've been taking care of other people all your young life," he said aloud, because Jeb wasn't around to contradict him. He gazed up at the simple house in the distance. "You just aren't very good at taking care of yourself."

John Eustace blinked. He loved Jeb with all his heart. He'd do anything for him.

Susannah had long ago become accustomed to taking care of herself. Because no one else had ever done it, the responsibility seemed hers alone. By the time she'd graduated from college, she preferred it that way. Taking care of things herself left no room for disappointment.

As a result of her forced independence early in life, she realized she wasn't good at delegating, and the Arts Commission's spring fund-raiser had become a full-time job. Jeb should see her now. The night before she'd gone to bed at 3:00 A.M., and without a miracle, tonight would bring no improvement.

She had a dozen telephone calls to return and . . .

"Lady?"

On the bottom step of her front walk, Susannah paused. She turned around, finding the same small, dark-haired child she'd first seen a month ago, and several times since. The little girl wore what appeared to be the same jeans and T-shirt, though her face looked clean and her glossy curls brushed. The warmer mid-May weather now suited her appearance, but she'd never spoken before.

"Hello," Susannah said, sitting down on the steps to bring herself more on a level with the child. She smiled. "What's your name?"

"Miranda."

"What a pretty name. Do you live around here?" Perhaps she was a new neighbor. Susannah knew the people closest to her but not up or down the block.

"No," Miranda said, holding out a hand. "Do you have money?"

Taken aback, Susannah laughed. "I have a few dollars. Why?"

"You live in a big house. You drive a big car. I seen you, coming out of your garage." She pointed toward the closed doors in the hill nearby. The garage had an elevator to the hall near the kitchen, but Susannah rarely used it. She seldom used her car either, preferring to walk or take taxicabs and avoid the parking problem. "Are you rich?"

Feeling more uncomfortable by the minute, Susannah stood up.

"Do you need money?" she asked.

"Just for supper. My mom won't let me take money or stuff, though. She says we're just poor right now and we'll have a house when my dad comes back." Miranda paused. "Maybe it'll be a big, beautiful house like yours."

Susannah reached into her purse, pulling out several bills, which she slipped into the little girl's hand. "Where do you live now?"

Miranda pointed to the alley not a hundred feet from Susannah's house. "There's a old car there, and Mommy and I sleep inside at night."

With a growing sense of dread, Susannah asked, "Where's your mother now?"

"Looking for work." Wide, dark eyes met Susannah's. "My dad went away," she said, "because he couldn't get a job. We'll be all right."

Susannah had a feeling the words were a litany, repeated by Miranda's mother to comfort her late at night, in an alley, inside an abandoned car. The child was homeless, and Susannah's heart tightened as it had in New York when she and Jeb had fed the street woman, when he'd given her his coat.

"Of course you will." She reached back into her purse. "Miranda, I want you to give your mother this." She wrote on a page torn from her address book. "This is my phone number and where I live. Tell her to call or come to see me. Maybe I can help."

She didn't know how, but she couldn't watch this small child day in and week out without doing something. Something besides giving her money.

"You tell your mother to buy you both a good dinner tonight."

Miranda tucked the note and folded bills into her jeans pocket with care. She'd obviously learned at a very young age the value of money and what it could buy. Survival.

She gazed up at Susannah. "You're pretty. Can I come see you too?"

"I hope you will." Turning away, Susannah blinked. "Miranda?" she said without turning around. "I have a garden out back. If you like, you're welcome to come play there anytime." Off the streets, she thought. "Just ring the bell and ask first to make sure there's someone home."

She heard no response. When Susannah turned again, the little girl had slipped away, into the gathering twilight, heading for the alley she called home.

Inside her own house, Susannah slumped at her leather-topped desk, rubbing two fingers over the bridge of her nose. Jeb had seemed to consider her little better than worthless. Rich and unemployed, she led in his view a life without purpose. Doing good works. In Susannah's circle charitable activities provided meaning enough, acceptable meaning, and she would have bristled at his opinion of her, except that it had lately become her own.

Had Miranda been conning her? Were her worn clothes and guileless questions a pose to solicit money? Or were they a fact of urban life? And what on earth could she do to help?

Reaching for the first telephone message she needed to return, she suppressed a sigh. She had little energy for anyone else tonight, even less for a scheduled appearance with Michael at a theater opening. But her presence was expected. And so would she be expected in his bed later.

Susannah gave in to the sigh. She'd been putting him off on that raincheck for a month, and Michael had joked, with a hurt edge to his tone, that she'd taken the April Fool's joke about their sex life far enough.

She had no interest in sex.

Dragging herself out of bed each morning, she didn't wonder why. Jeb might think she was rich and idle, but she was really working too hard. Trying to prove what? That he was wrong?

Six weeks after the blizzard in New York, a month after his one phone call, she was still thinking about him. About being pampered in the limousine, in his bed where he had brought her coffee and morning kisses. Remember the bad things, she ordered herself. His child bride. That helpless, white-tailed doe he'd shot. The teenage groupies. Jeb had only been amusing himself with her and hadn't meant a thing he did or a word he said. Besides, she had more work to do.

Before she could dial the first number, Leslie sailed into the airy, first-floor study, and looking up, Susannah felt the room spin as if her mother's motion had disarranged it. Susannah had skipped lunch because she hadn't felt hungry; in fact, she still felt stuffy and bloated, not in the mood to deal with her mother.

Leslie stood at the desk, thumbing through the stack of mail she'd brought, some of it Susannah's. "A bill for me . . . another bill for you . . . a note . . ." Leslie examined the postmark on a friend's envelope. "I see she's still on Maui . . . bill . . . and what's this?"

Susannah was busily organizing her telephone messages, trying to quell her irritation. She almost wished her mother's mail wasn't being forwarded from her Connecticut home, just minutes from Drake's. Given half a chance Leslie would open Susannah's private correspondence, and the red envelope she was holding, the logo in bold blue and white by the return address, looked disturbingly familiar.

"Hand it over," she finally said.

"Since when do you enjoy country music?"

"I don't."

"Since New York?"

When Susannah slit the envelope, a pair of red, white, and blue concert tickets fell into her lap. She gingerly picked them up and read: Jeb Stuart Cody, Tour America. San Francisco Arena. Front Row Center, Seats 10 and 11. A note stapled on top read: *Thanks for the memories. Let's make some more.* No signature.

She heard her mother's arch tone. "Susannah?"

She hadn't seen him in six weeks. She hadn't talked to him in a month. She'd hung up on him then, but the handwriting looked like his. It certainly couldn't be Breeze Maynard's. She stared at the tickets. The concert was tomorrow.

"What sort of memories?" Leslie said, reading over her shoulder.

"Bad ones."

"Then why would he—?"

"I'm sure I don't know. And I don't welcome an inquisition." She hesitated, her palms cold and clammy. "We spent . . . a few hours together during a snowstorm. Lots of people did."

Leslie tossed her beige-blond hair. "He's a handsome man. Very charismatic. And that body . . ."

"Mother." Susannah only used the term when driven to the limit.

"I know those newspaper gossip items angered you, and I can't blame you for that. But, Susie, you're not getting any younger. If Michael doesn't suit—"

"Michael's fine." Susannah pushed herself away from the desk. "Which reminds me, I have to dress. Are you coming with us to the theater and the reception after?" She crossed her fingers behind her back. There'd be liquor at the reception, and she couldn't watch Leslie all the time. She felt strung out as it was, without having to baby-sit tonight.

Leslie studied her closely. "You don't look well. Your skin's gray and you've lost weight. Is something wrong?"

"Charity exhaustion." And after the fund-raiser came the Junior League fall fashion show, then the holiday cotillion and another debutante ball.

"The Whittaker family curse."

Studying her mother's designer jeans and Stanford sweatshirt, Susannah forced a smile. "Why don't you dress tonight—it would make you feel good to put on something pretty again—and join Michael and me?" She raised a brow. "Misery loves company."

"I think I'll stay in."

"And call Drake again?" One alternative seemed as bad as the other. Susannah had begun to worry about

Leslie's isolation. Perhaps she'd have to suggest that her mother return east to visit her friends.

"We've had several nice chats lately. I think he's warming to me."

Susannah rounded the desk and gave her mother a light hug, whether she welcomed it or not. "Don't get your hopes up too high."

"Or yours," Leslie murmured. Susannah had reached the door when she said, "Are you going to that concert?"

"No. But I won't let these tickets go to waste either."

Still holding them, she swept from the room, her heart thumping, her palms damp. She had no intention of seeing Jeb Stuart Cody, of falling back under his spell. But the possibility had almost wiped fatigue and the haunting image of Miranda from her mind.

In his dressing room at the San Francisco Arena, Jeb lay on the navy blue carpet, counting crunches. Thirty-six, thirty-seven. His belly tightened again just as the door opened and Breeze walked in, toting the walkie-talkie that seemed like a third arm before every show.

Tonight she wore a sage green, western-style blouse bedecked with silver studs, a matching thigh-length skirt with a studded hem that must have weighed ten pounds, and silver knee-high boots. Flopping down on his back, Jeb sucked in air and frowned.

"You're not dressed," she said, eyeing his bare chest and black silk running shorts.

"I'm afraid you are." His critical gaze ran over her again. Breeze had the height and figure to carry off almost any style, but in Jeb's mind her fashion sense had fixated the day her band was killed. Her usual satin made him think of the old-timers, of the image country

music once had as appealing only to hillbillies, before it
went mainstream.

"Showtime in ten minutes. Or were you planning to
stay here, pumping up"—she glanced at the weights he
had already used, now shoved under the dressing table—
"instead of putting on your normally fine performance?"

Jeb ignored the dig. His relationship with Breeze continued to deteriorate and he didn't want another fight.
Getting up, he fought a sudden wave of dizziness but
flexed an arm. "My fans expect to see some muscle."

"The city fathers expect to see some clothes." She
stalked to the wardrobe on the end wall. "What are you
wearing tonight?"

"I'm tryin' out a new image." Jeb brushed past her,
pulling out a pair of dark pants and a white dress shirt.

He'd moved too fast. Feeling dizzy again, he shook
his head. It felt fuzzy, and his workout hadn't helped as
much as he'd hoped it would. He opened a duffel bag
on the oatmeal-colored sofa and took out some socks,
also dark, then a pair of plain black cowboy boots with a
roping heel.

"Well, I do hope it fixes what's wrong lately," Breeze
murmured.

"What's that?"

But Jeb knew well enough. In the past month he'd
blown more than one lyric, forgotten more than one
song. His voice continued to be hoarse, and in Las
Vegas the week before he'd cracked on a high note, like
a thirteen-year-old kid. When this concert was over—
and hell, it was sold out, he reminded himself—he had a
week's break, planned for a trip back to Nashville and
more recording time in the studio. He was still light one
song, and his mind stayed blank. He couldn't seem to
write so much as a jingle. Breeze had been beating the

bushes all over the country for a ballad to plug into his overdue album, a ballad with "hit" written all over it, but the fact remained. He wasn't doing well onstage or off, and articles had started drifting into the tabloids with headlines like: "JSC: A Flash in the Pan?" and, "Cody's Star Falling?"

Those were the best ones. The worst involved Clary, linking him by innuendo to her death, presumably because of her intended, unauthorized biography of him. The feeling was, he'd wanted to stop her. "Jeb Stuart Cody—Hiding a Guilty Conscience?"

He felt sweat bead on his upper lip and, grabbing a pair of white briefs, headed for the adjoining bathroom.

Breeze stepped in front of him. "I postponed your *Newsweek* interview, by the way. I told them you were run-down from the tour. We sure don't need any more hostile press."

"Hell, the press is always hostile." He spoke blandly, not to show her how the reports troubled him. "The honeymoon's over, that's all."

"Stop makin' excuses." She marched toward the door, probably as worried as he was. "John Eustace called while you were sleepin' late this morning. He wonders if you might have a fever."

"He loves to fuss." Jeb nearly smiled except his heart was tripping all over itself, like a clumsy child. The press had loved him at first. The fans. His group. Now maybe, again, there'd be just his grandfather.

"I'm not so sure he isn't right." She hesitated, then drew an envelope from her skirt pocket. She tossed it at him and two tickets dropped out. "I nearly forgot. Miss High Society returned those by messenger. So you needn't fall off the stage tonight, lookin' at seats ten and eleven in the front row."

Jeb crossed the room and lightly gripped her upper arm.

"I've heard enough about me and Susannah Whittaker— from you and the press and the boys in the band, particularly Mack who's nothin' but a pot callin' the kettle black. So lighten up, before I decide to purge my staff."

She yanked her arm free. "Don't be a bastard."

"I'm sick, remember? This sore throat makes me damn cranky."

"Then get some antibiotic, Jeb!"

"The doctor in Atlanta said it's viral."

"Do you want me to call someone here?" He shook his head and her face softened. "I know you haven't been feeling well . . ." She'd backed down but he only turned toward the bathroom, not wanting her sympathy. Breeze's walkie-talkie squawked and she said, "Five minutes now," in a harder tone.

He had a show to do.

"Breeze?" She waited and he said, "Do me a favor." Bending slowly, so as not to make himself light-headed, he picked the tickets up. "Send someone outside in front of the theater and find a deserving-lookin' young couple hopin' to see the show. Give these to them."

"With Miss Whittaker's compliments?"

"If you like." He reached up to the wardrobe shelf above the hanging rack filled with shirts and jeans and pulled down a hat. A black cowboy hat adorned with only a black band and a silver ornament bearing his initials. He'd given in after all.

"Well, well. My, my. If it isn't the Wall Street Cowboy."

"Not bad, Maynard. Maybe we can use that too. A new slogan."

"Maybe bein' a Hat like Brooks or Alan Jackson will just save your ass tonight. But you might try to sing well, just in case."

"Fuck you," Jeb murmured, "and somebody else's husband."

Breeze took a step, then stopped. "The way things are goin', Mack's gonna kill you one of these nights, if I don't do it first."

Then she disappeared into the hall, leaving Jeb with his raging throat and his bad opinion of himself. Sing? He wasn't sure he could stand up. Fear settled over him, worse than any stage fright.

In a wash of white light Jeb stood onstage, his shoulders squared, his legs spread, his hands faintly twitching at his sides as he gauged the exact instant when his guitar would come sailing through the air and he'd catch it, hold it high.

The lights changed, from white to patriotic red, white, and blue. Behind him a sweeping spot arced back and forth over the blowup of his image. Huge letters spelled "Tour America" like a blinking neon sign. Red. White. Blue.

The guitar came flying and Jeb snatched it from the air. Smack. His hands burned as he lifted it over his head. The lights, though he couldn't see that, would glint off its brass trim and make a mirror of the highly polished wooden surface. The guitar was worth thousands, but tonight he wished for his first guitar, a sale special from the local music store, his mother's gift to him that tenth Christmas before his daddy had gone to prison. He wished for the confidence he'd felt then, strumming his first chords, writing his first song, hearing his mother's and Clary's first praise.

He swallowed past the dryness in his throat, the raspy fire that wouldn't go away. He'd tried antibiotics and throat sprays, but they hadn't helped or cured. He'd have to wait it out, the doctors said; but Jeb wondered whether John Eustace might have found something in his medical bag to ease the hurt. The terror.

Dear God, don't let me blow it.

"How y'all doin' tonight?" he called out.

"We're doing fine!"

"All right, then."

His band exploded into the opening number—"Country Justice." Jeb scrambled wildly for the lyrics and, blessedly, found them. But he felt cold sweat trickle down his spine. Despite the appropriate response to his usual greeting, the crowd seemed lukewarm and he felt shaky, still light-headed. He had a bad feeling.

At the end of the song, the women screamed and at least one pair of panties rocketed toward the stage, but so did several paper missiles.

Jeb signaled his band to head right into "Do You Love Me?" a drastic switch of tempo from the first number. Silky and seductive, poignant, it ought to warm things up and cool them down at the same time.

As he sang Jeb made eye contact with Terry, his bassist, who grinned. Then with Mack, who didn't. He looked back over the audience and unfastened a shirt button.

The fans went wild.

He had them now. Everything would be all right.

With the black hat on, rakishly tilted over one eye, the small silver stud winking in his ear, he knew he looked sexy and dangerous. A combination the ladies loved, that the men would try to emulate. Wall Street Cowboy. He grinned during the few instrumental bars between choruses. Breeze would owe him an apology before the night was out. If only he didn't feel so dizzy . . .

His gaze sought the middle seats in the front row, ten and eleven. Breeze had done as he asked. A twenty-ish boy with a scraggly mustache and a skinny, sweet-faced girl about the same age occupied the seats. They reminded Jeb of himself years ago, of his wife Rachel. But he wanted to see Susannah Whittaker sitting there.

Jeb fumbled a phrase.

And someone booed.

He'd taken her in, hadn't he? Treated her right. He'd called her about Clary's witness but she'd already known, and hadn't called him first. He'd sent her the tickets.

"Jeb, for Christ's sake." Mack's half whisper reached him just beneath the music.

He had no idea where he was in the song.

Stopping the band, he leaned closer into the microphone, his eyes fixed on the front row. "I apologize for the distraction, but I happened to see a lovely lady down here." He gestured toward the sweet-faced girl. "Come on up here, darlin', and help me finish."

Blushing, stumbling up the steps to the stage, the sweet-faced girl charmed the audience. Jeb hated himself for embarrassing her, but she saved the night. With one arm around her shoulders, drawing her close against his side, he sang to her and only her. His breath control was gone, his chest felt reedy, but when the end of "Love Me" came, the audience surged to its feet.

Jeb felt the sweat dry on his spine.

He kissed the girl lightly, then guided her back to her seat, taking the mike with him and singing the next song, a two-step, from the floor. His security people hated that, but he needed the crowd with him.

At intermission Breeze thumped him on the back.

"I knew you could do it! This is a sophisticated town

with an audience to match, but after tonight they're gonna be country all the way!"

"Yes, ma'am," Jeb said with a grin.

He downed a Coke for energy and to keep his head clear, then opened his second set on his knees in a classic baseball slide up to the mike and into the first verse of "With My Heart in Hand." After that came the haunting "Huntsville Prison," and next his children's song, which always went over well, and then "Mama's Songs."

All showstoppers. Jeb had some misgivings about the one after that. He'd sprayed his throat between sets, but no one seemed to notice the slight voice-crack finish on "Mama's Songs" because it was emotional and Jeb turned it into a classic country break, worthy of George Strait. But he didn't know whether to do "Kid Sister" or not.

The tabloid headlines hinting at foul play in Clary's death made him wary. Before he made up his mind, Mack and the boys were already through the intro and Jeb automatically picked up his guitar.

The lights went low and a golden spot held him captive.

A hush fell over the arena.

He struggled to keep his voice clear and clean, not to involve himself in the lyric. Their childhood, the things they'd shared, their love for each other. It had all gone sour, like spoiled wine. But he'd never thought Clary would die without saying good-bye.

His throat tightening, Jeb strummed the chords of the bridge, his fingers feeling stiff and awkward, reluctant. He stumbled over a phrase about leaving home with no promise of coming back.

"Sing it, will you?" a man called out.

And over the music someone else said, "He can't sing!"

Jeb's mouth opened but no words came out.

"She's dead because of him!" It was the same voice again.

Jeb bowed his head over the guitar. Breeze had been wrong. He should have done the interviews, set the record straight. But he'd been wrong too. He hadn't spoken about Clary, except for that television sound byte the day of the blizzard, and then they'd managed to make him sound more interested in the gate receipts that night than in her death.

It was what Susannah thought of him too. Right here in San Francisco.

With the last line, he raised his head, looking straight out over the audience, his eyes beseeching. "Kid sister . . . I should have taken better care of you. . . ."

"You took care of her all right!"

Bewildered by that one voice again, Jeb stepped forward but Breeze suddenly grabbed his arm. "Come on, let's get you out of here."

"I didn't do anything," he murmured, the guitar still in his hands. Someone removed it from his grasp, and Jeb heard a commotion near the front of the stage, then hooting and catcalls. And the defending shouts of his fans.

He pulled against the hold on him. "Let me talk to them."

Applause grew in the darkness, but Jeb's security guards, one on each side now, replacing Breeze, hauled him away from the mike.

"I want to say a few words about my sister—"

The same voice shouted, hoarse but carrying: "What was she going to write about you, Cody?"

"Jeb, Jeb, Jeb," the crowd called. Feet stamped in rhythm.

Without warning a large man vaulted from the darkened aisle onto the stage. The thickly muscled guards let Jeb go, lunging at his assailant. Before they could stop him, the man smashed a fist into Jeb's face. Blood spurted from his nose. Another blow landed on his cheekbone, and he reeled back.

The fight ended there. The security men fought his attacker to the stage floor. Someone—Mack?—dragged him offstage. Dizzy, disoriented, he heard a thousand voices. Heard Breeze frantically issuing orders into her walkie-talkie: Bring the limo to the underground exit. Get more guards into the arena. Over the microphone a voice shouted, "Show's over, folks. Please leave in an orderly fashion. Anyone who does not do so immediately will be arrested. Mr. Cody has already left the arena. Please exit now."

"Jesus," Jeb murmured.

He saw pinpoints of light. He swiped a forearm across his bleeding nose.

The security men, several dozen of them, stood in a line across the front of the stage, their elbows linked, and Jeb's blood—that which didn't keep trickling down his face—went cold. Mack half urged, half shoved him from the stage into the wings. He didn't have time or the presence of mind to ask why the band had played "Kid Sister."

"I didn't do anything," Jeb repeated, as the other words flashed through his bleary brain. The long-ago memory.

He didn't.

8

Resting his head against the limousine's seat back, Jeb tried to level his pulse and settle the sick feeling in the pit of his stomach. He touched the scar on his upper lip. He'd been in fistfights before, one of them truly memorable, but never onstage in front of tens of thousands of fans and never without real provocation. Exhausted, he closed his eyes against the renewed dizziness that made his vision blur.

The sleek car moved swiftly along the quiet San Francisco streets. Moments ago it had pulled into the parking garage underneath his hotel only to find it thronged with curious onlookers, concerned fans, and angry hotheads eager for another round. Beside him Breeze had tensed.

"Reverse," she ordered and the limo's tires squealed, the car slewed backward along the entrance ramp and cornered crazily onto the street. "Stop here."

The chauffeur rocked the Lincoln to a halt, and Breeze threw open the rear door. Cool night air rushed in with the damp smell of San Francisco Bay. Jeb's skin felt clammy.

"Take a drive," Breeze suggested, looking around and gauging the distance from the limousine to the hotel's front entrance where another crowd had gathered. She leaned into the car. "I didn't want to tell you, but people got hurt. After we left the arena, more fights broke out and the police started swinging. Two men who attended the concert are in the hospital, one with a broken skull."

Jesus Christ.

Breeze had slammed the door and left him, risking her own skin to talk to that crowd and ordering his driver not to come back to the hotel for a few hours.

"Until things quiet down," she said. "Give me a call on the car phone first."

She'd given Jeb a thumbs-up sign through the tinted window glass, but his heart was still racing.

He rolled his head on the seat back. His throat felt as dry as the creek bed in August, and just as hot. Counting off the minutes, he touched his bruised cheekbone. His nose still hurt and dried blood had caked at his nostrils, making it a conscious effort to breathe normally.

He hadn't done anything. But neither, long ago, had his father. Or so he'd thought.

Jeb closed his eyes at the memory, which had tried to push its way into his mind again, after all this time, at the arena. The memory refused to dissipate now; even the cool May evening couldn't block it out.

He didn't do anything. . . .

A straw hat shading his eyes, the scent of fresh-cut grass teasing his nostrils, Jeb had been dozing by the creek that hot July afternoon, the sun beating down on his bare chest and legs, a cane fishing pole stuck between his toes and dangling over the dappled water. He hadn't caught anything but he didn't care. As John Eustace always told him, catching a fish wasn't the point; letting a man's mind drift was.

At the ripe age of ten, Jeb thought his grandfather had a point. But then John Eustace usually did, and he always made his points well.

Jeb admired that. He admired John Eustace's station in life too. His grandfather's office, in an added wing to his frame house in Elvira, had long been a source of boyish pleasure and fascination to Jeb, who spent many Saturdays there, happily prowling through John Eustace's medical books, running errands and cleaning up, and chatting with the endless stream of patients who filed through the plain but cheery office.

His mother feared that John Eustace would do one of two things—effortlessly guide her oldest son toward a medical education the family couldn't afford or turn Jeb into a hypochondriac.

He'd done neither of course. Mama should have known that. She'd scraped the money together the Christmas before to buy his first guitar, despite his father's objections.

His father, Jeb thought.

John Eustace had always called William Cody his least favorite son-in-law and a purely negative role model for the children, most of all Jeb, who craved some connection with his often absent father.

That afternoon by the creek he'd felt the cramping in his belly as soon as he heard Clary's voice calling down the hill. By the time she sailed toward him, her auburn hair flying behind her like a cape, he knew what had happened again. Jeb sat up, his heart thumping, the cane pole dropping from its loose anchor between his toes into the shallow creek.

"Cody! Cody!" Clary shouted.

Jeb got to his feet, not even savoring the cool feel of the grass against his bare toes or the hot lick of sunlight over his bare head. His straw hat had fallen off but he didn't look around for it. He stood watching his sister tumble down the hill in her too-short dress, which had long ago faded, her slim legs pumping; he stood watching the darkened blue of her eyes. Waiting.

Clary flung herself at him, winding both arms around Jeb's neck.

He didn't ask what was wrong.

"The sheriff came." Her voice was thick with unshed tears. Jeb held himself stiff, unwilling to enter the moment. For a few seconds more, this time, he would pretend that their world hadn't shattered. "He took Daddy away in handcuffs," Clary went on, "in his car, with that cage in back . . . like an animal." The tears glittered on her lashes, then spilled over onto her cheeks and Jeb's control broke. He pulled her close, convulsively wrapping his scrawny arms around her even thinner body and rocking her in his embrace. He could feel her tears on his bare chest, feel them trickling toward the waistband of his too-tight cutoff jeans.

"He's never coming back!" Clary cried, her slender body shivering though the day was hot, the air so humid it felt like a fist around his throat.

Jeb glanced over Clary's head and saw his cane fishing pole drifting, caught in the lazy current, toward the faster stream into which the creek emptied, toward the two-lane bridge that led into Elvira, to John Eustace's office.

Jeb tightened his arms around her, wishing he had

muscles like his father or even his grandfather. Wishing he could do something.

"He'll be back."

Clary was only eleven, but she liked things neat and pretty like Mama, and every time Daddy got arrested, she seemed to shrink, more each time, until Jeb felt as if he, not she, were the oldest child. Even her voice sounded small. "Will they let him out on bail?" she asked as if he knew the answer.

"Prob'ly," he said. "What do they think he's done?"

"Stole money." She lifted her head. "From the old fart who hired him to fix that barn floor over to Gatesville."

"What exactly do you mean, stole?"

"Like he went into that big house and broke the wall safe open and took a bunch of cash and, the sheriff said, some silver cups like they use at Derby time."

"Revere cups," Jeb supplied. They were prized by horse-country folks and used on special occasions to drink mint juleps from, prized by moneyed folks. Surely his father hadn't taken any such thing. What use would he have for them anyway?

"And jewelry," Clary added. "The sheriff told Mama some diamond bracelet and a couple rings, he said. They found everything, right on him."

"Maybe he found the stuff somewhere."

She leaned her head against his shoulder. "Mama's crying. She's cryin' real hard and the baby got scared, so now Ethan's cryin' too." Clary stepped back, dragging both hands with grubby nails across her wet cheeks, leaving streaks of dirt, which only intensified the blue of her eyes. "I told myself not to cry. I swore I wouldn't, but—"

He pulled her back into his arms, knowing that if his friends saw him, they'd jeer, but he didn't care. He hadn't cared the last time Daddy went away, or the time before that. He wouldn't care next time either, no matter how big he got. Not even when he and Clary were grown-ups like Mama and John Eustace.

"The other kids are scared too, Cody."

'I know."

"Are you scared?"

"No," he said gruffly. "Bein' scared won't help Daddy while he's gone." He hoped she couldn't feel his arms tremble. Jeb wondered why the sheriff had such resentment of his father, why he kept coming around and taking him away for things he didn't do. He wondered why the judge didn't see the light and send his daddy home again instead of locking him up and threatening, as John Eustace always reported, to throw away the key.

John Eustace said Daddy deserved to rot in jail, but he didn't like Daddy, never had, and Jeb supposed he never would. His grandfather didn't like Clary much either so Jeb discounted what he said about Clary and his father.

Mama said Daddy was innocent, and she never lied.

Mama loved him too, as Jeb did—even though his father had a temper, and expected things of him as the oldest boy. Expected him to be a man.

"He'll be back," Jeb said again. "Until he comes, I can take care of you." He stroked Clary's long auburn hair, which the sun had warmed like fire. "I'll take care of all of you." She shuddered in his arms, her slight body relaxing against his, and as they stood together by the creek, Jeb felt a strange peace wash over him, like the sweet smell of mown grass, the warmth of the summer day. "He didn't do anything," he whispered.

Not feeling peaceful at all on a cooler May evening, Jeb raised his head from the limousine's seat back. The car was drifting aimlessly, in and out of the low-lying wisps of fog that blanketed the dark city streets. His face ached, and he felt the same sense of injustice as he had that afternoon with Clary by the creek.

Innocent men, he thought.

Oh, he'd known his father wasn't perfect and neither was he. He had plenty of flaws. But those shouts . . . and the fist coming at him out of nowhere . . . and Susannah Whittaker, sending back the tickets, thinking the worst of him.

Jeb picked up the cellular phone, then put it down again. He didn't feel ready to call Breeze, though he wondered if she was all right, and safe in their suite. More likely, she'd settled everything fast and was at this very moment lying in Mack Norton's arms where she didn't belong.

As the limousine climbed a precarious hill that shamed the more gently rolling slopes around Jeb's native Elvira, he recognized the chic neighborhood— where he didn't belong. Snob Hill. Susannah's territory.

He had half a mind to drop in on her. Who did she think she was, returning his tickets by courier like a slap in the face? Money, he thought, couldn't buy class or the breeding his mother and John Eustace revered.

Jeb tapped a button and the privacy glass between him and the chauffeur glided down. If he showed up at Susannah Whittaker's, would she toss him in the street? Or be polite enough to ask him in? And if she did, could he convince her, as his father had never been able to convince the judge, of his innocence tonight?

He didn't suppose Susannah would bend, and he didn't know why that mattered to him, but it did. So did seeing her again, despite his best resolve after their last telephone conversation about Clary.

"Yes, sir?" The driver's eyes met Jeb's in the rearview mirror.

He gave the California Street address he hadn't realized he knew by heart, then sank back against the seat again, his nose and cheekbone throbbing, and the familiar dizziness rushing through his brain. Damn, his throat felt raw.

Jeb closed his eyes. He hadn't done a damn thing.

And if no one else might, Susannah Whittaker had better damn accept the truth.

Susannah heard the front door chimes through a haze of restless sleep. She'd gone to bed early but hadn't managed to more than doze in hours. The chimes rang again, echoing up from the front entryway, and she sat up. It was after one o'clock.

Mild alarm rippled through her. She was alone in the house. Leslie had gone back to Connecticut that morning and Susannah had canceled dinner with Michael tonight, pleading an upset stomach. True enough, she thought as she slipped from bed at the door chime's third peal. She pulled a paisley silk robe over her white cotton poet's shirt nightgown and padded barefoot down the stairs.

With every step, her stomach rolled. The nausea had been waking her up every half hour all night, and she wasn't in the mood for company. Leslie would have scolded her. Alone in the house, alone in the city, she'd say, easy prey for any passing pervert. Susannah needed a security system, or at least a dog. Couldn't she get one from that animal shelter where she volunteered? Susannah could, but she was gone too much and didn't like the thought of leaving a pet at home alone, as she had been left so often herself in childhood. Besides, she'd never been robbed and soothed her occasional fears at some strange night noise in the house by assuring herself she never would. She could take care of herself.

All of a sudden, she wasn't that sure. A dark figure stood outside the door. His broad shoulders filled the viewfinder but she couldn't see his face. He was standing too close or leaning—pushing—against the door. What if Leslie was right? Then he shifted to jab a finger at the bell again, and Susannah sucked in a breath, not at all sure of her safety.

Jeb Stuart Cody.

The light fell on his face, on its dark planes and angles, defining the faint streak of scar on his upper lip. Having promised herself she wouldn't face him again, she flipped the locks anyway and swung the door open, sensing something was wrong. He stood too straight, as if by conscious effort.

"I know it's late to come calling," he began.

She noted the swelling just beneath his eye. She could easily imagine the bar fight that caused it. The concert had been tonight. He'd have been wired afterward and looking for action, excitement. This time she'd managed to keep out of his way, to avoid becoming his amusement for the night.

Or had he come in anger that she'd returned his tickets?

He didn't look angry. She leaned a shoulder against the doorframe, hoping he would find her body a sufficient barrier to coming inside. "What happened?"

"A riot. 'An ill beginning of the night.'" His tone sounded weary and his shoulders slumped. "More Shakespeare." But his gaze, sliding over her from blond curls to paisley silk to bare feet, looked sharp enough. The look sent heat racing along Susannah's nerve ends—the same feeling she'd had in New York and been fighting ever since. "Don't you watch the news?" he said. "I suppose it was the main attraction on every local channel at eleven o'clock."

"I went to bed at nine."

His gaze warmed a few degrees. "Well, at least I'll get a fair hearing then."

As he swayed a little, Susannah couldn't help herself. She reached out a hand to steady him, then snatched it back, her gaze on the dark limousine waiting at the downhill curb. "At least you won't be convicted of DUI," she said.

"Are you going to let me in, or are we going to bring the court to order right here on the porch?"

"Cody, you're drunk. I don't want a drunk in my house."

"I haven't had a drop," he said, sounding offended. He swayed again. "Step back out of the damn doorway and find me a chair quick, unless you want to broom me up off the floor outside. I'm warnin' you, I weigh a lot more than you do, and lifting dead weight is no easy task."

Susannah moved aside. Maybe it hadn't been a barroom brawl.

Jeb stumbled over the doorsill into the house, shrugging off her hand when she reached out again. She could hardly pick him up if he fell, and he wasn't drunk, so perhaps he'd been hurt worse than she thought. Frowning, her queasiness forgotten, she followed him through the hall to the living room where Jeb fell onto her watered-silk celadon sofa still in his coat, immediately shutting his eyes. "I'll just rest a bit." He sighed. "'The troubled midnight and the noon's repose.'"

In the light she saw his bloody nose, and swallowed.

"What really happened?"

"T. S. Eliot. I'll tell you in a minute. Suffice it to say, there were few panties thrown onto the stage tonight."

Exasperated, in a soft rustle of silk, she sank down onto the floor beside the sofa, noting that his long legs hung over the opposite end, that his body, his shoulders covered the soft cushions. She studied his closed eyes, his battered face. The dried blood on his nose made him look like a little boy after his first fistfight.

"Is it just your face or . . .?" He might have internal injuries.

"I'm all right." He opened one eye. "I think I'm more sick than hurt."

She touched his cheek, which to her shock felt fiery. "Cody, you're burning. I could fry eggs on your skin."

"A little fever, that's all. I've had this virus for a month."

"And you haven't seen a doctor?"

"Sure, I've seen one. No, three of 'em. They all say the same thing." Shutting both eyes, he raised a shaking hand to his bruised cheekbone. "This'll be gone long before the virus, I'm afraid, so don't fuss over me like John Eustace. About either one."

"You should go home and sleep."

Jeb grinned weakly. "That's one thing I like about you, Miss Susannah. You're honest with a man, always let him know when he's not wanted."

He wanted her to feel guilty, but she wouldn't. "That mouse under your eye will be black by morning if you don't get some ice on it. I have plenty of ice, and I can clean that blood off your nose."

"Nice of you to offer. Especially when your voice tells me you can barely stand the notion of touching such a mess. But it'll keep. I got punched hours ago. Just let me rest here a while," he said again. "I didn't realize I had so much taken out of me, blood and all. I got out of the car in front of the house here and by the time I made it up those two damn flights of stairs to your door, I felt weak as old wash water."

"Well, you can't be sick here. You had no right to come—"

But Susannah was talking to herself. The smile slipped off Jeb's face, his left arm slid off his chest to dangle toward the carpet, and his mouth dropped open. She could hear the soft snores starting but didn't like the sound one bit. His breathing seemed light and labored.

"Damn," she said aloud, as Jeb might have, then rose to her feet and went upstairs to her medicine chest.

When Susannah came down, holding a bottle of rubbing alcohol, a box of Band-Aids, and a clean white washcloth trimmed in lace and threaded with ribbon, she found Jeb awake and looking at her.

"Sorry," he said. "Just a short nap." He eyed the alcohol. "What are you plannin' to do with that?"

"Disinfect your wound."

"No way. My mama never got near me with that stuff. Burns like hell."

"It's this or Leslie's bottle of peroxide."

"Who's Leslie?"

"My mother. She lives here sometimes. She's gone now," Susannah admitted, not knowing why she trusted him to know she was alone in the house, "but she uses peroxide to clean the sores she gets in the garden from not wearing gloves like a normal person."

"Are you putting me in the same category?"

"If it fits." But she couldn't stop the smile.

"You're not comin' near me with that peroxide either. That was my mama's other remedy and those frothy bubbles it makes on a person's skin purely make me—"

"I can imagine."

She set the alcohol on the end table, uncapped the bottle, and splashed some onto the washcloth.

Jeb nodded at the expensive lace-trimmed cloth. "Money doesn't mean much to you, does it?"

"Not much."

"I'd still rather you didn't ruin it with my blood." Susannah reached toward him but Jeb grasped her wrist. Even his fingers felt hot. His gaze looked sexy to her at first, until she realized he could barely focus. The look wasn't lazy or seductive; he was on the verge of passing out again.

"Don't be a baby. Tip your head back. This only stings for a second."

"Sting? All I want to hear of sting is a rock group."

"Jeb," she said, then, "Cody."

"Well, hell."

But he let her pull free and dab at the bruise under his eye. The skin had split but not badly enough to require stitches. She heard Jeb's breath quiver out with a raspy sound. "Your eye's one thing. That nose is another."

"It's not broken."

"And that chest . . ."

"You like my chest?" He smiled with his eyes closed. "Watch out, Miss Susannah. The list is addin' up. Pretty soon I'm gonna decide you like all of me."

"I'll never like you." She jabbed at the crusted blood under his nose, and Jeb winced. "We're the ends of the earth, like the North and South poles."

He laughed. "I'm feelin' better already."

Susannah turned the cloth to a clean spot. "Good. As soon as I'm done, you can get your chauffeur to help you down the front steps and into the car."

"'Heaven has no rage,'" he quoted softly, "'nor Hell a fury—'"

"'Like a woman scorned?'" Susannah said. "Shakespeare?"

"William Congreve."

"Meaning?"

"New York." He flinched as she worked at the dried blood. "Ouch. Try to leave me some skin, will you? Just because you misinterpreted my asking you to leave the hotel before the press made things worse—"

"I left because I meant to leave, not because you told me to."

"Lord, but you're ornery. If I didn't feel so damn light-headed, I'd consider taking a hickory switch to your backside, like my daddy used to do with us kids . . . when he was home." He smiled faintly, his eyes still closed. "Send you to your room to think things through a while. Make you feel sorry you returned those tickets I sent." As she turned the cloth again, he opened his eyes. The look this time was both lazy and seductive, and completely focused. On Susannah's lips. "Or teach you a thing or two."

She flung the bloodied washcloth down, her hand straying to the underside of her left breast.

"Don't think you can come in here and work your phony charm on me, Jeb Stuart Cody. Or get any sympathy because some obviously intelligent person decided to take a swing at you tonight and teach *you* some manners—"

"Have a heart, for Christ's sake."

"Why should I?"

His gaze darkened. "I'm sick and I'm hurt and I didn't deserve to have my concert broken up and other people injured just because . . . because . . ." He trailed off, as if he couldn't remember the rest of what he'd meant to say.

Sick, and hurt, she agreed. But for all that, and despite the bad things she tried to believe about him, what a beautiful man.

Jeb fell back on the sofa and his eyes drifted shut once more. "Susannah. I'll tell you everything. But not now. Jesus, I'm tired. Just let me sleep a while and I'll make you see how blameless I am. Later."

His noticeable weakness worried her. His apparent dismay about whatever had happened at the concert touched her. In spite of her misgivings, Susannah covered him with a cashmere afghan and let him sleep.

For the rest of that night Susannah didn't sleep at all. She finally urged Jeb up the stairs and into a front guest room, ghostly lit by the foggy moon shining through the windows. But when she went to lie on the unfamiliar bed down the hall instead of her own on the third floor, she tossed and turned. Her stomach rolled with her, and she could hear Jeb flopping back and forth too, as if he felt her nausea.

When he called out, she was wide awake and thinking of the bathroom.

"Mama!" he cried in a sharp voice. "It's all right!"

Susannah flung back the covers and raced along the hall to his room. Jeb sat bolt upright in bed, his feverish eyes wild, his arms flailing at the air, the covers kicked off.

She eased him back again onto the downy pillows,

pulling the goosedown comforter up to his chin. His skin still felt hot but drier now, which made Susannah forget all about her own stomach. She hadn't the vaguest idea how to care for him, but she'd do her best.

She looked out the front window as if for guidance, and saw his car.

"Cody?" she whispered in his ear, which sported a plain silver stud.

He batted at the sound, and moaned.

"Jeb, your driver's still sitting outside with the running lights on."

"Oh, God," he said, as if she'd reported a crime. His eyes snapping open, he stared at her without recognition for a moment, then his vision and his mind seemed to clear. "I'm still not used to people followin' me around. Waiting for me." He waved a hand in a shooing-away-flies gesture. "Tell him not to wait. Tell him to go back to the hotel. Tell Breeze where I am." He paused. "Tell her I'll call tomorrow." He gazed at Susannah, driving out the rest of her qualms. "Will you let me stay?"

"Yes."

She hadn't said the word before he dropped back to sleep.

All night she shuffled back and forth, plumping more pillows and piling on more blankets when Jeb's heat turned to shaking chills.

"Daddy!" he called once. "Don't let them take you!"

"John Eustace!" he shouted an hour later. "You're wrong! I can't come back! You're wrong . . . I love her!"

In the course of the night, from two A.M. until five, when the first light began to dawn, in his ravings she met Jeb's family—all of them. His mother, his father, his beloved grandfather with whom, apparently, he often disagreed despite the love between them. His one other brother and five of his sisters, all younger than Jeb.

And then at last, "Clary!" he cried. "God, Clary! Noooo!"

Susannah lay in bed, listening. Her heart beat thunderously; her heart ached. He must be out of his head with fever, and the rantings probably didn't mean anything rational or sane, but his cries came from deep inside and Susannah believed them.

She didn't bother with her robe. In the feeble gray light she dashed down the hall again into the front room. She grieved for Clary too, but she'd already cried her tears and railed at cruel, senseless fate; she'd even blamed Jeb for Clary's death, as if he'd caused it by not caring.

Now she knew better.

He might mask his emotions in daylight, but not onstage that first night and not in bed in her house tonight. He mourned his sister, and whether he would remember when the fever broke and sunlight flooded the room in which he lay, when his lazy gaze met hers again without confusion, his spirit still grieved.

Slipping into the room through the half-open door she hadn't dared to close all night for fear of not hearing him if he needed her, she bent above him, her blond curls tangled and brushing his cheek.

"Cody?"

He gave a solitary sob, dry as the feel of his hot skin beneath her fingers. Susannah smoothed his damp hair. "Ah, Clary. . ." He took a rattling breath.

"Jeb, it's Susannah. Whittaker," she added lamely, not certain what he'd think when he finally woke, lucid, and found her there. She didn't know what to think herself; she only knew she had to stay.

She offered him water from the silver carafe on the

nightstand, ice cubes clinking into a Waterford crystal tumbler. He gulped the water down, then resumed shaking. She'd made a mistake. In seconds he was shaking so hard his straight white teeth clanked together.

"Oh, Jesus." Eyes tightly shut, he hugged himself under the pile of blankets. Four of them, at Susannah's last count, all pure wool, spread over the warm weight goosedown comforter and Jeb's body, over the goosedown featherbed beneath his hips. "Cold," he muttered. "Damn cold."

Susannah grabbed another blanket from the linen closet in the hall, but it did little good.

"What can I do?" he suddenly asked in a reasonable tone, as if he'd read her thoughts. His eyes opened, focusing on her hands as they tucked the last blanket at his sides. "Susannah?" As if she hadn't been there all night.

"Yes, it's me. Go back to sleep."

She turned but he caught her wrist, his grip surprisingly strong.

"Get in with me. Don't be a prude." He tugged lightly. "It isn't as if we haven't shared a bed before, and the blankets don't help. I need your warmth." Still holding her, he shuddered, his fingers moving spasmodically on her wrist, his teeth chattering. "I'm in no condition, believe me, to violate your maidenly virtue."

Trembling now herself, Susannah eased into the bed without lifting the covers an inch more than necessary, and drew him close.

"We should take your temperature again." She'd already given him enough aspirin to kill the Terminator, but as far as she could tell, his fever was still high. Susannah had heard from her married friends that experienced mothers could accurately pinpoint a fever with one light touch on a child's forehead. Susannah longed for a child, but if she had one, how would she learn to care for it? And weren't adult fevers different?

"Just let me hold you," Jeb whispered, his lips moving against her hair. His arms held her as tight as she held him. He sighed deeply, but the rantings had stopped and soon so did the chattering, the shakes. When he slid one muscular leg between Susannah's, she let him. They lay pressed together while she watched the sun rise through the windows and begin to burn away the fog, and wondered why Jeb Stuart Cody—even in delirium—was the first man to make her feel cherished.

"All right," she said, her gaze blurring at the bleary sun. "Okay, Jeb."

As soon as she found him awake that morning, Susannah quarreled with Jeb. She wanted to call her doctor for him; he wouldn't consider it.

"Cody"—she was back to that, now that he could hear her—"you're not getting better. Last night, all night, you were much worse. You can't just get up now and go back to work."

Holding the morning newspaper, Susannah stayed in the doorway, and he gazed at her from his nest of pillows, his face dead-white, his gray eyes rimmed with charcoal shadows, his left eye nearly swollen shut and black as pitch. His tone sounded patient, sensible.

"I'm not goin' back on tour. I have a week off. I'll rest. I promise."

"You probably have bronchitis." Each time she'd pressed a hand to his chest, she had felt harsh vibrations.

"I'm not coughing."

"You will be." Susannah waved the newspaper. "You

haven't seen this." She'd read it, in horror, while Jeb slept like a corpse, his fever lower but still present, his breathing increasingly shallow and disturbed. "If you think you'll get any rest at all after this"—she rattled the paper again—"with the press camped on your door . . . My God, that man has a fractured skull."

He dropped his head back briefly to stare at the ceiling. "I know. Breeze told me. I'll pay his hospital bills. I need to call and tell her that." He looked at Susannah. "Damn, I thought I could convince you that I'm not the bad guy before you saw those reports."

"I don't think you're the bad guy. But the concert got out of hand. People were hurt. Seriously. There's a crowd in front of your hotel right now, with placards pro and con. Some of them are pretty nasty." They were about Clary.

Jeb didn't comment. He kept staring at her, as if he hadn't seen her until now, not since New York, as if she'd respond to those bedroom eyes again.

"What have you got on under that?"

Susannah looked down at her paisley silk robe. Then she looked up at his face, at the darkened gray eyes—or, rather, eye—the one that could stay open.

"It's called a poet's shirt. It's a nightdress."

He beckoned her to come nearer. "Perfect."

"Don't worry about it," she said, stepping back into the hall. "Now are you going to let me call a doctor or aren't you?"

"Sure."

She did a double take. He'd been so adamant. He'd talked her in circles. He'd even been about to try seduction again to keep her attention off him.

"He'll be waiting for a call anyway." Jeb glanced at the newspaper fluttering in her hand like Susannah's nerves.

He was unbuttoning his sweat-lank dress shirt as he spoke. "He'll have seen all that by now. He's probably foaming at the mouth. Get me a phone and I'll call him myself."

Susannah didn't ask who. At nine thirty, with his lean, hard body in a sprawl under the covers and his chest bare, his sun-streaked hair gilded in the morning light, he dialed the number. Long distance, Susannah noted before she fled the room to dress and armor herself against his fevered but probing gaze. At three o'clock that afternoon, while Jeb lay so heavily sleeping that she feared he'd slipped into a coma and considered trying to wake him, the doorbell rang. She answered, looking up into a pair of watery blue eyes that reminded her of a spaniel she'd once owned, and a shock of pure white hair that made her think, oddly enough, of ordering a bucket of fried chicken.

"Where's my boy?" The elderly man's tall, still strong body filled her doorway, as Jeb's had the night before. "Is he here? Have I got the right place?"

"Please, come right in." Susannah held the door wide. "You must be John Eustace."

9

Carrying a small cloth bag, John Eustace shuffled into Susannah's entry hall with a gait that obviously favored his left hip. He'd been holding his battered straw hat in his other hand and paused briefly at Susannah's mahogany Federal chest, placing it on top with care, as if it were his finest possession. He peered at his reflection in the hall mirror, at Susannah standing behind him.

"Upstairs?" he asked and she blinked.

The old gentleman apparently used as few words as possible, and she had an instinctual feeling that in those words he always spoke his mind. No frills.

"He's in the front bedroom on the second floor."

Susannah preceded him up the stairs, after John Eustace paused once more to wipe his feet on the oriental rug by the front door. She saw no dirt. The day was clear, the fog having burned off well before noon, but she had the impression John Eustace would clean his shoes if they were brand new and had never touched a sidewalk or a muddy yard.

He said no more until he walked into the bedroom. Jeb lay propped on the pillows, his eyes half closed, sweat beading his forehead and upper lip. He gave his grandfather a wan smile, lifting one hand in greeting.

"I knew I should pay no attention to that phone call this morning with your reassurances," John Eustace said with a snort, "except to get myself on the first flight out of Lexington." He hitched his way to the bed and looked down at his grandson. As Susannah looked on, John Eustace studied the black-and-blue bruise around one eye. "Confound it, boy." He pressed his palm to Jeb's forehead, then gave Susannah a look. "Hotter'n a jet engine's blast. Well over a hundred and two, I suspect. Next thing he'll be goin' into convulsions. You got a thermometer handy? Oral or rectal, doesn't matter."

"It sure as hell does." Jeb closed his eyes, as if the few words exhausted him.

"I have a digital thermometer," Susannah told John Eustace.

"Newfangled claptrap. Prob'ly not reliable."

Jeb's mouth twitched, and she said, "I'll get it."

"I didn't exactly ask you to come," Jeb was saying when she returned. Susannah handed the thermometer to John Eustace who slipped it under Jeb's tongue with a practiced motion that efficiently shut him up.

John Eustace fumbled in his small carpetbag. "You didn't call me to set my mind at ease about that riot last night and you know it, so don't bother to dissemble. Your mama would wash your mouth with soap if she heard you lyin' . . . or tryin' to." He pulled out the oldest-looking stethoscope Susannah had ever seen. Like the tapestry bag that held his medical supplies, it must have survived the Civil War. "Keep that mouth shut now while this young lady here and I assess your condition— which looks plainly miserable from where I'm standin'."

When he removed the thermometer, Jeb muttered, "You hardly are standin', old man. Why don't you plant your butt on that chair beside the bed and stop fussin' at me."

"You need someone to fuss over you. Right now I'm handy."

He looked at Susannah as if for the first time. In the front entry, clearly intent on finding Jeb, he hadn't so much as given her a once-over. Now his watery blue gaze covered her like a blanket, every inch, before he glanced away at the thermometer.

"One hundred and three point six degrees," he said with disgust. "How long you been sittin' on this infection?"

"You know. A month or so. The doctors say—"

"It's a virus? Maybe it was, but I told you to watch it didn't become somethin' else entirely." John Eustace passed the thermometer to Susannah. "Dump that in some alcohol. And take some advice from me, you and my grandson. Always get a second opinion."

"I did," Jeb said weakly.

"I mean, from someone who graduated medical school before the 1980s, no, make that the seventies. I swear, those boys don't learn the basic facts these days, just sail right into some specialty or other that makes more money than a man has any right to. In my opinion, not one in ten of them would know a case of measles or diphtheria if they fell onto it like a spike on an iron fence."

"PawPaw, don't lecture."

"You need a lecture, at least once a day." He brushed a

gnarled hand over Jeb's cheek, but the motion looked light as air. "While I'm here, I intend to get my time in." He sat down on the bed, nudging Jeb's hip, and pulled the sheet lower, baring his chest. "Let's see what else we got here." He probed and prodded Jeb's neck with fingers that looked gentle, paying particular attention just beneath his ears. "How long have these glands been up?"

Jeb ducked away, wincing. "I don't know. A few days."

"A week at least. Don't lie to me, boy."

"I'm not!"

"Does your throat hurt?"

"Off and on."

"Hurt to swallow?"

"A little. Yeah."

John Eustace looked thoughtful. "I don't suppose you've had any sleep lately. Or any decent food. Just singin' with that raw throat and gettin' pounded by somebody's fists." He rubbed the stethoscope against his blue-shirted chest to warm it, then stuck the ends in his ears. "Let's have a listen."

Susannah stood back, her hands clasped at her waist. Almost smiling at seeing the old man lovingly bully country music's newest superstar, she felt strangely relieved by John Eustace's presence yet also like an intruder. Her awkward ministrations the night before hadn't seemed to soothe Jeb half as much as his grandfather's scolding did.

John Eustace sat back with a sigh.

"Rattlin' and rumblin'. Sounds like heavy equipment in there, buildin' a highway." He turned from Jeb to Susannah. "Where's the nearest hospital? We need a chest plate."

"I don't want a hospital. The press—"

"I don't recall askin' you what you want, boy. And I

could care less about a bunch of reporters. You just let me and Miss . . ." His inquiring glance met hers.

"Susannah. Whittaker," she said.

"Drake Whittaker's girl? Jeb mentioned you but I'm afraid all I remembered was the address. Pleased to make your acquaintance." With a sudden smile that could have charmed rattlesnakes, John Eustace stood. "This boy never did have any manners, or he would have introduced us accordingly." He neatly ignored the fact that, in his obvious concern for Jeb, he'd stalked right past her into her own house without asking who she was. "It comes of not havin' a proper father and I do what I can to remedy that, but I can tell you, it's a difficult task." Heading for the door, he said, "Get your pants on, Jeb, while Miss Susannah and I find some transportation."

"I don't need a damn X-ray," Jeb said feebly.

"I'm here to tell you what you need. Whether you listen or not is your choice, but I'm makin' the decisions, so you might as well save your breath—what breath you have left in those miserable lungs."

Jeb caught Susannah's half smile. "Help me out here."

In the soft but steely voice she'd learned at her mother's knee, and with only a minimum haughty eyebrow, Susannah soon convinced John Eustace that they didn't need an ambulance. Jeb's limousine, which she knew from his earlier call to Breeze would be en route to the airport for her trip back to Nashville, would only attract attention anyway, quite possibly from the press who had staked out the hospital. Susannah's own car would suffice.

With John Eustace on one side and Susannah on the other, Jeb eased down the stairs wearing his clothes from the night before under an old trenchcoat that

Michael had given her to take to Goodwill on her volunteer day at their shelter. Jeb added her slightly too small wool fedora hat, pulled low over his eyes, which he hid with dark glasses. Out of bed he seemed even weaker than he was last night, which alarmed her.

If John Eustace hadn't come, she would have taken Jeb to the hospital herself. Somehow. Kicking and fighting, probably.

The hospital's diagnosis of pneumonia in both lungs worried her even more. When the doctor who read his films wanted to admit Jeb, she nearly panicked. He was obviously run-down from his concert tour—and grief over Clary's death, Susannah supposed. Couldn't people, even young people like Jeb, die from pneumonia?

"If I'm gonna die, it won't be in this hospital," he said.

And for once, John Eustace gave in.

"You won't die if I have anything to say about it—and I do. We'll take care of things," he agreed, wheeling Jeb out a side door. "At your hotel."

"I won't hear of it." Susannah didn't know she was going to speak until she said the words. "I have plenty of room for both of you." They had narrowly avoided a clutch of journalists in the hospital lobby, eager to follow up last night's riot story. The man with the fractured skull lay upstairs in Intensive Care, and although Breeze Maynard had issued a statement on Jeb's behalf, the reporters would seize upon his presence—at his hotel too. "You can sleep in the room across from J—Cody's," she told John Eustace.

"Thank you kindly. I have always believed that people mend faster as far from hospitals as they can get."

His easy acceptance didn't match Jeb's. When Susannah glanced at him, he was looking at her open-mouthed.

"Well, I'll be damn—"

"Watch your mouth, boy. There's a lady present."

"It's his favorite damn adjective," Susannah murmured. Following them out to her Bentley, she wondered what had happened to her normally staid, even predictable existence. She wondered what the lady from Greenwich and Nob Hill had gotten herself into. At the least, with John Eustace's arrival, Jeb Stuart Cody's place in her life seemed to have doubled. To Susannah's dismay, it wasn't a bad feeling.

The trip to the hospital took the last of Jeb's failing strength. He had no sooner fallen into an exhausted sleep in the clean sheets Susannah put on his bed, after a first dose of the antibiotic John Eustace had prescribed, when the front doorbell rang.

Michael stood on the porch, smiling expectantly. Wearing a tuxedo.

Susannah glanced behind her at the empty stairway to the second floor but it was blessedly empty, the house silent. Maybe she'd be spared awkward explanations. But with all the familiarity of a man she'd dated, more or less regularly, for the past several years, Michael stepped inside. He bent down, kissing Susannah lightly on the lips. Then he straightened to look at her rumpled silk blouse and designer jeans, the ones with the strawberry jam stain on the knee. She'd taken Jeb breakfast in bed that morning and dropped the jelly pot.

"You're not dressed," Michael said.

Susannah glanced at her watch. Six-thirty. The afternoon had passed at the hospital, and she felt disoriented. "Do we have plans tonight?"

He waved a hand. "Your plans," he said. "The Multiple Sclerosis dinner? That ten-minute speech you're giving?"

"Oh, my God."

"I'll wait in the living room." He gave her another careful look, then walked past her. "I'm beginning to wonder, Suse, about your legendary organizational skills. Maybe you do need Leslie here to keep you going." He turned. "Or are you still feeling badly? That stomach flu—"

"I'm fine." She hadn't felt nauseated all day. "Help yourself to a drink. I'll hurry. Give me fifteen minutes."

She heard a crash upstairs and a male voice cried out. Susannah tore from the room.

With Michael at her heels, she raced upstairs. At Jeb's room, she halted. He lay in bed, covered to his armpits, his upper chest bare, his eyes looking half-asleep but sexy.

John Eustace crouched beside the bed, picking up pieces of the antique porcelain chamber pot that Susannah kept on a walnut stand near the window. She'd thought of planting pink geraniums in it this spring. He turned, seeing her and Michael. John Eustace's cheeks turned rosy, making his hair look even whiter in contrast.

He held up a shard of white china hand-painted with primroses. "I suppose this was worth a small fortune. Jeb tells me everything in your house must be, though I haven't had the chance to see for myself. I'm truly sorry, Miss Susannah."

"I bought it at a flea market. I'm not sure it's genuine," she lied, not to embarrass him further. "Did you hurt yourself?"

"My hide is tough. Jeb's the one hurtin'."

"PawPaw."

"He needs to relieve himself, but I have prescribed complete bed rest until the antibiotic brings down this fever, so . . ." He picked up more porcelain pieces from the Aubusson carpet. Jeb's eyes were open now and he struggled to sit up. John Eustace pushed him back down. "You just lay there, boy, until I can help you. I thought there'd be no harm in usin' your more old-fashioned convenience, Miss Susannah. I do apologize."

"It's quite all right." Behind her Michael shifted his weight.

"Susannah, what's going on here?" he asked, and she turned, finding his gaze fixed on Jeb's bare chest.

She tried to explain.

"Are you crazy?" he said under his breath when she finished, steering her from the room into the hall. "If the man's that sick, he should be in the hospital. You're hardly qualified to nurse him back to health."

"You needn't be sarcastic."

"I'm being practical." He glanced back at Jeb. "For heaven's sake, he's not exactly a savory character at the moment. The newspapers were filled with that riot at the arena last night and he's apparently laid some poor chap up with a broken head."

She stiffened her spine. "That wasn't his fault."

"I suppose he got that black eye bumping into a door."

"Someone attacked him. He's sick, and he's hurt. And until he improves, I have offered my home." She saw Jeb watching them. "No one knows he's here except—now—you, and I'd prefer to keep it that way."

"I'll be the soul of discretion." He looked at Susannah, anger brightening his eyes. "Which is far more than I can say for you. If the press gets wind of your involvement, before the Arts Commission fund-raiser—"

"The press won't, unless you tell them."

Michael looked down at his shoes. "He's certainly had an easier time than I have, getting into your bed."

"He isn't in my bed," she said, which was a half lie. Last night she'd slept—what little sleep she'd managed—in Jeb's arms. Turning from Michael, she started up the next flight of steps to her rooms. "Wait for me downstairs. We can talk about this on our way to dinner."

While Michael nursed his whiskey in the living room and the strains of a Chopin prelude drifted up the stairs, Susannah flew back down to the second floor in her slip and robe to help John Eustace get Jeb to the bathroom. Then she dressed in navy blue velvet and diamonds, stopping in to say good night before she left.

Back in bed, Jeb looked wide awake and surly. "Who's the guy?"

"Michael Alsop."

"The San Francisco boyfriend?"

"My San Francisco friend."

"Don't fool yourself, Susannah. He has the brandin' iron heating in the fire."

She stood in the doorway, coolly watching him. The still-bare chest. The fever flagging both cheekbones. The hot gleam in his eyes.

"He's asked me to marry him," she admitted.

"And you said?"

She hesitated. She'd already done enough, inviting Jeb into her home; letting him stay; spending last night, as Michael said, playing unlikely nurse. "I haven't made up my mind."

"Think about New York while you're at it," he said and turned onto his side, putting his bare back to her.

The evening started badly and didn't improve. Michael's mood was one thing, but her own sense of unease at leaving Jeb was another. She worried about him all evening. And despised herself for having any response at all.

"He's not your type," Michael said at dinner in the

company of five hundred of San Francisco's social elite, with her half-written speech running raggedly through her mind, her stomach again in knots for the first time that day.

Had Jeb's fever risen with the night? John Eustace expected that. He'd asked Susannah for aspirin and an unbreakable basin, for extra washcloths and rubbing alcohol. Was he at this very moment stroking Jeb's hot skin, hoping to bring his fever down?

"I should hope not," she said, adjusting her diamond necklace with trembling fingers. "He's a public person and I'm very much private, except on occasions like this one." She glanced around the room, at the sparkle of jewelry and the gleam of gold, sequins, and glitter. Waiters cleared tables, and glassware clicked against china, against crystal. The overhead chandeliers made her weary eyes hurt. "We come from different worlds, and believe me, having seen a concert firsthand during that blizzard in New York, I wouldn't have his on a plate. Last night being the perfect reason why not. Let Breeze Maynard handle his problems. . . . As soon as he's able"—she lowered her voice—"Jeb Stuart Cody will be on his feet and out of my house."

"Breeze Maynard?" Michael murmured.

"She's his manager."

"I know. I saw her on the news while you were dressing. She hasn't lost her looks." He sounded hopeful. "Are she and Cody . . . ?"

"No," Susannah said, more emphatically than she intended. "They're friends. Like you and me."

Michael reached for her hand. "As good as that?" For the first time that evening, he smiled. "Maybe I won't be angry with you then." He caressed the back of her hand. "I might even begin to believe that nothing happened between the two of you in New York." He glanced toward the podium where someone was testing the microphone. "Maybe after you've given your speech and charmed society into turning out its pockets, you'll come home with me."

"I'll think about it," Susannah said, rising.

She headed for the lectern. Thinking. About Michael's persistent invitations and his budding jealousy, about Jeb lying in bed in her house. About New York.

By the time Susannah finished her speech, barely recalling what she'd said, her stomach was rolling ominously. No wonder, she told herself. She begged off after a quick nightcap with Michael in her own living room.

"I'm sorry. Really I am." She yawned in his face, something she'd never done before to anyone, ushering him toward the front door. "I need to catch up on my sleep, as you can see. And my stomach's still unsteady. That prime rib tonight with the yorkshire pudding didn't help. I plan to take some antacid and fall into bed."

"Alone?" He lingered with one hand on the door-knob.

"Don't insult me, Michael. Besides, we have a chaperon."

His mouth grim, he didn't kiss her good night.

Susannah locked up, then tiptoed up the stairs, holding her evening shoes in one hand, her skirt high in the other. Except for the Belgian lantern in the hallway, the house was dark. Hearing no sound from the second floor, she paused on the landing.

Leaving her shoes on the next step, she padded down the hall. John Eustace wasn't in the extra room near Jeb's and the door stood open. The bed hadn't even been turned down any farther than she'd left it, one corner of

the sheet and blanket folded back, the pillows plumped,
with a Godiva chocolate still waiting there. The crystal
decanter of apricot liqueur hadn't been touched either.

In Jeb's room Susannah found John Eustace sleeping
on a chair.

From the deep, even sound of his breathing, and
Jeb's, she supposed they were both asleep—after a particularly bad night? Susannah felt like a voyeur standing
next to the bed, watching Jeb's bare chest rise and fall,
watching his lashes flutter in the throes of some dream.
He might be all wrong for her, but sick or well, he was
still the most magnificent man she had ever seen. And
she'd come to like him, more than she'd admit. Much
more. She almost didn't care about Clary's stories. She
looked her fill, then turned away at last, her heart
thumping.

Hot fingers caught her wrist. Jeb's voice was a lazy
whisper.

"Have a good time tonight, sugar?"

Susannah glanced at John Eustace. "Yes. And don't
call me sugar."

"Better than last night?" He was smiling, just a little.

"Yes," she murmured.

John Eustace's face remained impassive, and at a tug
Susannah stepped closer to the bed.

"You're lyin'," Jeb said.

"I'm not one of your groupies. Or Breeze Maynard,
for that matter."

"Come down here."

"Cody . . ." but she had no will, and his name sounded
weak.

"Closer, dammit." With another tug, she felt her knees
give way. She bent, feeling as pliant as a beanbag toy,
and his mouth took hers. Hot, so hot, not all of it fever.

He drew her down further, his head falling back and Susannah's mouth covering his, opening to him, tasting heat and sweetness on his tongue, tasting cherries . . . and alcohol.

"John Eustace has been feedin' me expectorant cough syrup with brandy chasers."

"Mmm," she murmured, as he changed the angle on the kiss, pulling her toward him until Susannah lay across his chest in a puddle of navy blue velvet, the kiss delving deeper until she couldn't tell where her mouth ended and his began.

"You like that too, Miss Susannah?"

"Mmm," she said with a moan as he touched her breast through the warm cloth.

"I thought I'd remind you. Just in case you've forgotten about New York."

Gently, he pushed her away, and Susannah shot a glance at John Eustace, who seemed still to be sleeping in his chair, his head lolled to one side, his arms dragging.

"Forgotten about me," Jeb whispered. "Sweet dreams, sugar."

Susannah had no dreams over the next three days. And precious little sleep. She and John Eustace spelled each other nights while struggling to keep Jeb's fever down and took turns napping during the day. On the fourth morning John Eustace changed Jeb's antibiotic to a stronger, more expensive one, and by the next day he seemed to be improving.

A loose cough developed, clearing his lungs one racking spasm at a time. That night John Eustace and Susannah shared nursing duties again, shuttling back and forth on their shifts with barely a word exchanged until the early hours of morning when he lightly shook her awake at Jeb's bedside.

"How's he been?"

"Not too bad. I gave him the cough syrup about half an hour ago, then he dropped back to sleep." Susannah straightened, realizing that her hand lay in Jeb's, between them.

John Eustace studied their linked fingers. "He's resting easy now. I made some coffee, good and strong." He kneaded the nape of her neck with his knobbyknuckled, wiry fingers. "Come down to the kitchen before the sun wakes him up and I'll cook you breakfast, southern style."

Susannah didn't feel quite ready for grits and bacon grease, but she swallowed and went after him. In the past five days she'd come to like and admire him, though she couldn't be sure how he felt about her. He hadn't been any more forthcoming than Drake would be, or Leslie.

"Sit down there. Take a load off." He squinted at her in the pale dawn light. "You're lookin' peaked, girl. I may prescribe a tonic before I leave." He switched on the overhead lights and rummaged in the refrigerator, coming up with eggs and butter. "You feelin' all right?"

Except for the flutter in her stomach again, she thought. It had started several weeks ago in the late afternoons, and Susannah assumed it was fatigue, then nerves, but it seemed to be starting earlier each day. She supposed John Eustace had a point. She was burned out taking care of Jeb and trying to keep up with her own schedule. She didn't want a tonic, though. "I feel fine."

"Nevertheless. After we eat, you go on to bed and stay there till evening."

"Yes, sir." She grinned at him, and John Eustace laughed.

He threw a slab of bacon into an iron skillet and slapped it on the stove.

"What do you think of my grandson?" He kept his back to Susannah, while fussing, as was his inclination, with potato slices, fresh melon, and—as she'd feared—grits. Her stomach rolled at the sight of them, white and glutinous, bubbling in a pan. He must have brought them with him in that bag.

"I don't know him well," she said.

John Eustace snorted. "I didn't know my wife until we'd been married for twenty years. It takes time to know a person. What's your impression?"

Susannah didn't mention how they'd met. "He's talented, dynamic, a born performer. A much better musician than I . . ."

"Expected?"

"I didn't mean that."

John Eustace turned from the stove. "You come from upscale, moneyed folk, he tells me. A surgeon's daughter. A socialite mother, like yourself. You do anything for a living?"

She told him about her charities. John Eustace didn't comment, but she imagined that, like Jeb, he disapproved, that he considered her a do-gooder, for which she couldn't blame him. She felt like one these days. Aimless, dissatisfied with her efforts.

He flipped bacon in the sizzling skillet, its heady aroma making Susannah swallow. "Me and Jeb, we're of plainer stock. You know, he's never taken a guitar lesson?"

"I didn't know that."

"But he can play, and tell you what he's doin' in words—theory, he says—that make no lick of sense to me. Which puts me at a disadvantage, because Jeb spent so much time as a boy readin' my medical texts that he ought to have earned his degree just by taking the exams." He laughed a little. "Read my Shakespeare anthology, and anything else he could lay hands on."

Susannah smiled. "What was he like as a boy? Clary told me things, but not that much." And not that good, she added silently.

John Eustace looked over his shoulder. "I'd take whatever Clary said with several grains of salt."

She set aside the enormous glass of orange juice he'd put in front of her. She'd heard about John Eustace too from Clary, not by name but only as "my grandfather, that ornery old bulldog," and what she'd heard didn't match her experience of the past few days. His obvious dislike of Clary troubled her, and she jumped to Clary's defense.

"She was my closest friend. I loved her."

Did you have friends? Jeb had asked in a doubting tone, and he'd been nearly right. As a child, she'd been lonely. It was only after she started college and met Clary that she learned about friendship.

"Everybody loved Clary," John Eustace said, "at first." He carried their plates to the table, shoving one toward Susannah, and sat across from her. "You must have a good heart. A forbearing spirit."

He took a bite of egg piled onto some toast and chewed, then swallowed. He leaned forward. "My grandson has suffered some powerful losses in his life. He had a wonderful mama but a bastard for a daddy. That man purely loved to take skin off a boy's hide, one way or another. The law has seen fit to put him in prison now and then for other reasons, but I always tell myself a wise judge knows a rotten apple when he bites into one."

"Is his father in prison now?"

"Yes, ma'am. Doing fifteen to twenty on an armed robbery charge."

Susannah could feel her face pale. She knew practically nothing about Clary and Jeb's father, Clary never talked about him.

"Clary broke Jeb's heart," John Eustace said. "After that, I s'pose you've heard about his marriage, neither of them dry behind the ears. A couple of high school kids. It's a shame, in my opinion, that God makes us humans reproductive before we learn any sense or wisdom about this world, but there it is. And Jeb loved that girl." He tasted his coffee. "Sweet Rachel. She always thought he married her for the baby and because he missed Clary in his life, but he did love her."

It was on the tip of Susannah's tongue to ask what had actually happened to Jeb's wife and child, when she closed her mouth, not certain she wanted to know. And risk her own tender feelings for Jeb. Considering John Eustace's love for him, his resentment of Clary, she doubted she'd hear the truth anyway. Clary hadn't lied. Would she lie? Susannah had never considered that before.

She cleared her throat. "Clary thought he'd turned his back on her. For wanting an education. And later, for marrying my father."

"That what she told you?" John Eustace held her gaze. "Jeb never had the chance to go to college, not after Clary left him holdin' the bag at home with five sisters and a brother to finish raisin', but he has respect for learning. I taught him that, and in turn he's sent most of his kin through the university, one place or another."

Not quite surprised, Susannah remained silent. Her stomach felt iffy again, and she looked away from the plate of eggs, bacon and grits. She hadn't believed Jeb in New York about Clary's defection to college. It had seemed too slight a reason for such a rift between them. Not to be scolded by John Eustace, she sipped her juice.

She liked Jeb even more because of his ongoing concern for his family but didn't trust the feeling. She'd loved his sister as if she were her own, and didn't like wondering which stories to believe; didn't like having to choose between Jeb and Clary, as John Eustace seemed to want her to do.

He looked into his cup. "Jeb had some qualms about his sister marrying a man so much older than she was— we all did—but if that made her happy, he would have come to terms with it."

He omitted himself from the equation, which didn't surprise her now either. Like Jeb, John Eustace hadn't attended Clary's wedding to Drake, though the younger children had come to Greenwich with their mother, the only time except for the funeral that Susannah had seen them. She realized that once Clary left Kentucky, she had seen her family only once.

If Jeb didn't blame his sister for leaving home or marrying Drake, what had happened between Jeb and Clary? Between Clary and John Eustace?

John Eustace seemed to read her thoughts. "You and I are just getting acquainted. It's not my right to tell you family secrets. Clary made her choices," he said. "She lived with them." He paused, then added, "And died with them."

Secrets. She understood his reluctance to confide in a near stranger but couldn't let the subject go completely.

"She was still your granddaughter," Susannah said.

"I'm afraid so." He rose from the table and cleared their plates, hers barely touched. "Hill people are family people, and whether she left or not, Clary was one of us." With his back to her, he splashed coffee into the sink and changed the subject. "I've seen Jeb's eyes when he looks at you, Miss Susannah. I've seen yours when you look back at him." Turning, he pinned her with his watery blue gaze. "Do you care for my grandson?"

"I'm trying not to," she said honestly. "We're much too different."

"True," he agreed. "But then, opposites do attract. They can complement each other, and over time make people better, a union of two parts."

She didn't know what to say. John Eustace didn't see people as they were, she thought; he saw them as he wanted them to be. Even Jeb. Especially Jeb.

Maybe she did too. Before they met, she'd always seen Jeb one way—through Clary's eyes—but he was better than she'd believed, and for the first time in years she entertained the notion that Clary might have been less than perfect.

"I want—I need—to find out who killed Clary," she said at last. "Jeb doesn't. He avoids facing her death, but I won't be satisfied until whoever killed her goes to jail."

"You think you can change history? What's done is done."

"That's what Jeb thinks too. But he's wrong and so are you."

"You want to right a few wrongs, do you? Leave that to the police. It's none of your affair—or mine." When she lifted a hand in frustration, he cut her off before she could speak. "Have you ever heard the term, 'bad seed'? My granddaughter carried some curious genes, I can assure you." He forced a smile, as if about to lecture an uncooperative patient. "Now, Miss Susannah, you are a lovely young woman. I enjoy your companionship . . ."

A moment ago she would have glowed at the words. John Eustace did like her, and she wanted his almost parental affection, the sort she'd had so little of herself. But she was still a Whittaker and didn't take no for an answer.

"I don't believe your theory. It's not Clary's fault she died!"

John Eustace's tone took on an edge. "We have been gettin' on famously, and I'd like to keep it that way."

"I'm sure you would, but—"

"The man—or men—who killed Clary had some right." He swallowed, his face turning pale. "They must have."

"Then you think it was murder too!"

Did she have an ally after all? Even from the opposite perspective?

"Murder is a harsh term where Clary's concerned."

"My God. You're saying she deserved to die!" Shocked, she stood and walked to the windows that overlooked the garden. "That's a terrible thing to say."

"It's true. I won't discuss it further just now. But she blinded you."

Susannah wrapped her arms around herself. She wouldn't listen. Jeb had said Clary liked to play games with people, but even now, Clary was her closest friend, her best friend. She wouldn't tarnish that memory. But as she stood looking out at the neat flower beds and the path winding among them, the memories came. Had she suppressed them as Jeb did his grief? Or had John Eustace just shaken them from her?

Sometimes—occasionally—Susannah had wondered at the way Clary doled out hugs and praise according to her mood, like prizes for good behavior. She'd often wanted Susannah to herself, eschewing college outings with other girls, her temper flaring when Susannah objected to staying by themselves. Once Susannah had written home to Leslie, "Friendship can be stifling. At times Clary seems almost . . . clutchy."

"She blinded Jeb too," John Eustace went on. "So there you are," he said. "A place to start. A common bond."

She heard a noise upstairs and whirled at the interruption, avoiding John Eustace's eyes. His gaze seemed to look into her heart. She'd never felt as much concern from Drake, or as much opposition, on any topic. If he regretted what he'd said about Clary, she couldn't absolve him just now. But she didn't want to lose John Eustace's friendship either.

"I think he's awake. I'll see what he needs."

Jeb's grandfather called her back, his blue eyes troubled. When he lifted a hand toward her, it shook. "I know we don't agree about Clary—"

"And about Jeb?"

"I know what I see. You won't find a better man— educated or not, millionaire or pauper—than John Eustace Beauregard Stuart Cody. I believe you care more for my grandson than you know. But I don't want to see him hurt again."

Unable to stop herself, Susannah took a step toward him, placing her hands in his. "And I don't want him to hurt anyone else—especially me."

"Then there's the beginning to it, isn't there?" he said, and smiled.

$\overline{10}$

Naked, letting the night air cool her heated skin, Breeze walked through her palatial twenty-three room house without turning on the lights. She seldom returned to Nashville these days. Jeb's Tour America would take the rest of spring and into summer before his second album's release at the beginning of September, kicking off a new tour. Breeze daydreamed about the frantic planning, the months on the road, even the foul-ups. Her work as Jeb's manager kept her busier than she'd ever dreamed of being again, and—her chief reason for not hiring a road manager—kept her away from Nashville. From this house.

She kept meaning to sell it. She wished Jeb would urge her to sell, but he wouldn't. And if he did, she was stubborn enough at someone else's suggestion to dig her heels in and refuse. The imitation antebellum house, porticoed and white-columned, sat squarely in the middle of its wooded, parklike setting, an island among thick green foliage, invisible to the prying eyes of passersby. Set back from the road by nearly half a mile of white gravel driveway, behind square stone pillars and iron gates adorned with only the cryptic initial *B*, it had been her refuge once. Now it seemed more like a prison.

In the past week without Jeb she'd nearly lost her mind.

Without Mack too, most of the time.

Breeze swept past the doorway to the one room she'd avoided for days. She didn't need to look inside. Carpeted in white with stark white walls and ceiling, it was a shrine to her former life, its walls studded with platinum discs and gold records, as if they were sequins on a costume, with awards and photographs. Reminders that she'd failed to protect the people who loved her.

Breeze wandered outside onto the enormous screened-in porch that stretched along the mansion's rear like too many pounds on a woman's backside. It ruined the design of the house, but she loved the darkness here, the air, the sound of crickets and scurrying night animals in the yard. Blackness. Privacy.

She hadn't known what to do when Jeb sent her back to Nashville while he stayed in San Francisco, sick and hurting and eaten up inside because of Clary. He'd stayed in safe seclusion from the press and the continuing stories about the riot at the concert there, with Susannah Whittaker, no less. That thought alone might have sent her temper soaring, but Breeze also knew John Eustace. By now, he'd be changing Jeb's sheets and spooning gruel down his throat.

Breeze pulled her legs up onto the flowered chaise longue on which she'd settled. She'd been afraid for Jeb, afraid of his pneumonia, his failing voice, and his sinking spirits. However, since the phone call an hour ago about the witness to Clary's death, she'd been terrified.

"Hiding out here, are you?" Mack Norton ambled onto the porch, his features darkly shadowed in the moonless night, and dropped onto the chaise at her feet. "Peggy's going to divorce me," he said after a moment.

"Because of me?"

He smiled in the darkness. "Honey, you're one fine-looking woman and you're hell on wheels in bed. But, my wife is filing papers because, in her words, I am one piss-poor parent." He ran a hand through his hair. "I think she's got another guy. I swear I can smell Old Spice or somethin' every time I walk into that house."

"That's an easy answer, Mack."

"I wonder." He rose from the chaise and disappeared into the house. Breeze thought he'd gone to get a drink, which it appeared he badly needed, but he called to her from the downstairs hallway leading to her bedroom. "Are you comin' or not?" as if he didn't care.

"I'm coming."

Mack undressed by her bed. It flowed, all red satin quilted covering and overstuffed pillows, over a raised, white-carpeted platform, and she watched him from her vantage point two steps down and across the room at her mirror, brushing out her long hair.

"I had a call this afternoon from the police in New York," she said, "about Clary." She told him what she knew, and her mouth turned down. "This will kick up the fuss again. I'll bet they carried the story on the coast, for sure."

"I'm surprised Jeb hasn't called by now, looking for you to handle the media."

"Susannah Whittaker and John Eustace must be shielding him." She glanced at a nearby gold clock, shaped like a woman's body, her face above and the timepiece centered in her abdomen. Eleven o'clock. The boys had given it to her as a joke that last Christmas. "I tried to phone him, but the answering machine was on and I didn't want to leave a message. I'll try again later."

After she and Mack made love, which didn't calm her fears, Breeze slipped from bed.

With the air cooling further toward morning, she forced herself into the room at the opposite end of the big house, smelling the white roses Jeb insisted on keeping there as soon as she stepped inside. She didn't turn on the lights then either. She knew every photograph, every plaque, as if they'd been carved in her heart. They didn't belong to her, not really; they belonged to her boys.

Breeze stared at the darkened walls, remembering. She'd hit Nashville in the late seventies, not a particularly good time for country music. Except for the "outlaws," artists like Kris Kristofferson, Waylon Jennings, and Willie Nelson, who had fought the old-time establishment to gain creative freedom and maintain a traditional country sound, except for a few female singers like Emmylou Harris, the industry had been mired in a pop-country, elevator music sound stripped of all heart and soul. Breeze had once been compared to Harris, a comparison she treasured. Then, just as Breeze's career took off too, the urban cowboy phase briefly sent country music sales soaring, leaving the industry in an even more depressed state when it ended. Still, Breeze—and her traditional sound—survived, prospered. By the time new and younger talent arrived on the scene in the eighties, infusing it with what Jeb and others called the new traditionalism, her prosperity was already gone. Her band, and her music.

In the dark, Breeze knew the white grand piano too. It faced the window wall that looked onto the side yard, faced a wall of trees, dark as the grave in this last hour before the sun edged above the horizon. She went toward the piano, which glowed softly in the blackness like a beacon, and raised the keyboard cover.

Her hands trembled above the ivories.

She didn't play well, never had, and in recent years seldom touched the piano. Another reminder. She'd always composed there; it had been the birthplace of more than one hit song. Her palms grew damp and she moistened suddenly dry lips, still swollen from Mack's kisses. Kisses she'd barely felt tonight, or all week.

She'd heard the news. But it wasn't Jeb's career she thought of now.

Her fingers stiff, she placed them carefully on the keys, and standing there in her birthday suit, played a couple of chords. A-minor. Augmented. Diminished. She could hear the crowd now, the shouts and the applause. The music. She could feel the blood roaring through her veins, feel the love pouring back and forth between her and the audience. They cried her name in adoration, in ecstasy.

"Breeze! Miss B! We love you, Breeze!"

The way they called Jeb's name now.

Her hands stilled.

Bad news or not, she meant to keep him where he belonged. To blow the sky off country music, as she'd once done herself . . . and paid the price for.

Jeb wouldn't. Under her guidance he'd fly straight to the stars, through the stratosphere of country music and mainstream too. With a determined smile, she riffled off a few phrases, her fingers gliding more naturally now over the keys, keeping them soft and light, like the music itself until, after a while, it sounded almost like a song again, and she forgot that no one loved her, that she'd brought it on herself.

As Jeb might have said, more damn damage control.

Jeb tripped on the last step going downstairs and cursed under his breath. He didn't want to wake anyone. John Eustace, after six days of caring for him, had finally fallen asleep and was snoring to beat hell. Susannah had gone upstairs early too, pleading a sick stomach again, which concerned him—she'd had the same complaint all week—but he didn't check on her either. He needed to be alone.

The day before, his fever had finally gone, and he felt stronger, though still shaky. His hand shook now when he passed it over his eyes in the darkened living room. Clary, Clary . . .

Still hearing the late-evening news report in his mind, he groped his way through the room to sit at the ebony grand piano near the garden windows. He'd gotten bored lying on his pillows, listening to the Andres Segovia disc Susannah had bought him knowing his preference for classical guitar, reading the magazines she'd brought him, sipping the liquid diet she and John Eustace insisted upon. He'd peed buckets since the fever broke and wasn't used to inactivity in bed, particularly at this time of night when, after some concert, he would usually feel wired. So minutes ago he'd eased his way from bed on rubbery legs, down the hall and into a small den on the second floor where he'd turned on the television set.

". . . today in New York, the mayor's office and the chief of police announced they're back to square one on the Clarice Cody Whittaker killing in Central Park.

Following a thorough background check, the witness who came forward several weeks after the killing has been discredited." The woman had a long history of institutionalization in various mental hospitals, most recently Bellevue, where she had used her current alias, one of more than a dozen, it had been learned. "Police suspect her descriptions of the killers are also false. . . ."

No wonder Susannah had seemed pale all evening. No wonder she'd discouraged his requests for a television in his room. No wonder the phone had kept ringing, but no more than four times before the machine picked up.

He sat down at the piano, running his fingers lightly over the keys without quite touching them, so that no sound came out. After a moment, he realized he was playing "Kid Sister" and stopped. He stared down at the keyboard, clean and polished and perfect, without any of the chips or smears that decorated the ivories of the scarred upright in his mother's house. Clean and perfect, like Susannah.

In another day or two, three at most, he'd have to leave. Breeze would be on his back by tomorrow, after that news story, and if memory served, he had a two-night gig in Des Moines—or was it Dubuque? This hiatus would end, as his relationship had with Clary, with Rachel.

He gazed at the piano keys, forcing his thoughts from Susannah and trying to quiet the clamor in his lower body that the very thought of her provoked. He didn't realize when his touch became surer and sound floated over the room, the expensive instrument's tone clear as a warning bell, as a memory.

Ah, Clary . . .

"Deep River" wrung it from his soul, all adagio tempo

and yearning melody and measured chords, augmented triads echoing in the deep nighttime stillness.

He played it through three times, a benediction, before he felt slender hands on his shoulders.

"That's beautiful, Cody."

"It's an old gospel song. Part of my raising."

"Clary's too."

"Clary's too." Her arms slipped around him and she pressed, soft and silken, against his bare back. His voice had sounded thick and Jeb cleared it, hoping she'd think he was hoarse from pneumonia and not speaking much the last few days.

If he and Clary had reconciled, he and Susannah would have met years ago. Just as well, he tried to tell himself. She'd called him Cody, as if to remind him of Clary, but he didn't care. Clary was in the room with them now, between them, but for once, he didn't mind.

"How did you hear the news about her?" Susannah asked.

"Television."

"In the den," she said, as if she'd forgotten to hide some incriminating evidence.

"Doesn't matter. Breeze would've called in the morning. Your father—"

"I've already heard from him. You're right, but I wanted you to rest a little longer."

"Before the media grabs hold of me again? Or some other nut case takes a swipe at me, or a gun next time."

"Don't," she said.

"That's all it took at the concert here, all it took for Clary. Just one person with a grudge, an attitude, a history. One person who wants to bring me down, who wanted to hurt her, hurt anyone."

She rocked him close. "That riot wasn't your fault. Neither was Clary's death. And whatever happened to her, whatever either of us believes . . ." She hesitated, hugging him, his spine to her breasts. "It's time to let your feelings for her out before they kill *you*."

He shrugged away, staring down at his hands on the piano keys. "I thought that's what I was doing."

"Come upstairs," she said. "Your skin feels cool—and I want it to stay that way. So does your grandfather."

"So do I. I have to leave here." He made his decision. "Tomorrow."

"You need another day or two."

"That's not what the promoters will say, my booking agent, Breeze, or my band." He traveled with more than two dozen people, musicians and roadies. "They have families to feed and cars to buy, homes mortgaged until the next century. . . . I have responsibilities. The only thing I don't worry about these days is money."

He could feel the very air between them stiffen. "Stay down here, then, until your skin turns too cool and you end up in the hospital next time. Sit down here all night and play mournful music until your temperature spikes back up to a hundred and four."

"Settle down," he murmured, "or I'll think you care about me."

He turned on the piano bench, his jeans sliding over the polished wood surface, and opened his legs wide. He drew Susannah between them, resting his head against her satin nightshirt. He couldn't tell its color in the dark, but it looked shiny and warm, felt the same way, and he could hear her heart beating, strong and hard, in his ear.

Like Clary's, down by the creek the day they'd taken his father away.

"You really want to hear this?" He didn't have to say the name.

"Yes."

"I always meant to care for her," he said quietly, "but as it turned out, she sometimes cared for me instead. I was playin' that old gospel tune, remembering." He told Susannah about the sheriff and the caged car and the handcuffs, about Clary's tears and her trust in him. "Our daddy came home that next fall, about four months after they dragged him off that time. Right on time for hunting season. Mama was pregnant when he left. She'd lost that baby by the time he got back." Jeb frowned at the memory. "Mama still looked white and drawn, and he blamed that on me. Said I hadn't been man enough to see to things while he was gone."

He could feel Susannah watching him. "How old were you?"

"Ten," he said, "but he had a point. It wasn't as if we hadn't managed before without him, or wouldn't again. Soon enough."

He sighed against her.

"Daddy always went huntin' every fall. Bagged himself a deer or two, which Mama dressed and hung and then put into the freezer. He said for me to clean his gun that day, then come along with him." Jeb swallowed, his throat hurting again, his heart. "I never cared much for hunting helpless animals but he wouldn't take no for an answer. We marched off into the woods and he killed a doe instead of a buck that afternoon and brought her home stretched out over the hood of his old pickup." He swallowed again. "Hell, I'd seen *Bambi* like every other kid. That night in my dreams I kept seeing that doe, its fawn standin' off to the side and lookin' on while Daddy made me gut its mother."

"Oh, God."

"I haven't eaten venison since."

He wasn't telling her everything, which Susannah seemed to sense.

"And then what?"

He glanced up. "Clary found me. On my knees down by the creek near our house, spewing the contents of my stomach." She'd held him, cradled him. "'Daddy loves you,' she told me. 'It's just his way of makin' you a man.'" At Susannah's frown Jeb hesitated. It had taken him a while to see the mixed messages in Clary's statements. He wouldn't touch the other memories, later, when everything between them had changed. "Sometimes she took care of me instead, and did it better."

"I doubt that."

Jeb felt something ripple through him, like joy. She didn't blame him for the riot, or for Clary. Or for his own weakness.

"The next day," he told her, "John Eustace took me out behind the garage and taught me how to hit a target—one that couldn't bleed. He's a crack shot," Jeb said, "and to this day so am I."

Susannah touched him, and he looked up. Her eyes were suspiciously bright, their centers dark and wide.

"You ever go huntin' with your daddy?" he asked, hoping to lighten things. Hunting was the last thing a woman like her had ever done with a parent. Especially Drake.

"My father was a very busy man. He still is."

"Too busy for his own daughter?"

"Leslie—my mother—always says he belongs to the world. As a neurosurgeon, he enjoys an international reputation. Just like you." She said the words grandly, like a gesture, like some line in a play she'd rehearsed.

"You holdin' that against me?"

"A little, I guess."

A lot, he thought.

"My mother tried to make up for him, but she's never been able to . . . focus, really. On anyone's problems but her own. So I learned to take care of myself."

Her voice drifted on, telling Jeb about a childhood spent with pets and horses instead of family and friends. About private schools and holidays alone, especially one Christmas when Drake Whittaker attended a medical conference at The Hague and Leslie decided to go on to Paris to see the spring clothing collections.

"Poor little rich girl," he murmured, trying to pull her close again between his legs.

She resisted. "I didn't mean to sound self-pitying. I'm not."

"Life happens, that's all. However it happens."

"So it does." She gave a little shrug, then headed for the stairs. "Good night . . . Cody. Sleep well, unless you decide to make music the rest of the night." She paused. "If you do, the piano won't wake me. Or John Eustace either, I'm sure." She hesitated another second. "Have I ever told you you're a wonderful musician."

"It's mostly instinct. I learned long ago to trust my instincts."

He noticed she was cradling her left breast, just underneath, where the small tattoo lay near her heart. Jeb realized she touched it when she felt unsettled, or sad.

"If I don't see you before you go," she began.

"You'll see me."

He would still leave, he told himself. She could stare at him like that all night, with her eyes wide and her mouth parted, and in the morning he would still leave.

And try, as he'd always succeeded in doing before, with every other woman since Clary and his wife, not to look back.

Susannah lay blinking at the astronomy display on her darkened ceiling. She'd pasted the stars and planets there for nights when she couldn't sleep or stop thinking. They glowed at her now, and she imagined them winking, like fireflies.

She'd always envied Clary and Jeb their close-knit family, at least the early years. But Jeb had had no easier time growing up than she did. He hadn't married a girl as young as she'd thought. He hadn't killed that deer in cold blood either. How much of what Clary told her about Jeb was true? *It's just his way of makin' you a man.* Clary's words seemed contradictory—part comfort, part criticism of Jeb's masculinity. At ten years of age? How many other games had she played with him, or with Susannah? She wondered whether John Eustace's view was skewed after all.

Yet Clary had always seemed proud of Jeb. Proud but heartbroken by his rejection. Susannah had suffered that herself in New York, and she suspected she might again. Clary could have hardly resented his newfound fame, though; he'd worked hard for it. Maybe he needed it too much.

He'd had a father who spent more time behind bars than supporting his family; a mother who'd been left with eight children to feed, Jeb among them. He'd delivered newspapers, Clary had said; mowed lawns; dug earthworms for fishermen; run errands for his grandfather. She doubted that had been a lie on Clary's part.

His father, she thought. And Drake. Maybe John Eustace was right. She and Jeb had common bonds, including Clary.

Susannah rolled over in the big walnut sleigh bed, pulling the white cutwork comforter over her shoulders, feeling the satin of her nightshirt slowly warm, resting her head on the snowy cutwork pillowcase.

Too late, she thought. Jeb was leaving. Better that he should, that she chose someone like Michael, who wouldn't see her as a poor little rich girl, who wouldn't turn her inside out and make her want too much.

Susannah gave herself one last talking to as the moon shifted, slanting across the plum-colored walls, emerging from the clouds to shine, silvery and serene, through her bedroom windows. She'd opened them, hoping the fresh air might lull her into a dreamless sleep, which it finally promised to—until she was jerked awake by the creak of a floorboard in the third floor hallway.

Struggling with her tangled covers, she turned over.

Jeb slipped into the room without fully opening the half-closed door and wandered to her bed, appearing hazy and rumpled as if he were sleepwalking. But his eyes looked alert, searching her face, her form outlined by the sheets. He dropped down onto the polished floor beside the bed, and took her face in his hands. They felt cooler than the nights he'd tossed and turned in fever but not as cool as they had downstairs.

"I came to apologize. For saying what I did." Looking deep into her eyes, he shook his head. "No, that's not only why I came. Though at first, that's what I did think about you."

"What?"

"That you were spoiled and overprivileged, that you

had too much money and not enough feeling for other people."

She felt foolish. "Just because a person has money, doesn't mean she's not human. Or that she doesn't have emotions like anyone else."

His gaze held hers. "I know."

"Dreams," she added, "hopes."

"Pleasures?" He lowered his head to brush his lips against hers. Light and soft, slick and warm.

"Pleasures," Susannah agreed, feeling her whole body weaken. She should push him away now, stop trying to read in his eyes the message she wanted.

He kissed her again, lingering. "I think we like the same pleasures."

"It seems so."

Another kiss, slow and seeking. "I think we've been runnin' around the bed all week. Downstairs, upstairs . . ."

He was leaving tomorrow.

"You must have been more delirious than I thought."

"You weren't but you were running too." Jeb smiled. "It's cold out here." He shifted, banging a knee against the floor. "Damn, but I'm purely freezin' to death. Can I get in bed with you?" She opened her mouth to say no, and he added, "You let me before."

"You had a fever. Chills. I was warming you."

"See what I mean?"

"Cody."

"You let me in before that. In New York." He kissed her again, drawing his mouth back and forth on hers until she moaned.

"I don't know what you—"

"You know what I want." He trailed one finger from her cheek along her throat to the closing of her satin nightshirt and over its smoothness to her left breast. He touched the place where he'd seen the heart tattoo. "You want the same thing."

"It's just sex," she said in desperation.

He eased the covers back and crawled in, gathering Susannah close before she could say a word or even think of some rhetorical cold water to throw on him, and molded their bodies together, hers satin-covered to her thighs, his bare except for . . .

"Did you come up here like that?"

"Like what?"

"Naked." Below the nightshirt, her thighs felt silky against his rougher skin, which only made Susannah's toes curl. All her pep talks to the ceiling vanished from her mind as Jeb's leg stroked hers. Sometimes differences seemed just fine, like puzzle pieces. "John Eustace might wake up."

"He might," Jeb said. "He is a doctor and doctors, as you well know, thrive on practically no sleep at all. Even at his age."

He slid one leg between hers, cupping Susannah's head in the palm of his hand and turning her slowly toward him. Their mouths hovered an inch from each other and she felt the warmth of his breath, not quite even, matching hers. Everything about them suddenly seemed to fit.

"If he does wake up," Jeb went on, "I hope to hell he has sense, after lookin' in my bed, not to come after me. There is, as he always says, a lady present."

The reminder was for herself. "It's a good thing you're leaving tomorrow."

"But tonight . . ."

His mouth closed over hers, and she tasted brandy, heat.

"You're right, Miss Susannah. At first I did think all we

had goin' for us was sex." He turned his head, kissing her from a different angle. "I thought all I wanted from you was this"—he coaxed her lips open, trailing his tongue over them, then sliding inside—"to have my mouth on you, my hands." He ran one down her side, a pathway of heat, and moaning, she never wanted him to leave. Easing the buttons open on her satin shirt, spreading it wide and finding sleek bare skin, he exposed one breast and then the other. "To kiss your mouth and—" he slid lower, his dark hair slipping against her as he moved his head to find the small heart beneath her breast, "oh, God, this." With his mouth pressed to her skin, he quoted: "'On her left breast/A mole cinque-spotted, like the crimson drops/I' the bottom of a cowslip.'"

"Cody." Susannah tugged at his hair, but he only groaned.

"I thought we had discussed my name." And he turned his attention to her other breast, in just the same place. "That was Shakespeare, *Cymbeline*." With his lips stroking the soft skin there, he whispered, "Maybe one day you'll get another one right here, for me."

"But we don't—we won't—"

"At first I would have agreed with you." He nuzzled her bared midriff, then the indentation of her waist, then lower, across her bare belly. His breath, like Susannah's, came in short puffs. "I would have . . . said that all I wanted . . . was to kiss you—" he slid upward, pressing himself against her, "to use my tongue on you. That I only wanted to make you as soft as I am hard." Slowly, gently, he slipped a finger into her. "Jesus, you're wet."

"Cody . . ."

"I was wrong." He moved higher, taking her hand and drawing it low to cover him, guiding him closer, then touching, barely touching. "I didn't just want to get inside you." He pushed into her slowly, an inch at a time. "Oh, Christ. . . ." He dropped his head next to hers on the pillow. "You see, I did in the beginning . . ."

Susannah wrapped her legs around him, pulling him in, and he began to move, easy at first, then faster, harder, deeper. Their rhythm, their scents—his of brandy and skin, hers of desire and the expensive herbal shampoo she'd used—their parts and pieces fitting, joining, meshing . . .

"Cody . . . Jeb!"

"Oh," he said hotly, "Susannah."

He moved until she thought she couldn't bear any more of shared pleasures, then moved some more, his hands holding her hips, his voice a throaty whisper, praising, entreating. The pleasure built and grew. And grew some more. Then he tensed, all his muscles gathering in the same instant Susannah joined him, climax shattering over them in the same seconds like a shower of the stars on her ceiling that she had likened to lightning bugs. Fireflies.

"But then again. . . ."

Groaning, he didn't finish the thought. And Jeb Stuart Cody didn't finish loving her the rest of the night. Susannah couldn't have called it anything else. On her part, or his.

Hours later John Eustace paused on the landing in front of Susannah Whittaker's bedroom door, which stood ajar. Through the crack, he could just see morning light slanting through the room's windows and across the bare wooden floor, striking arrows of brilliance there, and straight toward the hall. Craning his neck only a little and feeling it catch for his nosiness, he glimpsed the corner of a rumpled bed, all in white, a brown muscled arm that surely wasn't Miss Susannah's. And of course he already knew that Jeb's bed was empty.

John Eustace smiled to himself, because he could still be romantic even at his age, then turned away. He clumped back across the landing to the stairs, imagining bare skin, dark and light, a ruffled cap of blond curls and his grandson's streaked, darker hair. Two heads lying close. A strong hand curved around a fragile breast. Legs twined together, one pair long and slim if slightly bowed—the mark of a horsewoman—the other long and straight and with that small, scimitar-shaped scar on the knee that had come from testing his grandfather's scalpel when Jeb was six years old.

Now Jeb's fever was gone. His lungs sounded clear.

It was time for John Eustace to head for Elvira.

He set one foot on the stairs, then the other, wincing at the burning pain in his left hip. It never felt right until noon these days but damned if he was ready for a plastic one. He took his time going down to the second floor, not wanting to wake the lovers.

Despite his argument with her, their differences, he liked Susannah Whittaker. He was leaving John Eustace Beauregard Stuart Cody in good hands, as the insurance slogan said. Something fine, he thought, might come from Clary's life, after all.

11

"*John Eustace is gone.*"

Susannah spoke against Jeb's shoulder, her lips pressed to his warm, bare skin, her body snug around his under the white cutwork duvet. She smiled at the groggy tone of his voice as he rolled toward her, disturbing the blankets, her new sense of security, and the scent of lovemaking. It rose around them like a morning perfume.

"Home, I guess," he murmured.

"He left around dawn. I heard the taxi and he's not the quietest person going down stairs." She paused. "I think I heard him earlier outside this door."

"Spyin' on us?"

"He was checking on you."

"Sure he was. Checkin' to see I minded my upbringing."

She grinned as he sleepily looked into her eyes with a half-awake, amused expression. "And were you?" she asked.

"Yes, ma'am. My mama taught me to give a lady what she needs."

Susannah touched his cheek, scratchy with morning whiskers. "Maybe I did and maybe I didn't. Need anything."

He laughed, soft and seductive. "Oh, you did. In the shower too."

At the memory Susannah kissed his shoulder. In her plum-and-ivory marble bathroom, in the middle of the night, Jeb had soaped her, head to toe, under the steaming water. While he sang to her, softly in her ear, his rich baritone filling the shower stall, she slicked the fragrant herbal bar over his skin too, at last joining him with her uncertain soprano, wondering how she'd survived so long without sharing such an experience, without having this man in her life. A man who sang for his living, but no less beautifully in the shower. Rinsing each other clean, they stopped frequently to kiss and touch, then kiss some more until it became impossible to dry off and get back in bed before making love again. Susannah didn't even think of protesting when Jeb had pressed her to the tile wall. . . .

Now she gazed at him, clean and dusky tan, against the pristine white cutwork sheets and pillows. The contrast between the bedding, which suited her as a female, and his completely male body, took her breath away. So did Jeb's lazy smile.

He gathered her close, lightly kissed her mouth, one hand between them at her breast. When Susannah winced, he said, "Still tender?"

"A little." All the time lately, she thought.

Pulling back, he studied her face until she wanted to squirm at his more serious regard. "I didn't hurt you, did I?" She shook her head. "Are you feelin' all right today? John Eustace remarked upon your pallor more than once and you look tired to me too."

"You kept me up all night."

"You kept me up all night," he repeated, going back for another, deeper kiss. He pulled her over him, settling her legs between his with Susannah's crotch nudging his. Jeb glanced down. "And look what we have here again."

"Trouble," she murmured but she couldn't resist pressing closer.

"Umm, there's trouble, then there's trouble. Like first impressions and the truth."

"Like spoiled rich girls and modest hill—"

"—billies?" Jeb nibbled his way along her throat, then sucked at the tender skin. His mouth felt hot but his tone had cooled.

"I was going to say boys from the Kentucky hills."

"Is there a difference?"

"Yes. Don't be insecure." He sucked a little harder, and she gave a small cry. "You'll make a mark on me, Jeb."

"Jeb, is it now?" His tongue soothed the spot, and her limbs weakened.

"Yes. I guess it is."

She felt his smile on her dampened throat, but he clearly didn't want to discuss their differences, or similarities. Jeb raised her chin, inspecting the mark he'd obviously made, with satisfaction. "This looks almost like a heart to me." Then his arms closed over her back and he waited, with a devilish smile in his eyes, for Susannah to lower her mouth to his.

When she kissed him, he tickled her. "Call me a hillbilly, will you?"

She shrieked.

"Are you sorry?" Jeb's hand darted from her waist to her ribs. "How sorry?"

Susannah laughed, shifting as far as he'd allow in his embrace, her lower body rolling against his. Jeb's breathing changed, becoming shaken and erratic. She twisted, flailing with arms and legs until he clamped them both tight, grasping her wrists in one hand, putting her legs in the vise of his. Giggling, breathless, Susannah gave him her open mouth for another kiss and Jeb rocked them, the kiss heating as he changed angles this way and that. Then all at once, Susannah felt her stomach lurch.

"Let me go!"

"Not till I've had my way with you again, woman. Just punishment."

"Jeb, *let go!*"

Her frantic tone must have registered. The kiss ended abruptly. His arms fell away, and Susannah bolted none too soon for the bathroom.

Miserable, mortified, she didn't hear him come in minutes later, his bare footsteps on the marble floor muffled by the sound of the toilet flushing a second time.

Jeb hunkered down next to her and Susannah, shaking, collapsed back onto her ankles, her arms still gripping the basin. A chill ran through her. "Didn't your mama teach you—while she was at it—not to embarrass a woman when she's kissing the porcelain god? It's a private matter."

"You all right now?" He ignored her weak jest.

"I will be. I think."

Her skin felt clammy. Her stomach was still roiling. And her mouth tasted as she imagined Leslie's must after a long, lonely Saturday night with a bottle. Dimly she heard Jeb rise and go to the sink, run water, and unscrew some kind of cap.

"Here. Gargle." He held out a paper cup. His voice sounded shaken. "It's mouthwash and water. Don't swallow."

Susannah obeyed, her fingers trembling when she lifted the cup. She felt so weak, hot and sick, then cold again. "Thanks."

"How long have you had this morning affair with the commode?"

"Off and on," she admitted, sweeping hair from her face. "You and John Eustace are right, though. I've been feeling lackluster lately. No appetite, a stuffy stomach—"

"Tired?" he said quietly.

She frowned. "I thought it was fatigue, because of too much work for the Arts Commission, or even because of how I felt after Clary's death, but it hasn't gone away."

"Since when?"

Susannnah thought for a moment. She'd been trying not to think about it, in the hope she'd recover naturally. "Several weeks." Her frown deepened. Or had she been avoiding reality? "No, since mid-April."

Jeb helped her to her feet, his tone flat. "And it never occurred to you what exhaustion and no appetite and tender breasts might mean?" He gazed at her with darkened gray eyes. "When was your last period?"

Her cheeks colored. "That's none of your business." But counting back, she realized she'd never actually had that period in April. Susannah could have groaned. Her schedule had been so jammed, and she'd thought her symptoms were a reaction—as they might well be—to those few days in New York. Now she was missing a second period.

"I grew up in a house with eight kids," Jeb said. "I saw

my mama carry one more than once, saw her bring 'em home from the hospital, saw her nursin' her babies. I've changed a few diapers." He paused. "I held her head a few times too in the morning. So unless I miss my best guess, you're pregnant, Susannah." His gaze slid away from hers. "You're a healthy woman with an active sex life. What else might it be?"

Some terrible disease, she thought. And then, no, a miracle.

Jeb turned, heading back into the bedroom. "Let me be the first to offer my congratulations," he said, walking toward the half-open door to the hall. "I'll even steep you a cup of tea to settle that stomach before I go. Once you've made your plans with the San Francisco boy-friend—"

"His name is Michael." On still shaky legs, she followed him down the steps to his room on the second floor. He yanked on jeans, a shirt and some socks, pulled on his boots, then threw his carry-on bag, which Breeze had sent, onto the neatly turned-down bed, and Susannah watched him stuff things inside. "If I am pregnant, Michael isn't the father of this child." She touched his arm, swinging him around with no resistance. "You are."

Pulling away, he stared at her. "No way."

With jerky motions, he zipped the bag shut and pushed past her. Susannah felt more than cold; she felt icy to the bone. He wouldn't acknowledge her, wouldn't look at her.

"Jeb, it happened in New York, during the blizzard." She stepped in front of him in the doorway. "Between you and me, dammit." She hadn't been with Michael in months, long before her trip east.

"Nice try, Miss Susannah."

"Don't try to pretend otherwise."

"I don't have to pretend anything." He looked past her at the hallway wallpaper. "I was married once, too soon, as it turned out, to know how to do right by the girl I'd made pregnant." He swallowed hard, his gaze shifting to the floor between their feet. "I watched her bleed to death. I watched my baby son die a few minutes after he was born—"

His voice cracked and Susannah nearly weakened.

"Jeb, I'm sorry."

"I promised myself then that it wouldn't happen again. I carry protection—always—and I use it." He looked at her. "I used it with you too." She could sense him watching her, her flat abdomen, as he quoted softly: "It seems that 'Passions spin the plot: We are betrayed by what is false within.' That's from George Meredith." He held the carry-on bag in one hand, the other tilting her face toward him. "I should have known I'd be right about you after all. Rich, spoiled, beautiful . . . and what else? Bored, sugar?"

Her voice shook. "Don't call me sugar!"

"Now that the Arts Commission fund-raiser is organized and the Christmas cotillion planning is underway, have you decided to make a project of Jeb Stuart Cody?"

Stunned, she could barely comprehend his words.

"Well, think twice before you go public on this one, before you bring a paternity suit against me and drag us both through the media muck." His eyes met hers. "Such things happen to everyone in the business. I don't know why I expected this to be different. Or you," he added, then shoved past her into the hall.

"Get out of my house!"

"I'd call Michael if I were you."

"Get the hell out of my life!"

"Such as it is," he murmured, going down the stairs.

Hastily pulling on a robe, Susannah pelted after him like a wild thing, her hair flying, her eyes seeing red, her whole body frozen inside. As if Drake had left her alone again on Christmas to open her presents by herself. She'd almost believed in Jeb. Almost loved him.

"I never want to see you again, you—"

"Don't worry about it," Jeb threw over his shoulder.

"—*redneck*!"

The front door slammed behind him and silence reigned. A silence that shouted louder than words to Susannah about her own foolishness.

Nearly a week later Jeb came offstage in St. Louis coughing his lungs out. He'd barely made it through the last song and, as he stumbled over coiled electrical cables and dodged props and people in the narrow backstage hallway, he felt torn between turning his chest inside out and cursing himself for going back to work too soon.

"Lie down," Breeze said, following him into his dressing room. "I'll get you some suppressant and make you a cup of tea with honey."

"Protecting your investment?"

Ignoring his sour mood, she touched a hand to his forehead as Jeb slumped into a chair.

"You can always go back to San Francisco," she said, handing him a thermometer. "If you'd prefer someone else's tender loving care."

"I'd prefer John Eustace." With the probe under his tongue, he rested his head against the chair. After their last phone call his grandfather had sent Breeze and Jeb to a hospital emergency room in some city or other—

Jeb couldn't recall which—clearly irritated with his grandson over Susannah Whittaker. Jeb's X rays had proved negative, and the mucus was still clearing from his lungs with annoying regularity, considering his profession, so he assumed, as John Eustace must, that he was on the mend.

"Except for that brain of yours," John Eustace had said. "Whatever your quarrel with Miss Susannah, I'd patch it up if I were you."

"It's basic," Jeb replied but would say nothing more.

If he told his grandfather about Susannah's condition, John Eustace would appear all right—with a shotgun—and Susannah Whittaker would have a wedding band on her finger before the week was out.

Jeb shook his head. He wouldn't trade an old tragedy for a new one. She was exactly what he'd first thought, and from now on he would trust his instincts.

New York, she'd said.

In a pig's eye, Jeb thought, discarding his own speculation of her not long after that, pregnant with his baby. He yanked the thermometer from his mouth.

"Normal," he announced.

Breeze stood at the small range in the dressing room's minikitchen, pouring hot water into a cup and dumping in a tea bag. She smiled thinly over her shoulder. "John Eustace said not to worry excessively unless it goes up again. And if it does, to call him. He said he'd be on the first plane to wherever."

Jeb suppressed a smile. If he could count on anyone, it was John Eustace, and these days Jeb could number on one hand the people he trusted. His grandfather, most of his band members, Breeze—some of the time—and . . .

He'd almost added Susannah.

Jeb straightened in the chair, giving himself a cursory

once-over in the dressing room mirror. He'd soaked through his shirt during the performance and dark circles showed under his arms. His lips looked bloodless, his face pale. He still felt like hell.

"You want me to call the car? You could skip that party at the governor's mansion. I'd make your excuses," Breeze said, handing him the tea spiked with honey and a bottle of prescription cough syrup with a spoon. Her eyes looked warmer, apologetic.

He should trust her all the time. But there was her own dishonesty with herself, which he despised, and there was Mack.

"So you and Norton can spend the rest of the night tryin' out new songs behind my back? That is, until you feel like fallin' on each other."

She rinsed the thermometer in alcohol and shoved it back into its case. "If you'd take any interest in your own album and come up with a song yourself, we wouldn't have to." She met his eyes in the mirror. "You haven't picked up that guitar offstage since you came back from San Francisco."

"Quit talkin' about that."

Her gaze slid away. "You slept with her again, didn't you? Whatever happened, Jeb, has you tied in knots worse than before. I hear you pacin' every night—"

"I hear you screwin', so we're even. Neither of us is gettin' any sleep."

Hurt flashed in her eyes. "I can move in with Mack if you want. You could get a smaller suite, save yourself some money." She gave him a bitter smile. "You're going to need it if you keep on like this."

His show had been off-center tonight. His breath control was still gone, his voice hoarse. Fear gnawed at his insides.

Breeze seemed to read his expression. Her tone softened but her words didn't. "The album's stalled, one cut short. If you don't make a decision soon, the label's going to make it for you. You'll record what they say you will. Is that what you want? After we fought, like a lot of other artists, for control over our material?"

"My material," he said. "You're out of business. Remember?"

Breeze stared at him for a moment, then shook her head. He watched the affection for him fade from her eyes.

"I don't know why I work for you," she said and left the room.

"Shit," he said aloud. Then he called after her, like a little kid in some fight with a buddy. Like Susannah Whittaker in her front entryway that last morning. He'd slammed the door but he'd heard what she called him. It had been sticking in his craw ever since. "You think I can't hear you every night, Maynard?"

She poked her head back in the door, as he'd expected. Her eyes shooting fire.

"Hear what? Besides my love life?"

"You poundin' on that piano. It's a damn fine melody. Maybe you'll let me hear the words some night." At her silence Jeb turned on the chair. "C'mon, Breeze. You're wrong," he said, "about a lot of things."

"Not about San Francisco, I'm not."

Then she disappeared. When he yelled after her again, she didn't come back. Just as, long ago, Clary hadn't. Susannah wouldn't either—not that he needed her to.

With one hand pressed beneath her left breast, Susannah watched from her living room windows, watched the dark-haired child playing in her garden. Miranda, who had appeared earlier at her door, skipped along the stone path, stopping here and there to bend and examine a late tulip or to straighten and meet a huge purple iris at eye level. She could hear the little girl singing to herself, which tugged at her heart. Miranda had a sweet voice and dark hair—reminding her of Jeb.

Susannah had no sooner heard the front door slam a week ago than it opened again, admitting Leslie. Wearing an oversized white tunic sweater with black spandex leggings, she shoved her suitcases into the front hall with a toe shod in elegant ebony riding boots that had clearly never been near a horse.

"Is my vision failing me in middle age, or was that the illustrious Jeb Stuart Cody stalking down the front walk and into my cab?"

So that's where he had disappeared so quickly.

Susannah mumbled some agreement, then turned toward the stairs. She'd put on a robe but had nothing underneath.

"You went to the concert," Leslie guessed.

"No. I didn't."

"Well, thank heaven. That riot was all over the New York papers. I can only imagine what the coverage here must have been like. Your father nearly had a fit when I told him about the tickets. It was the only issue on which we agreed."

Susannah groaned but continued up the stairs, her stomach unsteady again. She'd been in no mood to deal with her mother's craziness about Drake, or anything else. And she vowed to keep her own problems to herself until she made some decisions.

That had been a week ago and Susannah was still

muddling through the morass her quiet, well-bred life had turned into the instant Jeb Stuart Cody entered it.

The baby was his.

She had no doubt of that. She'd gone over the facts in her mind a million times. New York. The blizzard. His hotel suite. The wide bed with the Indian star quilt. Protection, he'd said. But she'd read the literature since he'd rejected her for the second time and stormed out of her house, rejecting his child. Condoms provided no more than an 85 to 90 percent safeguard. Condoms could fail, and Jeb's obviously had at some time in those few days together. Probably the first, she thought. In the past week she'd replayed every love scene with him like an old movie, if a rather steamy one despite the snowstorm, and swore she could remember warmth flooding through her at his climax.

Warmth. Semen. Life.

She and Jeb had created a baby from a crazy couple of days when she hadn't even been certain she liked him. She wasn't proud of her actions, but the fact remained.

Her doctor had confirmed it only that morning. She was pregnant all right. By Jeb Stuart Cody. And she was alone.

She knew how sensitive he was about his marriage. Having learned about the deaths of his wife and child, she couldn't blame him for that, though his rejection still hurt. Again. Especially because she didn't expect him to marry her. Even if the other fact remained as well: She loved him. If she hadn't known it before his stay with her, before the night they'd spent in her room and in the shower, if she'd fought the knowledge after he left, she knew it now.

She didn't need marriage, she told herself. Or love. She had her own money, her own house. Susannah stared out at the sun-washed garden, at the light glinting in

Miranda's dark hair, turning it shades of brown and gold—like Jeb's. The little girl had plunked down on the stone walk and was digging a spoon Susannah had given her into the rich earth by the path. The simple sight tightened Susannah's chest and she looked away. Miranda would be all right. And so would she.

Avoiding Leslie's usual messes, she wandered upstairs. How right a nursery would look on the third floor in the room across from hers with a Jenny Lind crib, a braided rug on the shining wooden floor.

She wanted this baby even if Jeb didn't. Oh, how she wanted it.

Like everything else in her life, she could do this on her own.

Late the next night Jeb knocked on Breeze's bedroom door, intent upon patching up their argument from the night before. She hadn't spoken to him since. When she answered in a sleepy tone, he went into the dark room and, although he knew they were alone in the hotel suite, closed the door behind him. He leaned against it. She'd stayed out late but had come home to sleep, a sure sign she'd been quarreling with Mack too.

"I'm sorry," he said.

Breeze's long blond hair swept over the front of her light-colored, filmy gown that looked as soft as butter in the moonlight filtering through the gauzy draperies.

"Tell me what happened in San Francisco," she said.

"I developed pneumonia. Susannah Whittaker took me in so the press wouldn't find me after the riot." He crossed his booted feet at the ankles, folded his arms over his chest. He kept his tone lazy. "John Eustace helped her tend me until I got well."

"I know that. Don't be a smart ass. What else?"

Jeb thought he'd just blurt it out, but couldn't. He glanced at the room's dark furniture, the chair and love seat upholstered in turquoise silk, then at the big bed covered in a matching, quilted spread. The St. Louis suite had four bedrooms, not six, and no helipad on the roof, no swimming pool. He liked the elegant Adam's Mark, though, and the view from the suite's windows, especially the living room, of the nearby stainless steel Arch, was magnificent. He should know. He'd been sitting in the dark there for hours, searching for the courage to face Breeze. Jeb looked down at his feet.

"Susannah's pregnant."

"Christ, Jeb."

"I didn't say it was mine."

"Is it?"

"Hell, no," he said, moving away from the door, "but I suppose you ought to know, in case she decides to try and make my life miserable in court . . . or in the tabloids."

Breeze sat up, flinging her hair back. She stared at him for a moment, as if searching for some deeper truth he didn't want to confess, then she got out of bed and glided past him out into the suite's living room.

Jeb followed.

"What do you want to do about this?" She'd automatically accepted his innocence, aligned herself with him again. "What are we up against here?"

He knew what she meant. "Susannah's not as tough as she'd like people to believe, or as enamored of me as you've been thinking. She says she doesn't want to see me again, and it sure sounded genuine when I left her house."

Pausing only to flip on a single lamp on an end table,

Breeze paced the comfortable room. More dark walnut furniture, silk-papered walls, soft turquoise sofas and striped chairs. She was frowning, rubbing one thumb into the palm of her other hand.

"How do you feel about her? And I don't want some throwaway remark."

"We had something goin', but it's history now." He traced the scar on his lip. "I'm sure not tyin' myself to some woman with a kid in her belly that's not mine." He winced at his own words. "I think I made myself clear. Besides, I've got enough trouble with the tour and the album. I don't need any more."

Jeb stood with his back to the windows, to the awesome sight of the floodlit Arch, the darkened Mississippi River beyond.

"That's all that matters, then?" Breeze said.

"Yes, ma'am."

Apparently satisfied, she gave him the first true smile he'd seen in days. His second St. Louis concert had gone even worse than the first, worse than his last meeting with Susannah Whittaker. Jeb was getting scared. He watched Breeze sit down at the piano, an intricately carved walnut baby grand, then waited while she ran through a few bars of the tune he'd been hearing late at night when Breeze was alone, and when Mack Norton stayed with her. It sounded like the kind of poignant melody that people would hum long after they heard it. With the right lyric it had all the makings of a hit single.

"Sing me something, Jeb."

He stood behind her, his hands on Breeze's shoulders, and let her play. He hummed along for a while, trying out a phrase here and there, getting himself into a mood. Usually he composed on the guitar but didn't go to fetch it from his bed, where it lay on the Indian star quilt.

When the words came, he tried to stop them. ". . . some-thing," he sang, "from a poor boy like me." His stomach tightened and he trailed off.

"Go on."

Shaking his head, he lifted his hands from her shoulders and stepped away from her, away from the words forming in his mind.

"It won't gel just yet," he murmured. "I'll work on it."

A hit single, maybe even the missing song he needed for the second album, the title if it turned out right. Or maybe he'd scrap the insistent lines, just as he and Susannah Whittaker had scrapped each other.

"Jeb?"

"I'm goin' back to bed."

She caught up with him in the hallway. Their rooms were next to each other, and he stood for a few seconds, looking down into her eyes, filled with trust, with belief in him. Even John Eustace didn't believe in him just now.

"Don't worry," she said.

"I'm not." Not in the way you mean, he thought.

"I know exactly how to deal with a woman like Susannah Whittaker."

"Maynard, stay out of it."

She planted a lingering kiss on his cheek. "Rest easy, cowboy." She slipped back into her room, leaving the door open like an invitation.

12

The next morning as the hot St. Louis sun penetrated the suite's living room windows, while Jeb stood under the shower in the bathroom at the other end of the hall, Breeze Maynard punched San Francisco's area code into the cordless phone, then an unlisted number she had committed to memory the first time Jeb gave it to her while he was staying with Susannah Whittaker.

Her answering voice sounded soft, uncertain. Or was it ill?

"What do you want," Breeze said without a greeting, taking the phone to pace the room, "to keep you quiet?"

"Miss Maynard," Susannah acknowledged coolly, as if she'd been expecting the call.

"Jeb tells me you're pregnant."

Silence.

Breeze turned toward the windows, admiring the sparkle of the Arch in the sun only a block or so away, the echoing glint of light on the water below it. "There's no use pretending, Miss Whittaker. Even socialites get themselves knocked up." She could hear the sharp intake of breath, could sense the struggle for control. "He also tells me it's not his."

"That's what he chooses to think."

"No surprise, I might add. Last year at least three country stars of my acquaintance were dragged through the same kind of mess by women they barely knew."

"I have no intention of dragging him, or myself—and most of all, not his unborn child—through anything." She paused. "But you tempt me. I almost wish I were inclined to trail his image across the front page of every paper in this country."

"That's just fine if you're prepared to supply him with enough free publicity to send his CD into quintuple platinum this summer. And help me launch his next tour in the fall. Go right ahead—and see what a job I can do on your blue-blood reputation."

"Why do you dislike me so?"

Breeze shot a look toward the closed bathroom door. "It's been a while since Jeb and I rolled around in the sheets, but he's not exactly forgettable. If you know what I mean." She waited a beat, then said, "You have proof of this pregnancy?"

"That's my exclusive, Miss Maynard. Why would I share it with you?"

Breeze's respect inched upward a notch. Her tone had been strained, whether by anger or illness, but Susannah Whittaker had chosen a pretty classy way of telling her to go to hell.

"How far along are you?" she pressed.

"About eight weeks."

Breeze felt a spasm of envy. Not that she'd want a baby with her on tour, not now anyway.

"Then I imagine I'm keepin' you from a morning bout of sickness. Or some other tiresome symptom." She dropped down onto a thickly cushioned chair upholstered in striped turquoise silk near the fireplace. "But I suppose a woman like you, easily bored into an affair with a celebrity—into an unplanned pregnancy, no matter who's really responsible—can overlook the brief incapacity you're sufferin' for the larger picture."

"Meaning what?"

"I've read that the rich live mostly on paper, so it wouldn't surprise me to learn—if my investigators browsed through your financial holdings—that you're livin' on some kind of edge. Perched there on California Street, just ready to topple."

She could hear Susannah gasp.

"What will it take," Breeze went on, "to ensure your silence on this matter . . . and your future distance from Jeb Stuart Cody?" She hesitated for effect. "Free publicity aside, actually I'd be very disappointed to find mention in the press about a child, or even a firsthand account of Jeb's seclusion with you after that near riot in San Francisco—"

"How dare you!"

"Everyone has a price, Miss Whittaker. Money, or whatever. Frankly, I'd rather pay it now than have some tabloid tempt you into forgetting your high-minded ideals."

"We're talking about an innocent child. *My* child," Susannah said and slammed down the phone.

Still holding the receiver, Breeze heard a small sound in the room. Faintly smiling, she glanced over her shoulder and saw Jeb standing in the hallway, a thick hotel towel wrapped around his lean hips, a furious look on his handsome face.

Too late, Breeze realized her mistake. Instead of the

victory she'd wanted, she was staring straight at more damage control.

Days later Susannah was still shaking.

Breeze Maynard's insinuation had been insulting. But what if she had been penniless? Some girl like one of those at the concert in New York during the blizzard, who'd stayed and asked for Jeb's autograph? Even the one whose breast he'd signed? What if she'd been some hapless waitress in some hotel bar, who'd given in for a night to his star luster? His charm? And then found herself pregnant, out of a job? Except for the money, the fantasy wasn't that far from her own situation.

Unable to pay her rent, she'd have to beg shelter from her family, who would disapprove, maybe disown her, or end up on the streets, like the not-so-old woman she and Jeb had met in the snow, her hands gloveless, her body covered only by an old sweater. The woman he had insisted they feed.

But she wasn't poor or homeless. Thank heaven.

Still, Susannah couldn't shake the images.

She marched resolutely down California Street toward home. She'd asked the taxi driver to let her off several blocks up on Polk Street where she picked up food at her favorite deli. But in truth, she knew she'd wanted the walk home to think, and to look for Miranda. As Susannah neared her house, she automatically glanced toward the alleyway and its abandoned car— Miranda's home.

At first she didn't notice the slender woman polishing the car's hood. Then the woman straightened and caught her gaze. Susannah stopped on the sidewalk, forcing a smile.

Introducing herself, she said, "Are you Miranda's mother? She's been coming to visit. Playing in my garden. I hope you don't mind."

"I've told her to stay . . . home." The woman's blue-gray eyes had immediately turned wary. She probably thought Susannah was a social worker.

Susannah walked closer. Miranda's mother appeared fragile, but strength radiated from her direct gaze and from her small-boned but wiry hands. She twisted them together at her waist. Her worn jeans were held by a length of braided cord instead of a belt, and her blue knit top seemed a size too small, but her clothes were clean, her hands too. "I'm afraid I've sent Miranda home more than once with muddy fingers. I apologize. Next time I'll make sure she washes first."

"I don't want her coming there."

"I can't see the harm in our friendship," she said. "Miranda enjoys the garden and it's safe there, off the streets."

"I'm sure you'd think so." The woman eyed her critically, noting Susannah's tangerine linen designer shift, her expensive, heeled sandals with their orange and green and cream straps. "But I don't. My daughter and I stay together. That's our safety."

"Mrs. . . ." She trailed off, not knowing her name.

"Cheryl." The woman folded her arms, as if guarding the entrance to her alley, to the abandoned car. "If you feel like calling the authorities, I can't stop you. But if they take my baby—"

Susannah touched her arm, and the woman recoiled.

"I won't tell anyone." She held out the string bag she carried, stuffed with a loaf of Italian bread, some cheese, and cold cuts. "But please," she said, following Jeb's example, "I'd like to buy you dinner."

The woman, Cheryl, turned her back. "We don't need your charity. Leave us alone." She stalked back down the alley toward the old black car. "Leave my daughter alone. We'll be fine. My husband will find a job soon and we'll be just fine."

Moments later, still shaken by the encounter, Susannah stood in her dressing room, closets flung open on both sides. Tonight was the Arts Commission fund-raiser dinner dance, and she could already hear Leslie, bustling along the hallway on the second floor, skirts shushing, stopping at a mirror to check her appearance.

Nervous, she knew. Drake's recent rejection of Leslie in Greenwich must still hurt, as powerfully as Jeb's did. But Drake, after some considerable arm-twisting, had agreed to attend tonight as Leslie's escort possibly to please Susannah.

Standing naked, she riffled through the closet racks once more, coming up with the gown she'd intended to wear in the first place—specially made for the occasion.

Of floor-length bottle-green silk, bare on one shoulder and caught at the other with an antique gold clip, the dress made her feel sensual—and slim. Putting it on the first time, she had glanced at her stomach in the mirror, wondering whether she imagined the slight rounding there. Too soon, she thought, taking another, even more critical look. It would be all right after all. And the designer gown made her hazel eyes appear pure green.

Once dressed, Susannah brushed her hair high, securing it at the crown with another gold rosette, letting wisps of curl fall where they would. She hoped the vaguely Empire look suited her. With full battle makeup on, maybe no one would see the smudges beneath her eyes from lack of sleep, the pallor of her skin from morning sickness, which she'd so far managed to hide from Leslie.

Now that she'd decided to play single parent for the rest of her life, she couldn't wait for the first trimester of pregnancy to be over.

The doorbell rang and she answered on a cloud of expensive perfume.

Her father stepped inside, looking fit and elegant in a silk tuxedo with garnet studs. Susannah embraced him, this otherworldly creature her mother still adored. To Susannah's constant dismay, so did she. Usually to the same result.

"Susie." After only the lightest brush of her lips on his cheek, he held her off. "You look smashing tonight. Nervous?"

"I've been rehearsing my speech into a mirror for weeks. I won't even need the prompter."

He turned slightly, shutting her out. "I believe Michael's right behind me. I saw him hunting a parking place on the street. I hope you don't mind, I took the other space in your garage."

"You know it's always yours."

"Drake!" Leslie trilled from the top of the stairway. She made certain all gazes were upon her before she started down in a flurry of burgundy chiffon, cut enticingly low at the bosom and hemmed high on the leg.

Susannah watched her parents kiss the air, then turned at Michael's ring, grateful for something else to do.

From that moment the evening went downhill, and long before she'd given her own remarks at the banquet and settled back to listen to the guest speaker, a renowned art critic from New York's Metropolitan Museum, Susannah wished she were in bed. She kept yawning, hiding her rudeness behind a hand.

"Tired?" Michael leaned toward her at the table over dessert. "We'll slip out early. After tonight you'll be able to catch up from all the excitement." His gaze held hers.

She focused on his tuxedo front and the line of onyx studs.

He'd been dropping references to Jeb since the night they'd left Jeb sick in bed on her second floor. Susannah had yet to fully explain. She'd have to soon; he or Leslie or Drake would notice her growing condition. Perhaps especially Drake, whose medical training, like John Eustace's, made him a keen observer.

Tonight, she promised herself.

But she couldn't short-circuit her duties as chairperson of the fund-raiser, and it was well after two A.M. before they left, with Leslie and Drake quarreling, this time in the rear seat of Michael's car.

"We could get a taxi, Drake," Leslie was saying. "These young people may want to look in on one of the parties."

"We're going home," Susannah said, hoping to avert the fight.

Drake's voice tightened. "And so am I."

He'd insisted on staying at a hotel, as usual, not with Susannah. Michael pulled out of the line of limousines, taxis, and cars in front of the de Young Memorial Museum in Golden Gate Park, where the banquet had been held in the dramatic tribal arts gallery, his hands firm and steady on the wheel of his new black Jaguar.

"I thought we'd have a nightcap," Leslie insisted. "Somewhere private, with a romantic view of the city."

"I have an early plane and I'm still on east coast time."

"But Drake . . ." Her mother stroked his tuxedo sleeve. Susannah could see her in the vanity mirror on the sun visor as she checked her dark circles. "I do so want us to be friends, if nothing more."

"How many times, Leslie, must I say it? I loved my wife and she's dead, and part of me died with Clary. What you and I once had is over. Please stop."

"But if we only tried a bit harder . . ."

He shrugged away, lit a cigarette, and stared moodily out at the passing city streets. "Why in hell can't you understand? You keep that damned house a stone's throw away from ours in Greenwich, though all your friends long ago began to see you as a hopeless hanger-on, a desperate romantic—"

"Drake." Susannah glanced at Michael whose face looked stony.

"It's true," her father said. "That's the trouble with women her age. They expect marriage to last forever."

"Love," Leslie murmured.

"Whatever we had ended when you plunged yourself into that bottle. I won't go through that again—no matter what your reasons or rationalizations may be. So please do me the courtesy of dropping the subject." He snuffed out the cigarette. "My apologies, Susannah. Michael."

"It's been a long night," Michael said without conviction.

At his hotel, after a curt good-night to Leslie, Drake climbed out of the car, promising to call Susannah soon. She could hear her mother in the rear seat, sniffling into a burgundy lace-edged handkerchief that matched her dress.

Susannah thought Leslie had dressed too young; attempted to peel away the years to seem more like Clary, whose elegance she could never have matched. What sense could there be in her continual attempts to interest Drake again? When he'd said "our home," he hadn't meant his with Leslie, though it was the same house; he'd meant his with Clary.

At Susannah's house Leslie declined her offer of a midnight cappuccino.

"I believe I'll go on to bed." Still obviously upset, she kissed Susannah, then Michael. "Drake was simply tired from surgery all day yesterday, then the flight from New York. The time change," she said and drifted up the stairs.

Slipping off her shoes with a sigh, Susannah went into the living room, turning on lamps and plumping pillows with a vengeance. Michael stopped her.

"Sit. Relax. I'll fix us a drink."

"Perrier, please." She cast a look toward the stairwell to make sure Leslie had gone up. "With a twist of lemon and one of lime. But you have whatever you want."

"Coming up."

"The key to the liquor cabinet's on the underside of that bottom shelf. Where the glasses are." He already knew, she realized.

They sat on the sofa in strained silence, sipping their drinks, until Michael seemed to notice her too-bright eyes, her fingers clenched around her glass. He reached out, turning down a lamp to its lowest setting. "She can't help herself, Suse."

"I know."

"Neither can he."

She turned toward him, unmindful of her gown, pulling one leg up onto the sofa and tucking it beneath her. "But they say such terrible things to each other."

"What's new?" he said, obviously trying to make her smile.

"I guess I spent too many years listening to them. I can't bear to hear it anymore."

"Look on the bright side. They're not together very often."

"I suppose," she said, taking another sip of sparkling water.

"Suse, what's wrong? Besides World War Three on the domestic front?"

She squirmed a little. "Nothing I can't handle."

"Cody?" he said.

Susannah rubbed her knee through the green silk. She'd refused any number of Michael's invitations since the day he'd seen Jeb in her house. She'd promised herself she'd explain tonight.

"In a way," she admitted.

"You're in love with him."

Her throat tightened, and so did her grip on the green silk. Dampness from her fingertips spotted the fabric.

"It hardly surprises me," he said after a silence. "I could see how he looked at you. I wanted to think I imagined how you looked at him, but I was wrong."

"If it helps, I don't think I'll see him again. We quarreled before he left. I don't think it would be right for either of us."

"But?" he said, clearly hearing the omission.

"I—" She twisted the silk until he closed his hand over hers. Susannah looked up at him. "I can't keep this to myself. I shouldn't, because I'm really quite happy about what's happened and if you and I are to remain friends, I think you should know." She cleared her throat. "I'm going to have a baby."

"You're what?"

"I'm pregnant."

She could see him calculating, coming up with the answer.

"It's Jeb's," she said for him.

"My God. You're sure?"

"Absolutely."

He squeezed her hand. "Does Leslie know?"

"No. You're the first—except for Jeb." And Breeze Maynard, she thought.

"What does he plan to do about it?"

"Nothing."

Michael swore softly. "What are you going to do?"

"I've always wanted a child." She smiled but didn't look up at him. "I'm not getting any younger. Thirty-one, unmarried . . . I don't suppose people will throw stones, but . . ."

"Look. We've been together in our fashion for years." He grasped her shoulders, waiting for her to glance up. His blue eyes were serious, the light, musky scent of his cologne seemed to cover her like a security blanket. "Let's get married. It's not as if I haven't asked you before. Marry me, Susannah."

She couldn't speak. She simply stared at him, amazed by his offer. It certainly beat Breeze Maynard's by a mile.

"My parents would be ecstatic and you like them, I know you do." She nodded and he said, "So will yours. Once they get used to the idea of a grandchild, maybe it will even draw them together."

She shook her head. "No, Michael."

"Why not?"

Susannah flung out a hand. "You know how they are. You saw them tonight, heard them. And they loved each other, once."

"So?"

"You just gave me the best reason why we shouldn't marry. What do you think would happen to us? We love each other, Michael, but we're not in love." She took his face in her hands, met his frustrated blue eyes. "If you married me, pregnant with another man's baby, where do you think we'd end up in five years? or ten? even two?"

"Nobody can answer that, Susannah."

"I know, but I can't take the risk . . . of hurting you, of becoming my own parents."

He eased away, gently removing her hands from his cheeks, then rising. He stood over her, his gaze saddened, his mouth a straight line.

"I hate him for doing this to you."

"Don't blame Jeb."

"What kind of man is he?" he said, then answered himself. "A self-centered, ego-driven, no-class superstar, the flavor of the month."

"Michael, please don't say things you'll be sorry for."

"Please don't defend him."

She rose, and in silence they walked to the front door where he turned to her for a light kiss good night. To Susannah it had the flavor of ashes.

"Think about my proposal," he whispered.

"I've given you my final word."

"I'll ask again in a few days."

Susannah said no a second time, and Michael went away looking hurt but concerned. She hated stepping on his feelings, but she'd told him the truth. Settling for less than either of them deserved would only corrode their friendship in the end.

Had she been honest about Jeb too? She hadn't said she loved him, not in those words. She'd let Michael assume it, though.

"Studley Do-right," she murmured.

She gazed down at the warm, squirming puppy on

her lap in the old cane-backed rocking chair. It was cud-dle time at the private animal shelter where Susannah volunteered once each week, and she decided she just might need the contact today as much as the mixed breed dog that reached out to lap her wrist with a raspy tongue.

Susannah cradled him close, teasing him with the name she'd just given him. Sassy and audacious, he was a charmer—like Jeb—and if she let herself, she could fall head over heels for the puppy too.

The dog nearly overflowed her still slender lap, mak-ing Susannah smile. She'd always loved dogs and cats, guinea pigs and horses, with the whole-hearted affection she reserved around her parents, for fear of rejection. He looked so mournful, gazing up at her with those dark eyes—like Miranda's. At nearly three months, by the veterinarian's calculations, Studley was entering the awkward stage—dog adolescence, she supposed—and Susannah feared that no one would adopt him. Sooner or later, he'd be transferred to the county dog pound, and she didn't want to consider what would happen to him then.

For an instant she seriously thought of taking him home.

The dog peed on her lap.

Holding him up high in the air for a scolding, she laughed into his chocolate-brown eyes and he slurped at her face.

"Apologies will get you anywhere." She fondled his sleek caramel coat once more, slipping him a dog treat from the pocket of her camel pants, which felt damp.

Leslie complained each Friday that Susannah was asking for trouble, driving her biscuit-colored Bentley into the run-down Western Addition neighborhood, where roving gangs could be a problem, "simply to pet a bunch of mangy animals that must be laden with fleas and God knows what diseases," but Susannah continued to ignore her mother's protests.

"Live in my house, Les," she always said, "live by my rules."

Brave words. Leslie knew how to get around them of course, and Susannah actually had few stringent rules about anything, but she felt her mother needed the occasional reminder. She also needed a kick in the behind about her own life, but that was another issue. These days Susannah felt too weary and nauseated to push Leslie toward some purpose, or even toward the weekly AA meetings she somehow always "missed."

She realized she'd been avoiding Leslie, not wanting her to notice Susannah's pregnancy until she felt ready to tell her.

Susannah gave the pot-bellied puppy a kiss on the nose, then placed him back in his wire cage among the bank of other cages, other homeless puppies, and gently closed the door. He whined piteously.

"I'll be back." She hoped he wasn't there when she came, that he'd find a home in the meantime. Then she prayed that he wouldn't.

She enjoyed her work at the shelter, but lately her emotions could be precarious, and something, as it was in the dog's life, seemed to be missing.

Like Leslie, she supposed, she needed some new purpose. Something other than gestating that would fulfill her in the years ahead, make her into a fully functioning, happy parent for her child.

On her way home the puppy stayed in her mind. Like Jeb Stuart Cody. It seemed odd to compare him with an abandoned dog, but she'd seen the rash of unfriendly news reports: Jeb had walked offstage one recent night in Phoenix, using his lingering cough as his excuse, but, the report stated, it was widely regarded that he was losing his famous voice. Only the day before, in Philadelphia, for the first time he'd canceled a performance. And his second album? Jeb told an interviewer it was "in the can" and would be released as scheduled in September, but speculation abounded in the media: He'd scrapped the album and was slowly, inexorably, sliding downhill.

Susannah guided the Bentley around the corner onto California Street, and Clary's last words came back to her. *Help him.*

She wheeled the car into her underground garage and cut the engine, leaning back against the ivory-colored leather seat. If Clary had liked games, if she'd lied at times about Jeb, the night Susannah found him playing "Deep River," the night they'd made love, she had assumed *he* was telling the truth. But was he? Maybe game-playing—manipulation—was a family trait. Or possibly, because of his rift with Clary and the loss of his wife and child, he was scared of a new commitment. Still, she cared about him.

In spite of her suspicions, she cared about Clary too. Susannah had loved her friend, her stepmother, and missed her still. She felt a continuing sense of frustration that Clary's killer was still at large, that no new clues had been uncovered since the police discredited the lone witness. She settled a hand over her barely rounded stomach. Clary and Drake had tried to have a child; but it was Susannah who was pregnant now, who would deliver a presumably healthy baby around Christmas.

Clary's niece or nephew.

Through Jeb, her child had a blood link to Clary and at last Susannah thought she knew how to help. Unlike

Clary or Jeb, she'd been privileged all her life. Susannah remembered the homeless woman she and Jeb had found in New York; remembered her own willingness to give the woman money; remembered him saying, "We're talkin' about a laying on of hands here." They'd fed her. And he'd given her his coat.

Whether they agreed about Clary or this child, he was right in that. Susannah had known nothing then about true charity. Remembering Miranda's mother, she supposed she still didn't. But as she'd already done at the animal shelter, she could learn.

She'd honor Clary's memory and, as she'd asked, help Jeb too, even if he didn't want her help. Or her.

13

Susannah went house hunting. In the two weeks since she'd made her decision, she'd seen an appalling number of properties in appallingly bad condition in, according to her mother, the most appalling part of town, but as she climbed her own front steps with the late afternoon sun at her back, she was grinning. Today, she'd lucked out. Decision-making, beyond what she normally practiced in what Jeb had referred to as her "good works," had become almost second nature, like racing for the bathroom every morning, and she realized she had rarely felt more in charge of her own life, if not her body.

At eleven weeks her stomach could still be unreliable, though yesterday morning she'd managed to keep down her usual soda crackers, and this morning her worship service with the porcelain god had been brief.

Leslie had been horrified when Susannah announced her plan. "A shelter?"

"For homeless women and their children. I have the money to get started. I probably won't even have to tap into Grandmother's trust. I'll look for supplemental funding from government agencies."

"Do you realize what you're undertaking?"

"Not yet," she'd said, "but I will."

Susannah scooped up the mail, depositing it on the Federal chest in the foyer and walked through the house to the garden where she found Leslie fighting for possession of a small canvas gym bag with Studley Do-right. Susannah's second decision had seemed the easiest; she'd brought the puppy home from the animal shelter after her first day of house hunting. Now she'd change Leslie's mind about the women's shelter.

Her hair tangled, her face glowing with sweat, Leslie glanced up. "There you are. Of all the mutts, you had to get this one." Releasing his hold for an instant, Studley barked a greeting at Susannah. "My ears have a headache," Leslie said, kneeling in a freshly dug flower bed. The dog clamped his jaws around the gym bag again and bounded off with it into the bushes. "Oh, blast!"

Susannah laughed. "You and Drake never let the dogs inside in Greenwich. You're not used to sharing quarters with such an outspoken or demanding companion."

Leslie struggled to her feet, brushing back strands of hair, which looked damp and stringy, from her face. She brushed at her white leggings, dark smudges at both knees. "You might think again about keeping him."

"I have thought, more than twice." She glanced meaningfully at her mother. "It's as much his home as it is yours." She tried not to stumble over the next words. "He's just a baby."

"That dog was barking when I left for class at noon and he's still barking."

"Class?"

"Self defense." Leslie stripped off her purposely baggy red sweater, revealing a red-and-white striped leotard underneath. "You might consider it too. Especially as you seem so bent upon exposing yourself to danger." She paused. "I had to chase that dirty child from the garden again when I got home." She gestured at the nearby mound of rich earth where Susannah's new impatiens plants had been. "She and your . . . animal dug up all these." Leslie waved at the limp flowers nearby in a heap.

"When she came last time, I was transplanting." But Susannah couldn't feel angry. Her own daughter might be playing there soon enough, and Miranda's continuing visits, usually without her mother's permission, Susannah suspected, made bright spots in her days.

Despite Leslie's negativism about Studley and Miranda, she couldn't contain herself any longer. "I found it," she said.

"Found what?"

"A house. This morning. In the same block as that brown frame two-story you didn't like."

"Near the animal shelter? In the Western Addition?"

Driving past with no intention of stopping the Bentley again in a neighborhood her mother considered an invitation to murder, she'd seen the house. Ignoring Leslie's frown, she went on. "The exterior paint isn't even that bad, still white and just flaking a little, but for now maybe some touch-ups will do, until the funding gets straightened out." She took a breath, willing Leslie to share her enthusiasm, her sense of rightness about this. "I made an offer. The agent says I'll have acceptance by tomorrow."

The stately three-story clapboard with its rambling stone chimneys and broad front porch, the brick herringbone-patterned walk, the abandoned flower beds, had instantly drawn Susannah's gaze. She could already envision them filled with perennials. Flanking the front walk by the steps she'd have shrubs, or maybe flowering plum trees. In the spring . . .

"Oh, Susie. Probably no one else wants it."

"It's perfect, I tell you."

Studley emerged from the bushes, crawling on his belly with Leslie's gym bag in his teeth. He dropped it in front of her. His gaze traveled soulfully from Leslie to Susannah.

"He didn't hurt it," she said, bending to pat the puppy.

Leslie didn't glance at the bag or the dog. "We were talking about your project."

The word reminded her of Jeb. "It's not my 'latest project.' It's permanent."

"Have you spoken to Michael about this?"

Susannah managed not to cringe. She and Michael weren't on the best of terms, but as her lawyer he had agreed to look into the legalities of setting up the shelter while she began exploring alternative funding and ways to refurbish the house. Eager to begin, and according to Michael naive, she prayed that none of the issues would take long.

"Yes, we've spoken. He's doing his usual first-rate job."

"Of course he is. But what does he think about the shelter?"

Susannah sighed. "He thinks I'm out of my mind. Does that make you happy?"

She turned and went back into the house. Leslie followed her inside, so Susannah bypassed the liquor cabinet. She couldn't drink because of the baby anyway, but she also felt sure she'd seen Leslie casting longing looks toward the supply more than once.

"Hostility doesn't become you." Leslie dropped down onto the carpet across from Susannah's chair. "I don't understand what's happening. Michael has stopped coming by, and you haven't been out with him in at least a week. I sense he's deeply hurt. You could do worse than to marry Michael Alsop."

Studley shambled into the room, then plunked down beside Susannah, apparently exhausted from his fight with the gym bag. He laid his head on her knee. Stroking his glossy coat, she could feel the loose skin over warm muscle. "Michael and I are friends. It would be wrong for us to marry, as wrong as . . ." She trailed off, then began again because it needed to be said. "As wrong as it is for you to chase after Drake."

"Chase after—? Clarice is dead now." She started to put her sweater on the sofa, then, eyeing the dog, draped it across her lap. "Drake didn't mean a word he said the night of the Arts Commission dinner. He can be a selfish man. He needs a woman—not a girl—to guide him."

"Oh, Mother."

Surprised, Leslie glanced over. She didn't seem to realize Susannah had used the term, reserved only for moments like this one of exasperation.

"Well, he does need me. No matter what he says."

Susannah headed for the liquor cabinet. Keeping her back to Leslie, she felt for the key under the shelf and unlocked it, taking out a bottle of tonic. She poured it into a glass full of ice and added a lime. "Would you like one?"

"No."

"Mother, we'll never agree on this. I'm sorry I brought it up." She sat down again. "I know you didn't have any great love for Clary and I suppose I can understand that, but I wish you could be happy about the shelter. If it prevents one woman, one young girl or child, from meeting a similar fate on the streets—"

"Clarice was hardly a street person."

"But she was vulnerable . . . as we all are."

"In that neighborhood, I should say so. Since when have you become such a feminist and social activist?"

Since she'd met Jeb, Susannah thought.

"Since my closest friend met a violent death in a city park."

"Spare me another rehash of the tragedy. I've heard it often enough from Drake. It's police business to solve her puzzle. Whatever happened, happened." Having echoed John Eustace's view, Leslie jerked to her feet and began pacing the room. "Frankly, Susannah, there were times when I could have killed her myself."

"I can't believe your insensitivity," she said, her throat tightening, her pleasure at finding the shelter's new home gone, her disappointment in Leslie so fierce she might have touched it, like a sore. "I mourn her. My father mourns her."

"And you think this shelter"—Leslie said the word contemptuously—"will heal you both? I don't read about Jeb Stuart Cody beating his chest in grief."

"You won't," Susannah said. "He'll work himself to death before he admits how much he misses her. If he admitted that, he'd have to deal with it." Like the baby, she thought.

Leslie stared at her.

"You seem to know him much better than I thought."

"We had a brief . . . thing," Susannah admitted. "In New York. And while he was here in San Francisco, when you were in Connecticut. It ended the day you saw him getting into the cab."

Leslie's keen gaze slipped over her and Susannah's

grip tightened on Studley's fur. "I wonder who's planning to work herself into a state, trying not to deal with something." She focused on Susannah's abdomen. "Or is my hearing completely gone after two weeks in the same house with that dog? You've been sick most mornings lately." She paused. "How far along is it?"

She flinched at the hard tone, the harsh words. "The baby's due near Christmas."

"Then there's time. Barely. If we make arrangements now. . . ." She started for the entryway, then stopped. "You are certain? You've seen a doctor?"

"Yes."

"Someone discreet, who can be trusted not to notify the press?"

"Leslie." Gently pushing the dog aside, she stumbled to her feet, feeling sick again and light-headed. Her mother, Breeze Maynard. She'd looked at things from both sides now, as the song said.

"There's no other solution. You're a woman of quality, breeding. Mr. Cody—I assume it's his because Michael would be careful—is the sort of man who tempts one to thoughtless indiscretion, but he is not our kind."

"Oh, for God's sake."

"Need I remind you, your grandmother was one of society's most highly regarded hostesses. The Founders League of this city still holds an annual dinner named for her. You are also—again by your own misguided decision—a single woman. You can't possibly think of having this child, of raising it on your own."

"Roughly one-quarter of this country's single female population does exactly that."

"Not people of means, influence, importance. Your father—"

"Is that why you and Drake brought me into the

world? Because it was the right thing to do? Because *The New York Times* would print the birth announcement, listing my forebears for six generations? Because five hundred people would attend the christening and bring all the right gifts from Tiffany's and Bergdorf's?"

"How dare you speak to me that way."

"You certainly didn't love me."

"Susannah."

She marched past Leslie, through the doorway and up the stairs.

"I'm going to have this baby," she said from the landing. "I'm going to keep it and love it with all my heart. I don't give a damn what anyone—if anyone is so inclined in the 1990s—says. And I am going to open the shelter because *that* is the right thing to do."

Studley frolicked through the living room and up the steps to her, and she bent to take him in her arms. "The dog stays. If that's a problem for you, I'd suggest you return east to live—and to find yourself—as you please."

"Susannah!"

"I wonder who's really more selfish," she said. "Drake, or you."

"San Francisco Socialite Cares for Homeless."

At the end of June Jeb carried the latest issues of *USA Today* and a prominent news magazine off the plane with him at Nashville. He carried them to Breeze's home and into his room there for the weekend stay during which he would record the last song for his second album. He carried them with him that night to a small club on the city's outskirts that invited people via a hand-lettered poster in the window to "come in and set a spell."

Jeb sat, the articles about Susannah's shelter under his drink glass, as if to anchor her there, his guitar across an unoccupied chair.

"You treat that thing like a baby," Breeze murmured, careful not to brush Jeb's arm. She'd been careful ever since he'd caught her flaying Susannah Whittaker by phone with that offer to buy her silence.

The silence hadn't been broken, which didn't surprise Jeb once he'd cooled down. He knew her well enough to know that she had a code of honor John Eustace would prize. In anger he'd accused her of the opposite and had been fighting himself ever since not to pick up the nearest phone and call her.

Except it wasn't his kid.

He fingered the guitar's bridge, adjusting the saddle to his liking. "This thing is a baby," he told Breeze. "The closest I plan to come to being a father anyway."

She threw him a look, gauging his mood. Her recent caution with him had Jeb walking on eggs around her, afraid he might be the one to provoke another quarrel.

"I thought that's what you wanted," she'd said, hanging up the phone that morning to find him listening in the doorway, wearing only his towel.

"If I want you to fight my battles for me," he'd told her, "I'll let you know."

"And I'll do the same."

Meaning Mack. She and Mack weren't getting on, and the return to Nashville, brief as it would be, had her even more on edge. Jeb glanced at Mack, sitting at another table in front of him and Breeze, with the other members of his band—Skeet and Terry, Cameron and Bull. Mack had his back turned and was starting on his third beer, fifteen minutes after they'd arrived at the bar.

Jeb felt like getting wasted himself. Instead, he picked up his guitar, settling it across his left thigh and hooking his left boot low over the table's frame in the classical playing position he seldom used. It was a damn sight more comfortable than standing onstage with the guitar strap biting into his shoulder all night. In the silence during the house band's break, he strummed a few chords.

A microphone whistled at the front of the room. The lead singer of the honky-tonk's band, no more than twenty years old, tapped the head with a grimy-nailed forefinger. "Well, look what we got tonight, folks." He peered into the darker reaches of the smoke-filled room, which smelled too of spilled beer and cheap whiskey. "The man hisself. Jeb Stuart Cody."

Jeb wore the black cowboy hat he'd tried a few times onstage, Breeze's "Wall Street cowboy" image, pulled low to shield his eyes. His plain, worn jeans and white shirt hadn't drawn much attention when they walked in, though someone had recognized Mack and Breeze. He should have known, Jeb thought. He didn't welcome the attention he'd craved for ten years of playing in dives like this one. He just wanted to sit there, knocking back a Corona light, and letting his muscles turn to water. Tomorrow he'd be at the studio by eight o'clock. Tonight he wanted to block out the world again—and his own growing guilt over Susannah. So why had he brought the guitar, and played even one note?

"Come on up here, Jeb. And show us how it's done."

Breeze prodded his bicep. "Go on, try out the new song."

He'd only played it two or three times, in other towns, in other bars, and the reception had been good, if not as outstanding as he would have liked. He'd fiddled some more with the lyrics, let Breeze play a bit with the melody.

What the hell. He'd come here on purpose.

Grabbing the guitar by its neck, Jeb surged out of his chair and up to the makeshift stage. As soon as he took the one step up, the crowd exploded into applause and adrenaline rushed through his bloodstream like a drug. The lead singer clapped him on the back, whispering into Jeb's ear that he admired him more than any of the others—Strait and Brooks, Tritt and Billy Ray Cyrus, even the oldtimers like Hank Williams and George Jones. Jeb could feel himself grinning.

After his usual greeting, he launched into "Lou'siana Lady" and heard feet stomping. Jeb worked the guitar strings, adding plenty of hammering on. When the song ended, even Mack gave him a thumbs up.

"You ain't heard nothin' yet." Jeb settled onto the stool that had been offered, hooked a battered boot heel over it, and tuned his guitar. The room fell silent, expectant, and Jeb milked the anticipation, making small talk and telling a few harmless jokes acceptable even to the ladies.

He hadn't lost it. The ongoing reports about his voice, which was slowly healing, the catcalls he still heard at each performance about Clary, the sagging ticket sales, the speculation that he'd never release the new album . . . all junk. As Breeze always said, he'd keep rising to the top like warm, sweet cream on a new bucket of milk. He didn't need anything else. Anyone. Another few minutes, and he'd forget Susannah Whittaker too.

"As long as I have a captive audience"—he leaned closer into the mike, letting his voice drop low and husky to set the mood—"my manager and I thought it'd be a good idea to let you have a peek at my latest song."

He knew his mistake the instant he opened his mouth, adding his voice, soft and sultry, to the melody Breeze had written.

"Little rich girl," he sang through two verses and the chorus, telling a story, as all good country songs did. He sang of a woman with a haughty air that protected her vulnerable heart. He sang of riches and privilege, contrasting it with poverty and want. He sang of a woman who had everything, and nothing. In the last line, he sang, "Little rich girl . . . you could learn a lot from a poor boy like me."

After some fancy fingerwork to tie things down, he bowed his head over the guitar, awaiting the verdict of the crowd, which took a while. That didn't bother him. An emotional song, a poignant one, often caused people to need a bit of space and time. When the clapping began, he lifted his head.

"I'm glad you liked it."

Breeze was grinning too. His band rose, as if they were one person instead of five, to their feet, leading a mass tribute, the kind he'd dreamed about years ago. After long moments, Jeb signaled to the honky-tonk band, mouthing "Huntsville Prison." He followed that with "Mama's Songs," "Do You Love Me," and then, giving in to the request, with "Kid Sister."

Jeb hadn't performed the song since San Francisco and fumbled the first phrase. His heartbeat kicked up.

"Sing it, man!"

A drunk called out, "Maybe he's got him a guilty conscience, like they say."

Mack leaned forward from the front table. "Let's go, Jeb."

"I'm staying this time," he said and started to sing.

After the first bars the crowd settled down. The

applause at the end proved decent if not hearty. Someone asked for a repeat of "Little Rich Girl," and a woman yelled, "Who's it for, Jeb? That society girl?"

Breeze leapt onto the stage, taking the mike and shaking a finger. "Shame on you. Don't you know that's just wishful thinkin' for a country boy? Besides, he's got his hands occupied, and everything else"—she glanced meaningfully at his crotch—"with sweet country stuff like y'all out there."

Shrieks and whistles.

Laughter.

Applause.

"Time to go," she whispered. "Mack's right."

Jeb held up his guitar, letting it flash in the harsh spotlight.

"Sorry, folks. Breeze tells me I have to get up early tomorrow to finish my new album. Thanks for listenin'."

He jumped down, helping her back to the table, and before the crowd could swamp them, Mack and the others skillfully circled them for the quick trip out of the smoky club into the clean, sweet June night. Mack pushed him toward the car.

"See?" Jeb said. "No riot."

"Aren't you the lucky one?"

Turning, Jeb held out his hand for Mack's keys. His guitarist was swaying on his feet, the smell of stale beer strong on his breath. "You had enough. I'm driving."

Mack grumbled, then gave in, probably at the grateful look in Breeze's eyes. Gunning the engine on Mack's seven-seat minivan, Jeb thought, No, I'm not lucky. He'd left the articles about Susannah behind on the table, but he hadn't cleared her from his mind.

*   *   *

Holding a tray loaded with a bowl of cold gazpacho, a plate of cheese and crusty sourdough bread, and a glass of iced sparkling water, Susannah was poised to go up the stairs when the doorbell rang.

Studley rushed from some activity, probably forbidden, in the dining room and out into the hall, barking and circling like a dancing dog in a circus.

"Hush," Susannah ordered, trying to sound stern as she set down the tray. Having paid cash for the shelter, she'd closed on it that morning and had spent the afternoon there making lists and meeting with various contractors. The task of getting the house in shape for its opening looked awesome, but she'd been organizing events most of her adult life, and this one, though different, had enough similarities to give her confidence. Plus the fatigue that kept washing through her in waves tonight. But she'd make the deadline she'd set, or more than one contractor would wish he had.

Sweeping Studley aside with one bare foot, she opened the door.

"Miranda."

The dark-haired little girl stood on the porch. At eight thirty it wasn't yet dark, but soon would be, and Susannah wondered at the shyly expressed request.

"Can Studley play with me in the garden?"

Susannah suppressed a groan. Her mangled impatiens had been replanted but seemed to be suffering a second transplant shock, and only the day before she'd found time to edge the walks with scores of bright portulaca. Remembering Cheryl's words, she hesitated. "Does your mother know you're here?"

"She's getting supper."

The simple statement didn't fool Susannah. To Miranda, getting supper meant her mother was out 'scavenging from restaurant trash dumpsters or begging on the street. Susannah had seen her often enough. Worse, she might even be driven to shoplift from the corner market. If she did and got caught, what would happen to Miranda?

Studley jumped against Susannah's leg, as if to beg for the little girl's company.

"All right, but just for half an hour. I want you where your mother can find you before dark." Miranda scampered inside, down the hall, and through the living room to the garden doors.

"I'll be good," she said. "No more digging."

"Keep an eye on Studley for me." Susannah paused in the door. "And Miranda, before you leave, I'll give you something to take home."

"Mommy doesn't want anything."

She knew she shouldn't override the woman's authority but couldn't help herself. "Not even a couple of ice cream bars for dessert?"

"Yes!"

Watching child and pup race each other into the garden, she smiled. The plants could take care of themselves. It had taken weeks to see Miranda's carefree smile, and it didn't come often. Let Miranda's mother deny her the treat—if she had no heart at all.

In the plastic grocery bag Miranda later carried "home," Susannah put ice cream, but she also put yesterday's leftover chicken breast cooked in wine and herbs, courtesy of her housekeeper, and a container of salad with honey-mustard dressing, plus half a loaf of the sourdough bread. Let Cheryl deny her child a proper meal, if she could.

She had settled herself in bed, earlier than usual, her feet and back aching from standing all day but her stomach quiet—absolutely steady—for the first time in weeks when the phone rang. Susannah reached for it across the expanse of white cutwork duvet and piled pillows. Apparently, she had finally passed the first trimester of her pregnancy in every way.

Now if only she could last another six months—against her mother's disapproval and Michael's ongoing coolness. Susannah hoped it wasn't Michael calling now, with another form to send over for application to some city, county, state, or federal funding agency. She already felt as if she was going blind from filling out forms. When she answered, she wished she were deaf.

"Hey. Susannah." The deep, sonorous voice went through her like a magic sword through stone. "It's me. Jeb."

As if she wouldn't know. "Why are you calling?"

"I know it's not my responsibility—"

Her heartbeat lurched. "Jeb, I've heard your view on my 'predicament.'"

"I didn't call to talk about that. Exactly. I called to say that, although it's not my personal responsibility to apologize for that telephone call a few weeks back, it is my duty as Breeze's employer to take the blame."

"I don't need your money."

"I know that," he said. "Hell, she knows it too. She just gets impulsive sometimes and overly protective. Like John Eustace."

"It took you long enough to call," Susannah said, though by now that didn't surprise her.

His voice warmed. "I guess it did. Again. I'm sorry."

"Well, now that you feel better . . ." Her hand poised above the telephone's cradle, ready to drop the receiver into it.

"I saw you in the paper, and in *Time*."

Her spirits dropped, ready to hear his disapproval too.

"You got some good press there."

"Better than a paternity suit," she said for him.

"I guess I deserve that." He hesitated. "Are you really going through with this thing? Opening a shelter for women and children? That's a pretty mean part of town."

"I'm a pretty mean lady these days."

She heard his sigh. "You aren't going to let me off the hook here, are you?"

After he'd walked out on her, rejecting his own baby? "I've had my exposure to the infamous Cody charm." She fought the impulse to say she would live with its results, if blessedly, for the rest of her life. "What did you want, Jeb?"

He avoided the question. "What kind of shelter?"

Susannah sighed. "Not one of the barracks-style kind, with dormitory rooms and rows of iron double-decker cots, drugs everywhere, no privacy, and people stealing each other blind."

"What kind then?"

"The cozy kind, if I can manage it. Eight bedrooms, four on each of the two upper floors, all private, each for one woman and her children, up to a total of four in a room. Fresh paint, pictures on the walls, a community kitchen with three square meals a day—no one showing up on the doorstep at seven o'clock for the night and leaving in the morning for the streets again."

"Sounds costly," he said. "Sounds good."

Leaning back against the pillows, Susannah warmed to her subject, as she hadn't been able to before, with anyone else.

"I'm hiring a resident housemother of sorts to oversee things. She'll have her own room downstairs off the kitchen with its own bath—at one time the maid's quarters when that area of the city was more upscale." She felt certain he'd ask whether she ever meant to step inside herself. "I'll be overseeing the renovations, conning cookware and dishes from area manufacturers and merchants, linens, games for the children, clothing, books . . . that sort of thing."

"A real laying on of hands. Almost too cozy. How long a stay will you allow?"

"I haven't decided, but I'm looking at other shelters and how they're set up, both private and public. Mine is patterned after several I've seen, all church sponsored. They seem to work especially well, even though it won't be possible to take in as many women as at the barracks shelters."

"At least they'll survive," he said. "With dignity."

He actually understood. "Yes. It's a great house too, Jeb." She sat straighter in bed, unable to suppress the urge to tell him in detail. "And I hope to have counseling for permanent housing, jobs, retraining, health care, especially prenatal and infant . . . In my mind it's kind of a halfway house for the dispossessed. So many of these women don't fit the stereotype. They're not druggies or crazy, just down on their luck. Like that woman we met in New York. I closed on the house today," she finished, "ordered new wiring and plumbing, a new kitchen, and landscaping."

Jeb whistled softly. "And you think all that's going to be done by—when?"

She told him the date, only a month away, but he didn't laugh.

"You'll make it too," he said.

Faith in her from Jeb Stuart Cody? She wouldn't have believed it, but he was the first person not to call her crazy. She waited for him to say she was self-serving.

"The Clarice Cody Whittaker Shelter?" he said.

"Yes."

His tone dropped lower. "God bless you, sugar."

"Don't call me sugar," she said but couldn't stop the smile. "Since we're apologizing, I'm sorry I called you a name."

"Redneck?" he said. "Sometimes I act like one."

Sometimes he made not anger, but pure need, run through her. She relaxed against the cutwork pillows again, wallowing in them, and could have sworn Jeb's masculine scent—clean skin, soap, and hormones—still permeated the fine cotton.

"Susannah? How are you doin'? Otherwise, I mean?"

"I'm taking care of things."

She could almost hear the shock in his silence. "You haven't had an abor—"

"Myself. My baby."

"I don't hear any wedding bells," he said, sounding relieved.

Susannah counted to ten. Did he honestly think this child was Michael Alsop's? Or was that Jeb's way of getting out of the situation he'd helped get them in? Every day or two in the media, Susannah read or heard about his rumored sexual exploits as well as his career troubles. But maybe the dalliances were no more true than that the San Francisco riot had been Jeb's fault. When would he find the time? she wondered.

"I'm not marrying anybody." Scared or not, let him have his illusions. "Michael and I decided to stay friends. But I'm keeping the baby if that's what you meant."

"A family of your own," he murmured.

Susannah hadn't thought of her own lack or of filling it with this unexpected miracle. He was right.

"My own family," she agreed.

"And you're okay?"

"I feel—" she touched her abdomen, circling it with

gentle fingers, "wonderful. My doctor says I'm built for the task, so . . ." She stopped, embarrassed.

"Well, that's good. That's just fine. I'm glad you're all right."

She turned her head against the pillow, against the wave of yearning. Damn him anyway. She needed to hate him, just a little, as she had because of Clary when they met. But Susannah decided she must be a more liberated woman than she'd ever thought and much less a product of her upper-crust upbringing than she'd given herself credit for. It would really be better for the baby if she didn't hate its father.

"About the shelter," he said.

"What about it?" She could talk to him all night, if he liked, about the shelter, of which she already felt proud.

"I thought maybe I'd put in an appearance."

Her pulse skittered. She didn't want a sideshow.

"It's named for my sister," he continued. "I wouldn't rain on your parade or anything, I'm not grandstanding here. If I were you, I wouldn't tell the press or make mention of it anywhere." He paused. "I'd just slip into town, quietlike, for a few hours, show up and maybe sing a couple of songs . . . that is, if you'd want me to."

Susannah bit her lip to stop its quivering. She had the most insane urge to cry—for herself and the baby, for Jeb who, whether he realized it or not, had just admitted how much he missed and loved his sister, no matter what had happened between them. "I think Clary would like that, Jeb."

"But would you?"

She couldn't quite say so. "You're more than welcome to come."

"Don't wear yourself out in the next month," he said. "I'll see you then."

Rubbing her cheek against the cutwork pillow, she inhaled his imaginary scent. By the end of July she'd have a belly for sure. She'd have the armor around her heart in place.

"See you then."

"Take care, Miss Susannah," he whispered and disconnected the call.

14

Susannah stepped back, narrowly avoiding the snakelike coil of orange trouble cord on the dining room floor of Cody House. Despite the shelter's more formal name, she always thought of it as simply that, though she never allowed herself to think why. Two weeks after she'd talked with Jeb and received his surprising endorsement, the renovations were well underway and with a smile of satisfaction she sidestepped a carton containing the room's simple new chandelier.

On a physical level she couldn't fully participate in the refurbishing, especially since the weather had turned warm, yet for the first time in her life she felt truly useful. Only yesterday her flyers had gone out to social agencies, to other shelters, to people on the street. Among them, Miranda. Susannah hoped the little girl had taken it to her mother and that Cheryl would read it. Humming a tune under her breath, she checked off the chandelier on her clipboard and, pausing to chat with workmen, headed for the kitchen.

Plaster dust. The chipped asphalt tile flooring half torn up. The counters stripped away and thrown into the yard for later removal from the property, the new base cabinets and wall units in more boxes stacked along one wall. The smell of fresh paint.

Susannah flung open a window above where the sink had been. She'd wanted to help with the painting but didn't because of the fumes, unhealthy for the growing child inside her, so she contented herself with organizing. Tomorrow the window frame would go as well, and a new garden window with shelves for house plants would be installed.

To her amazement the renovations continued more or less on schedule—due, so Michael said, to Susannah's skill at arm-twisting.

In the corner of the kitchen she counted off cartons of dishware and glasses; pots and pans and two boxes containing a state-of-the-art blender and streamlined coffee machine—donations from the merchants and manufacturers she had managed to charm. She hummed another line or two and went down the short hallway to the counselor's room and bath, where new fixtures stood. The cream-bordered-in-navy-blue ceramic tile had been laid over the ancient octagonal black-and-white ones, and the new floor looked both serviceable and lovely, even though the grouting had yet to be applied.

She stopped dead at the house's back entrance. Through the screen door she saw an overflowing Dumpster, the old kitchen cabinets . . . and Michael Alsop, who was striding from the driveway toward the door with a faint smile.

"Good morning." Susannah opened the door. He carried a box, plain and unmarked. "Do you have time for a cup of coffee? I bought at least a gallon when I stopped for doughnuts on the way over."

"A quick cup," he said.

"Styrofoam," Susannah warned him.

When they stood, leaning against an as yet unpainted wall because there were no chairs, he swigged at the coffee and she smiled over her own cup. Freshly shaven and showered, his brown hair neatly brushed, wearing a crisply pressed khaki summer suit and conservative tie, he looked attractive but very much out of place.

"What do you think?" She waved her free hand.

"It's coming along," he acknowledged.

"Even Leslie noticed."

"She's been here?"

"Several times. I know," she added. "I'm astonished too."

Michael's gaze drifted over her, noting the Kentucky T-shirt she wore over jeans. Jeb's shirt, which had become her favorite. He couldn't see that the top jeans button was undone to give her breathing room.

"I've brought you a present." He'd set the carton by the card table that held the coffee, plastic spoons, and a jar of creamer.

"May I open it now?" He nodded and Susannah, who loved presents, went down on her knees, tearing at the flaps with both hands. After plowing through tissue paper, she breathed out a sigh. "Oh, Michael. Thank you."

The richly polished wooden sign had three dimensional letters, white outlined in dark green, the colors of the house, shutters, and trim: THE CLARICE CODY WHITTAKER SHELTER read the first line and underneath, FOR WOMEN AND CHILDREN.

"For the front porch, I thought, by the entrance." He hugged her briefly, then marched toward the back door. "By the way, it looks as if we have a better than even shot for that new federal grant I mentioned yesterday. They're sending forms." With that faint smile and the briefest warming of his blue eyes, he stepped out into the warm July morning. "Good work, Suse."

The words followed her through the house, Susannah carrying her coffee and humming again, from the kitchen to the upstairs rooms, taking inventory as she went. The painting done. The beds delivered. Half the bureaus in place, the rest slated to arrive that afternoon.

"Morning, Miss Whittaker," an electrician greeted her in the upstairs hall. He set a ladder under the light fixture. "Looks like this wiring will be finished today. The upstairs power's off now, so if there's anything you need . . ."

"I have the best work crew in the Bay area," she said, patting his arm on her way past, "and the generosity of friends. What else could I need?"

Downstairs, sunlight streamed like quicksilver over the newly finished living room floor where the donated and well-worn but beautiful oriental rug would go, and the practical leather sofas and chairs that would last the shelter's lifetime. Susannah planned to soften their effect with throw pillows, garnet and green and ivory.

The front door opened, letting in a rush of air warmer than usual for mid-July in San Francisco, and Leslie swept inside. She looked at Susannah's T-shirt.

"You aren't inhaling those fumes again, are you?"

"I'm careful," she said, "and isn't it a little late for you to play mother hen?"

Leslie shrugged. "Perhaps. The front walk slates look wonderful, Susie. So does the porch with those railings nailed back on and painted." They had exchanged few words since her mother learned about Susannah's pregnancy, and those words had been carefully considered. She couldn't help wondering what Leslie wanted now, and all dressed up too for a change. Her dark linen suit and spectator pumps looked even more out of place than Michael's business suit, especially because Leslie had been given to leggings and bulky tops.

"Michael stopped in for coffee . . . and brought this." Retrieving it from the kitchen, she showed her mother the name plaque.

Leslie's gaze was thoughtful. "I still think you and Michael may end up married."

"I still don't." She thought of the lingering hurt in his eyes, the lopsided smile. "Neither does he, I'm sure."

"Things change." Leslie brushed at an imaginary piece of lint on navy blue. "I've come to rescue you. We're to have lunch at one with the director of California's social services. I've brought a dress for you in the car, though the Lord knows where you'll freshen up or do your makeup."

"I can use the counselor's bath." She tried to suppress her excitement but failed. "Where did the invitation come from? I've been calling that office for weeks, with little more than polite 'someone-will-call-you-backs' in response."

Leslie struggled with the smile. "You're not the only one who can pull strings. Where do you think you learned that? I called in a few favors, invoked your grandmother's name once or twice, and Fisherman's Wharf—the director—await us."

Susannah stared.

"It's noon already. Put away your clipboard and get dressed." The smile flickered before Leslie controlled it.

"Oh, and this," she added, delving into her handbag for a folded sheet of familiar paper.

Susannah took it and read.

"That dirty little girl rang the bell this morning before I was out of bed. That dreadful dog of yours scraped half the front door finish off before I could answer."

"Miranda," Susannah murmured. But better still, Miranda's mother. In a neat, clean hand with no spelling errors, Cheryl had filled out the form at the bottom of Susannah's flyer. She and Miranda hoped for admittance to Cody House.

With a fresh lilt in her step, she left Leslie to admire the living room floor's just-dry coat of polyurethane and took her best black linen summer dress, suitably loose-fitting, to the rear bathroom with the only mirror and working sink in the house. Soon, she could hear Leslie berating a plumber about something. Susannah, applying mascara, found herself humming again.

Jeb Stuart Cody's "Kid Sister."

Against his better judgment, Jeb tucked the telephone receiver under his chin and punched in numbers. In the two weeks since he'd talked with Susannah, his thinking about her had become even more constant.

In Baltimore he'd nearly taken a twenty-ish girl up on her offer of a key to her room, "a good time and privacy," in the same hotel. The suspicion that she could be underage had kept him celibate.

In Kansas City his left hand had shaken, badly, as he tried to steady it on a nubile shoulder while with his right hand he signed the gleaming, tanned skin. Breeze had hauled him out to the tour's waiting bus just in time.

In Toronto he'd accepted a raft of slips of paper with

names and phone numbers on them, which he still hadn't thrown away.

In Ypsilanti he'd surrendered to a come-on in some afterhours bar. And could still recall the taste of the woman's mouth—Seagram's Seven Crown and Coke—the feel of her breast in his palm. Two-and-a-half sheets to the wind by then, he'd barely managed to avoid a fist in the face from her neglected boyfriend. Or husband. Jeb hadn't stuck around to find out which.

In Oklahoma City in mid-July, near the end of Tour America, he was still wondering whether that blond had reminded him of Susannah Whittaker.

He had no excuses this time. He wasn't calling to apologize, only to hear her voice.

"Hello?" She sounded sleepy soft and slurred.

"Hey, yourself." He dropped into a chair in his hotel suite's living room. The lights were out, the room shadowed, and Breeze had gone with Mack. "I'm sorry if I woke you. Are you in bed?" He waited for her to ask why he was calling but she didn't.

"Yes," she said.

Heat rushed through him. Susannah's room, he remembered, with that big bed and those pristine white sheets, all fine Egyptian cotton, and those fussy pillows with the fancy holes cut in them. The look of her, sleek and slim and sexy, lying there close at hand.

"Jeb, it's nearly midnight."

"Two A.M. here."

She paused, as if unwilling to ask. "Where are you?"

"The Sooner State." He stretched out his legs. "You'd think it would be laid-back, quiet. But since I finished my album, the press has been hounding us. The weather out this way's hot as a tin roof in August, skipped right over July apparently, and I'm bone tired."

"You should be sleeping."

More heat.

"Couldn't," he admitted, stifling a groan. "My internal clock's all messed up. Nobody's fault, but at the moment it seems like Breeze and the promoters planned the least efficient travel routes they could find, east one day, west the next, north then south. Lord, even my hair feels weary." He smiled. "Besides, as you know, I never can sleep after a show."

He could hear the smile in her voice too. "Tired and wired?"

"You wouldn't want to come out here and give me a nice back rub, would you?"

"No." He could almost hear her fighting herself, as he had been, wanting to hang up, wanting at the same moment to keep talking. "When does the tour finish?"

"Two weeks. Just before your shelter's grand opening."

Susannah seized the opportunity he'd given for a retreat to neutral territory. With her every word about the shelter's renovations, he sensed her growing anticipation, the sense of achievement. Even her mother had been helping out, though Susannah said she couldn't think why.

Jeb rested his head against the back of the chair, his eyes closed, envisioning her house as it took shape, envisioning her.

"I'm proud of you, Miss Susannah."

"I'm proud of me too." Her voice sounded husky. "What will you do when your tour ends?"

"I'll head back to Nashville and home base. The new album comes out September first, then we kick off a tour of the Southeast and West until Christmas."

She'd be having her baby then.

"That's not much time off," she murmured.

"No, and Breeze tells me I've been sorely remiss in my song writin'."

Except for the latest, he added to himself but didn't mention "Little Rich Girl." He wasn't sure Susannah would appreciate his lyrics though she'd find out soon enough.

"Jericho was only waiting for the last cut, chafing and cursing all the while," he said. "But the new ballad's a good one and I hope it'll do well."

It had already been mixed and mastered with the rest, he told her, and any day now they'd start rolling out CDs. The press furor would really start up then. And Breeze would spend the last part of her summer fending off maneuvers for a quick look ahead of the album's release, a slipup in the first single's appearance date just before that.

He swore he could hear Susannah roll over in the crisp white sheets. "Sing me the song," she said, and Jeb nearly did groan aloud.

"Right now?"

"Even I can understand a ballad. What's it about?"

"Different," he said. The half lie didn't sit well, and Jeb straightened in his chair.

"No honky-tonks? And cheating wives?"

"No eighteen-wheelers," he said, stalling. "Or rodeo cowboys old enough to know when to quit before they lose the good woman waitin' for 'em at home."

"Garth Brooks. 'Wild Horses,'" she said, "from his *No Fences* album."

"Do I detect a new country music fan?" The thought pleased him immensely. Too much.

"I've listened to a few things," she admitted, "but my lips are sealed."

Jeb shifted again. The white sheets, her soft skin. And

now, the remembrance of her mouth. Shut tight when he would have teased it open with his lips and tongue . . . Oh, Miss Susannah.

What the hell. He'd given in to the temptation to call, but it ended there. By the shelter's opening she'd be four months gone. She'd start showing soon, her belly growing taut. It was a sobering thought, yet curiously fascinating, and he couldn't stop from asking again.

"How you doin' . . . yourself, I mean?"

Susannah laughed. "Why do I suddenly feel as if I'm in the audience at one of your concerts? The spotlight homes in, the smoke drifts, the guitar flies through the air, your hand reaches up—"

Jeb laughed too. "Private performance."

And in a drawl that mimicked his, she answered, "Well, then. I'm doin' fine."

"All right," he said, just above a whisper.

He hung up moments later, the sound of her simple good-night in his ear, the echo of his own self-doubt in his brain. He went to bed hours later in the empty suite, thinking of warm sheets and a woman he couldn't claim. When he finally slept, he dreamed—of a rounded belly, a baby, and blood.

"I could kill you, Mack."

In his dawn-lit sitting room Breeze stood at the window, her arms folded over her breasts and the whisper of her white nightgown, her hands clasping her elbows as if to shield herself from further hurt.

With an inarticulate sound, he set the phone receiver back in its cradle, then rose from the club chair where she'd found him, and crossed the room. Standing behind her, he set both hands on her shoulders and Breeze flinched.

"Five o'clock in the morning's a strange time to call your wife."

"I had a dream about the boys." He made small circles on her bare shoulders, but Breeze fought not to lean back, to turn her head and take his mouth in a kiss that would let her forget again, for a while. "They've been attending day camp this summer, the first time away from Peggy and home, and I dreamed they jumped into the swimming pool's deep end. Nobody saw them. Nobody heard them cry . . ."

Breeze turned in his arms.

"You'll be seeing them in a few weeks," she said, feathering her fingers across his cheekbone. "They can come stay at my house too. Jeb says he'll take an apartment for the summer so we can be alone."

"Is that what he said?"

"About the apartment, yes. Not the rest," she admitted. She looked into his eyes, still shadowed, still haunted. Despite the divorce proceedings, their quarrels had become more frequent, more fierce.

"Or don't you want to spend time with me alone?" she asked.

Mack ran a hand through his already-rumpled hair. "I don't know what I want," he said, "but then, neither do you."

Breeze stepped back. She knew what he meant. Last night Jeb had tried out "Little Rich Girl" for the concert audience and invited her onstage. Despite his merciless teasing, she'd stayed in the wings, but the adrenaline still pumped through her veins and she hadn't slept well. If she had, she would never have heard the low rumble of Mack's voice in the sitting room or the clear mention of Peggy's name.

"You're full of it, Mack."

He watched her brush past him, her nightgown's diaphanous skirt riffling against his bare legs.

"Maybe I should get back to the suite," she said. "Jeb's probably lyin' there alone, watching the morning come and missin' me."

"Jeb's not missing you, don't bullshit me." Grasping her arm, he hauled her around. "Or try to make me jealous. Jeb's walking around with a hard-on for that Whittaker woman." He tilted her chin up. "I've known him longer than you have and I see all the signs—inside as well as out."

Her gaze slipped downward over his strong bare chest to his snug white briefs.

"You boys always do have the disadvantage of being obvious."

"Dammit, Breeze." His mouth homed in on hers, hard and demanding, or was it desperate? He wrapped her tight in his arms. "Damn you and that mouth of yours. Don't you know what's right between us?"

"I guess I do," she whispered, trailing a hand over his chest and belly to the fullness between his thighs, making him grunt.

"Let's concentrate on that then."

But it wasn't enough, she realized, could never be enough. She just didn't know what would, except all the things she couldn't have and didn't deserve.

Hours later Jeb, having survived his dreams, sprawled across the diagonal on the king-size bed, fighting his way up from heavy sleep but unwilling to wake enough to pull the star quilt over his chilled body. Then he heard a small sound and realized he wasn't alone in the room. His heartbeat lurched.

Rolling over, he opened one eye and saw Breeze standing beside the bed in a filmy white nightgown that made her look like some sexy ghost.

"Jesus, you scared me." But he tore his gaze away from her and yawned. "Don't sneak up on a man like that."

"You must be cold," she said. "Your whole body's covered with goosebumps."

"Nice of you to stare." Jeb opened both eyes to look at her more closely. "Are we signing a peace pact here, or what? You and I haven't had this many words to say to each other at once since I left San Francisco." Her gaze dropped and he said, "What's wrong, Breeze?"

"Just about everything."

Jeb sat up, tucking the quilt under his armpits. From the suite's living room he could hear the Ibanez guitar album he'd left on the CD's repeat, playing itself over again as it must have all night. "Is this an all-out blue funk, or can you be more specific?"

She sank down onto the edge of the mattress. "It's Mack."

"Why am I not surprised?" While he'd slept off his nightmares, dawn had come and then full morning. The bedside alarm read eight o'clock and sun streamed through the windows because he'd left the draperies open. The light filtered through her gown, giving him a too-good view of Breeze's spectacularly narrow waist and generous breasts. "You mind gettin' into a robe— there's one on the back of my bathroom door—before we solve your romantic problems?"

She stood abruptly. "Forget it." And started across the room.

"Get back here, Maynard," he said, wanting to kick himself.

She didn't go for the robe but sat down again, faintly smiling.

"Glad to know someone wants me."

Jeb raised his eyebrows. "My, my. I think we have headlines here. 'Breeze Maynard Feels Sorry for Self.'"

Her lower lip quivered. "Why shouldn't I, after overhearing Mack on the phone with his supposedly soon-to-be-ex-wife? My God, five o'clock in the morning and he's cooin' in her ear like some lovesick turtledove."

"Marriage is an intricate thing, Breeze. Mack's not ready to give it all up."

"Maybe he never will be."

"And how much does that matter to you?"

She stiffened. "Don't call me a whore, Jeb. I may not be a tight-ass like Susannah Whittaker, or look the next thing to a virgin like she does when it pleases her, but I take my men one at a time with decent intervals between and a reasonable amount of thought beforehand."

"I'm talkin' about futures. Do you love Mack enough to stay with him once the divorce is over, to think about marryin' him and settling down? Having kids together? And growin' old in each other's arms?" He paused. "That's what we're talking about, not Susannah who is none of your business."

"Pregnant as she is by some other man, so you tell me, she's not yours either."

"True enough," Jeb said but looked away. He'd felt close to her last night, in spite of the miles between them, the child she carried—too close for comfort.

She plucked at a loose thread on the star quilt between them. "I know you don't approve of me with Mack any more than I approve of you with that Whittaker woman."

"That's over," he said.

"Then why are you participating in the shelter's opening?"

"You know why." He'd lived with the sense of his sister's betrayal for too many years, and maybe that had insulated him from her loss. He still found it hard even to say her name. "Because of . . . Clary."

She looked at him. "Tell that to Susannah. Tell it to your mirror if you want, cowboy. But don't tell it to me."

"All right." He rolled over on his side, his back to Breeze. "Now that we've settled once again on the fact that you disapprove of my life and I disapprove of yours, why don't you go order us some breakfast while I get another half hour's sleep?"

"I hate it when you dismiss me like that."

Jeb had a comeback on the tip of his tongue when he heard the soft catch in her voice. From the sound of it, instead of predictably causing her to throw a hairbrush at him, "I love it when a woman knows her place," would have surely made her cry. And Breeze didn't cry often. Jeb turned onto his back and saw her eyes brimming.

"Ah, Maynard."

"Can I please crawl in with you?"

He tensed, the covers warm over his bare body, still feeling unsettled about Susannah.

"Bad idea," he murmured.

"Just for a few minutes."

She seldom begged either, and it tugged at his heart. With a sigh Jeb flipped the corner of the quilt back. "Enter at your own risk," he said, then drew her down beside him into the crook of his shoulder.

She snuggled nearer, raising her face to his. "A kiss would feel nice too."

"Worse idea." His heart thudded loud enough to drown out Ibanez.

"I need one. Badly," She knew how to bargain in bed too, which he'd nearly forgotten.

Dipping his head, he pressed his closed lips to hers, then pulled back before she could land another one. "That's all, dammit."

Mack had hurt her, and she'd suffered too many hurts in her life. Sometimes she didn't know what was good for her, as his sister hadn't either, but at the moment Jeb did. He urged her closer, aligning Breeze's soft, lush body with his, tucking her head into the hollow of his neck and letting her cornsilk hair warm his chest. In that position, despite her hurt and his lowdown ache for Susannah, they fell asleep for the rest of the morning like children, as he and Clary had done so many years ago after their father took a switch to one of them, or got carted off to jail.

15

"*Clary would be* pleased if you came," Susannah told her father a few days before the shelter's opening.

She'd flown east at his request to help sort Clary's belongings in the hope that he would honor her wish that with Drake at the opening, she'd feel safe from Jeb's searching gray gaze and her own response to him. In the past two weeks he had phoned Susannah with fair frequency, always sounding as if he'd broken some promise to himself yet couldn't keep from it.

Susannah knew the feeling. She spent each call with one finger poised above the disconnect button, knowing she should use it but unable to cut him off like that.

Oddly, he had become her biggest supporter about Cody House—because of Clary, she supposed, and his own inability to express his grief—but in return Susannah felt she had somehow helped him through the last, exhausting days of his first national tour. Maybe that had been for Clary too, she decided.

"I have some tough cases coming up," Drake finally answered. "A bigshot oil man from Texas with a brain aneurysm as big as a golf ball, a Broadway actress with a tumor pressing on her optic nerve . . . I'm not sure I can make the trip to California just then."

"Please try."

Hiding her disappointment, Susannah went upstairs at dusk to the room Drake had asked her to clean out for him. She supposed he'd want her to do the same with the beach house at Hilton Head sooner or later. She'd taken his willingness to pack Clary's things away as a good sign that he was healing, but now she wasn't so sure. Why be surprised when he hedged about attending the shelter opening? He'd simply thrown obstacles in her way, as he always did. And as soon as she'd turned away, he mumbled something about checking on patients and left for the hospital, leaving her to face Clary's abandoned office on her own, to deal with Clary's absence by herself.

The room smelled stale, abandoned. After throwing open a window, Susannah shoved cartons around. She'd packed half a dozen the day before, thinking the brisk activity might keep her too from remembering Jeb's last phone call and the yearning inside when he said good night.

She also hoped it might help her forget her unkind words to Leslie, whose growing involvement in the homeless center threatened to make Susannah lose her mind. Leslie never did anything by halves; either she avoided life entirely or flung herself headlong into it, plowing everyone else out of her way. When she'd actually told California's social service director at their most recent meeting, "I'm so grateful for your interest in my shelter," Susannah's temper had blown. And she'd booked the first flight to New York.

She opened a desk drawer, dumping its contents into an empty box. Drake had asked that nothing be thrown away yet, that the office cartons and personal clothing, designer dresses and gowns, stay in the attic, "just for a while."

Susannah repressed an image of her father, sitting alone in the dusty, cavernous high-raftered space on the third floor under a single bare light bulb, sobbing into his hands, which held Clary's wedding dress.

A black-and-white mottled notebook slipped off the carton's edge onto the floor, and she retrieved it. The book had landed open, facedown, and as she turned it right, her heart trembled at the sight of the familiar, flowery handwriting, all loops and spirals with circles over the i's. "Clary," she whispered.

She scanned the page, and a shaky smile formed.

The entry, written during their college days, contained wickedly accurate satire of a troublesome professor in a lit class they shared. Laughing, Susannah flipped the page, then another. These were her good memories of Clary, the good stories. She sank down onto the floor, crossing her legs, which wasn't as easy these days as it had once been, and letting her lap cradle her abdomen.

Setting the notebook in the carton at last, in the fading daylight she took up another, plain black and cheaper looking, to which Clary had clipped a note: "Useful for my book. See pages turned down."

As she had been unable to resist talking to Jeb, Susannah couldn't keep from looking at the marked passages in what seemed to be a journal from Clary's childhood. Maybe she'd learn more about Jeb, about the complex relationship he and Clary shared.

The love between Jeb and Clary sounded innocent and warm, the kind Susannah might have cherished with a brother. Looking through the book, she chose entries at random—some unmarked—but she'd read only a few pages before her stomach began to churn at the description of Clary's adolescence.

He touched me again. I've asked him not to, because it isn't right, but he does it anyway. Touches me where my chest has gotten soft and bumpy, where my legs meet and the darker hair has started to grow. Mama tells me these changes are normal at my age, but I still feel funny about them and the way I feel when *he* puts his hand on me.

"Dear God," Susannah said aloud. Her hand shook as she turned another page. Clary wouldn't play games, wouldn't lie to her diary, would she? Susannah's mind whirled. Jeb's young wife. Those girls clamoring for autographs, his teasing, his hand on a bare shoulder, the pen moving across the swell of a teenage breast . . .

Last night I learned what being a woman really means. *He* touched me there, kissed me, and put himself inside me. Am I bad? There's no use asking Jeb. If Mama knew, she'd cry. If Daddy knew, he'd surely beat me. And John Eustace . . . ? Lord knows what he would do.

"Susannah?"

Hearing Drake's voice in the hallway, she slapped the book shut. She was carrying Jeb's child, but Susannah couldn't think of anything worse than the words she'd read, not even Clary's murder. Clary hadn't hurt Jeb. No wonder she'd never told Susannah exactly what he'd done to her to make her leave Elvira.

And what if he hadn't stopped there? What if the speculations were true, and he had met Clary in Central Park, quarreled . . . then shot her to death to keep this dreadful secret? He'd known about the gun . . . He knew how to shoot.

She didn't realize how long she'd hunched on the thick apricot carpet of the room in which Clary had planned to write Jeb's biography, but a glance out the window at darkness as Drake stepped into the room told her it must be after nine o'clock.

"Susie, you look pale."

He dropped down in front of her, his silvery hair glowing in the soft light, his blue eyes slightly less glacial than usual. Taking both her hands in his, he rubbed them.

"I . . . worked too hard," she said, avoiding his gaze. Hoping she wouldn't humiliate herself by getting sick in front of him. She pulled her hands free as soon as he helped her to her feet.

"I'm sorry you didn't talk to me sooner about this," he said, gesturing toward her growing abdomen. "I might have put some sense into your head."

He'd been furious when Leslie told him, because even at thirty-one Susannah hadn't found the courage to disillusion him about her—and lose what little love he offered. To his credit, he'd contented himself with one brief lecture about irresponsibility, then proceeded until now to ignore the entire matter.

"How were your patients?" Susannah brushed off her jeans. She'd learned long ago to imitate his evasions of unpleasant subjects by changing them, but the ploy didn't work.

"The least you can do is sue Cody for putting you in this fix, and force him to support his child."

Her stomach rolled again at the mention of Jeb's name. "We reached our own agreement."

Drake sighed. "I have half a mind to throw a wrench in his spokes with a carefully planted story in the newspapers. Then see how long he avoids responsibility, if he wants to keep his career."

"Drake, please don't."

As if it might shout the truth aloud, she tossed the notebook onto the pile in the open carton. What had Jeb said in New York that last morning? . . . *the things people like you always say about poor country boys . . . abusing dogs and sheep . . . any animal that would hold still . . . sleepin' with my own* . . . Oh God, she thought.

Drake followed her down the stairs. "I've made reservations at the Spinning Wheel for dinner, your favorite table by the lake. Your geese are gone now, but—"

"I can't," she said. "I'm not hungry."

He studied her. "Are you sure you're okay?"

"Talking about Jeb upsets me," she said, which was even more true now. "I'll throw the rest of Clary's office things into boxes, then I'm flying back to San Francisco. I have a few things to oversee before the opening."

"I cleared my schedule. I'll be there."

"You will?" She looked up. "Thank you."

"You were right. Clary would want me to."

Though relieved that both her parents would attend, having missed so many school functions and horse shows in her girlhood, she didn't need Drake now as much as she had when she arrived in Greenwich. She'd hoped then he would reinforce the armor around her heart when she saw Jeb again; but all she needed now was the memory of those journal passages from Clary's childhood—which, as she'd always said, seemed as different from Susannah's as good from evil.

Two nights later, her nerves in shreds, Susannah opened the front door of Cody House to find Jeb on the porch, carrying a guitar, and smiling. "Glitz," he murmured, taking in the beaded black shoulder straps on her dress, her glittering bodice, but not letting his gaze slip lower than her breasts. "I might have expected as much."

He stepped inside, glancing toward the party sounds coming from the living and dining rooms. When he bent to kiss her in the entryway, Susannah stepped out of reach.

"At least you know what to expect." Not meeting his eyes, she looked over his shoulder at the still open door. Outside, a dark limousine waited at the curb, engine purring. "If your driver would like to come in for a drink or some food . . ."

"He's all right for now." Frowning, Jeb closed the door. He propped the guitar in a corner. "I hope you have a good alarm system in this neighborhood, but don't worry about him. He carries a gun."

"Always? Even when we—?" In the car, she thought, in New York.

"Yes, ma'am."

Escaping his puzzled look, she turned on one black high-heeled pump and led the way into the living room, where a cheery fire blazed in the black-and-green marble hearth and people seemed to be stuffed, like the filling in the cushions, into every available space. Let him wonder at her coldness. She could feel Jeb at her back, but no one had yet noticed him.

Leslie was talking with Michael in a corner, and Drake had pushed Susannah's new resident counselor, a pretty redhead, close to one wall for what appeared to be an intense conversation. Susannah didn't have time or the inclination to see that as a positive sign of his recovery from Clary's death. Determined to get this over with, she brightened her smile by twenty watts or so, then plunged toward the center of the crowded room.

In the dining room opposite, another thirty or forty people lingered over the tables spread with ham and turkey and roast beef, with salads and fruit, with cakes and pies and puff pastries, with huge urns of coffee. Near the desserts, Susannah caught sight of Miranda's shiny dark hair, and one small hand reaching up for a wedge of jelly roll.

Susannah seized a glass and rapped a fork against it.

"Everyone, may I have your attention?" Thank God she and others had already made the formal remarks. A few curious glances met hers, and Leslie turned, her smile freezing like a twin to Michael's. "We have a surprise guest who probably needs no introduction."

She watched Drake's icy blue gaze drop to subzero.

When Jeb moved closer, when she sensed he would have touched her arm, Susannah inched away. She kept her tone cordial, nothing more. "Ladies, gentlemen, please welcome Jeb Stuart Cody, Clary's . . . brother."

The word nearly choked her. At the expected applause Susannah gestured him to the center of the living room. Jeb's smile grew slowly into that all-out display of charm that could get him under any woman's skirts.

Tonight he looked like anything but a poor country boy. He wore a beautifully tailored dark suit complete with vest, and a shirt so white it made her blink. His subtly patterned silk tie couldn't be faulted; his hair had been brushed to a soft sheen, and it curled a bit at the nape of his neck. Susannah could barely look at him.

Cheryl, smiling, wearing a simple but neat red dress and a ribbon in her hair, called out. "Sing something for us, Jeb."

He'd been right about the glitz, but it was a mixed crowd. A sprinkling of sequins and silks, a smattering of workmen looking uncomfortable in jackets and ties, a few wives and children. Social workers and socialites. Apparently some knew country music, but all of them knew Jeb Stuart Cody.

"Why not sing that new song you mentioned?" Susannah said.

He colored slightly and cleared his throat.

"I'd rather start with something established, if you don't mind." He retrieved his guitar from the entryway, then settled onto one of the sofa arms, tuning the sleek mahogany-inlaid-with-pecan instrument while he carried on some light patter, tonight about the shelter's worth, about his pleasure at taking part in its opening. He didn't mention Clary, which for once suited Susannah.

Then he began to play. And to sing. And finally, murmuring Clary's name, he sang "Kid Sister."

Susannah could have heard a single heartbeat across the room when he finished, the last note trailing off in his husky baritone, his head bent low over the guitar, and more than a few eyes appeared damp. Dry-eyed herself, Susannah glanced up at the same instant Jeb did, and nailed her with his stare.

As the applause rose, she looked away from the question in his eyes.

When the clapping faded, he worked his way through the crowd, accepting praise in an offhanded but gracious way, appearing to be what she now knew he wasn't—a decent man—and appearing at her side before she could leave the room.

"If you want something to drink," she said, focusing her gaze on Miranda, who was playing under the table with Studley, "there's punch, coffee, tea, bottled water, juices . . . everything but liquor."

At that instant the party under the table decided to move. Squealing with laughter, Miranda in a frilly pink dress—donated by someone—barreled into Susannah's legs, followed by Studley who wrapped himself around Jeb's, leaving hairs all over his pants.

"What's this?" he asked, breaking into a smile.

The little girl gazed up at him. "My name's 'Manda."

"Hi there, 'Manda."

"It's Miranda," Susannah said. "Miranda Colby."

"And this is Studley Do-right." The little girl had said the dog's name perfectly, and Jeb laughed, but Susannah could feel her spine stiffen.

"Did you name the dog?" he asked Susannah.

"Miranda, why don't you take him out into the yard?" It was newly fenced in with a swing set and sandbox. "The lights are on outside, and I'm sure he'd love you to throw his new rubber ball for him."

"You're a good singer," Miranda said, staring up at Jeb.

"Thanks." He hunkered down in front of her at eye level. "How'd you like to do an encore with me?"

"What's a encore?"

"Another song, because you liked the other ones so much."

Ignoring Susannah, Jeb took the dark-haired little girl by the hand, the two of them looking almost like father and daughter, and walked her back into the living room where he introduced her to his guitar and to the crowd. Susannah wanted to snatch the child from him. Over his bent head as he showed Miranda how to play a note, Leslie sent Susannah a message that she could clearly read: *Did you invite him here?*

Susannah went into the dining room to fuss with the devastated platters of food.

At first she shut the strains of "Deep River" from her ears—remembering that night in her home when he'd played the piano—then from her heart. Poor Clary.

What had she ever done to deserve such betrayal? What had Susannah done by falling for Jeb herself?

The moving song produced silence, then murmured appreciation.

She would have used the moment to slip away, but Jeb must have spotted her. She'd no sooner set foot in the hallway, intent upon reaching the relative sanctity of the kitchen on the pretext of making more coffee, when his hand settled on her bare shoulder.

A wave of yearning, of loss, then of revulsion rolled through her.

"If you're hungry, there's plenty of food."

"I'm not. Hungry or thirsty."

She didn't turn. "Then perhaps you'd like to mingle. I'm sure everyone would welcome the chance to talk with you. If you'll excuse me—"

"I don't believe I will."

Susannah whirled, her gaze meeting his. Dark gray, and stormy. His easy smile had disappeared but he touched her shoulder again. "I beg your pardon?" she said.

"Don't use that high-society talk on me, sugar."

"Is there a problem, Susie?" Drake stepped close, an inch or so taller than Jeb, his blue eyes frosty and his mouth a grim line.

"No problem," she said.

"Not a'tall," Jeb drawled, his accent deeper, clearly deliberate.

"I'm asking my daughter."

"Then you heard what she said. This is a private—"

"You don't need any more private conversations with Susannah." Drake's voice was low but deadly. "Get your hand off her before I find it necessary to escort you from this house."

Jeb stroked his upper lip, the scar. "You and what Sheriff's Department?"

"Jeb," she murmured.

He glanced at her, then at Drake. "Why don't you go back to the party and drape yourself around that little redhead with the freckles everywhere? Or isn't she young enough for you?"

"You surly bastard."

Jeb grabbed Drake by his tie. "I never did like you. I should warn you that, where you're concerned, my temper is on a mighty short rein."

"Susannah, leave us alone."

"The two of you, please. Don't make a scene."

"We can take this into the yard," Jeb suggested, "or I can rearrange your lines and creases right here, Dr. Whittaker, whichever you prefer."

Drake's voice dropped even lower. "No wonder Clary left Kentucky and that hellhole she grew up in with the likes of you."

"Clary left for other reasons! Nothing was ever simple between us. Maybe she and I convinced ourselves—for public consumption, because it was less painful—that she left because she wanted more than Elvira could give. Maybe I resented you for keeping her away. That's for me to work out now. She's gone, but sooner or later, we both would have had to face the real reasons—and she just might have learned that the life you offered was an empty one." He looked at Susannah. "Your own daughter is a living example and I thank God she's finally worked her way out."

Drake covered Jeb's strong hand with his on the tie. "You think I don't know who the father of her baby is? The man who won't accept his own child and raise it?"

Jeb's gaze flickered, then managed—as he'd done in

the entryway—not to look at Susannah's slightly rounded abdomen. She could barely breathe for what he'd just said about Clary.

In the distance a fork clanked against someone's plate, reminding her that they were conducting a public display. The rest of the room had fallen silent. Drake noticed too. Prying Jeb's fingers loose from his tie, he stepped back, pasting on a sickly smile that wouldn't fool anyone.

"If I were you, Cody, I'd watch my back."

Michael was staring at them too from the other room, and as Drake joined him, the intent gazes of onlookers following, Jeb grabbed Susannah's elbow.

"Where can we talk?"

"I have nothing to say to you."

"Well, I've got plenty to say. So where?"

She cast a glance at her father, at Michael. "Jeb, you'd better go."

"Not until I understand why you greeted me at the door with as much enthusiasm as if I were carrying plague." He steered her along the hall.

"Upstairs," she said, resigned.

It hadn't been the best choice, but Susannah didn't realize that until they stepped into the first bedroom at the top of the stairs, Miranda and her mother's, and Jeb closed the door. He leaned against it, blocking escape, and folded his arms, drawing the dark suit fabric tighter against his biceps. The hint of muscle, of power and sheer male presence, made her regret not suggesting the kitchen instead. Susannah fought not to look at the nearby beds.

The flutter of awareness through her body shamed her. How could she even think of him and bed, much less respond to him? She wanted to turn on a light, but

Jeb blocked the motion and she saw him only by moon-light. The very air in the room seemed his, warm and sultry, all scented masculinity and, tonight, some expensive woodsy cologne.

"I'm sorry about that downstairs," he said, "with your father. Even sorrier that you've obviously led him to believe your baby is mine."

Susannah took a step. "Get away from the door."

"What was it, Miss Susannah? A way to get even with me for not believing your story? A way to keep from pinning the blame on a more socially acceptable prospect for his son-in-law? Because the San Francisco connection doesn't want to marry you?"

"How many times do I have to tell you? His name is Michael."

"I don't give a damn what his name is. Just stop draggin' me through his mud."

"Let me out of here."

When she reached him, Jeb dropped his arms. But only for a second, before they came up around her like an ambush.

"Or maybe you'd prefer that it was me who fathered this baby?"

Even his voice sounded of sex. Susannah felt herself trembling. His touch. She couldn't bear it, couldn't fight it.

"You have an inflated sense of your virility. Now let me go or I'll—"

"What?" Jeb cut off the threat, his arms tightening and his mouth coming down, hard, on hers. "You can't keep away from me any more than I can keep away from you," he whispered into her mouth. She tried to close it, but he only changed the angle, intensifying the contact. Susannah felt his growing hardness against her gently rounded belly, felt the blood rush through her veins, her senses. Moaning, desperate to escape her own reactions, still she clung to him, aroused by his first touch, despising herself. He gentled the kiss a fraction of a second before Susannah ground her heel into his instep.

"Jesus Christ!"

Caught off guard, he nearly let Susannah slip out the door. She had one foot in the hallway when Jeb spun her back inside, up against the door, which closed as he pushed her into it. Jeb turned the lock. "Now listen here, Miss Susannah. I'm gettin' serious."

"I hate you!"

"And here I thought we were gettin' on well enough."

"I despise everything you stand for, everything you've done in your miserable life."

He raised his eyebrows. "Such as?"

Susannah stared down at his brass belt buckle, at the scant inch or so of space between them before the name tore from her like a sob. "Clary."

She might as well face him now. End it. Then cut him from her life, as Drake would excise a tumor.

"What about Clary?"

She shook her head, unable to speak.

"What about my sister?"

"That," she whispered. "She was your *sister*. Just a girl when you—God, to think I ever let you touch me." She wiped a hand hard across her mouth, erasing the taste of him, the sick taste of him and her own guilt.

"When I what?" She could feel his gray gaze, searching her face for some clue. "When I *what*?"

"Abused her." She swallowed. "Sl-slept with her."

"What the hell is this all about?" Susannah looked up, seeing the stark expression on his face. "You really think I—?" He shook his head as if to clear it. "*Christ* . . . my own *sister*? You could think that after what you and I have done with each other, what we shared?" He braced his arms at either side of her head, dropping his low until their foreheads touched, his voice barely audible. "Christ, you could think that of me?"

"I read her journal. It's all there."

"Tell me," he said to the floor.

"I can't. It's too terrible to repeat."

"Tell me one thing."

"She said . . . she said you touched her . . . all over." Susannah swallowed. "She wrote, 'I learned what being a woman really means.'"

Jeb went white around the mouth. He pushed away from the door. "It's not true. Not a word of it." He ran a hand over his hair. "Christ, John Eustace always said she could tell a lie better than any person he ever knew, but I always thought . . . I told him she was good, just inventive, that if he loved me, he'd better never say another bad thing about Clary or I'd—" he broke off, then tried again, "I'd stop loving him."

Wanting to open the door and run, Susannah stood frozen at the look on his face. The horror, the sorrow. He couldn't fake such a look. No one could. Dear Lord. What if she'd been wrong? But if Clary hadn't written the truth, then what was the truth?

Jeb walked around the room, picking up a throw pillow from the bed and putting it back, hefting a glass paperweight that must belong to Miranda's mother. His fist tightened around it. Then he fired it at the wall. The glass didn't break but dropped with a thud to the industrial-grade blue tweed carpet. Sinking down onto one of the beds, he dropped his head into his hands.

After a moment, Susannah sat beside him, not touching. Her words seemed inadequate. "I—I may have misinterpreted something."

"You may have?" He didn't look up.

He stripped off his suit jacket and rolled up his sleeves as if preparing for surgery, like Drake, or for battle. Susannah stared at him, feeling lost and deceitful herself.

"Let me tell you what I know," he said hoarsely, "what I promised I would never tell anyone." He looked into the middle distance, his words halting. "Clary was a real pretty girl. You know that as well as I do. She had a flirty way about her, sure enough . . . and wasn't above using that to get her way." He glanced at Susannah. "Hell, she used that to get your father interested too, I suppose. Anyway, about the time she started to develop, to look like a woman, our daddy got arrested—again—for breaking and entering or burglary, I don't remember for sure. It happened too many times to keep 'em straight." He raked his hair again. "But this one time, the sheriff came out, as he always did, to haul Daddy off to jail, and he brought this new deputy with him, a big guy half again my size even now, with a swagger to his step."

When he paused, Susannah said, "Go on."

"He helped take Daddy away and Clary cried, carried on as she did, hoping the sheriff would change his mind and let Daddy off the hook. He didn't of course, but I guess the tears touched somethin' in the deputy—he must have been about twenty-five at the time to Clary's thirteen—and he came back out to the house the next day, wonderin' if she was all right, so he said."

"What happened?"

"Nothing, then." Jeb shook his head. "But Clary kept growin' and changin', and a time or two later, I forget just when, she asked if she could ride along with Daddy in the patrol car, just to keep him quiet. The deputy'd come alone that time, so he took one look into Clary's big blue eyes, at that tangle of auburn hair she had, and said, 'Sure, why not?'" Jeb focused on the placid seascape print by the door. "I warned her to mind her business, but she said she knew how to help Daddy and to mind my own. That was the first fight I think we ever had and that's when everything changed."

"You were—?"

"Thirteen myself by then. Still skinny, big hands and feet. No muscle to speak of. Anyway, Clary started seein' him, which drove me wild. The start of all our problems. She'd sneak off soon as Mama fell asleep, exhausted from caring for the little ones, and come home later and later. And later," he added, his gray eyes dark. "I guess if you read the journal, you know the rest." Jeb stroked the scar on his upper lip. "Dick Sheridan," he said. "Richard Gage Sheridan. That bastard had a wife and kids at home, another on the way, but he took my sister like a common slut. Took her and took her and . . . took her."

"Oh, Jeb."

"If she kept Daddy out of jail by givin' away her innocence, I never knew about it. He's in the state pen right now, rottin' away on an armed robbery charge, and Clary's—" he dipped his head low again, like his voice, "Clary's dead."

"How helpless you must have felt," Susannah whispered back.

"I was just a kid. What could I do . . . until it was too late?"

"That's why you hated her marrying Drake, isn't it? Because he seemed like just another older man, dirtying her? Taking her innocence? And someone else—desperate and depraved—walked up to her in Central Park and took away her life."

He looked up. "You see why it doesn't matter to me much whether she was murdered or mugged? It's all the same effect, leading to that end, from the time she turned thirteen."

Frantically, she thought back over the journal entries. "Clary never actually used your name in any of those . . . episodes. She always wrote 'he' and often underlined it. From the way she wrote about you earlier, the love, I assumed . . . "

"Maybe she wanted you—or anyone who happened to read it—to assume that."

"Jeb, I'm sorry." Oh God, how wrong she'd been.

"Hell, what else would you think of a redneck like me?"

"I never meant that."

"Yes, you did." For the first time since he'd walked into Cody House, he looked at Susannah's slightly swollen abdomen. The look was brief, assessing, but not accepting. He didn't want her. He didn't want their child. And right now she couldn't blame him. "I loved my sisters, and I never hurt them—not one of them."

His voice floated to her, as if across a vast distance, which couldn't be bridged.

"As someone called Anonymous once said, 'You should make a point of trying every experience once, excepting incest and folk-dancing.'" Getting off the bed, Jeb walked to the door. "I've spread enough gladness for one night. Guess I'll get my guitar and get out of your father's way. Yours too," he added.

"Jeb."

"No wonder you wiped off that kiss. Sorry, but whether you believe it or not, I don't usually force myself on women."

"You didn't," she said, but he was gone. He went lightly down the stairs, as if to lift the cloud of confession with each step, and Susannah stayed behind.

In the darkness, in the silence, she sat with only herself for company. Or so she thought. When the first light movement rippled through her abdomen, she nearly missed it. Then, placing a hand over her belly, she waited—and the soft, butterfly kiss from within brushed through her again. The baby had moved. Jeb's baby . . .

She was still sitting on the bed, which by later tonight would be Miranda's or her mother's, when she heard Jeb's rich voice and Clary's name. He was talking to those people downstairs who, like him, had come to honor her. Then she heard his guitar, a sweet, soft melody, and the words he hadn't wanted to sing earlier.

"Little rich girl . . . you could learn a lot from a poor boy like me."

He'd once said he saved his best notions for his songs. He'd given her one, a ballad that even she could understand. *Christ, you could think that of me?* She'd been so wrong about him. He'd been so right about her.

Susannah sat in the dark, not quite alone, and cried.

16

Alone in the music room in Breeze's Nashville mansion, Jeb dimly heard the phone ring in some far-off room but ignored it. There were enough people, including servants, that someone else would answer. He resettled the guitar across his thigh, and in his mind listened to the scrap of melody he'd struggled with all morning. A hot August morning, already over ninety degrees with humidity to match. Hazy sunlight filtered through the triple pane windows into the air-conditioned room, and outside he could just hear the trill of songbirds in the nearby woods; a hearty splash coming from the swimming pool; the shouts of Mack's children at play, probably their favorite water polo.

The melody line, the same he'd been working on since Clary died, disintegrated, and Jeb strummed a heavy chord in frustration. "Dammit." He decided he didn't like the embryonic song; but then he didn't like much these days so he didn't throw it out.

He hadn't found the large apartment or airy house he

wanted before Tour America ended, before that disastrous night in San Francisco at Susannah's opening, and after that he hadn't cared. Breeze didn't begrudge him a place to stay, and for now that's all he wanted. Except her daily prodding to keep at his songwriting. If he'd been living by himself, he supposed he would never take the guitar from its case the whole summer.

He touched me.

Jeb didn't believe in keeping secrets, but he wished he'd never kept that one. Wished Clary hadn't turned ugly fact into heinous fiction, or inferred it anyway.

He thumbed another note, then set the guitar aside.

Susannah Whittaker. Poor little rich girl. Past history.

Hell, he didn't need her either. He'd have to be crazy to involve himself with that family of hers; she could look down her nose at his beginnings if she liked, but at least he'd known love along with poverty. Susannah was more deprived than he'd been the worst day of his life. Hell, why regret that kiss in the upstairs bedroom at her shelter, even if it was the last one? She needed it.

Sometimes lately he wished he hadn't been so hasty, or so adamant, in saying no to John Eustace's plea that he come home this summer. Of course, all he had to do was pick up the phone, alert his grandfather to his arrival, reserve a seat on an airplane . . .

"Jeb." Breeze's voice brought his head up, interrupting his thoughts. She sounded subdued as she came into the cathedral-ceilinged, Southwest-style room, her voice carrying even so in the acoustically near-perfect space.

"Phone call for me?" he asked, glancing around for the nearest extension.

"In a way."

She shut the door behind her and, with a frown, crossed to him.

His first thought was of John Eustace. "Somethin' wrong?"

"Yes. Not your grandfather."

Jeb started to rise from his stool at the music stand, but she stopped him, drawing him back down and kneeling in front of him. She wore a damp yellow bikini, her long blond hair pulled high into a ponytail and secured with a plain rubber band. No sequins, Jeb thought but didn't smile. His heart was suddenly thundering.

"Bad news?"

"From New York," she said and he swallowed.

If she'd said the west coast, he would have thought, Susannah. Her baby.

"The police called. They have a new clue, and it looks like murder. Someone Clary knew." Breeze's gaze imprisoned his.

"What kind of clue?"

He listened intently to her story. A young couple in Central Park, making love off the path near the spot where Clary had died, had discovered, right under where they were lying, her daily schedule book in a matted pile of last winter's fallen leaves. A leather book, Breeze told him, with her initials stamped in gold and a notation inside. They'd turned it over to the police.

He studied a sheet of staff paper on the music stand, not seeing a single note. "Why didn't they find it before? They must have combed that area a million times in the first days after she died. What if it's a plant, just like that phony witness who came forward but turned out to be a mental case? Like the guy who threw his fist in my face in San Francisco?"

"The police think the killer tore the book from Clary's hands and threw it, that it landed well off the path where these people found it, in a clump of bushes and trees. It got covered when the first wind picked up, and then only a few days later, the blizzard happened . . ." She trailed off, clasping his hands tightly between hers. "The leaves packed down. Snow and rain. It was a hard winter in the East." She paused. "The police have already authenticated the book, Jeb. They've shown it to Drake Whittaker for one thing, and traced it back to the manufacturer she ordered it from. They even have her signature and credit card number on the order for imprinting her initials. And inside the front cover is one of the new business cards she had done not long before, at the same time she announced her contract to write the book about you."

He hadn't asked the one question whose answer he really needed to know. "What did the notation in the book say?"

Breeze cradled his face. "I don't know. The police want to talk to you."

"I thought it was over," he said, remembering the grilling he'd gotten the night of Clary's death when he established his alibi. He'd been with Breeze, polishing a song for his album, and preparing for his New York concert. "They already checked out my whereabouts that afternoon."

Breeze hesitated, swallowing. "They feel I have too much of a vested interest in your innocence to be that credible. Because I'm your manager and sometime cowriter." She paused again. "Because we were lovers."

He smoothed her hair back from her temples, then tugged lightly at her ponytail. "What's the plan?"

"Mack's calling for airline reservations. We leave for New York on the first available flight."

Jeb pushed her gently away and rose from the stool. His hands felt clammy and his heart raced. He could almost hear the sheriff's car flying up the drive, doors slamming, voices shouting. Dick Sheridan's too. He could see his daddy in the rear seat, handcuffed and silent, his eyes glittering with rage—and fear.

"I guess I'd better pack," he said.

"Jeb?"

"I'm fine. I can handle it," he said as if to himself. "I've been called things just as bad as a murderer." Maybe Susannah came from better stock, after all.

"No one's calling you a murderer."

His legs felt badly jointed, stiff, but he managed his way to the door. "Just keep the press off my back, if you can."

"I've already called a conference for right after we land," she said.

"I don't want to talk to 'em."

"I'll take care of everything."

"Damage control?"

She stopped him before he opened the door. "That's my job—but just so you'll know, cowboy, I happen to love you."

He dropped a light kiss on her mouth. "Don't tell Mack, but I love you too." He paused, then went into the hall and up the stairs to his room, his pulse racing like a chased rabbit. He knew, he just knew, Breeze was watching him. And crying. Jeb called back over his shoulder, not to embarrass her by turning around.

"Hey, it's free publicity."

Susannah read the news that same afternoon. Leslie handed her the papers the minute she walked into the house, feeling hot and sweaty from a day at the shelter, which didn't have air conditioning, usually unnecessary in San Francisco's mild climate. The unexpected late summer heat wave had left her limp and edgy, though she knew it wasn't only because of the weather.

Her back aching, she lowered herself into the first chair she came to, her gaze fixed on the headline across the tabloid: "CODY QUESTIONED IN SISTER'S DEATH. New Clue Reopens Case."

The vague story underneath said little more than the headline. She'd made terrible accusations herself, not that long ago. Susannah threw the paper aside, then went to the built-in bar between living and dining room for a cold drink. Leslie hovered in the background, obviously awaiting her reaction to the news about Jeb, and eyeing the bar.

She realized that, for the first time in days, she'd done something as soon as she reached home other than check the liquor cabinet. The grand opening of Cody House had been Leslie's last good day, as Susannah termed it. That night Drake took the pretty redheaded counselor out for a late supper, and Leslie fell into a depression. After hurting Jeb, Susannah didn't sleep well herself and easily heard Leslie moving about downstairs well after midnight. The chink of ice cubes in a glass remained one of her most vivid childhood memories, and quickly brought the pain flooding back. The fear.

The next day she marked the bottles. No need to water down Leslie's supply in the hope of regulating her drinking and avoiding some vicious quarrel with Drake. With only the two of them in her house, Susannah didn't bother. Nor did she replace the empties.

She turned from the bar with a glass of mineral water.

"Drink?" she asked, her gaze wandering the room.

Clearly, Leslie hadn't expected her home so soon. A tall glass with an inch or so of melted ice in the bottom sat, like a guilty child, on one end table by the sofa.

"I had some lemonade. It's dreadfully hot today." Leslie picked up the newspaper again, rattling the pages. "Well? What do you say now to your Mr. Cody?"

"Without more information than this, I say nothing."

She couldn't help it. She tried to sit back down in the chair she'd vacated, tried to sip at her water and give Leslie the benefit of the doubt, but couldn't. She went straight to the end table and picked up the glass. Like broken shards, keen disappointment stabbed through her.

"Susannah. Really."

The lingering aroma of whiskey reached her nostrils without having to sniff, and when she handed the glass to Leslie with the one word "Lemonade?" she could smell the truth on her mother's breath. Leslie didn't flinch.

"If I wanted a jailer, I would have stayed in Greenwich with Drake. Or I'd turn myself in with Jeb Stuart Cody to the Manhattan police."

"You missed your self-defense class this morning, didn't you?"

"I had a headache. I decided to rest."

"And you failed to show up at the shelter at four o'clock to stock pantry shelves."

"I fell back to sleep after lunch and didn't wake up in time."

The familiar excuses didn't sway Susannah. She'd had far too much experience with Leslie's dissembling when she drank, with her failures.

"I don't know what you expect of me," Leslie said, going to the bar and dumping the remnants of her glass in the small stainless steel sink next to it. "I went to that clinic in New Mexico when you and Drake conspired against me—"

Susannah reached her limit. "When we tried to help you!"

"—and as you well know I followed the program, even though I was simply not like all those other people with severe problems."

"Drug and alcohol dependence," she said.

"And though I nearly died of boredom, not to mention restriction, I emerged with a clean bill of health, which I didn't need in the first place. I have maintained a sensible life-style ever since, exploring my potentials, and what do I get for it? Suspicion."

"Can you blame me? Or Drake? How many times, as a child, do you think I came home to find you passed out across your bed?" The memory made her blink. "Or once, half gone in the swimming pool with a drink still in your hand?"

"I was lying on the floating lounge. I couldn't have drowned if I'd wanted to."

Susannah huffed out a breath. "You won't even acknowledge the problem. Not even now, when you've already lost your husband."

"Drake is temporarily out of his mind. A midlife crisis. Even you, Susannah, should be able to see that when it's in front of your eyes. If Clary wasn't enough, how do you excuse the little redhead . . . your own employee?" She took ice from the freezer, cramming it into the glass and adding a can of lemonade. "Drake will come to his senses. Men are weak, that's all. Driven by their genitalia."

"Oh, for heaven's sake."

"When he looks around one day, he'll realize what he threw away. And come after me. Which is why," she said, "I spend so much time here instead of in Greenwich. A man appreciates having to chase after a woman until she catches him—as the saying goes."

The old saw made Susannah see red.

"You spend time with me because none of your Connecticut friends speak to you."

Leslie took a long swallow of lemonade and grimaced.

"I do believe that shelter has had an effect on your mind. First, you throw Michael over, abandon your normal charities for a bunch of homeless women and noisy children, then you revile your own mother . . . and refuse to see the truth about Jeb Cody when it's in every newspaper in this country."

Susannah was shaking. "On the contrary, I'm happier than I've ever been. When I was a girl, in day school near Greenwich, I had no friends. Until I met Clary, and Drake divorced you, I was afraid to bring anyone home. Every child I invited to the house saw you with a glass in your hand, saw you laughing at nothing funny, saw you crying—"

"Susannah."

She briefly clapped a hand to her mouth, as if to stop the words, the thoughts.

"I needed you and you weren't there. You never worked a day in your life outside your home, but you weren't there. And I miss you." She didn't look at Leslie's face. Setting her own glass aside, Susannah left the room.

Upstairs, she closed her door and lay down on her bed, letting her shoes drop to the floor. Studley slept at the foot of the bed, so deep in some twitching dream that he didn't hear her come in.

Susannah lifted the receiver and dialed her father's number.

"I was just about to call you," Drake said, though she wondered if that was true.

"I've had a quarrel with Leslie. I hurt her feelings, but

I think you should know—she's drinking again. Blaming it on your date in San Francisco with my counselor."

"I should have known."

"She thinks you'll come chasing after her when you've regained your senses."

He was silent for a moment, during which Susannah wondered whether they shared anything but her mother's addiction. "How are you? Holding up?"

"I'm all right."

"I suppose you've seen the headlines?"

Willing to let him change the subject, Susannah asked about the clue. "The accounts here are little more than teasers to sell papers, I suppose." She told him what she knew.

"I can't tell you much more. Only that the police have found Clary's daybook with some incriminating writing in it."

Susannah thought of the journal and could have groaned.

"Do you know where Jeb is?" she asked, realizing the question might set off a storm, which it did.

"I believe he's a guest of NYPD, midtown. Where I hope they nail his ass to the chair under a hot white light and run his mind in circles until he confesses that he murdered my wife."

"Drake, surely you don't think Jeb—"

"What else should I think? When she decided to do that book about him, he killed her to keep her quiet. Or had her killed. That's motive, Susie. They've been at odds for years. God knows what he's hiding under his good-old-boy public image."

Susannah gripped the phone with white fingers. Not that long ago, briefly, she would have agreed. "That's all you can tell me?"

"The police are notoriously closemouthed with evidence, and this is the first solid piece of it they've had. I'm sure they're not about to reveal their cards to anyone, not even Clary's husband."

"Thank you, then." She poised a finger over the disconnect button.

"Suse? Take care of yourself. And Leslie."

"Don't I always?"

When she hung up, having learned little more than she'd known when she called, Studley's tail flopped rhythmically against the white cutwork duvet and his eyes opened, staring balefully at her.

"Come here, mutt." Susannah opened her arms and he lunged into them, licking her face until she had to laugh. "I love you too. Want to come with me tomorrow and see Miranda?"

Studley lapped at her nose.

"All right, all right." She settled the pup against her side, his one paw draped over her rounded belly, and he was soon asleep again. Downstairs she could hear Leslie moving around, then the clink of ice again, the dull thud of a bottle being set down. She'd switched from lemonade and Susannah sighed. She'd be pouring her mother into bed tonight, but first . . .

She opened the nightstand drawer, fumbling for her private phone book. Within seconds, she realized she didn't know Jeb's home number, or any number for him. Not that he'd be there, according to Drake.

She pressed a hand to her abdomen, feeling the baby move under her palm. Those first, light flutters had by now given way to genuine kicks, and ordinarily she would have smiled. Instead, she bit her lip and said, "Daddy's in trouble, sweetheart. What can we do to get him out?"

Nothing, she thought at first.

Then she eased away from Studley, letting his head and silky ears loll onto the cutwork pillow, and went to her stereo system.

In the CD cabinet she quickly found Jeb's first album.

He had an address, all right. A phone number. Several of them. JSC Enterprises, Inc., for Cody products and his fan club, occupied offices in Nashville, Tennessee, and under Personal Management, she read Maynard Artists. They'd stonewall her, no doubt about that, but that wouldn't stop her. Susannah had spent much of her life employing her Whittaker hauteur to get what she wanted, and she would. Even if that meant climbing over Breeze Maynard.

Her fingernails biting into her palms, Breeze again surveyed the shambles of her Nashville home. In the vast living room, only the walls of glass remained undisturbed, reflecting the night's blackness outside and the tumbled furniture, the thrown piles of books and magazines, the upended ceiling-high plants that flanked the fireplace. Unpotted now, their roots lay exposed and rich dirt spilled onto the polished floor. Before sickness could overwhelm her, she turned away, because these were only things, objects, and the rest of her life had crumbled too.

She walked down the hallway past the library, its books helter-skelter on tabletops, floor, and shelves, past the downstairs family room and bedrooms, to the kitchen where drawers still hung open and cabinet doors alternately gaped and others, obviously having been slammed shut, seemed to hide secrets.

Didn't everything, everyone?

Breeze had no love of the police. Such authority always reminded her of the day she lost her band and ultimately her career. Now the law-and-order eagles threatened Jeb, and like John Eustace, she could hardly think straight for her anger and her sorrow.

She and Jeb had spent only three days in New York, then come home to this.

Her black satin nightgown swirled around her bare legs as she whirled in the kitchen's center, barely avoiding the ceramic-tiled island in her haste to escape the violation that still quivered in the air, through every room, and through her soul. On smooth bare feet she hurried back along the hall, needing, needing. . .

Refuge.

Jeb's cooperation with the New York police hadn't cut much ice. They questioned him until, he said, his brain turned to pudding, then questioned him some more. His lawyers had done their best, but after two days Jeb volunteered to take, then insisted upon, a lie detector test. He didn't think it had gone especially well, but the police finally released him, content that his alibi still held, or so Breeze had assumed.

Then she'd walked into her house and found the house's interior utterly destroyed.

Still terrified at the invasion of their midnight privacy, the maid and gardener had told her of the search warrant. The local authorities had gone over every inch of Breeze's mansion, looking for what, she couldn't say— the murder weapon, Jeb thought. Of course they uncovered nothing, but she still couldn't sleep at night.

Mack Norton, she thought. More bad news.

In a flurry of black satin she sailed along the southern hall into the other wing of the house and the ground-floor music room. She didn't hear any sound from within, and no beam of light showed beneath the door. Had Jeb gone up to bed?

She eased the door open, slipping inside, and calling him.

"On the couch." He lay with an arm flung over his eyes, bare-chested but wearing jeans, his legs sprawled out and his boots off. Breeze tripped over one on the floor but didn't swear. She'd been tripping over things for the three days they'd been back.

"Couldn't sleep?" she asked.

"Couldn't eat. Couldn't drink. Couldn't find major C on the damn guitar." He lowered his arm to look at her in the dark. The soft night air whispered through the room from the open French doors leading to the patio and the pool, and the scent of gardenias wafted in. Moonlight spattered the walls, the floor, the stool where Jeb had been trying for days to write a song. "Just couldn't . . ."

"Want me to get you a blanket?"

"No. Thanks."

"It's a nice night, maybe you could fall asleep smellin' the garden and hearin' the crickets sing."

"Breeze, let me be."

She straightened, unable to see his eyes or expression. But his voice sounded tired and empty. "I'm sorry," she said, trying not to feel offended. "I guess you'll have to get your pudding brain back in gear in your own fashion."

"Hey." She hadn't taken a step when he called her back. "You're right, I can't even think. I hardly know my own name right now. I've been lyin' here with a full bladder for an hour, and I swear I can't recall where the nearest bathroom is."

"Through that door, cowboy." She pointed at the far wall and the powder room.

With a heavy sigh, Jeb eased himself upright, then

across the moonlit floor. When he came back, he seemed to glide toward her, without effort, and into her arms.

"I can't tell you how sorry I am they trashed your place. Because of me."

"Not you," she said, "some silly scribbles on a sheet of paper. Lord only knows what Clary really meant, or if she meant anything at all."

The notation had been written the day she died. Scrawled across one page of her schedule book at an angle. In big letters, two of them. *J.E.*, Jeb had told her after his questioning, and the *E* trailed away, as if Clary were interrrupted in the act of writing it. "Writing the rest," Jeb had said. "J.E.B." Or maybe Clary had written it after being shot, just before she died. Which was Breeze's theory.

"How do you know?" Jeb said. "You never met her."

"But I know you, and through you, I know her."

He rocked her in his arms. "God, what's going to happen next?"

"Whatever happens, we'll turn it to our advantage."

He laughed softly. "Maynard, I have to tell you . . . I am not in the mood for some Pollyanna lecture, even though I admire you for bein' so positive after Mack Norton dumped you like yesterday's socks."

"He did, didn't he?" When Jeb said it, it didn't sound as tragic.

"Not even a fair fight, if I heard correctly."

She rubbed her cheek against his bare chest. "'Peggy needs me,' he said. 'She and the boys need me.'" Waiting for her when she got home, Mack had toured the ruined house with her, then laid his bombshell.

"He never wanted to leave her in the first place," Breeze murmured.

"Did you really want him to?"

"Maybe not." She turned her head and kissed his chest. "Maybe what I've always wanted is right here."

His hands in her unbound hair, Jeb pulled her head back. "Breeze . . ."

His mouth was still open on her name when she covered it with hers. Jeb had always been the best kisser of her experience, but he ended it almost before it began.

"Big mistake, Maynard."

"Jeb—"

"Trust me."

Embarrassed, she struggled out of his embrace, her voice shaking. "It's Susannah Whittaker, isn't it?"

"Hell, no."

"You think I don't see you, every time you come back from some encounter with that woman? Your heart's in a sling, cowboy." She forced a smile. "A sure sign of love, if you ask me."

"I didn't ask."

"I'm goin' to bed," she whispered.

"Come back here. I'm not finished with you yet."

Obedient, Breeze went back into his arms but refused to meet his eyes.

"We had something good once," he said, low and soft. "We still do, though it's different now. I don't want to lose that, Breeze. If we go ahead with this thing, tumble around on the sofa and the floor the rest of the night, in the morning we're both goin' to hate ourselves, maybe hate each other a little too—and right now, no matter how I feel about Susannah Whittaker or don't feel, I pretty much despise myself anyway."

"You'll forget New York and that humiliation with the police. I'll forget the Nashville troopers breakin' into my house and runnin' their hands through my lingerie drawers." She tipped her head back to smile weakly at him. "And I'll forget Mack Norton too."

"He's goin' to be touring with us next month."

"I'll forget him. Compartmentalize him at least."

Jeb laughed. "I bet you will. I almost pity Mack."

"Peggy had better have enough horse liniment around to soothe his ego, if not his skin. I plan to take a few stripes off him just for fun."

Jeb hugged her, and they talked close together on the sofa in the darkness, as they'd done so many nights together, first as lovers and then as friends. They spoke in near whispers about Mack, then about Clary. They remembered Breeze's band, and Jeb's wife Rachel, his so briefly newborn son. But he cut himself short before mentioning Susannah Whittaker again. At last he kissed Breeze, sweetly, tucked her into the crook of his shoulder lying on the sofa cushions and said, "Sleep."

"You too."

"I'm half there already," and in the next moment she heard his breathing slow.

Exhausted, he slept deeply, but Breeze lay awake, stroking his hair until the darkness outside began to lighten and the birds began to sing. She had a feeling it was her last night with Jeb, however platonic, and just as she planned to make him the biggest star country music had ever seen, Breeze meant to make it last.

At times like this, it seemed almost worth never singing again herself.

17

Susannah, who didn't usually consider herself to be a slow study, finally realized that Jeb would not return her calls. In the past two weeks, since his questioning by Manhattan police, she'd left messages with his record producer in Tennessee, with his fan club based in Nashville, with Breeze Maynard's management company there. All addresses and phone numbers plainly printed in the liner notes for his first album. But reaching Jeb proved a different matter.

At first she thought he'd gotten the messages but, after their last encounter at the opening of Cody House, Jeb had decided to ignore them. And her.

Breeze Maynard's press conference on Jeb's behalf should have tipped her off: the taut, professional manner softened only by Breeze's voluptuous figure in garnet satin and her long blond hair, swinging free every time she moved to make a point. Her careful phrasing and, during the questioning session after her formal statement, Breeze's protective stance, her defending words.

With the continuing hostile reports in the papers, on television and radio, Susannah supposed Breeze had simply deepened the moat around Jeb's castle—wherever that might be. Certainly on a personal level she'd be in no hurry to relay Susannah's messages to him.

She reread the latest article in the San Francisco evening paper, then tossed it onto the sofa beside her. Leslie had already taken to her bed, pleading a headache, which Susannah suspected might be genuine enough, but the result of an afternoon bout with a bottle rather than the gym workout she'd probably invented. Leslie hadn't shown up to help at the shelter in days, despite Susannah's constant urging.

She needed help. One resident counselor and a pregnant founder weren't enough. With the shelter's bedrooms filled and applications still coming in, Susannah rarely had the chance even to sit down.

Now, she regretted not accepting Michael's invitation to have a casual late dinner. "I'm worried about you," he'd said, stopping by the shelter late that afternoon. "All work and no play. Take the night off, won't you?"

"I can't." She needed to watch Leslie.

Michael had left the date open. "Call me if you change your mind."

Susannah picked up the phone. In the past months she'd developed a new respect for Michael, who remained a staunch friend, and whose hurt over their broken romance—such as it had been—seemed to be healing. In deference to her own hurt, he'd even stopped goading her about Jeb. And Michael was the only person in her life who understood about Leslie.

Yet she didn't dial Michael's number.

Punching in the long distance digits for the office number she'd gotten from Elvira information, she waited for what seemed an interminable time, once she'd made up her mind not to let Breeze Maynard keep the upper hand. She should have thought weeks ago of calling John Eustace, who entered her mind often. If anyone could get through to Jeb, his grandfather could.

His gruff voice, sounding full of gravel, made her smile for the first time in days.

"I suppose you're callin' about my grandson."

"I was thinking of you too," Susannah said, smiling at his bluntness and trying to cover her own transparency. "Wondering how you've been."

"Creaky and cranky as an old wagon wheel." He paused. "I haven't heard from him all summer, if you're wondering."

Surprised, she felt her smile fade. "I imagined by now you and Jeb would have had at least one more of your visits together."

"He's off the road. Never considered comin' home. Prob'ly staying in Nashville with Breeze Maynard, who guards him like a brace of bloodhounds sniffin' out danger."

"Would you happen to have her home number?"

"Won't do you any good."

Susannah didn't have to ask why. She could hear the echo of her own frustration in his tone.

"That woman won't let his own grandfather through since that mess in New York. I don't blame her," he added, sounding sad. "Jeb's in a peck of trouble and anything she can do to simplify things is all right with me."

"But you'd be such a comfort to him."

"Jeb and I are not seein' eye to eye on certain matters at the moment, and I'm sure she thinks I'd only send his blood pressure sky high. So she takes my messages but never delivers them, I'm sure. Not the first time it's happened," he said, "so I know it won't be the last. Breeze operates on the principle that the less I know, the better. And it's true, the press sometimes comes snoopin' around Elvira hoping for information I don't have—thanks to her vigilance." He paused again, then said, "Leave it to Clary to turn everybody's lives upside down and inside out. His most of all."

The mention of Clary's death, in a way that condemned her, made Susannah stiffen. Knowing his view of his granddaughter and remembering their quarrel, she wouldn't be drawn into a defense of Clary again, particularly after finding her journal and getting Jeb's side of things.

"I'm sorry to hear about your problems with him," she said.

"And what about your own, Miss Susannah?"

"Well, I . . . Things haven't turned out well." She didn't know what else to say.

"Last time we talked he said the problem was basic."

Susannah covered her abdomen with a protective hand, agreeing with Jeb. "I suppose it couldn't get much more basic."

"With the problem identified, you're both halfway in the right direction to getting it resolved." He waited but she said nothing. "I'll give you Breeze Maynard's unlisted number and wish you well. I enjoyed our time together in San Francisco, and I stand by everything I said then with the hope you don't hold that against me." When Susannah assured him she didn't, he said, "My grandson has his pride, you know. And the word 'basic' stuck in his throat like a broken chicken bone. If you want my opinion, you'll be hearin' from him when Jeb stops nursin' his wounds over Clary and the police.

When he gets back on the road and starts doin' what makes him feel good again."

"You think I shouldn't call, then?"

"That's purely up to you, Miss Susannah." His voice roughened again, and she could hear the love he tried, as Jeb sometimes did, to hide. "But I will tell you this: my grandson does whatever he thinks necessary for the people he loves—just not for himself very well. You think about that a while, you hear?"

Jeb heard the phone ring, an irritating alarm that he did his best to ignore. These days the telephone meant trouble more often than not, so he scrawled another few notes on the staff paper in front of him and went back to his songwriting. Or what passed for it. He hadn't finished a piece since the words for "Little Rich Girl" and had begun to fear he never would.

The doubt made panic streak through him, and he threw his pencil at the music room wall in frustration. Outside another Nashville late summer afternoon had already hit record temperatures, and Breeze's central air-conditioning worked overtime. Still, Jeb sat spraddle legged in jeans at the music stand, only his chest bare and his feet, which he hooked over the high stool's chrome footrail.

"Lord in heaven, why don't you strip and get into the pool?" Breeze dashed into the room, looking cool as an ice-cream cone in a pink, green, and white–striped swimsuit. "If I were a man and had legs like yours, I wouldn't cover them up in that hot denim."

Jeb concentrated on his guitar strings. He didn't want to leave the house, hadn't left the grounds in a week. "You have great legs."

"Thank you kindly." She pushed the guitar off his thigh and set it on a vacant stool. "That was Jericho on the phone. Specifically, your new producer." The first one had quit after Jeb's most recent questioning by the New York police. "I've just called the office to start polling the radio stations for airtime, on his advice. The booking agents too, the tour promoters. We're all in agreement." She held his gaze. "It's time, Jeb. You know it is."

"Thank y'all for consulting me," he said. "I'm just the boss."

"You and I talked about this already. Releasing the single gets us a jump on the album and some good publicity." It was standard practice, a teaser for the album to follow. "You should hit the charts even sooner than last time."

"Might."

She planted both hands on her bare hips. "You said yourself the flare-up over Clary provided free publicity."

"More than I bargained for." He'd stopped reading the papers, hadn't turned on the television in days. "Christ, Maynard. Suppose the single does well right off? The phones will be ringin' here every minute until we take off on tour. I have a semi permanent headache right now and we still have the show to smoothe out, the placement of 'Deep River' in the lineup to decide."

"Stop walkin' around it, Jeb. You just don't want Susannah Whittaker to hear 'Little Rich Girl.' Which you might have considered when you wrote the lyrics."

"She probably already heard it." That night at the shelter, he thought. "But I'd rather we released another cut, yes."

"This one gets the album's title out there. Your choice. The ballad's emotional, sympathetic. Advance ticket sales for the tour are down. Need I tell you, you could use a little sympathy from the public just now?"

Jostling Breeze a little, Jeb pushed past her to the music room's French doors looking onto the lawn. He stared out the glass at the corner of the swimming pool just visible, at the deep woods that ringed the property and sheltered him from prying eyes, from the notoriety that was turning his fiery, newfound fame into ashes.

"I'll have their support, as soon as I'm onstage again." His stomach clenched tight. "I'll put on such a show they'll have to love me."

Breeze made a sound of exasperation. Turning on her heel, she left the room and he could hear her bare feet slapping along the Mexican-tiled hallway. Jeb was at the door ready to close it so he could try to work again when she slammed back in, carrying a large canvas sack.

She dumped its contents on the floor.

"Hate mail. And there's another just like this that I couldn't carry. This morning's delivery. I have two temporary secretaries in my office here and another two at the one in town, just sorting through the usual dirt for any real threats that the police need to know about— threats against your life, Jeb—so you tell me again you don't need a miracle of good press as soon as you can get it. And some damn tight security when we kick off this tour."

"All hate mail?"

"Three-to-one on the good days. After my press conference in New York, for instance. And when the police released you to come home. Other than that, mostly vicious and quite inventive."

Jeb sank onto the stool, running both hands through his hair.

"I never hurt Clary," he said, remembering Susannah's

accusations too. "Never touched a hair on her head, a square inch of her skin, except with love." The right kind, he thought. The purest kind. "I sure didn't kill her. But my God, who did?"

Breeze stepped over the scattered envelopes. She pulled his head to hers, touching foreheads.

"I don't know. Let's just hope the police find him soon."

He hadn't cared at first. Even the thought of knowing the truth, putting a name and face to it, had seemed too painful, like remembering Rachel and the baby. Like going back to Elvira. Susannah had changed that, pulled him out of himself.

"Don't give up now," Breeze said.

"You're a fine one to be telling me not to quit."

She pulled back, frowning. "Are you tryin' to feel better by hurting me?"

"I'm trying to make you see that if you'd stayed where you belonged, you might have worked through what happened to the band and come out all right yourself. On top of the heap, still up there with Reba McEntire, Emmylou Harris and, now, Trisha Yearwood and Kathy Mattea. Maybe you should start thinking about that, stop worrying about me so much."

"I think you're tryin' to hurt me."

"Breeze . . ." She was halfway down the hall before he slipped off the stool. "Breeze, dammit, wait."

"You just do your job, cowboy, and I'll do mine. 'Little Rich Girl' gets released tomorrow."

Susannah had heard the song before, that night at Cody House while the rest of the party went on below and Jeb's voice floated to her up the stairs where she sat crying, regretting her lack of faith in him, on Miranda's bed.

She stood in the room's doorway now, listening to the soft strains of "Little Rich Girl," which had been playing on every radio station for days. Earlier the disc jockey had given it number seven on the country music charts, and climbing, though not as quickly as expected. The mellifluous voice droned on, sounding almost gleeful about Jeb's problems with the press and his fans and of course the police, and Susannah had stopped listening.

"That's Misser Cody's song," Miranda said, glancing up from the Barbie doll on her lap. Around her lay a collection of doll clothes and as Susannah watched, she selected a red print miniskirt and yellow halter top. Miranda pushed one black pump, one blue one onto the doll's feet, her tongue clamped between her teeth.

"Yes," Susannah finally said, "it is."

She went downstairs to monitor a noisy game of Monopoly among the school-age children who had just started classes that week and were munching on the freshly baked chocolate chip cookies Lisa, Susannah's resident counselor, provided. Downstairs too the radio played Jeb's song—her song.

Susannah drifted into the kitchen, snatched a couple of cookies for herself with a big glass of milk for the baby, then peered out the dining room window once more for Leslie. Her mother had promised to take the younger children to a nearby playground before dinner.

"Want me to go?" Lisa came into the room and immediately noticed Susannah's frown. "You're going to develop lines and scare that brand-new baby as soon as it pops into the world."

She managed a laugh. "You're right. Yes, I'd love it if you'd take the kids to the park for an hour or so. But Miranda's happy enough on her bed with the doll your sister's children handed down. Thanks, Lisa. It's good to see her smile."

"Her mother had a secretary interview this afternoon. I hope it went well."

"So do I."

While the kids were gone, Susannah tended the cooking pots in the kitchen where Lisa had started beef stew and left fresh bread dough to rise. When her stomach growled, she decided to stay for dinner. The house had become so cozy, and the boisterous company might keep her mind off Leslie. And Jeb.

Even Breeze's home phone number had produced nothing, as John Eustace predicted. She'd already left enough messages to paper the shelter's dining room wall and had even sent one letter, mainly an apology for the last time she'd seen him.

After dinner, Susannah lingered. She talked with Lisa in the kitchen while they helped the mothers clean up. Then she sat in on a Ouija board game, observing only because she'd always been half-afraid of the occult on the theory that she was better off not knowing the future. Finally, still unwilling to go home and find Leslie lying on her bed or the sofa, fully clothed and reeking of drink, she went upstairs for the nightly tucking-in rituals for the youngest children.

"Now I lay me down to sleep . . ."

"Can I have another drink, Mama?"

"I have to go to the bathroom."

"When can Daddy come live with us again?"

In the doorway of Miranda's room, Susannah paused at the last question. The other children's voices, so predictable in their last-minute requests before sleep, struck her as both comforting and as good practice for her own forthcoming motherhood. She pressed a hand to her stomach, feeling the baby kick lightly against her palm. "Night owl," she murmured, hoping her unborn son or daughter heard the nighttime rituals and would become drowsy too.

But Miranda's question made her smile slip.

In Susannah's explorations of the social welfare system, in her visits to other shelters, she had learned how devastatingly divisive the need for help could prove. With Miranda's father in the picture, the family wouldn't qualify for dependent aid, at least not to the extent they were able to get it now, and according to her own shelter rules, they wouldn't be allowed to live at Cody House.

She'd meant the rule for safety as much as anything else; to ensure that she helped those people who seemed most helpless, homeless mothers and their children. But perhaps she'd been hasty as well as inexperienced.

"Daddy's still looking for work." Miranda's mother smoothed back the hair from her daughter's face. "He's still in Illinois. He'll come as soon as he can."

"Then we'll have a house again?"

"I hope so."

"I like it here," Miranda said.

"I know, sweetheart. But we can't stay forever."

Cheryl sat down on the bed, gathering Miranda close for a kiss, and Susannah remembered the first times she'd seen the woman, brittle and wary, pale and thin. After a month of good food and ample rest, Miranda's mother looked almost pretty.

"Read me a story, Mommy?"

Susannah meant to walk away. She needed to check on Leslie but would resist the urge to phone Jeb again, to leave another message. She'd left too many of them over the years on Drake's answering machine at work, with his service, and in more recent years, had called his beeper number more times than she cared to admit, rarely getting an answer. But in the hallway now she froze as Miranda's mother began reading from a popular children's book. The soft tones, the repetitious phrasing of the story that never failed to delight a child Miranda's age, drew Susannah back herself.

Cheryl saw her.

"I hope you don't mind," Susannah said. "I've always loved that story."

She smiled. "Me too. Come in. Sit down."

Hesitating, Susannah succumbed to Miranda's pleas that she "sit by me, on my other side not by Mommy. Studley too," she said.

"Studley's asleep by the fire downstairs."

"Then you sit." Miranda patted her blankets.

The story went on, about a small black kitten who never used his basket but kept exploring, poking, climbing into everything but that—and always getting lost. Then found again. Miranda clapped her hands each time the kitten came back home.

By the story's end, she seemed ready for sleep, but Susannah felt once more on the verge of tears. She'd cried in this room before, cried as she hadn't done in years, except when Clary died. Now she blinked and straightened, sending Cheryl a smile of thanks.

"I enjoyed that."

"I'm glad you joined us," she said, then leaned down to kiss Miranda good night. The little girl's arms held tight before she let go and looked up at Susannah. When Miranda's mother nodded, Susannah bent, with some difficulty over the bulge of her stomach, and kissed Miranda gently.

"Sweet dreams," she said.

Miranda gazed at her. "Are you going to read to your baby too?"

"Every chance I get."

Susannah went swiftly down the stairs, retrieved her light wool blazer from the coatrack in the front hall, and after quick good-nights to Lisa and the teenagers in the living room, slipped outside. Blindly, she walked to her car and poked at the lock with her key until she swore. Leslie had never read to her as a child, had rarely tucked her into bed. By nighttime she'd often been too far gone in misery for kisses and last-minute requests and rituals, except her own. No telling what she'd find at home tonight—how many years later?

As she pulled away from the curb, Jeb's song was playing on a stereo somewhere in the house again. He'd become a favorite, especially since his appearance at the shelter's opening. The ballad drifted to her through an open window, making Susannah gun the Bentley's engine. Earlier the disc jockey had informed her that Jeb would kick off his second U.S. tour the following day—Saturday of Labor Day weekend. Susannah didn't even know where he might be now.

One thing was sure: No matter what else awaited her at home, there'd be no message from him.

On the same Friday afternoon before his new tour—Jeb Stuart Cody: Country Roads—began, Jeb dogged Breeze's footsteps toward her first-floor office and into it, wincing at the brighter light and the heat from a bank of computers that the air-conditioning couldn't keep up with, flinching at the sight of the cabbage rose chintz upholstery and draperies, the pale pink walls, in which Breeze had decorated the large room. She kept her back to him, as if to pretend he wasn't there. But he'd been thinking about what she said a few days ago and had made up his mind.

He glanced at the temps who swiveled around from their computer keyboards. "Mornin', ladies." Returning their quick smiles, which had lately been missing from his life, he turned Breeze toward him. "Part of my job is appreciating my fans. Show me some of the mail that's come in—the good stuff. I'll sign some eight by tens while I'm here."

"You'd be better off finishin' that song before we leave."

"Just get me the mail."

Breeze looked mutinous. "If it'll spare me a lecture in front of my staff, gladly."

Jeb was two-thirds of the way through the dizzying pile of postcards, letters, manila envelopes containing handmade gifts, and phone messages—even the good stuff came in mountains—when he stopped. His gaze fixed on a stack of pink paper slips. "What the hell—?" He riffled through the messages, then looked up at Breeze and the other two women in the office. "Is this what normally happens to my telephone messages? You just throw 'em in with the mail from everywhere, or what?"

Breeze's gaze homed in on the slip in his hand.

"That sack came from the Nashville office."

"When?"

She shrugged, avoiding his gaze. "This morning, I guess. Or yesterday."

Jeb looked down at the familiar name and phone number. He slapped the message down on a desktop, then the others in rapid succession like cards dealt from a deck. "Look at the dates here, Maynard. Last week.

The week before that. How many times was she going to
have to call before you made mention of her trying to
reach me?"

"I don't personally take each call, Jeb." She turned her
back to the computers, lowering her voice in the apparent hope the others wouldn't hear, though Jeb didn't
care. "Don't stand here and humiliate me in front of the
secretaries. Those messages are not in my handwriting."

"I suppose the ones that came here to the house you
simply forgot."

"She hasn't called the house." But her cheeks colored,
and Jeb lowered his head to hers, forcing her to look at
him.

"You're lying."

She tapped the messages. "She hasn't called in days."

"And where was I when she did?"

"Working," she said. "In bed early, hiding your head
under a cabbage—how do I know? You must have been
somewhere I didn't want to disturb you."

"Like hell."

"She's no good for you, Jeb."

But Breeze was talking to thin air. He had whirled at
her first word and stalked from the office, along the hall
and upstairs to his room, to a private phone. More hate
mail or not, Susannah had called.

When Susannah reached home that Friday night, the
house was dark except for the porch light and one over
the garage. She pulled the Bentley into her space, next
to Leslie's recently leased black Lincoln Town Car,
which barely cleared the end of the small garage, and
cut the motor.

Going through the garage and up in the house's private elevator to the kitchen area, she walked along the hallway to the front entry and thumbed through her mail. Bills and circulars. Nothing from Jeb.

"Leslie?"

Unable to avoid the issue any longer, she called up the stairs.

"Mother?" she said, getting no answer.

Her palms instantly damp, Susannah hurried up the stairs. Leslie wasn't in her room or the den. She'd nearly reached the top of the flight to the third floor when Leslie came hurtling down, her arms outflung, her face streaked with tear tracks. "Susannah, I thought you'd never get home. Where were you?"

"I stayed for dinner at the shelter. I called. No one answered here."

"He is a heartless man!"

Drake, of course. Susannah opened her mouth but didn't get the chance to say anything. The sharp odor of whiskey nearly knocked her over, as Leslie flailed out in some drunken gesture of grief. Reeling back, Susannah lost her footing on the stairs, felt herself begin to fall.

Crying out, Leslie tumbled after her, grabbing for Susannah. A hand grazed Susannah's jacket sleeve, then slipped away into thin air. Susannah went sprawling, bumping her way down the rest of the flight to the second-floor landing. Her head thunked against the newel post and she groaned, instinctively wrapping both hands around her middle.

"Susie! Are you all right?"

"I—" she gasped for breath, dark stars whirling at the edges of her vision, "I'm not sure."

For some moments she lay there, struggling to breathe, praying not to feel the slow trickle of blood between her legs that would tell her she was indeed hurt, her hands.

"I didn't push you. I swear I didn't," she said with a
moan.

"I'm okay. Really I am." *Please God, let it be true.* Her
head pulsed with pain.

"I was upset with Drake. He called, incensed about
Jeb Cody's new song, and when I suggested we talk it
over in person, he began shouting at me. To leave him
alone. To stay out of his life. That he—he didn't love me
and never would."

Despite the low-down ache in her back, her belly,
Susannah struggled upright and put her arms around
her mother.

"I only had a little drink." Leslie enunciated with care.
"Just one, before he called. He said I was a drunk, a piti-
ful drunk, and no one could want me." She peered up at
Susannah. "You still want me, don't you? I only had one
drink."

Able to breathe again, Susannah held her close, at the
same time assessing her own pain. The pounding in her
head gradually eased, then she said, "Les, you had more
than that. A lot more."

Her mother shoved away from her, eyes bright. "I
said I was sorry you fell! I told you how dreadfully Drake
treated me. And you talk to me just like him," she said,
stumbling to her feet.

Susannah got up and, holding her stomach, followed
Leslie into the living room. At the bar, she turned to
face Susannah, a half-empty bottle of Tanqueray in one
hand. "After that, I deserve a little comfort. I am surrounded by insensitive people, my own family . . ."

"Don' t you see what's happening?"

Leslie didn't answer.

"You've turned Drake against you. You're turning me against you." Susannah reached for the bottle. "Where were you all afternoon? And this evening?"

"Here. Where else would I be?"

"And you couldn't answer the phone?"

"I answered when Drake called. I'm sorry I did."

"Oh, Mother."

She tugged but Leslie refused to let go of the gin bottle, and Susannah gave in. As she released it, the momentum carried Leslie back, into the small corner between the bar and the dining room arch. Rubbing her shoulder as if Susannah had done her some terrible wrong, she uncapped the bottle.

"Don't do it," Susannah said.

The liquor sloshed into a waiting glass, already full of melting ice. She hadn't been upstairs that long then. Why had she been on the third floor at all, which was Susannah's territory? Leslie lifted the glass and drank.

"You're killing our love for you," Susannah said, "but you're killing yourself too."

"I am obviously my own responsibility, then. All alone. Me, myself, and I."

She staggered toward a chair, more intoxicated than Susannah had seen her in years. Her addiction had been growing worse again, each drink leading to the next and the next until there would be no space between them. No peace.

"What were you doing in my rooms?"

"Susie, don't be paranoid." Her words slurred. "I promised Drake I'd look."

"Look for what?"

"I wasn't spying. I swear I wasn't. But he said . . ."

Her mother's head lolled against the chair back, and Susannah grasped her shoulders. "What did Drake say?"

"Said . . . Clary. Jeb Cody . . . find . . . evidence."

Her blood chilled. "What kind of evidence? What could possibly be in my house?"

"Don't know. But Drake said—"

"What, Mother? Tell me." Susannah gently shook her and Leslie's eyes opened wide, looking full of hurt and betrayal.

"He said . . . Susannah knows."

She sank back on her heels, her pain forgotten now, her disappointment in Leslie. Even the baby's welfare took second place for the instant it took to realize Jeb's dangerous position—a position she had unwittingly put him in. *I hope they run his mind in circles until he confesses that he killed my wife,* her father had said. The police hadn't found anything. But Susannah had. And from the white look on her face in Clary's office that day, Drake would have sensed it too.

He might not know what she'd found—not yet.

But the damning inference that could destroy Jeb's career with scandal, and make him look worse to the police, sat in Drake's attic. Even by innuendo it would be enough for any reporter, any fan. Perhaps, at this very moment, Drake was up there in the attic's cavernous space, under the bare light bulb, but not as she'd imagined him, holding Clary's wedding gown.

The journal.

She had to get to the journal, to Drake . . . before he released it to the world.

18

Susannah's flight from San Francisco didn't leave until noon the next day, and by the time she stopped her rental car, leased at JFK, in Drake's driveway, the dashboard clock read well after ten P.M. Even that late, the Labor Day weekend traffic from the airport had definitely taken its toll. Her body felt stiff and achy too from her fall down the stairs the day before. As soon as she stepped from the gunmetal gray sedan, avoiding a quick glance at the attic windows of the house, she could feel her knees buckle.

Stiffening her legs and squaring her shoulders, Susannah left her beige raw silk jacket in the car and marched into the house. She hadn't brought any luggage, only the olive green, figure-skimming dress she wore and a small carry-on bag with a nightshirt, fresh lingerie, and a toothbrush. She didn't plan to stay long—not at all if things went badly with her father.

She found the foyer, the living room, Drake's den on

the first floor, empty, but the four-car garage to the left of the house had been closed, a sure sign that she'd find him home.

Going up to his room, Susannah prayed he'd be there, in bed, fast asleep and dreaming with a smile on his face. She should have known better. Once Drake suspected Susannah of knowing about Jeb, he would not only have set Leslie to searching for evidence, he would have gone hunting himself. And just as he sought every last mutinous cell of a patient's tumor during surgery, he wouldn't rest until he found the journal.

Panting lightly as she climbed the stairs to the third-floor attic, she felt the baby roll over inside her, disturbed by her efforts and her mounting anxiety.

"Drake?"

The attic door stood open, but the single bare light bulb she'd imagined had been augmented by two large table lamps set upon packing crates. Clary's things, Susannah thought, her heart sinking. Drake didn't hear her come in but kept rummaging through a carton, flinging papers, books, pens and pencils aside.

She crossed her fingers behind her back, that he hadn't found the journal yet.

From the looks of the attic, now strewn with opened boxes, he had been at his search for some time, perhaps since he'd talked with Leslie the night before.

"Drake," she said again and his head came up, glinting silver in the light, his eyes hard as frost. He didn't seem surprised to see her.

"Why don't you make it easy for me? Point out the right box and save the trouble of sealing everything up again."

"I don't know what you're talking about."

The bluff didn't work. "Come now. You're as white as

you looked the last time I saw you among her things. It
wasn't because you worked too hard, was it?" His gaze
fixed on her abdomen, which suddenly seemed too
prominent to Susannah, like a red flag in front of a bull.
"Didn't you think, Susie, about the consequences of toy-
ing with a man like Cody before you went to bed with
him?" He flung aside a sheaf of magazines. "Every time
I remember losing Clary, I think of him."

"Jeb's been having a hard time too since Clary died.
You know that. Hurting him won't bring her back."

"I don't want to hurt him. I want to destroy him." He
glanced up again. "And I know how. After ten years of
playing every low-down dive and honky-tonk in the
south, waiting for his big break, how much do you think
success means to him?" He paused. "If he hadn't
screwed Breeze Maynard when she hit the skids, he'd
never have gotten anywhere. So what does a low-class
slime like him do when he starts eating three meals a
day and sleeping in a real bed? When women—including my own daughter—begin throwing themselves at
him like promotion giveaways at a shopping mall?"

"Please," she said, putting a protective hand to her
stomach, "stop. I never dreamed you were so bitter."

"Bitter? I lost my wife. My daughter can no longer
appear in polite society without people whispering
behind their hands. . . . If they knew who had fathered
that child—"

Did he care for her, then? If he did, maybe she could
change his mind.

"What will you do, Drake? Tell them? No one thinks
that much these days of a single mother. That's common
enough, even accepted." She shook her head. "You can
search this whole attic, but if you find something else
you consider to be incriminating, what will you do?" She

walked toward him, her gaze lowered not to look at the carton in the farthest corner. "Give it to the press? The police? How would that help Clary? Or me?"

"It would help to have Clary's killer behind bars."

"Jeb didn't kill her," Susannah murmured, defending him though weeks ago she hadn't been as sure. "He couldn't kill anyone."

Shoving one carton away, he pulled another close. Trembling, Susannah watched him sorting, sifting, with each movement coming nearer to that one box.

"Whatever you think you'll find here, I'm sure Clary never meant for anyone else to see. If you really care what other people think . . ."

But did he? She glanced away. Drake had divorced Leslie after two decades of marriage, had then married a girl twenty-seven years his junior. Her mother's money was old money, blue-blood money, but Drake's was new. As a self-made man, he could easily turn his back on society, and with his professional reputation people would still flock to him. He obviously didn't care enough about appearances that she could change his mind about a scandal.

Shifting her gaze, Susannah found her father studying her in the attic's garish light. He spun around, looking toward the darkened corner where she'd put Clary's box. Too late, she realized she'd been unconsciously staring at it.

"No," she said, but he had already taken two steps.

Climbing over boxes and around wardrobes, he tore open one carton, then another while Susannah stood frozen, knowing she'd given herself away. He opened one journal, reading for a moment before he shut it, steadily plowing through the rest of the stack she'd carefully made, with that one plain journal from Clary's adolescence on the bottom. Away, she'd hoped, from curious eyes. She thought Jeb was wrong, that Clary hadn't meant for anyone to ever read it. Including Drake.

"Good Lord in heaven." He looked shocked and white, as horrified as Susannah had been, then he scanned the page again. Angry with Jeb that day, she'd even bent the corner over, making it easy to find. "My God, Susannah. You read this?"

"Yes, but Jeb told me—"

"You mean to say he knows she wrote this?" Closing the book, he held it tight against his chest. "That's the last bit of evidence I need, in my own mind."

"Drake, it's someone else." Quickly, she tried to tell him about the sheriff's deputy who had abused Clary, but she could almost see Drake shutting his ears. "Don't you see? She must have been afraid of Richard Sheridan. She never even used his name."

He pulled away, heading for the stairs. "She was afraid, all right. But not of some small-town sheriff. How long do you think it'll take those Manhattan detectives to put two and two together? To realize that she kept silent all these years in fear of her own brother? When Clary found the courage to write that book about him—"

He whirled around, nearly colliding with her, bringing the sharp memory of her fall the day before. His icy blue gaze burned, full of rage and determination.

"Please don't do this," she said, "not to Clary—"

"She was his victim, for Christ's sake."

"—and not to me."

He had already weighed tarnishing Clary's memory against his own need to avenge her death on Jeb. He didn't care about high-society's opinion as Leslie would. Susannah had no more weapons, except his tenuous love for her. She'd never tested it before.

"Jeb Cody's the finest man I ever knew," she said. "If you take that journal to the police and to the press, I'll go to him—whether he wants me or not. I'll stand by him." She pushed past Drake, her fingers itching to grab the journal from his hands, to run with it. "You'll never see or hear from me again."

"You actually love him?" he said hoarsely. "Susannah!"

Stumbling once on the stairs, she scrambled down the flight and then hurried to her room. She didn't turn on the light, didn't want to see its Louis XIV elegance, the ivory and gilt-edged furniture, the canopy bed, the silk-papered walls. She'd memorized this room long ago, in the darkness on too many nights, alone. Tonight, she wouldn't stay. Retrieving her carry-on bag, Susannah went down to the first floor and out the door to her rental car.

"Or would I even be a sacrifice for you?" she whispered.

Breeze promised to keep her mouth shut when Jeb opened his new tour in Atlanta on the Saturday before Labor Day, on a late summer evening when the Georgia temperature seemed to approach the boiling point. With the release of "Little Rich Girl" before his second album, he and the band had ridden the New York publicity blitz to number seven—respectable, and gaining momentum—on the country music charts, and Jeb's spirits lifted. He had to give Breeze that much, he'd said.

"We're all right," he kept telling her and the others from the minute they boarded his new navy-and-silver tour bus outside Breeze's Nashville headquarters, reporters' flash units blinking on every side, until they completed the sound check in Atlanta's coliseum before the first show of a three-day series.

Ticket sales remained lower than she would have liked. There would be no sold out performances.

Despite her efforts to hype his image, Jeb's general press continued to fluctuate between hostile and supportive, but he had read enough of his good mail to discount the rest, so he said, as nerves on her part.

Backstage, wearing red, white, and blue satin trimmed in silver fringe, she counted off the minutes until the opening act's final chords vibrated through the huge amphitheater before Jeb's band struck up the first notes of "Lou'siana Lady," a sure crowd pleaser—though she'd wanted him to use one of the new numbers. He said it was his lucky song, but Breeze's heart rose in her throat.

"We're on," Mack said behind her.

Breeze didn't look at him. "I'm not worried."

"'Course you aren't. Neither was Jeb when I left him hangin' over the john."

She spun around. "Is he sick?"

"Not now," Mack said with a grin, then herded the others with a rebel yell onto the stage, exchanging high-fives with the opening act as they passed coming offstage.

Applause deafened her, one of Breeze's favorite sensory experiences. In spite of her fears, she couldn't help grinning when she turned to find Jeb standing there, looking pale green.

Breeze ran her gaze over him, from broad shoulders in a custom-sewn white shirt with the sleeves rolled back, to snug black pants and shiny black boots. He liked the fashion statement, he said; when he worked hard, the sweat didn't show under his arms. She slapped the black Stetson on his head. "There you go, Wall Street." She sent him out onstage at the dimming of the lights. The crowd screamed, and in the same instant the band whammed into "Lady" like a desperate man into a ten-dollar prostitute.

Jeb sailed through the first set, looking relaxed and confident, even as he sang "What'll I Do When He Takes You Back?" from the new album.

He wailed on the next intro, with some tricky guitar work on a beautiful cherrywood twelve-string borrowed from Mack. Then Breeze blinked at the tender lyric to "Surprise Me," the album's fifth cut.

"We've got 'em now," he said, coming offstage after "Do You Love Me?" had brought the house down, his face dripping wet and his hair curling around his collar. "What'd I tell you?"

Then, at the end of the second set, things fell apart, right after Jeb sang "Little Rich Girl." Breeze wondered whether it reminded people of the Whittakers, all the press coverage with Susannah, and that Clary's death still went unsolved. That, as some thought, Jeb held the answer. Whatever had happened, someone shouted a request for "Kid Sister," which Jeb had informed her he would not sing on the tour.

Mack called out, asking for a different request. But when he signaled the band to swing into "The Last Time I Called You," the music died away after the first two bars.

"What's the matter with 'Kid Sister'? You scared to sing it?"

"Let him be!" someone yelled.

"You a coward, Cody?"

Jeb held up a hand for silence, stepping forward to the very edge of the stage.

"I've decided not to include that number in my tour this year, not because I'm afraid people will think I'm hidin' something." He gripped the microphone with white fingers. "I have nothing to hide. We had our problems, but I loved my sister, loved her more deeply than I can say. As y'all know I wrote 'Kid Sister' for her—and to sing it right now just makes me sad." He stepped back. "My apologies. I hope you understand."

"Sing it, damn you!"

Jeb looked around, his gaze finding Breeze in the wings.

"Sing it," she mouthed, echoing the crowd. He'd had them in the palm of his hand. If he walked off now, as he appeared about to do, the tour would be in trouble before they finished the first night. The papers tomorrow would scream accusations or, at the least, whine that Jeb Stuart Cody was headed back for the oblivion from which he'd come.

Jeb started walking and the boos began.

She and Mack exchanged frantic looks.

At his nod, her mouth went dry, but she took one step, then another, until she reached the curtain and pushed past the obstruction of herself, out onto the stage in front of the huge backdrop—this season, banks of enormous monitors that played Jeb's performance image as it happened. Another two steps and she was striding, her patriotic satin skirt swinging, her silver bootheels stamping out her determination to save him.

Head down, Jeb passed her as Mack's voice blared over the microphone. "Breeze Maynard, ladies and gentlemen!"

Chills ran down her spine.

Her pulse raced double time.

The wooden stage under her feet. The hard lights. The darkness beyond. The rustling and shifting of bodies, the smells of perspiration and excitement, of popcorn and hot dogs, of mustard and cotton candy. The first smattering of applause besides that of the band, the growing thunder of it. It was like a carnival, a three-ring circus, and standing at the mike once more, Breeze became its center.

When she opened her mouth and began to sing, the world went right again, as if for too many years it had been spinning off its axis. The first notes sounded rusty, like an old pump handle bringing up a seep of water from some old well, but then she felt her vocal chords relax, her body loosen, and heard the true, sweet melody, the poignant words of "Kid Sister" coming from her own throat.

Oh, Jeb. Forgive me.

She finished to a standing ovation, to the roar of approval that had so long been missing from her life, her soul. Blinking, she bowed from the waist, the long spill of her blond hair touching the floor, then whipping back again when she straightened, a silken flood along her spine.

Taking her bows and gesturing for the band to take another, she hoped Jeb would appear, but he didn't. The generous applause died down, and people began filing from their seats, up the aisles toward the coliseum exits.

The other band members congratulated her, and Mack paused to give her a quick hug.

"You haven't lost it," he said, his voice husky.

"I was only helping Jeb." She looked around for him.

"Sure."

Mack hurried off to join the others, Skeet and Terry, Cameron and Bull, who headed for the dressing rooms and cold beers without their usual joking and laughter. The nearer she came to backstage, the more her steps slowed. The area, which usually teemed with technicians

and theater management, with journalists and hangers-
on, seemed strangely quiet, oddly empty, until she took a
few more halting steps.

Seeing Jeb, Breeze stopped. He had made it as far as
the wings and stood facing the wall, leaning into it, his
head pressed to the sterile gray concrete, his arms
crossed over the back of his head as if to shield himself,
his body shaking. Her throat tight and hurting, Breeze
took a single step, but he must have heard her.

"Go away. I don't want you to see me."

Like an ostrich poking its head in the sand, he must
have hoped the others would ignore him. But not her.
Never her.

"No, Jeb."

On an anguished sound, he turned, coming away from
the wall, and into her outstretched arms. "I loved her. I
loved her so much . . . but Jesus, not the wrong way."

Breeze didn't know what he meant, but she didn't
have to. She drew his head onto her shoulder, pulled his
arms around her waist. He clutched her tight. "Let it all
out, baby," she said.

She could barely understand him through the racking
sobs. "I can't do it anymore, Maynard. You heard 'em
tonight. Until they find who killed her, they'll never
believe me." He shuddered. "When we were kids and
Daddy used to take a belt to me or a block of wood,
Clary would hold me just like this and say, 'He don't
mean it, Jeb,' even when she knew he damn well did.
But she always made it better . . . just like I did for her
until. . . ."

"I know."

"After Rachel died, then Clary . . . When I met Susannah, I hoped . . ."

"It'll be all right," she promised and hugged him, as

fierce as an old teddy bear, letting him cry for the first time since Clary lost her life, and he'd shut away his grief in some mental mausoleum.

After long moments, Jeb seemed to come back to himself. He straightened in her arms, not looking at her. "In a second, I'm gonna be hiccupin' like some five-year-old with hysterics."

"Feel free."

Raising his head, he looked at her until Breeze said, "What?"

"If I can't meet your eyes tomorrow mornin', will you still respect me?"

"Always." She wiped a hand across his wet cheeks. "It's hard not to respect a man I love with every breath I take."

"Somebody already wrote that song." He gave her a shaky smile. "You know, Maynard, you were damn good out there tonight. 'An admirable musician,'" he murmured. "'O, she will sing the savageness out of a bear.' *Othello*," he said, and then, "Thanks for savin' my ass again."

"Anytime." She wound one arm around his waist, fitting her body and her steps with his as they walked along the empty hall toward his dressing room. "Though I do believe you nearly did that on purpose, cowboy."

Having missed the last flight west, Susannah spent a miserable, sleepless night in a motel near the airport. Before dawn at the terminal, she jockeyed for a seat on the first flight out. It was booked, but she poked her Whittaker hauteur right in the reservations clerk's face and, after one significant glance down at her own swollen belly, obtained a first-class window seat on the 8:00 A.M. flight to San Francisco.

Susannah didn't know where else to go. Or how to warn Jeb about Drake.

She and Jeb hadn't spoken since the shelter's opening, and she didn't know where he was; whether he'd welcome her hunting him down.

She would deal with Leslie as she could, then wait out Drake's need for revenge on Jeb for Clary's death. When weighed against his paternal love for her, would he decide in favor of the living? Choose Susannah over a memory? His track record throughout her childhood and into her thirties didn't give her much hope.

But until he either released Clary's journal to the press, or enough time passed in silence for her to guess that he wouldn't, she simply had to wait. She didn't know what else to do.

Susannah found her front door unlocked, and her pulse sped. Leslie was usually so security-conscious.

"Les?" she called out.

To her surprise Michael appeared from the living room, a cup of coffee in hand, his hair rumpled. "Welcome home. Your mother had a bad night." He ran a hand over his unshaven jaw, which lent him a rougher, more masculine look that reminded her of Jeb. "She called me around midnight, distraught over some quarrel you two had, but by then she was pretty far gone and I couldn't understand much of what she said. Something about Drake and Clary, his looking for something . . ."

"She'd probably been drinking all day again." Susannah started up the stairs. "I'll straighten things out."

"She's out cold, Suse."

She found Leslie curled into a tight ball on her bed, her clothes askew, one hand pressed like a flower in a book between her cheek and the pillow. Like cheap cologne, the aroma of stale liquor drenched the room.

Susannah touched her mother's matted, beige-blond hair. "It's me, Leslie. I've seen Drake, and with luck everything will turn out right." Leslie opened one bleary eye and she added, "I shouldn't have said what I did. I love you. No matter what."

Leslie rolled onto her back. "Jeb Cody called."

Susannah's heart instantly raced. "Did he leave a number?"

Leslie muttered, "Called more than once. Not the first time, but then . . . Prob'ly he did, but no paper . . . I said remember." She stared up at Susannah. "Sorry . . . Can't now."

"Are you certain it was Jeb?"

Leslie's jaw cracked in a yawn. "Speaking or singing . . . no mistaking that voice."

"Mother, I'm not angry—not now—but this has gone far enough. You need help."

Leslie turned onto her stomach, burying her face in the pillow. "Michael will take care of me."

Susannah watched her fall asleep, then headed downstairs, feeling both despair—for her mother—and hope, because Jeb had called. Halfway through the living room dread stopped her cold. What if he'd called, not in answer to her messages or to make amends, but to tell her that Drake had contacted him?

Michael handed her a steaming cup of coffee. "She'll be okay, Suse. She's never handled tension well."

"Leslie doesn't handle life well," she said, not wanting to mention Jeb.

He put an arm around her shoulders. "You can't make her accept help, you know."

She leaned against him, grateful for his strength.

"A few years ago I watched her bottom out. I took her to that dry-out spa myself. I had such hopes that she'd turn herself around." She paused. "But she didn't. She's always had a bottle somewhere and I knew it. Even in this house."

"Perhaps especially in this house."

Susannah drew back. "What are you saying?"

"That you expect her to fall from grace. So she does."

She pulled away, going to the window and staring out, sipping now and then at her coffee, which burned her tongue.

"You're a fine one to talk. She called you last night and you came. And here you still are, brewing coffee and making her excuses."

"Not exactly," he said, then crossed the room to her. "I came because I'm her friend as well as yours." Taking her coffee cup, he set it on a table. "Susie, alcoholism's a tough addiction to crack. You're no different from any other family in that regard. You and Drake both cover up for her, set your sights too low—and help ensure the addiction."

Susannah covered her face. "I know what I should do. But the hardest thing is to give her some space, a little time. Let her realize the problem and its solution for herself. Let her risk losing the people she loves. I tried to tell her that. To let her be frightened, and alone." She waved a hand toward the stairs. "Look what happened."

"I know. But what's the choice?" He took her hands down. "She's leaned on your father, but especially on you. She'll lean on me if I let her. Let's take a page from Drake's book—make her take responsibility for herself, Suse. Force her to become the grown-up she should be, and stop picking up her toys."

Michael had included himself, she suspected, mainly to spare her feelings. Easing away, she went to the telephone on the dining room sideboard. He was right.

She'd guarded her own heart too well, had sheltered Leslie's drinking and Drake's egotism, telling herself they were the only parents she had and to make the best of it.

She'd give Leslie that space now, and she wouldn't wait to learn whether Drake loved her. There were two people who would know Jeb's tour itinerary: Breeze Maynard and John Eustace. Without hesitation, she dialed the old man's Kentucky number.

"I s'pose you've seen the television news," he said when she identified herself.

Susannah hadn't, and her stomach tightened. When she learned that Jeb had walked offstage last night, the first night of his new tour, her heart sank.

"I hoped he'd come to his senses by now, at least about Clary, but I was wrong," John Eustace murmured.

With a promise to see what she could do, Susannah thanked him for the Atlanta number he gave her and hung up. She dialed again, and waited. When Breeze Maynard came on the line, Susannah clenched a fist.

"I need to speak with Jeb."

"He can't come to the phone."

"I'll wait."

"He's sleeping, Miss Whittaker, but—"

"I should leave my number—again? Oh, and I'm sure you'd tell him I called." She paused. "Wake him up. I'll speak to him now."

Breeze's voice dropped low, as if her hand covered the receiver for privacy. "He really is sleeping. Worn out. The doctor gave him a pill."

Susannah's patience fell, her voice rose. "Try to wake him!"

"You misunderstand."

"No," she said, "I don't think I do."

Breeze Maynard's tone turned husky, but urgent. "I meant to call you myself, but the press has been busy all morning and afternoon here, and last night—"

"I heard about last night. From John Eustace."

Susannah's fist unclenched, then tightened again. She'd come a long way from the high-society beginnings of which Breeze accused her. A failing, in Breeze's view.

"I understand this: You are a jealous, overly protective woman who doesn't want Jeb to think for himself where I'm concerned."

"You couldn't be more wrong."

The soft statement brought Susannah to a halt, her diatribe forgotten.

"Jeb needs you," Breeze said, "more than he needs anyone, even John Eustace." Briefly, she filled in the details of Jeb's last concert, of the moments backstage. "I've never been more worried about him," she finished. "I know you and I have had our difficulties, but I believe—I'm trusting you in this because I have no choice—that we both have Jeb's welfare at heart."

"Yes," she agreed.

"Then please help him, Susannah."

She didn't ask how. They were Clary's words, her own inclination. The choice seemed even simpler now: not to fret over Leslie or to wait for Drake, but to follow her heart. She owed allegiance not to her parents, but to her baby's father. The man she loved.

"Jeb's tumblin' down a well," Breeze Maynard whispered, "and I don't think there's any bottom."

19

Susannah wasted no time in packing and no more time with Leslie, who wouldn't be swayed just then by anything she said. She hailed the first cab she saw and asked the driver to take her to the airport, but soon realized she couldn't leave town again without making one stop first.

When her taxi whipped to a halt in front of Cody House, Susannah struggled from the rear seat, leaving her small carry-on bag behind. "Wait for me."

Miranda greeted her at the front door.

"Look, I made cookies with Mommy. Want one?"

Susannah took the misshapen lump of dough, which looked underbaked, chewing enthusiastically because she hadn't taken time to eat all day. The cookie tasted strange. "Mmm, delicious. I've never had better chocolate chips."

"It's peanut butter with walnuts."

She swallowed. "The best, Mandy." She followed the

little girl into the kitchen, where Studley danced around the table. The puppy had taken up residence at the shelter, wallowing in attention, and Susannah rarely had the heart to take him home at night. In the past few days she'd been grateful for his place here. "I'm flying to Atlanta," she told Miranda's mother. "I hope you all won't mind baby-sitting Studley."

"He's fallen in love with the neighbor's standard poodle." Susannah laughed with her, then Cheryl's smile faded. "I wish the shelter's policy toward humans was as welcoming."

Susannah frowned. She'd done everything she knew to make the residents happy, and Lisa had already helped several of them find permanent housing and jobs. In little more than a month two women and their children had moved out, replaced by new homeless families.

"Male humans," Miranda's mother added, with a meaningful glance at her young daughter, who clung to Susannah's legs, a cheek pressed to her pregnant abdomen, "listening to the baby," as she always said.

Susannah asked the little girl to walk Studley in the yard, and the two skipped outside, the dog yipping at Miranda's heels.

"My husband," Cheryl said as soon as they were alone.

"He's in San Francisco again?"

Dropping spoonfuls of dough onto a cookie sheet, she nodded. "No reasonable job presented itself in Illinois, or anywhere else he's tried. He's running out of money—the last savings we had—and for the past two nights he's been sleeping in Golden Gate Park."

The early September nights were cool, and Susannah empathized.

"I wish I could bend the rules, but they're to benefit everyone."

"Yes. I know." She paused. "And I'm . . . grateful." She bit her lower lip, then said, "Maybe that job interview I had on Friday will turn into an offer. They promised to let me know by Monday. Tomorrow. If I start making money, Miranda and I could move into an inexpensive motel, and Steve could join us."

Susannah didn't know what to say. In Cheryl's eyes she could read loneliness and need, the same she felt for Jeb.

"Let me think," she said. "If your interview doesn't pan out, maybe I can come up with something."

"Thank you, Susannah."

"Don't thank me yet."

With a faint frown still shadowing her face, she said good-bye and hurried out to her taxi at the curb. Studley and Miranda waved her off, and Susannah settled back against the seat, wondering whether she could really help anyone—Leslie, or the women at Cody House. Wondering whether she could help Jeb either, or if she was still what he'd always seemed to think, a do-gooder.

Doin' all right, Jeb told himself halfway through his second Atlanta concert. After last night embarrassment alone could see him through. No one had asked to hear "Kid Sister" yet, and in the second chorus of "The Last Time I Called You" his voice sounded true and strong, so Jeb figured he could pull it off for sure.

In a half-unbuttoned chambray shirt and a new pair of tan leather chaps that highlighted his jeans-clad crotch, he gave the crowd what they'd come to see, and expect. A high-energy, razzle-dazzle performance.

"Little rich girl," he sang last, past the sudden lump in his throat.

He'd tried calling Susannah on Friday but got no answer. Later that night, he and Breeze had concentrated on final details for the tour, so he didn't have another chance to call. On Saturday a woman had answered Susannah's phone, saying she wasn't there. Then he'd fallen apart onstage.

The standing ovation at the concert's end brought a grin to his face when he hadn't felt like smiling in some time.

"Thank y'all for comin' tonight! God bless!"

Mack clapped him on the back. Skeet slapped his butt, locker-room style. Cameron, Bull, and Terry circled him, everyone talking, laughing. "This tour's gonna show 'em all how it's done!" He looked up at Breeze striding across the stage, her eyes clear and proud.

"You might like to know," she said, "Nashville called. The new album's number four on the Billboard chart." Mainstream, she didn't have to tell him. Maybe last night hadn't been such a disaster. "You gonna trust my judgment from now on?"

Jeb's grin widened. "When it pleases me."

Breeze herded the band toward the dressing rooms, and Jeb looked away from the concrete hall. At least he hadn't proved himself the gutless wonder his daddy always claimed he was. He'd done his job tonight.

He froze in the act of picking up his standard mahogany guitar. He spun around again, his gaze homing in on that gray wall, on the woman leaning against it, a small bag at her feet, her eyes fixed upon him in what appeared to be both wonder and uncertainty.

His pulse slammed like a door, banging back and forth.

Jeb walked toward her, his steps steady enough, his knees wobbling as he'd once seen a frozen daiquiri do, just before it slipped sideways and fell from a bar waiter's tray into someone's lap. Near enough to touch, he kept his hands at his sides, one in a death grip around the neck of his guitar.

"Well," he said. "Miss Susannah."

Her gaze traveled over him, over his face and body, lingering at the juncture of the leather chaps, then back to his mouth. "I missed the show, Cody, except the last song."

Jeb swallowed. "I hope you didn't come all this way just to slap my face for singing about you."

"I've grown to like country music"—she raised her eyes to his again—"and a certain country singer."

His mouth went as dry as the bottom of an old well.

"Have you now?"

"The song is right. Jeb, I can learn a lot from you." He saw her swallow. "I'm so sorry for what I said the night Clary's shelter opened. I jumped to the most terrible conclusion, and I'm sorry."

"Do you believe what I told you?"

"Every word."

His mouth might be dry, but he could have drowned in those eyes of hers. Those soft, frightened eyes. She looked about to say something, but didn't. He took a step that would have brought them together, then stopped when he saw people coming toward them. With his free hand, Jeb caught Susannah's.

"Come on, let's find us some privacy."

Tugging her after him, he strode down the hall, nodding curtly to the people they passed, sidestepping a young girl's request for an autograph. In that moment Jeb didn't care about his career, about courtesy. Opening the door to his dressing room, he pulled Susannah inside, tossed the guitar down, shut the door, leaned up against it, and hauled her into his arms.

"God, I don't care why you came. I'm just glad you're here."

His mouth settled on hers with a familiarity, a sense of homecoming, that left him breathless and weak and, in seconds, wanting her more than he'd ever wanted anyone in his life. He wanted Susannah more than he'd ever wanted Clary's sisterly love, more than he'd ever wanted Rachel and their child.

Dragging his mouth from hers, Jeb pressed warm kisses along her throat. Susannah sagged against him, and he took her weight, then realized that she didn't quite fit, as she used to do.

Lifting his head, he let his gaze slip over her, from blond curls to dazed, still-serious eyes, to the sweet fullness of her bottom lip, then down over her breasts—fuller now—to the swell of her stomach, obvious in the dusty blue knit jumper that hugged her belly, outlining the child within.

Jeb felt as if he'd been knocked backward through the wooden door into the hall and was about to land, hard, on his backside. She looked so beautiful that he blinked, expecting her to change with the motion, to become slim and straight again, but not nearly as sensual as now.

"Say something, Jeb."

She had tensed under his hands at her shoulders, as if she feared he might push her away, reject her again.

"Have you ever thought of takin' a buggy whip to me?"

Her eyes softened. "More than once. If I knew where to find one."

He wrapped his arms around her, tight, and let her cling. Jeb buried his face in the clean scent of her hair, smelling like his mother's herb garden, and felt his arms tremble. "I love you," he whispered for the first time, and then, "So. You've decided you like me some?"

"I love you too."

They kissed some more, with small murmurs and moans, lips and tongues exploring, tasting, until Susannah gasped at the building pleasure, and so did Jeb. Breaking the kiss, he pressed his mouth to her temple, running his hands over her still-slender back to her thickened waist, then up again. He spoke against her skin because he didn't want her to see his eyes.

"When a man first learns that a woman is pregnant, he finds it hard to believe, to accept as a reality. She still looks the same"—he stroked her back again—"feels the same."

He hesitated and Susannah said, "Are you trying to apologize?"

"Don't stop me now." He caressed her through the knit jumper. "Then little by little, day by day, he usually notices the changes. Her breasts, her—"

Someone hammered at the door, the vibration going through his back.

"Jeb? You in there?" Breeze called. "There's a line of people at the rear door wanting autographs."

He turned his head. "Tell 'em to go away."

"And the mayor of Atlanta, cowboy."

Breeze banged on the door again, and Susannah stepped back, taking all her warmth with her.

"Open the door," she said.

"Damn." Jeb's gaze focused on her belly. "Can we continue this later?"

"We can." She leaned to kiss him, heat flashing through his body, then peeled him away from the door. "Right now, your public waits."

Once they'd seen each other again, they couldn't take their eyes off each other. During the hour of autographing in the coliseum's rear hall, during the brief reception in Jeb's dressing room with the mayor, the picture taking and hand shaking, Susannah sought his gaze across the jammed room and caught Jeb searching hers every time she looked up.

She tried to stay in the background as she always had with Drake. She and Jeb had things to say, but until they did, she didn't know whether, or where, she belonged in his very public life.

But Jeb drew her forward to meet the mayor, saying, "This is Susannah," as if that were explanation enough.

At the first camera flash, she knew she'd lost any power she held over Drake. The morning papers would show her with Jeb, and who could misinterpret the look in his eyes even if the husky warmth in his voice didn't accompany it?

The room grew warm, and Susannah's skin flushed, her eyes drooped. Out of the way again, she leaned against the dressing room's far wall.

If she stayed with Jeb, she would never know for sure about Drake. If he released Clary's journals, she'd conclude that his need for revenge against Jeb had overridden his concern for her; if he didn't release them, he might only mean to spare the family further embarrassment, deciding that her pregnancy by Jeb—their continuing affair—was sufficiently mortifying, as Leslie considered it to be.

Either way she would never know whether Drake loved his daughter more than he loved a tarnished memory.

But if her actions helped save Jeb and his career . . .

She smiled at him across the room. In answer, his gaze darkened, traveling over her, lingering on the swell of her stomach. Stifling a yawn, Susannah pressed a hand there and watched his eyes follow the motion, watched him shift his weight as if to ease discomfort. He raised a glass, taking a last swallow of the champagne Breeze had opened, then excused himself from the group around him and started toward her.

Susannah wished she could sink into the paint, not to have other, curious gazes assess her, wondering why Jeb took such an interest in a pregnant woman.

"Tired?" he said.

She nodded. "I flew from San Francisco to New York and back, then to Atlanta, all in a day and a half. I may be a bit jet lagged." She'd explain that later.

"No doubt." With a hand at her waist, he turned, catching Breeze's eye. At his slight nod, she began deftly and graciously clearing the dressing room, bringing each person in turn to say good-bye to Jeb.

"Thanks for stoppin' by," he said over and over with that charming smile, adding a personal word for each visitor until the room had almost emptied.

"You too, Breeze," Jeb added.

To Susannah's surprise not a flicker of dislike crossed her face.

"I hope you'll stay," Breeze said, then left them too.

Jeb shut the door, and Susannah glided into his arms. The public relations aftermath of his concert had only heightened her anticipation.

"Now as I was sayin'," he murmured, sliding one hand up and down her back, then around front to cover a breast. "A man feels these changes in a woman . . . her breasts"—his hand slid lower—"her belly. Changin' and changin' until he can hardly keep from knowing the fact."

"The fact?" Susannah's skin felt fiery.

"That he's going to become a father," he said. "That he already is."

"Jeb, I didn't come here because—"

"Shh." He lifted both hands, watching as Susannah did, entranced, until they lightly cupped her abdomen. Jeb's fingers twitched, then opened wider, cradling her, loving, accepting.

It was the one thing she hadn't counted on, and Susannah took a ragged breath.

"Jeb, I don't want you to feel—"

He dropped to his knees, whispering. "Don't talk. Right now I'm meetin' my baby."

She gazed down at his bent head, feeling stricken, feeling cherished, as she had in San Francisco when he was feverish, at the most unexpected moment. "Oh."

"That all you can say now?" He raised his head to look at her. "Just, 'oh'?"

Susannah could only nod. And promise herself that she would walk through the fires of hell itself to save this man, burn everything behind her, including Drake and Leslie, reduce everything else she had to ashes, to love him, to keep him loving her in return.

Jeb laid his cheek against her stomach, as Miranda often did, as if he were listening too. Susannah hoped the baby would move but it didn't, and after a long moment, ignoring some commotion in the hall, he smiled up at her.

"I suppose we ought to make some plans."

Susannah heard a stumping sound outside, which Jeb didn't notice. Touched but confused, she stroked his hair. She'd never leaned on anyone else before. "I made up my mind a long time ago," she said, "to have this baby and love it. I didn't come here hoping you'd—"

"Miss Susannah, I could use your cooperation. Where I come from, a man owns up to his responsibility. He takes care of the woman he loves. We have a wedding to arrange."

Without warning, the door opened and a shock of white hair appeared, then a wiry, well-used body in a worn dark suit and bolo tie, with a gnarled hand poised on a mahogany walking cane. Wearing an aggrieved expression, John Eustace gimped into the room. Having obviously heard what they were just saying, he cast a quick glance at Susannah. Then one at Jeb.

"I purely hope so, boy," he said, "or I'll have to fetch my shotgun."

"*Basic*," John Eustace had said next, "is the operative word all right."

He'd badgered Jeb and Susannah to set a date, to make things legal. Jeb was more than willing, but Susannah kept resisting.

"I may not be marriage material," she told him, avoiding his eyes. "My mother—my mother is an alcoholic, and my father is an egotist. I didn't learn from them how to be married, how to love."

"You're doin' just fine."

"My parents don't have the same track record as yours."

"My daddy has spent half his adult life in prison," Jeb replied. "Maybe he and Mama didn't have the same chance your folks did to get sick of each other. They spent most of their time together honeymooning, half a dozen times, and making babies to cement the deal, but—"

Susannah didn't smile. "I don't want us to get sick of each other, Jeb. To give up on each other."

"Neither do I. We don't have to be like either set of parents."

"Let's just see how things go."

Jeb chafed at her hesitation, at his grandfather's obvious disappointment in him for not being able to convince Susannah to marry him. She came from a more sophisticated background than he did, Jeb allowed. In Susannah's high-society world, divorce was common, if no less painful, and people sometimes bore children out of wedlock without batting an eye. Celebrities did too these days, he admitted—just not Jeb Stuart Cody.

But as always, he saw the vulnerability in Susannah, the protectiveness with which she cradled her growing abdomen and their child. The same way she'd touched her breast and the heart tattoo. When John Eustace left for the Atlanta hotel where the tour was staying, she finally admitted her fear that Drake Whittaker would try to ruin Jeb's life and his career.

"Why didn't you tell me this before?" he asked.

"I told Breeze. Backstage. As soon as I arrived."

"You told—?"

"So she can prepare a publicity defense, in case Drake releases the journals."

"Susannah, Christ." He paced the dressing room. "You and Breeze make quite a team, protecting me from the world. What gives you that right, either of you?"

Looking miserable, she shrugged.

Jeb went to her, taking her shoulders and softening his voice.

"I love you. And you love me. That's all we need." He waited until she looked up at him. "I don't care what Drake does, and neither should you."

"He could destroy you, Jeb. I gave him that power."

"Clary gave him that power," he said, then let her go. "I'm a grown man, Susannah. I'll deal with my own problems." He stared at her. "What's Drake's number in Greenwich? I'll talk to him myself."

"It's after midnight."

"I don't give a damn."

"Please, Jeb."

"Hell." He slung an arm around Susannah's shoulders, drawing her close. "I'll get him tomorrow." He gave her a heated look, his tone deliberately tender. "Let's get you to the hotel."

He knew she needed rest, but his body hummed with wanting her. Maybe she'd get a second wind, they'd order something light from room service and feed each other, lying on his bed under the star quilt, kissing between bites . . .

In the limousine whizzing across town Susannah fell asleep in his arms, and Jeb could only smile, stifling a groan against her silky hair. At the hotel he carried her inside to the private elevator that opened directly into his suite on the top floor, laying her gently on the wide bed for which he'd had such plans. He undressed her but she never moved, and despite his need for her, Jeb contented himself with holding her while she slept, silent and apparently dreamless, until dawn.

Jeb had one hand on Susannah's bare thigh, his other twined in her sleep-tangled hair, his mouth a half inch above hers and descending when Breeze rapped at the bedroom door.

"Nobody home," he called softly as Susannah stirred.

"Six A.M. wakeup," Breeze informed him, poking her head in the door. She stared at them, and Jeb held Susannah close. "The limo's out front. You have a photo shoot this morning with *People*. 'The Sexiest Man Alive.' Then an interview with the local press. Sound check at five. The concert. And the bus pulls out at midnight for San Antonio."

"Who plans these damn tours anyway?"

"You know who, cowboy."

Her head disappeared, and he cursed under his breath. "All right, I'm up. I'm up."

Without opening her eyes Susannah groped for him under the sheet. "That's true."

Grunting, Jeb covered her hand with his. "How about we save this for later. I promise."

As his feet hit the carpeted floor, she squinted at the clock. "And I thought being a famous surgeon's daughter was rough."

"Wild horses," he whispered.

She looked unconvinced, knowing as well as he did that they'd have little privacy until the bus reached Texas and another hotel. The thought only made him want her more. Before Jeb left the suite, he asked her for Drake's office number, but when he called from the coliseum where the photo shoot took place, Drake's receptionist told him the surgeon was unavailable, adding that Drake would be in surgery until evening. If he cared to leave a message . . .

Jeb didn't. Hanging up, he considered Susannah with new regard. This was how she'd spent her childhood, most of her adult life. Early on Drake Whittaker must have made himself unavailable to his wife and daughter—more unreachable than Jeb's own father, rotting in prison—and he doubted Drake would change. Considering his own, even more public life, he wondered whether Susannah would ever agree to marry him, or how long she'd even stay with him on tour.

Jeb connected with Drake late that night when the tour bus stopped for gas two hours outside of Atlanta. He called from a public phone, not wanting Susannah to hear, or the band. He came right to the point about Clary's journals.

"You know damn well that's circumstantial evidence at best, and at the worst, conjecture—fiction on her part. I loved my sister, yes, but in the same way any brother loves his sister. Nothing more, nothing sick." He paused. "I sure as hell didn't kill her. If you want to ruin me, go ahead and try. Send copies of that journal to every newspaper in this country and see what happens. I can command as much free air time as I please, but if I'm lucky, the media will tire pretty quickly of the whole thing— three days, tops—and you'll be left with no hard proof and no one to listen."

"Except the police."

Jeb's stomach tightened. "They can bring me in again, question me until my hair turns gray, but they'll still end up with nothing that would hold up in court."

"Having heard about your father, I'm sure you'd know that."

Hunching over the receiver as Mack Norton passed by, Jeb lowered his voice. "I may not have blue blood running through my veins, but I love Susannah, who is carryin' my baby. If you love her, you won't do anything more to hurt her." He waited a heartbeat, then said, "I wish you and I could find some kind of harmony for her sake—and Clary's memory. But I leave that up to you. I've said my piece." And he hung up.

He stood for a moment, breathing in the cool night air and the smell of diesel fuel from the nearby pumps. Jeb looked up at the clear sparkle of stars overhead. That was why she wouldn't marry him. He'd said it himself. Drake was why, not only because he'd neglected her but because she'd never know, unless she waited to see what he did with Clary's journals, whether her father loved her.

When he reached the tour bus, he lingered in the front lounge, which he normally found restful with its soothing color scheme of oak with turquoise and green furnishings and plush carpeting, where the kitchen, living area, and the convertible band bunks were. The wooden privacy blinds were open to the passing night, and the boys had grouped with Breeze and John Eustace around the table, preparing to play stud and drink beer. Breeze fussed with her green plants on the counter while she waited for the microwave popcorn, and its smell, which Jeb had never liked, dampened his spirits even more. He wished it could dampen his frustration with Drake, his desire for Susannah. Helluva of place to try and make love, he thought.

"Hey, Jeb. Want to sit in?" Mack waved a fistful of cards.

"No, thanks. I think I'll get some sleep."

"Or somethin'," Skeet murmured, and Jeb, resisting the urge to wipe his smile away, headed for the back of the bus.

"He looks like a thunderhead," Cameron observed.

"Woman trouble," John Eustace said, which made the others laugh, especially Bull who sounded exactly that—like a bullhorn.

Terry's cackle overrode it. "He may come flyin' back down that hall in a minute."

But it was Breeze who slammed the microwave door and said, "Leave him be."

His band had tried teasing Susannah earlier, but she didn't seem to know how to deal with them. Jeb suspected she thought they disliked her. From their comments—the kind of cheeky banter they exchanged with him, with Breeze—he knew better but also knew he wouldn't convince her of that, any more than he could pressure her, because of Drake, into marrying him.

Hell, he'd waited long enough to ask, Jeb thought. To accept their child. He supposed she deserved time to ruminate on such a decision.

Trying not to make noise, he slipped into the darkened stateroom that occupied the rear third of the bus and stretched across its width. Tugging off his boots, he let them fall with a soft thud to the thick, seafoam-green carpet, pulled off the rest of his clothes, then crawled in beside her on the queen-size feather bed.

Susannah snuggled against him, her back to his front, and Jeb draped an arm around her, nuzzling the nape of her neck. She groaned.

"Did I wake you?" he whispered.

"You always wake me."

In that instant Jeb knew for certain that he couldn't live without her. That he would take his chances again with love, and fate. Convince her—somehow—to do the same with him. He felt his muscles begin to relax, felt himself settle in to the gently rolling rhythm of the bus lumbering along the highway. He'd never found the motion erotic before. "I've been thinkin' about you all day. All night onstage too."

She sighed. "I was dreaming about you in those tan leather chaps. Feeling a little jealous that all those women threw roses and grabbed your legs when you got close to the lip of the stage. And tossed underwear at you."

"Doesn't mean a thing." He let his hand drift over her, breast and belly, easing up her nightshirt, the Kentucky one, which seemed to be Susannah's favorite, and pressing his fingers against her warm, tight skin, circling. After a moment he felt the baby kick, and smiled. "Feel that?"

"All too often," she said with a smile in her sleepy voice.

He wouldn't mention his talk with Drake. Just keep this time for them.

"It's a good sign, isn't it?" he asked. "That the baby's healthy and vigorous."

"The baby's fine," she whispered, "and so am I. The doctor says—"

"Doctors can be wrong. Even John Eustace."

"We'll be all right, Jeb." She moved closer in to him, her bottom snugged against his crotch, making him even harder.

He stroked her belly, stroked their child to sleep.

"I want you," he whispered, pushing himself against her. "Now." He slipped one hand between her legs, his callused fingertips lightly rasping the soft skin. "Now?" he asked. Susannah made a sound of agreement, opening herself to him, and Jeb felt his heartbeat hurry. "Is it all right?"

She was past five months now, the baby starting to crowd her ribcage, but she was carrying well in front, and still felt slim except right there.

"It's more than all right."

One of the boys out front hooted in triumph, and he heard the slap of cards on the table, someone scraping back a chair, then opening the refrigerator for another beer. Jeb turned his face into her shoulder, kissing her cheek, his mouth warm and damp and open on her skin, making her moan. Aware that they weren't alone, he covered the sound with his fingers, then as natural as a sunrise, slipped inside her, whispering from Shakespeare's *Henry IV*, "'Commit the oldest sins the newest kind of ways,'" and the rhythm began, the bus's gentle, steady rocking taking them higher and higher, closer and deeper, until his fears and his passion exploded with hers, their climax going on and on in a series of soft moans and whispers of love, with Jeb pleading—when he'd promised not to—that she marry him and put him out of his misery.

When they lay quiet in each other's arms, Susannah rubbed his bare chest with the silk of her hair, the soft flutter of her curls against his skin. She toyed with the gold hoop in his ear, and the bus's motion tumbled them closer.

"The rear of this thing's the worst place to ride." Jeb palmed her breast, his thumb making lazy circles over her nipple. "I was goin' to change the stateroom, have it put in the middle instead, but I think I've changed my mind."

Susannah agreed with him, then grew serious. "Jeb. Did you talk to my father? When we stopped before?"

"Yes." He drew her head to his shoulder. "But don't worry about Drake."

Shifting, she peered at him in the darkness, her features striped by the strobelike flash of headlights passing in the night. "I'm not worried exactly. He'll do what he wants. But I am wondering—about Clary." She held his gaze. "How must she have felt when she wrote that journal? When that man touched her? She was little more than a child then."

He winced. "I used to think so, though John Eustace never agreed. He thought Clary was born grown-up, and wily in her ways. I never believed him." But lately he kept remembering things he thought he had repressed, or explained away, years ago.

In the darkness the intimacy, the confidences, seemed as natural as their earlier lovemaking, and he realized he'd never felt as close to anyone as he felt now to

Susannah. He'd glimpsed her life with her mother and Drake; he owed her a deeper look at his too. Remembering two nights ago, when he'd left the stage and cried, seemed to make telling the secret easier.

He pressed her head back onto his chest, so she couldn't see his eyes.

"When I first suspected that Clary's relationship with Dick Sheridan wasn't exactly right, I didn't know what to do. She claimed he forced her, and I promised myself that, when I got older, if he hurt her again, I'd go after him."

Susannah tensed. "And did you?"

"When I was sixteen," Jeb answered. "Daddy was away again of course, as Mama always put it, and Clary'd come home that night reeking of liquor, her blouse torn and a big bruise on her arm." He shuddered at the memory. "I took off runnin', ran the mile into town straight to the sheriff's office where I knew he was on duty."

Her voice was hushed. "What happened?"

Jeb gave a harsh laugh. "I should have known he'd be waitin' for me. The minute I burst in the door, he muscled me out back behind the station. Where I met several of his closest friends, who just happened to come by." He fingered the scar on his upper lip.

Susannah caught him. "Is that where you got this?"

Nodding, he said, "Two of 'em held my arms while Clary's deputy punched me. When my head dropped down onto my chest, another one yanked it up by my hair and nearly broke my neck, holdin' it back so Sheridan could finish his work." He paused. "They left me lyin' on the curb a few blocks down, which is where John Eustace found me on his way home from deliverin' someone's baby."

Susannah stretched to kiss his scarred mouth. "John Eustace cleaned you up."

"I had three broken ribs and a broken wrist, two black eyes and a torso that turned purple from bein' kicked in the stomach when I finally went down." His smile was grim. "Clary took care of me too, so Mama wouldn't see. I don't know what excuse she made . . . a schoolyard fight, I suppose." He sighed, tightening his arms around Susannah. "I stayed in bed for a week. Clary waitin' on me day and night, the way I'd taken care of her whenever she came home hurt. Then I got back on my feet and saw . . ."

"Saw what?" Susannah said when he didn't continue.

"How wrong I'd been." Wanting to block out the painful memory, he urged her onto her back, and with a desperation he hadn't felt in years, took her mouth again. "I need you." He hovered over Susannah, one hand working its way between them to her stomach. "I need you both."

To his relief she gave him what he wanted. "Oh, Jeb . . ."

"Hey, Cody! Susannah!" A fist pounded on the bedroom door and Mack's voice called out. "Keep the noise down in there. We cleaner-livin' folks are tryin' to play a little poker here."

Jeb could feel Susannah stiffen beneath him, could almost see her cheeks burn in the darkness.

"Do you think they hear us?"

"No, I think my band is just testing you for their seal of approval." Grinning, he hugged her tight, astonished when she sounded pleased, delighted.

"Really?"

"It's just their way. Don't pay 'em any mind."

But she pushed at his chest and raised onto an elbow. "Mack?" she called.

"Yeah?"

Jeb could hear muffled laughter, even from John Eustace.

"You'll have to excuse us. As you well know, this man makes women scream," she said, "and I am no exception."

The front room exploded with hoots and cheers, and, his chest shaking with silent laughter, Jeb hauled her back into his arms. He looked down into her eyes, watched the smile play in them as well as on her lips. The hell with her mother and Drake, with Clary's journals, with his own patience.

"So are you gonna give up and marry me, or what?"

20

Three weeks later, at the end of September, Susannah married Jeb in the still-blooming garden against a backdrop of still-green trees at Breeze Maynard's Nashville home. They waited until then because of Jeb's tour, which had kept them moving through the South and West from San Antonio to Mobile to Charleston to Santa Fe; and because of the continuing catcalls during some of Jeb's concerts and the press coverage of her pregnancy, they kept the wedding small. They chose Nashville not only for privacy and the setting's beauty but for convenience, which Susannah tried not to resent.

She focused on her love for him. How could she not love a man who, during the first concert after she joined him on tour, had sung "Oh, Susannah" just for her? Who had since added it to his show every night?

She focused on her pride in him. Jeb had been nominated in four categories for the annual Country Music

Association awards: Best Single for "Kid Sister"; Best Album for his first, *Jeb Stuart Cody;* Male Vocalist of the Year; and the Horizon Award, for the entertainer whose career had taken a giant leap that year.

The trip back to Nashville the day before the wedding provided the first break in his tour schedule, and three hours after she'd said, "I take thee, John Eustace Beauregard Stuart Cody," she was sitting with Jeb on the aisle waiting for the awards ceremony to start.

Susannah gazed around her at the glittering audience filing into seats at the famed Grand Ole Opry. Like most things concerning Jeb, it wasn't what she expected. A kind of barn, she'd supposed, thinking of the original theater. Instead, she studied the large, well laid-out auditorium, beautifully lit, with a huge, pentagon-shaped stage.

She'd expected to see lots of jeans and boots, not formal dress. She saw some of both, but the boots shone and the black jeans were topped with tuxedo jackets, some with elaborate sequined designs across the shoulders and back yoke, even down the sleeves. Turning her head, she found plenty of regulation black tuxes, plenty of designer gowns.

Susannah wore her cream-colored, sand-washed silk wedding dress, cut low to reveal a hint of cleavage and skillfully designed to make a fashion statement of her pregnancy, its long sleeves of the crocheted lace that also trimmed a deep-cut, floor-length hem slit just high enough to permit easy walking. With the gown that afternoon she'd worn an antique lace mantilla, her something old and borrowed from John Eustace, whose wife had worn it at their wedding more than half a century ago. Tonight, in honor of another occasion, she adjusted her off-white Stetson.

Jeb grinned. "I didn't know you'd bought that hat. In Dallas last week?" She nodded. "Or that you'd wear it."

"Mack tells me I belong now, that I'm one of the band."

"Someone's gonna kick you right off the Social Register, Miss Susannah."

"Mrs. Susannah." Then her smile faded. "I have all the society I need right here, and all the family too."

Her mother hadn't come to the wedding, not that Susannah blamed her. Leslie had checked into the Betty Ford Center the day after Susannah left and was reportedly doing well. Drake hadn't come either, but neither had he yet given Clary's journals to the press. She supposed she could thank him for that much.

Jeb caught her hand. "Mountain Mama, you sure look at home. I think we'll buy a place to live down here as soon as the tour's over."

"I wouldn't mind." His hand felt clammy. He was wearing the correct black tux, pants and jacket, into which she'd nudged him. No hat. "Nervous?"

"Not as long as you keep holdin' on to me."

The music came up, and the emcee appeared on-stage to a burst of applause. Clint Black, handsome in his trademark dark jeans and hat and hunky as ever, strode to the microphone with that big grin and those dancing eyes. Susannah squeezed Jeb's hand harder. As much as she liked Clint and his music, the superstar singer couldn't hold a candle in Susannah's heart to her new husband.

If only Clary could have seen him tonight . . .

Susannah wished, as she had for the past three weeks, that Jeb had finished talking about Clary that night in the bus. Though he hadn't said so, she sensed there was more. She'd pump John Eustace for information, she decided, and this time he'd tell her. That wouldn't take away the disillusionment Susannah felt about her friendship with Clary—in fact, she feared it might make it worse—but at least she'd know the truth. Then she'd ease Jeb's sorrow over Clary somehow.

If only they knew who had killed her.

Jeb had worried about tonight's ceremony—whether someone in the crowd or fans mobbing the front entrance might boo him or shout the taunts with which he'd become too familiar in the last months.

Worried for him, Susannah heard little of the opening monologue, though she laughed at all the right places, taking her cue from Jeb. On her other side three seats in, Breeze looked resplendent in a gauzy mauve gown, its scooped neck and bodice of sequins glittering in the darkened auditorium. Then she glanced at Michael, sitting between Breeze and John Eustace who sat next to Susannah. John Eustace had given her away that afternoon in Drake's place, "because nothing could give me greater pleasure."

When Michael smiled at her, she blinked. He had shown up in Nashville that afternoon, missing the wedding by half an hour, with his Armani tuxedo, his return ticket to San Francisco, and a mysterious, gift-wrapped package for Jeb and Susannah that he wouldn't let her open until "the time is right."

After the awards, he'd said. When she and Jeb could be alone.

Now he let his gaze slide away, let it slip once more over Breeze, his obvious approval of the ex-singer making Susannah smile. Well, well, she thought. Her speculations set aside for later, she focused on the awards.

"They're for last year's work," Jeb said in her ear when he lost the crystal trophy for male vocalist.

"Stop squirming. You can't win them all."

"One down, three to go." He kissed the nape of her neck. "Then we can get the hell out of here and consummate this marriage."

"That will be like closing the barn door after the horse gets out."

"I look forward to it." Jeb laughed, tickling her ear. "First the hat, now you even sound like country."

"It's gotten in my blood."

Jeb lost Best Album but when Lorrie Morgan announced the winner of Best Single, and Susannah heard "Kid Sister," she broke into a grin before the words were out.

"You won! Jeb, you won!"

He rose from his seat to the first flurry of applause. Someone across the aisle clapped him on the shoulder, and Susannah looked at Mack, who was beaming. "Thatta boy, Jeb."

"Go get 'em, cowboy." Breeze leaned across to touch his hand.

Looking dazed, Jeb stood in the aisle for a second, which seemed like an hour to Susannah, just holding her gaze with his. Then, as if coming to his senses at the growing roar around them, he bent down, avoiding the tilt of her Stetson, to kiss her lightly on the mouth, one hand at her shoulder, the other briefly covering her silk-clad belly.

"You feel like butter," he whispered, "and velvet."

"I love you. Go on up, Jeb."

He bounded onto the stage, all exuberance and pride, and Susannah knew she had never loved him more. Until he spoke into the microphone.

After thanking Breeze as co-songwriter and Jericho Records and his band, then John Eustace for always believing in him, he looked out over the audience, at Susannah.

"I guess by now most of you know how special tonight is for me in another way. For those who don't, I got married about four hours ago and my bride's sittin' right there." The spotlight caught her, blinding her. The applause rained down again, and several people called best wishes. "Thanks," Jeb murmured. "You too, Susannah." He waved his award. "Now let's get this show over with, so we can shut ourselves in a bedroom somewhere and I can show you how much I really love you."

Breeze noticed that Susannah was still blushing near the end of the ceremony when Jeb, the last of the five acts for the Horizon Award, returned to the stage to sing "Kid Sister." But before he began, he stopped the band and signaled for silence.

"I wouldn't be here tonight if it weren't for the people I mentioned before—especially one of them again." He smiled and Breeze's heart immediately lurched. "I've had my good times and my bad, most of 'em this year, but long before that, I had Breeze Maynard on my side." His smile grew at the smattering of applause. "Breeze, you've been standin' in the wings long enough." The applause intensified; a few people shouted their agreement. "Before we carry this show past its scheduled three hours, get on up here and help me sing this thing."

The band covered her hesitation, but it didn't nearly cover the tide of applause. Beside her Michael Alsop put a warm hand on her back.

"He's right," he said. "The world misses you."

Breeze's throat tightened. She couldn't say a word, much less sing. But Michael pushed, and so did John Eustace, grinning, and before she knew it, she was shaking out her skirts, then striding to the stage. Jeb helped her up the steps to the microphone.

"I know, you are goin' to kill me someday. I'll just take my chances. Because I saw your face when you sang that other time to help me, only for a second, but I saw it." He signaled again and the band struck up the first bars of "Kid Sister."

The notes, the lyrics . . . they were the best of her and Jeb. She knew that now, but she'd seen him with Susannah, had watched him with her as they said their wedding vows, and she felt no sadness at the realization.

With their arms around each other's waists, their heads close together, Breeze and Jeb sang Clary's song, their voices instantly blending, his strong baritone with her equally strong contralto, every note and nuance perfect, as she had rarely experienced perfection since losing her band and giving up her own career. Tonight she and Jeb finished the tender duet, for which she'd written the gentle music and he the poignant lyrics, to a standing ovation.

At the continuing applause, the cheers, her heart hammered in a hard rhythm, as if the audience held a mallet, and she was their nail. Pounding her back in where she belonged. Jeb held up her hand, linked with his, the small diamond stud in his left ear flashing, his smile not quite on center. Breeze blinked, then at his urging bowed with him, their shoulders touching, her hair fluid as a waterfall, sliding overhead and grazing the floor at their feet before she straightened with a smart snap, her trademark snap, and felt gravity take over. The tears spilled, a raceway down her cheeks.

Slipping her arms around him, she held Jeb tight. "Thanks, cowboy."

"You're welcome, Maynard." He swallowed. "Breeze . . ."

"Don't you dare say you're sorry." Raising her head to the ongoing sounds of tribute, Breeze kissed him, then admitted to herself at the same time, "In Atlanta that first night of the new tour, I did this to save you. This time," she said, "I did it to save myself."

Holding a hand over the mike, he looked into her eyes, his voice hoarse. "It's good to have you back." Then Jeb took his hand away and, to her absolute delight, shouted: "Breeze Maynard, ladies and gentlemen! The great Miss B!"

Without music, it was the sweetest song she'd ever heard.

Halfway toward dawn John Eustace stashed himself in the far corner of someone's living room and watched his grandson introduce his bride to the rest of Nashville's music community—or so John Eustace supposed. The wedding cake–style mansion belonged, he thought Jeb had said, to a prominent record producer. Or had that been at the first party, the second, the third? Jeb's double trophies for Best Single and the prestigious Horizon Award had made escape or a proper wedding night impossible.

John Eustace longed only for a comfortable bed—his own, in Elvira. He'd never stayed this long on tour with Jeb before, and in the past week he'd begun to yearn for his native Kentucky hills with ever increasing fervor. God only knew what his patients had suffered at the hands of that young upstart who zipped around town in his flashy BMW, dispensing blinding white smiles with his newfangled brand of medicine.

He stared into his glass of orange juice, his hip aching as if the hundreds of people milling about the overly decorated room had walked across his body. He couldn't see a vacant chair or overstuffed sofa in sight.

"John Eustace?" Susannah's warm voice captured his attention. "You look lonely."

"Homesick," he admitted, glad that she'd slipped away and come to him. "I always try to tell Jeb I don't get the same thrill he does, livin' in a sideshow, but he's never understood yet. I don't expect he ever will." Looking at her, he smiled without having to force it. "I'm glad I'll be leavin' him in capable hands tomorrow."

"Tomorrow?" she repeated.

"Miss Susannah, this should be your honeymoon." He glanced around at a shrill burst of laughter. Near the green velvet draperies with gold swags, a woman's dress hung off one shoulder, exposing the swell of a breast and her matted hairdo hung askew, one bobby pin dangling. "You may tolerate this kind of craziness, which looks to me like a frantic last gasp before the Black Death sweeps through—and I hope you do enjoy it, as you've married it—but I cannot." He touched her hair. "I'm stayin' at a hotel tonight. If I ever get any sleep, in the morning I'll hop the first plane home. With my blessings to you and my grandson for everlasting happiness."

Susannah laid her head on his bony shoulder. John Eustace pressed her closer, relishing the warm feel of her cheek, her hand in his, her rounded abdomen against his side. With his other hand he stroked her soft, warm curls.

"Have I said welcome to the family yet?" he nearly whispered.

"Only a dozen times. I cherished every one of them. And speaking of family . . ."

A couple pushed by them, heading for the bar, and Susannah edged John Eustace deeper into the corner toward the velvet love seat they'd vacated. "Let's sit down while we have the chance. There's something I need to ask you before you leave."

John Eustace obeyed but as soon as he sat and set aside his walking cane, his side began to hurt even more, not only at the shift of weight.

When she said, "I've been thinking all night about Clary," he wasn't surprised. He'd been expecting more from her on that score.

Susannah's retelling of Jeb's long-ago fight with Clary's sheriff was quick and to the point, her own emotions apparently suppressed. "After he recovered from the sheriff's beating," she finished, "Jeb said he saw something—only he wouldn't say what. I think it was something that finally turned him from Clary."

She looked at him questioningly, and John Eustace looked away.

"Will you tell me?" she said.

He shifted, pain shooting through his hip. "That's Jeb's place."

"It's too hurtful. I don't want to press him, John Eustace," she said. "Not tonight, and tomorrow you'll be gone." She didn't add that they never knew when they'd see him again.

He listened to glasses clinking, to the music, loud and raucous from another room, to the low hum of conversation only a few feet away. He was glad the darkened corner hid his face. "Clary and I never saw eye to eye, as you know. I doubt my version would strike you as kind, or fair, to her."

"I'd like the truth."

John Eustace appreciated her honesty. He had learned long ago that few people could be called entirely honest, and thought Susannah was one of the few—like

Jeb. His heart swelled with love for the woman his grandson had married.

Trapped, he shifted again. She was family now. What choice did he have?

Staring into the middle distance, he chose his words carefully.

"The night I picked that boy up, I thought I had never seen a more betrayed look in anyone's eyes than I did in Jeb's. I was wrong. I was also afraid in those first hours that he'd been done damage enough to kill him. Internal bleeding," he said, more comfortable with the physical details, "perhaps a ruptured spleen." He didn't look at Susannah, but her hand took his. "Thank God, his injuries were mostly cuts and bruises, except for a break or three, and a pair of the best shiners I have ever seen."

"He told me about Clary, taking care of him."

"As she should have," John Eustace said. "She caused Jeb most of his problems growin' up, no matter what he thought." His mouth hardened. "By the time she turned five years old, no matter her sweet smile and soft voice, I knew where most of her genes had come from. That girl could make my hand itch to swat her, by no more'n sayin', 'Good morning, PawPaw.'" He shook his head. "Just like her daddy."

"What happened when Jeb got well?" Susannah said.

"Jeb decided to go back for more. He had no more sense then than any other hot-headed sixteen-year-old boy. I always told my wife that boys from puberty into their twenties are purely insane and she would ask me what I thought to do about it. Still," he said, "I wish I'd been around the night Jeb followed Clary to her latest assignation with that deputy sheriff—Elvira's full-fledged sheriff these days, I'm sorry to tell you." He waved a hand. "But I wasn't around."

Susannah clutched his arm. "Was he—Did the sheriff—?"

With effort he steadied his voice. "No, child. The sheriff didn't touch him."

"PawPaw."

She used his nickname for the first time, but he couldn't enjoy it. Just as he hadn't enjoyed the past three weeks with Jeb on tour; hadn't found it easy in the last months to look in his own mirror.

"Jeb found Clary with the sheriff. On a dark road a few miles from home. In the backseat of his patrol car. With all their clothes off, if you'll pardon my frankness." He hesitated. "Clary was all over him."

"*Making love?*" Susannah said, holding his gaze. "You mean he wasn't—"

"Abusing her?" John Eustace laughed, harshly. "That man never laid a hand on Clary without her wantin' him to. I'm sorry to spoil your image of my granddaughter."

"I asked for the truth," she said, her face pale, "but it's so hard to imagine."

"Then she never showed you her worst side. Clary was a selfish girl, an even more selfish woman. I suspect she wouldn't have wanted you and Jeb to even meet." He placed his hand over Susannah's. "Clary had a cunning sense of how to pit people against each other. Her daddy and Jeb. Her mama against her daddy. Your father, against my grandson. And you . . . ."

"She'd have sensed Jeb and I would like each other."

"She prob'ly sensed he'd fall in love with you." Without looking down, John Eustace felt Susannah's other hand glide over his. "She must have known Jeb would love you more than he'd ever loved her, or anyone else."

"Even Rachel?"

"He loved that girl too, but in a sweet, youthful way. Seeing her die as he did"—John Eustace held Susannah's gaze—"of a nasty obstetrical condition called placenta previa, which means the placenta pulled away prematurely, causing massive hemorrhage, and virtually drowning their child in blood—froze something inside him . . . until he met you."

"That's why he's so afraid for me and this baby." Susannah shuddered. "Oh, John Eustace. Clary must have sensed I'd love him too."

"I think you could win bets on that."

"How could she deny him happiness?"

There was no sane answer. His hip ached, his heart. He'd done what he could and would live with that knowledge for the rest of his life. "Jeb never understood my dislike of Clary, just as I couldn't understand his closeness to her. Except she didn't show him her real nature either until the end. After he saw her with the sheriff, I saw the true depth of betrayal in his eyes. That's what hurt Jeb most, I believe. Clary had lied and let Jeb take the beating. And not long after that, it's what probably sent him in Rachel's direction—to the first love of his life."

"Thank you for telling me," Susannah whispered.

He looked away and saw Jeb coming toward them, alone for the first time all evening, his stride confident. Swallowing, John Eustace knew at an advanced age that sheer pride in someone, sheer happiness for him, could bring tears. He leaned close to Susannah. "I think I see jealousy on the hoof. I'd better take my leave and find another pitcher of orange juice, without someone wantin' to dump vodka into it."

"John Eustace?"

Struggling to his feet, he met her gaze. "Yes, child."

"I'm proud to be part of your family."

The words slashed him open like a scalpel. "I hope you always will be, Miss Susannah." As Jeb reached them, he added, "You just take care of my favorite grandson . . . and that first great-grandbaby."

"I will."

"What's all this?" His gaze sharp, Jeb stopped John Eustace when he reached for his walking cane. "You monopolize my woman, then scurry off at bein' caught?"

He'd seen them talking. Probably seen the quick blur of tears too.

"A pregnant woman needs her rest, her strength. I was hopin' you'd come to your right mind at last, had enough of all the hoopla, and were comin' to take this lady home."

"As a matter of fact, I am."

"Then my presence has just become unnecessary."

Jeb looked harder at him, possibly seeing the signs he'd learned to expect. John Eustace exchanged glances with Susannah, silently asking her not to confirm Jeb's assumption that he would be gone by morning.

Looking from her to Jeb, John Eustace stored up images for the lonely nights in Elvira with his memories, with his pain. Then he squeezed Jeb's broad tuxedo-clad shoulder, and Jeb handed him the cane.

"Your wedding night's nearly over," John Eustace said. "Don't you think you ought to make something of it?"

Walking away, he told himself he had seen love before, had felt it in his youth and for fifty years of marriage thereafter, but he had also seen sorrow and felt that too. He hoped not to have any more in his life, not to lose the one person he couldn't bear to lose.

✿   ✿   ✿

"Am I talkin' to myself?" Susannah heard Jeb say.

Lying beside him in one of Breeze Maynard's high-ceilinged bedrooms, she smiled at the last moonlight streaming across the king-size bed, turning his bare body and hers to silver. Even after John Eustace's revelations about Clary, she couldn't stop smiling, would have smiled at a hurricane—or a blizzard. She'd think about Clary later.

"I'm awake." Unable to wait, feeling the rightness of it as if finishing something they'd started in New York, they'd made love in the limousine on the way home, wearing most of their clothes. As soon as they reached the house, laughing and kissing, climbing the stairs, they peeled off Jeb's black bow tie, Susannah's shoes. More kisses, a few more steps. His onyx studs and pleated shirt, her creamy dress. At the top of the flight, Jeb pressed her against the railing. More kisses while he fumbled with his pants, then her silk lingerie and hose. Naked at last, they'd barely reached the bed before Jeb entered her the second time.

Satisfied, replete, Susannah yawned in his arms.

"Keep talking," she said. "I'm not that sleepy. I'm getting used to life on the road. It even feels strange not to be moving. All that's missing is the rhythm of the bus."

"Better than a vibrating motel room mattress."

"Sexier," Susannah murmured, trailing a finger down his chest.

"We could have had one of the drivers take us for a spin." Jeb's hand dropped to her round belly. "Talk about sexy." He stroked her. "You planning to play basketball?"

"I'm fielding my own team."

He nuzzled her neck. "Can I play too?"

"You already have. That's how I got in this condition."

"We're gonna have to play a lot more to make a whole team."

Breeze had given them her house for the night, and the rare isolation pleased them both. It hadn't hurt Breeze either. Making the offer to stay away all night, "somewhere or other," she had slyly looked at Michael. "I'll either be partying . . . or I'll be partying," she'd said.

Michael had kissed Susannah in full view of Jeb. "I thought you were crazy, falling for this guy." Drawing back, he'd smiled at Breeze. "But country music's not so bad."

Susannah's stomach rumbled now and she grinned at Jeb. "I hate to tell you, but we'll have to play later. I worked up an appetite."

"You're hungry?"

She played with the diamond ear stud he still wore. "For food."

"Well, let's feed you then. Put on another ten pounds."

Amid much false grumbling about his disappointment that she'd meant food instead of sex, Jeb slipped on a pair of black silk running shorts and led her downstairs in the last minutes before dawn. "I suppose your lawyer friend could make an argument for annulling our marriage," he said, rummaging in the refrigerator without bothering to turn on the kitchen lights. "I realize we didn't get around to making love until three A.M., the morning after the wedding. If you have any second thoughts about the road—or me—good old Michael could probably cut you loose."

Susannah ignored Jeb's flash of insecurity. Sidling close to him, she tugged her cranberry-colored panne velvet robe tighter and reached for a platter of cold cuts—turkey, ham, roast beef, and tongue. "Do you think Breeze and Michael really . . .?"

Pulling out bowls of potato salad, cole slaw, a deep-dish apple pie and one of pumpkin, a huge wedge of wedding cake, he feigned ignorance. "What?"

She piled the meat on a tray with rounds of pita bread.

"Do you think they may be in bed together somewhere even as we speak?"

"How do I know?" Adding bowls and plates and a bottle of sparkling water and a bottle of champagne to the tray, Jeb carried it down a hall and into a large Southwest-style room lit by the pearly gray dawn.

"Jealous?" she asked.

"No, ma'am."

He drew her down onto a sofa, cushioned in teal, rose, and sage green, and low to the floor. In silence they loaded meats and salads into the pita bread. Maybe he wasn't the only one who could feel insecure. Jeb had spent the summer in this house with Breeze. Had they shared a room? Made love?

"I haven't made love to another woman," Jeb said, "Breeze included—haven't even wanted to, since I met you. My press image—whether bright as brass or tarnished as it has been lately aside." He paused. "Aren't you going to ask me why?"

"No," she said, taking a bite of her overstuffed sandwich.

"I'll tell you anyway." Jeb popped the cork on the champagne, deftly catching the overflow in a plain water tumbler. "Couldn't find any clean wineglasses," he said, then casually, "Couldn't get you off my mind, out from under my skin from the first minute I laid eyes on you in New York, your eyes shooting sparks, mad as blazes about Clary. Maybe it started long before that, when she sent me your picture from school."

Susannah set her sandwich aside.

"I couldn't either. Forget you," she said.

Jeb pushed the tray away, put his sandwich down with hers and their glasses. Making room on the sofa, they lay next to each other, turning naturally after a first kiss, so that her back touched his front. Nudging her robe open, Jeb sleeked both hands over her bared belly, murmuring to her, kissing her hair.

"When I lived in Elvira with my daddy and mama, when I learned to play guitar, I always wondered if I'd ever be this happy anywhere else." He touched her face, guiding Susannah's mouth around to his. "I think this is the happiest night—or morning—of my life. At least until the baby comes."

Susannah sensed his eagerness, heard his serious tone. "Boy or girl?"

"Either one. Just healthy. Both of you. That's all I want."

Remembering John Eustace's story about Rachel, she turned fully to face him on the sofa, her mouth raised to his, her body eager too, her hand reaching low to touch him.

He grunted. "Easy there. I take it you're hungry again. Make it last this time." But he gazed at her with uncertainty, making her love him all the more.

"You're still worried, aren't you? That you'll hurt me or the baby?"

Despite their previous lovemaking, his shrug told her all she needed to know. So did his eyes.

Coming up on her knees, after waiting for Jeb to do the same, Susannah stroked him through the dark silk running shorts and he groaned, the sound echoing off the room's vaulted ceiling, bouncing off the window glass. Then his hand found her too, began to cruise over her, until her moistness covered his fingers and she moaned. Jeb didn't smother the sound.

"Nobody's here," he whispered, removing her robe, his movements mirroring hers, quick, then slow, then quick again until she felt heat streak through her like the moonlight across the bed upstairs, like magic.

"We can make as much noise as we like."

"Then show me how much you love me." His tone strained, he caught her hand.

"No. This way," she said, "this time." When he didn't protest, she eased his silk shorts off, letting them fall to the floor with her robe.

His eyes glazed and vulnerable, he wrapped her hand around him. "Tight," he said. "Harder." Then, "Please. Oh, dammit, you're gonna cause my death. I didn't— Don't stop—want to *hurry* . . ."

"Jeb!"

His fingers flew over her, his touch sure and perfect. Susannah did the same for him. In the next instant she felt the swift flow, the satiny spending, and it carried her with him, on a series of cries with the dawn light spilling through the uncurtained windows of Breeze Maynard's house.

Such happiness, Jeb told himself, couldn't last.

It lasted until noon the next day when Breeze came into the house carrying a look of satisfaction, and the box Michael had brought. From Drake Whittaker.

Jeb wasn't sure he wanted to look inside.

What kind of surprise would he find? Another shock? He didn't need one, and neither did Susannah.

"I know all about Clary with the sheriff," she'd admitted over a late brunch. "John Eustace told me," and she covered his hand with hers. "Please don't be angry with him. I badgered him to tell me, so blame me if you must."

"I can't blame you. I'm just sorry you had to hear all that."

"I'm sorry she hurt you, Jeb." She squeezed his hand. "I'm sorry I believed everything was your fault instead for so long."

Jeb stared now at the gift-wrapped package from Drake as if it were a ticking bomb.

"We can take it with us," he said. "Open it later." Their short honeymoon would end that evening when the bus pulled out for Baton Rouge, then Galveston, the next leg of Jeb's tour. "Or we can leave it here."

"Let's open it now," Susannah said.

The package had been addressed to both of them, which in itself made Jeb uneasy. Susannah yanked at the white ribbons, tore off the silver-and-white paper, then slipped a letter opener under the box flaps inside, which had been taped down. The plain brown carton bore dirt streaks and dust. Some present, he thought, but her eagerness seemed to grow.

"Susannah, maybe we shouldn't."

For all he knew, Drake Whittaker had a weird streak. Like all public figures, Jeb had received his share of strange "gifts," seen his share of oddball "presents."

The box flaps snapped open and Susannah made a sound.

"Jeb, look!" But all he saw was a stack of musty-smelling papers. "They're Clary's," she said, her smile incandescent. "Don't you see? There won't be any scandal. My father sent us the journals!" And she flung her arms around his neck.

The queasy feeling didn't leave him, though. It didn't leave him that afternoon while they plowed through the notebooks, and he revisited his sister's childhood, his own. Like the sad-sweet memories, it didn't leave him in the bus that night, rumbling south through Tennessee into Mississippi, while he and Susannah read some more and Jeb came to terms with his feelings for Clary, who had been his companion in childhood but not beyond. When he read the entries that had upset Susannah, he knew the same sick feeling would never completely leave him.

They'd spread the journals around them on the state-room's bed, and out front he could hear Mack, Skeet, and the others teasing Breeze about Michael Alsop, who had kissed her good-bye with promises to call, who had sent her twelve dozen roses, a dozen for each hour, the cards said, that they had spent together. And then . . .

"Jesus Christ."

"What is it?" Susannah asked.

"His name."

"Whose name?" She leaned over his shoulder to see the open journal page. "Clary didn't use a name. That's why I thought . . ."

"Here she does," he said, pointing. He'd been reading about the months after their rift, after he'd found her with the deputy sheriff and discovered what a fool he was to believe in Clary. Susannah hadn't read past the earlier entries before.

"Gage?" Susannah read, still not understanding.

"Like many southern men, like me," he said, "Clary's sheriff had a string of names, family names. Richard Gage Sheridan."

"Jeb, I don't see—"

"Richard. Gage. Sheridan," he said again and tapped the name on the page written in Clary's hand. "Just as she called me Cody, she called most men by their last names, but she couldn't with him." Jeb paused. "He was married, and a father." He thought of Mack, of the times he'd given Breeze a hard time because Mack had a wife and two little boys. "So Clary always called him Gage—his middle name."

When Susannah would have spoken, he pressed a finger to her lips. "Remember that page of her daybook they found in the park? She'd scribbled two letters on it," he said, his sense of urgency and horror growing with each word, "and the police tried to blame me for them. J.E., they said. But, Susannah, the police were wrong."

She simply stared at him, as if he'd lost his mind.

Jeb spun the book around. "Look how she makes her G's, the little ones not the capitals. They look almost like capital J's."

Susannah's head touched his, and he heard her breathe out, "Ohhh. Oh, Jeb."

"That's all she had time to write. The two letters. Or maybe the ink didn't flow. But they weren't the first two of my name or anyone else's. They were the last two of Gage Sheridan's. G.E." Jeb slapped the journal shut. "Damn him."

"Do you think he still saw her? After she married Drake?"

"What do you think?" Jeb held her gaze, the bus lumbering along in rhythm with his distracted heartbeat, making him feel not sexy, but sick. "You think Gage let her leave Elvira and that was the end of it?" Jeb shook his head. "I don't think so. And from what I know now of Clary, the hard way, she couldn't let him go either. Married to a man older than Gage? A busy man without enough time for her? And what about that beach house Drake bought . . . in Carolina, wasn't it?"

"Hilton Head."

"It would have been an easy enough trip to the Atlantic coast. That's where lots of people down home go. Where he went to see her. I don't imagine Dick Sheridan came to New York—not more than once," he said, feeling cold now.

"You think he killed her."

"I know he didn't know how to stop himself once he got started. I don't suppose he reserved that temper of his just for me." Tracing his scar, he looked down at the closed journal, but he could still envision Clary's hand-writing. "I saw bruises on her more than once."

"Let's call the New York police, Jeb. Tell them what you think. Show them the journals."

The panic faded, and a sense of calm settled over him. He'd never felt so calm. He hadn't been home in years, too many years. As John Eustace always told him, it was time.

"Sure," Jeb said. "After I take a little trip of my own."

21

On a sunny autumn afternoon Susannah sat beside Jeb in a rental car, as he drove into Elvira. In the week since he'd read Clary's journals, on the road in Baton Rouge, then Galveston, he'd been loving, even tender, yet somehow removed. She could only hope that these two days—the first break in his tour schedule—near John Eustace would finally heal him. Until then, she knew, in the deeper ways that counted, she and Jeb were merely going through the motions.

He whizzed along Elvira's tree-shaded streets of neat suburban homes, past a modern, yellow-brick building.

"Was that your elementary school?" she asked.

"No, they built a new one after Clary and I reached junior high." He smiled thinly without taking his gaze from the road. "You should have seen ours. One story, four rooms, a board floor that hadn't seen varnish in half a century. It burned down one night, saving the town from having to raze it."

Susannah wondered whether he was kidding, playing to her former opinions of his background. She had to admit, Elvira came as another surprise. When they glided past the sheriff's office without slowing down, Jeb's mouth pressed into a tight line, his knuckles white on the steering wheel.

"I'll drop you at PawPaw's first."

"Not your family's house?"

"Nobody there," he said. "Sometimes the younger kids come home, at holiday time, but even they've been putting up at John Eustace's the past few years." Susannah couldn't help envisioning a slum, with falling plaster and broken steps. "I'll show you," Jeb said, but when he pulled into the short gravel drive off a paved side road not far from the center of town and its main street, she simply stared.

Jeb helped Susannah from the car. After shutting off an elaborate security system, he guided her inside the traditional frame house to a small entryway with a room off to each side, and the stairway in front of her.

She could almost be overcome by memories, second-hand, from Clary and Jeb. *What was it like, growing up there?* she'd asked months ago, and he'd said, *Crowded.* But though plain, the house seemed spacious enough.

"Living room"—he waved to his right—"dining room, turned into my folks' bedroom"—he waved to the left—"kitchen at the end of this hall." He led her upstairs. "Three bedrooms, one bath. Which might have worked better if I'd had six more brothers instead of sisters." He caught Susannah's expression as she squeezed out of the small but clean bathroom. "You thought there'd be bats flyin' around, didn't you? Holes in the roof and ceilings? Drip pots to catch the rain? Broken linoleum floors, dirt everywhere."

"No, I didn—"

In a bedroom doorway he dropped a kiss on her mouth. "The same way I expected your house to have gilt and marble and alabaster cherubs carved in the door-frames."

The upstairs furniture was simple, and the walls were painted white, with framed children's drawings and a few religious pictures, featuring children with Jesus.

He took her hand, gently tugging her downstairs and outside to a sloping lawn, still green and thick in early October. As they walked downhill, she saw a hummock of dirt covered by grass and slowed her steps, nearly stopping. Jeb turned, following her gaze.

"My wife's not buried there. My son either."

Another misleading story of Clary's, she thought.

With a faint shiver, Susannah trailed him down to a clear, gurgling creek that ran over rocks and stones from around a curve in the hill, then past the house, below it, and toward the nearby road, where it tunneled under a bridge. Across the road half a dozen houses scattered another rolling hillside typical of the state but new to Susannah, who had seen more brown California hills than green in her adult life. On Jeb's side of the street, three or four more houses occupied the hill and their own generous two-acre plots.

In the peaceful setting she found it hard to imagine Clary's sheriff and their torrid relationship, or Jeb's father in handcuffs, being pushed into a patrol car.

"Seen enough to convince you our baby won't inherit any serial-killer genes?"

"Are you calling me a snob?"

"Former snob," he said. "Are you sayin' that's my own insecurities talking?" For the first time since she'd known him he looked ashamed, and she realized how difficult this trip had been for him. How even more difficult it might become.

"Maybe we should go," she said, touching his arm. "Rejoin the tour. What good will confronting Dick Sheridan do?"

"Susannah, we've been over this before." He walked back up the hill in the afternoon sun, his hair a myriad of shades: gold and russet and deep, rich sable. "You could've stayed with Breeze and the band."

"I don't want you hurt," she said, marching after him.

"I don't want *you* hurt. That's why I'm droppin' you at John Eustace's." He waited for her at the car. "I'm hoping Sheridan will be on duty tonight and we can finish things."

"Jeb, this isn't your fight!"

He slammed the passenger door shut as soon as Susannah moved her unwieldy shape onto the front seat. "My sister is dead! Dammit, you've been tellin' me to face that for the past six months! Your own father gave me the proof I needed to know Clary was murdered. You wanted me involved. Now what in hell would you have me do? Turn my back on her—again?" He went around, climbing into the driver's seat and slamming that door too. "She wasn't what I once thought she was, but who the hell is?"

Her tone insistent, Susannah touched the nape of his neck. "Jeb, you don't have to take care of her anymore."

He shrugged away. The look he gave her nearly shattered her heart.

"Is that what Drake taught you in that big house in Greenwich? To care for people only when it's convenient? Or socially proper? Or self-serving? Like that shelter of yours in my sister's name? Frankly, you're the most homeless person—emotionally—I ever met!"

Stricken, she stared down at her hands in her all but nonexistent lap. The baby kicked hard against the backs of her wrists.

"God. I'm sorry," he said. "I'm sorry."

But he wouldn't change his mind. Riding toward John Eustace's house, Susannah twisted the shiny wedding band on her finger until it chafed. And wondered whether she had married Jeb, loved him, come to trust in him and in their future together, a family, only to lose him in the end. If not to Richard Sheridan's fists or gun, then to a memory. Ironically, to Clary.

They'd had their first married fight, Jeb thought, reluctantly leaving Susannah at his grandfather's house, and John Eustace knew it. He hadn't seemed exactly glad to see them.

"Don't be a damn fool, boy. Richard Sheridan didn't kill Clary."

The journals didn't convince him, and neither could Jeb. The old man always had been as stubborn as a too-tight cap on a canning jar. Looking away from the pained expression in John Eustace's watery blue eyes, he opened the front door.

"Take care of Susannah."

"Jeb, please," she said, nestled in the crook of his grandfather's arm.

Running lightly down the front steps, he nearly turned back to catch a glimpse of her face, her eyes, the tangle of blond curls in which he loved to bury his fingers.

"I'll be back," he said, half to himself.

Jeb didn't drive directly to Richard Sheridan's office in town. He had several other things to do—things he'd been needing to do for years, needed to do now in case nothing worked out the way he planned. He supposed John Eustace knew that too. He stopped first at the iron-fenced cemetery behind Elvira's Baptist church.

On his mother's grave Jeb laid a small spray of autumn flowers, purchased on Broadway at the florist and craft shop still run by one of her friends.

"Mama," he murmured, "you were a fine woman. You did right by your children, but no doubt about it, you may have raised a fool for your oldest son."

Holding a second bouquet, he stared across the expanse of grass-covered mounds. Jeb sought the granite headstone he'd never seen before. John Eustace had bought it as directed with Jeb's money.

He stood, legs slightly spread, his hands in his back pockets, his head down as he read the stone's engraving:

Rachel Miller Cody. 1964–1980
Jeb Stuart Cody, Jr. Died at Birth, 1980

For long moments, he stayed, remembering the young girl he had first loved, her brown hair and eyes, her sweet smile. That's all he could remember. No image of her features, nothing of that first love remained.

"She's with the angels now," John Eustace had said when she died, the baby too.

And so she was. They were.

Jeb laid the other flowers across the mounded earth, the lush green grass, and in the deep bronze light of late afternoon walked back to the rented car, away from his youth.

Next, he drove the twenty miles to the state prison where his daddy lived.

The meeting didn't go well, but Jeb hadn't expected it would.

"Thought you'd get me out, did you?" William Cody said through the phone that connected them on either side of the glass partition in the visiting area. "Sing your way to fame and fortune, so you could pay off some judge on my behalf? Well, you're rollin' in money now, I suppose—and I'm still behind bars."

Jeb stared at the grizzled face opposite, at his father's straggly gray hair and dull eyes, for one second afraid he was looking in a mirror at his own future reflection. "I can't get you out."

"Hell, what do I care? I got three meals a day and a bed to sleep in. Plenty of friends." He shrugged. "And o'course, you may not know that prison is a real education." Leaning into the receiver, he nearly whispered, "Next time they won't catch me. I'm smarter now."

"If you were smart, Daddy, you'd be on the other side of this glass." Jeb rose from the hard-backed chair. He didn't like his father any better than he had the last time they saw each other, years ago while he was awaiting sentence for armed robbery, and Jeb knew he wouldn't visit again; that there was no point. "I'll send you some cigarette money. And a couple of my CDs when I get a chance." By the time he reached Elvira, full dark would have fallen. By then, Jeb figured, Sheridan would be on duty, waiting for him; as he must have been waiting for six months. Taking a step, he stopped and looked at the man who had fathered him but had never been a father to him. "There's nothin' more I can do for you, Daddy. I already raised your family."

Ignoring the low-down pain in her back, Susannah paced John Eustace's office. She had wanted as much as Jeb did to know what happened to Clary. Convinced from the start, as he hadn't been, that Clary had been murdered, she'd wanted the killer behind bars, but not if that meant risking Jeb's safety.

"Stop wearin' a hole in my rug," John Eustace said.

His laconic attitude irritated Susannah. "Are we going to stay here, doing nothing, while he walks in to that sheriff's office?"

"If there's something to be done, I'll do it."

"What?" she said. "Drive by after it's all over? Patch Jeb up again?"

John Eustace's hands shook as he opened the glass-fronted case in the office which adjoined his home. Susannah thought he was checking his medical supplies—bandages, gauze, tape, disinfectant—until she looked again and saw that the case held racks of guns. "Jeb is in no danger."

"If he is, you'll be too late!"

But John Eustace wasn't going anywhere. Selecting a dark wood-handled pistol from the rack, he exchanged its short barrel for another, longer one—roughly eight or nine inches—then limped through the room and outside. "Have you ever fired a gun?"

Following him, she suppressed a shudder. "I once chaired a committee for the control of handguns. I've never had any interest in shooting."

He made his way across the yard, tacking a clean bull's-eye to a heavily padded area on the rear of the garage. "Target shooting's different," John Eustace said. He held the pistol in one hand, testing its balance. "When Jeb was a boy, his daddy tried to interest him in hunting."

"I know. He told me."

Susannah stood near the back porch steps, frowning at his obvious attempt to divert her from worrying about

Jeb. His choice seemed a strange one. She stood several feet away while John Eustace loaded the pistol, explaining each motion, then sighted down the long steel barrel at the bull's-eye. His eye keen, his gaze steady now, he pulled the trigger, ripping a hole in the target, off-center.

"I've lost my edge," he said with a faint smile. "Jeb outshoots me every time." He gestured her closer, pressing the gun into Susannah's hand. "Never taught a pregnant lady to shoot before. Just look down the barrel, line up your spot—that center hole will do nicely—and squeeze the trigger. Gently. Go on now."

The gun kicked, flinging Susannah's arm up. The shot clipped a corner of the garage, sending splinters flying, a piece of roof shingle.

John Eustace studied the damage. "Of course in self-defense a man—or woman—might not have time for niceties, like taking aim. Up close, you wouldn't worry about hitting that bull's-eye. Theoretically speaking."

After a few more rounds each, with John Eustace placing his dead center, Susannah trailed him back into the house where he cleaned the pistol as if preparing for surgery. The sweet scent of gun oil filled the room, and she could still smell the gunpowder. "Can't we phone the police in the nearest town? The state highway patrol?" she asked. "Sheridan nearly killed Jeb once. If he's cornered now, he might try again. Please, PawPaw." Susannah rested her hand over his on the pistol.

Not meeting her eyes, John Eustace stared at their hands.

"All Jeb will get from Sheridan is a laugh in his face or a fist in his jaw—if Jeb should be so foolish as to press the issue." He glanced at Susannah, and a shiver ran down her spine as she watched the economical movements of his hands, swabbing the pistol's barrel with a wad of cloth soaked in the pungent oil. Something he'd obviously done many times. "You know how I feel about this, Miss Susannah." He flicked a sad smile at her. "Jeb's better off without her. And I'm not sorry Clary's dead."

Spraying gravel, Jeb stopped the rental car in the parking lot behind the Waylan County Sheriff's Office. Trying to forget his visit with his father and to concentrate on seeing Susannah soon, he crossed the lot to the rear door, the one most often used since Jeb was a boy. The same door through which he'd been thrown one night, the same yard in which he'd been beaten bloody. Only one light burned in the small building, and slamming the back door, not caring whether Sheridan heard him, he wondered if half his anger now wasn't for the boy he'd once been.

Even without Clary's death, he would have come back. Someday.

Jeb walked through the galley kitchen and down a short hall into the office, which took up half the front area of the building, the other half occupied by a few cells behind a steel outer door.

"Evening, Gage." The desk chair shot upright, spun around. "Nappin' on the job? Somebody could stroll in here and blow you clean away, into some permanent dream. You'd never know it. Like Clary."

Sheridan stared. He'd gained weight, though not as much as expected, and in fact looked fit, the buttons of his uniform shirt neatly closed over a still-flat belly, and in his mid-forties now, the sheriff's face bore few lines that would have shown his longtime drinking habit. Maybe he'd stopped, Jeb thought. As Sheridan came fully awake, his brown eyes grew more alert. His reddish hair, its color common in the southern states, hadn't thinned, and he still wore it squarely trimmed at the nape of his neck. A slim black ribbon slashed diagonally across his silver badge. For Clary? Jeb wondered.

"Well. Jeb Stuart Cody." Sheridan laughed a little. "The famous man himself."

"Thought I'd pay a visit." Jeb ignored the chair kicked out for him. "You're sheriff now, John Eustace tells me. Elected by the people, no less." He smiled. "You always were a real politician."

"I heard about your sister," the sheriff said. "I'm sorry."

Jeb studied his boot. He didn't believe Sheridan was sorry at all, especially when he mentioned New York, the dead-end police investigation there.

"I heard the police detained you for a time, questioned you pretty hard."

"Aren't you going to ask me if I did it?" Jeb said.

"What do you want from me?"

"An apology would be nice. For starters." He stroked a finger across his upper lip where the small scar reminded him, each time he shaved, of Clary's sheriff. He leaned forward, bracing his hands on the desktop. "A man tries to rearrange a kid's face, just for lookin' out for his sister—whom the man's been screwin' before she's of age—and the man wonders what he wants now."

"That was years ago." Sheridan shot out of his seat. "If you've come home just for an apology—"

"I said for starters."

"All right, I apologize." His expression was puzzled, a bit fearful. "I was a hothead in those days. I never should have touched you."

Jeb's fists clenched. "You never should have touched her."

"Hell, I know she was young, but we—we loved each other. I swear we did."

"Love? Your wife and kids know that? Or didn't you ever get around to telling 'em?" Jeb took a step. "Too late now. When I get through with you, it'll be front-page news. *Night Line*'ll be beggin' your lawyer to appear. There'll be people lined up in front of the courthouse in New York, just prayin' to be selected for the jury."

"What the hell are you talkin' about?" The fear disappeared from Gage's eyes and anger replaced it. "You gone over the edge like that daddy of yours? I may have taken you down a peg or two for interfering, but I never hurt Clary."

"I saw the bruises!"

"She liked it rough, that's all." He stared at Jeb, one hand on the holster at his hip. "Clary used to ask me to kiss her hard, squeeze her tighter." He paused. "And I admit, it set fire to me too . . . but I didn't hurt her in the way you mean."

"You killed her!"

Sheridan's face turned white but he said nothing.

"Don't tell me you didn't keep seein' her after she married Drake Whittaker." Jeb stepped closer, his fists tightening. "She married an older man, and you must have looked pretty good after awhile. Whittaker's a selfish bastard, gone all the time, not exactly attentive to his women. After a couple of years Clary must have been ripe for another go-round with you. So she wheedled Drake into buyin' her a house on the beach at Hilton Head, and you two took up again. Only this time you didn't need the backseat of a patrol car on some dark road."

"You got a dark mind, Cody." Sheridan turned away. Jeb expected the sheriff to whirl, his .357 magnum aimed at Jeb's chest, but when Sheridan faced him again, he deliberately placed the gun on the desk. "I don't know what's got in your mind about me and Clary and how she died, but you're wrong. I loved that girl. I still love her in a way I've never loved my wife or any other woman. I can't explain it. I stopped tryin' long ago." He looked at Jeb, as if pleading. "I miss her too. I've felt so helpless here. I wish I knew who killed her— if it *was* murder, which no one's proved."

"Clary's journals can," he said.

The sheriff looked blank. Briefly, Jeb explained the entries, then the daybook page found in Central Park.

"My name? Gage?" Sheridan said, shaking his head. "I swear to you, I was nowhere near New York that day." He glanced at the dark ribbon over his badge. "I was at a deputy's funeral. One of my boys stopped a drunk driver who turned out to be high on crack instead, and packing a nine-millimeter automatic. My alibi's sound," he said. "My wife went to his funeral with me, then we sat up all night with his widow." He frowned. "If Clary wrote my name, or part of it, it was a last message to me, I'd guess . . . a good-bye when she was dying." He swallowed. "Christ, I never thought we'd end that way."

Jeb's resolve faltered. From the ashen color of Gage's face, the sorrow in his dark eyes, he didn't look like a guilty man. He looked like a grief-stricken man who, until now, had been fighting not to show it, had been unable to show it. Like Jeb.

"They're not letters from my name either," he said. His fists relaxed. He'd missed something in those letters. "But I feel in my bones they're a clue. Clary wrote everything in her journal." He looked at Sheridan. "Everything. She left a message on Susannah—my wife's— answering machine the day she died. Susannah, who is

Drake Whittaker's daughter, thinks it was before she went to meet someone, someone she feared might harm her." Jeb frowned. "Someone she knew."

"And knew well, I'd say." The grief eased from Sheridan's features, and he looked thoughtful. "Most people are killed by somebody they know."

Jeb repeated the letters aloud, as he'd interpreted them. "*G . . . E.*"

"George? Gerald?" Sheridan thought some more. "How about Geoffrey? Like the English spell it? There must be a lot of fancy spellings in that circle Clary ran with after she married Whittaker."

"I don't know," Jeb said with a sigh. "Clary and I weren't on good terms when she died, as you know. I wish to hell we had been. I sure didn't know who her friends or enemies might be."

Sheridan hesitated, as if afraid to make the suggestion that might set Jeb off again. "What about your wife? She and Clary must know the same people."

Jeb stared at the man he'd hated much of his life. Like Susannah, Jeb had been the victim of Clary's stories too, and it was difficult to separate truth from fiction. Still, he had to admit, Richard Sheridan had the logical thought processes of a longtime lawman. He knew how to conduct an investigation, start to finish.

"I'll talk to Susannah," Jeb said.

Sheridan traced the handle of his gun with one finger. "While you do, I'll make a list of folks around here. Who knows, maybe someone felt jealous of Clary's wealth—her escape from the hills?" It had been Jeb's thought once. "Or took a long-ago dislike to her looks. Simple as that. Someone," Richard Gage Sheridan said, "from Elvira."

❖   ❖   ❖

Jeb pushed the accelerator to the floor, careening around the last corner and barely slowing for John Eustace's driveway. He rocked the car to a stop, its nose to the bumper of the old man's treasured blue Buick, and hit the front porch steps running. God, he hoped Sheridan was wrong, prayed he was wrong. But the fear had grown in him with every mile.

At first he thought that, despite the car in the drive, no one was home. His grandfather and Susannah might have gone walking, a favorite nighttime pursuit of PawPaw's, especially when his day "didn't set well." He stepped through the living room archway into John Eustace's office—which he'd never shut off from the house with a proper door separating his professional from his personal life—and found them there.

Susannah didn't look at him, but John Eustace glanced up from something he'd been showing her. Jeb couldn't see what it was. Susannah stood between them in the shadowed room lit only by the ancient green piano lamp on John Eustace's desk.

"When you goin' to learn not to slam doors, boy, or burn out your brakes and tires before their time?"

Jeb leaned against the doorframe, crossing his arms. Maybe he was wrong. Please God, he was. "I didn't touch your car. Didn't even kiss its tail this time. It'll go another hundred and fifty thousand miles."

"Should outlive me then."

Jeb noticed his face looked pinched, and pale. And Susannah hadn't moved.

"You all right, sugar?" He stepped closer, trying to see around her. The soft light shone in her blond curls, and he ached to twine his fingers around the stray wisp at the nape of her neck. "I'm sorry for what I said before. About the shelter and Drake. About you." He stumbled over his apology until John Eustace looked up again, his watery blue eyes pained. Jeb's stomach tightened. He'd known this old man, loved him, all his life. He fought to keep his tone casual. "You two plannin' my downfall, or somethin'? Susannah—"

"I'm fine."

Her voice sounded thin and soft. She shifted her weight, as if to ease some discomfort—perhaps from the baby's movements inside her—and Jeb saw the gun in John Eustace's gnarled hands. Like a shot of bad whiskey, cold shock hit Jeb's stomach.

John Eustace said, "After you took off on your mission, I decided Miss Susannah needed some distraction. It's never too soon to teach a woman how to protect herself." He smoothed the gun's mahogany handgrip with one finger, as he might have caressed a baby's cheek. "I'm afraid she didn't exactly take to the sport right away." He glanced at Jeb. "Remember when your daddy made you go huntin'? And I told you it wasn't the gun that killed that mama deer but the man who pulled the trigger?"

"You said I'd find the skill itself useful."

The next day John Eustace had started teaching him to shoot. He'd taught Clary too. "I believe Clary liked it more than I did. Why don't you put the gun back in the case, PawPaw, and we can talk in the living room."

"Susannah should sit down," John Eustace agreed. "I'm disappointed in you, boy. Upsetting her, runnin' out like that . . . I see Sheridan left you in one piece this time."

"We found some common ground."

"Did you now?" He stroked the gun again, as if seeking comfort.

Susannah turned her head slightly, her eyes wide with

what could only be fear. Jeb looked away, sickened, knowing she had reached the same conclusion he had, that she didn't want him to make another foolish move.

All the way to the house his brain had been trying not to hear the same ending to some crazy song. G.E., he had thought, for Gage Sheridan. The police still thought the letters were a *J* and an *E*, for his own name. And they were partly right. But until Gage had said, "someone from Elvira," the thought never crossed his mind. Or he hadn't let it.

J.E. . . . for John Eustace. Who had hated Clary.

"What kind of common ground?" his grandfather said, not meeting Jeb's gaze.

"I think you know," he said at last.

Oh, PawPaw. Tell me I'm wrong.

But John Eustace seemed not to hear. Deliberately he picked up a polishing rag. "I was telling Susannah that cleaning's as important as closing up a surgical wound with neat stitches." He paused. "But she took offense to something I said just before you walked in."

"John Eustace. Tell me about Clary."

"Oh, God," Susannah murmured.

"I should have known you'd find me out." The old man looked up at Jeb. "It won't take long. I'm tired—we all are—so I'll make it short." Slanting the gun to the light, as if looking for fingerprints, he said, "Clary had begun calling me here in Elvira, for some months before she died. She had that idea to write a book about you, which I tried to discourage, but then one day she phoned to tell me—gloating, I thought—that she had signed a contract with some big New York publisher and would be announcing her intentions to the press."

"I know about her press conference. Go on."

He studied the gun. "I'd never liked much of what

Clary had to say. I doubted I would in print either. She made some noises about wanting to see you again . . . lies of course. I doubt she meant to seek your approval about the book. She always did what she pleased, but I told her you were on tour and suggested we talk it over first."

"Where?"

"I was coming north for that concert of yours anyway at the convention center, so I suggested we meet in New York. I took an earlier plane that day than I'd planned, and Clary arranged to come into the city from Connecticut. It was her idea to meet in Central Park."

His grandfather's matter-of-fact tone, the lack of denial, seemed to make Jeb's own realization worse, and Susannah's profile showed her pallor.

John Eustace sighed. "She was a truly beautiful woman, Jeb. But still rotten inside. As soon as I saw her, auburn hair flying, those eyes bright with her usual malice—no matter that she would have called it spirit—and all swathed in mink, I knew why Drake Whittaker had fallen for her. I knew she also had no true intention of making peace with you. She'd never stopped loving you, she said, but Clary never loved anyone—"

"She did," Susannah said in a choked voice.

"—but herself."

"She loved Gage Sheridan," Jeb said.

Slowly, carefully, John Eustace reloaded the pistol. "Gage never did have any sense. If he believed that, he's an even bigger fool."

Jeb had felt betrayed years ago, by Clary. But he'd never imagined the sense of loss he felt now, rolling through him in sickening waves. His grandfather had become obsessed with Clary. He reached out, beseeching, not wanting to hear the rest of the story, but John

Eustace tightened his grip on the gun, and Jeb saw how very close it was to Susannah.

"We quarreled of course. I can't recall a time when we didn't quarrel, Clary and I, just setting eyes on each other. I asked her to leave you be, to cancel her contract for the book, or at least to give you and Breeze Maynard and your lawyers first look before publication." John Eustace watched his own white knuckles on the gun. "She laughed in my face. Said she'd left Elvira long ago and wasn't about to get under my thumb, or anyone else's again. Said she had Drake Whittaker wrapped around her finger and Gage Sheridan too. She had everything she wanted. Money, position, power, beauty."

"What happened?"

"She said . . . she said I couldn't block her from seeing you. If I tried, she'd write things about you . . . untrue things, sick things." His eyes met Jeb's. "I told her she was evil. That she had her daddy's blood in her veins and none of my daughter's, that I hoped she'd rot in hell." He shivered, seeming to grow smaller, weaker, in front of Jeb's eyes. "I told her if her book came out and damaged you, I would gladly kill her myself."

"You couldn't have," Susannah said, looking at his hands. "The police never found a murder weapon. From the ballistics report on the slugs they found, they know it was a Wesson, with a two-inch barrel, but—"

John Eustace's gaze flickered, and Jeb's followed from the gun in his grasp to the cabinet on the wall, glass fronted and filled with rifles, shotguns, the target pistols John Eustace favored. His soul, his faith in John Eustace, seemed to drain from him like blood from a corpse in a mortuary. Mounted on the cabinet wall, as clean and shining as the nine-inch target pistol in his grandfather's hand, as apparently unused, was the smaller barrel that went with it; the one that had killed Clary.

"A Dan Wesson," Jeb nearly whispered. "With inter-changeable parts, including the barrel. PawPaw gave one to me and one to . . . her." Jeb had lent his to his brother, Ethan. "This is Clary's, isn't it?"

"She brought it to our meeting. She pulled it on me," he admitted. "Yes, it's hers. She never had any control of her emotions, her anger—just like your father—not from the time she was a small child. She hid that from you many times, Jeb, but never from me. I think that's what hurt you most, that she never let you see her true self and so it came as a surprise when you found her with Gage Sheridan that night."

Clary had raged at John Eustace in Central Park. Clawed his face. Said she hated him.

"You shot her," Jeb said. "Left her there for dead."

"Yes. The only time since I took the Hippocratic oath not to do harm that I deliberately turned away from someone in need." He didn't look at Jeb or Susannah. "We struggled over the gun. It went off, hitting her right in the chest. I knew she wouldn't live. Her eyes went wide and startled and I must admit, I ran."

"She lived long enough to write your initials," Jeb said.

"Not then, I remember she'd had the book open on her lap while we talked. But she didn't make any notes, had no reason to. I wouldn't give her what she wanted—access to you again."

"That wasn't your place, PawPaw."

"I had to protect you, Jeb. She turned mean, as she always did with me. She scrawled something in that book of hers and I took it, flung it away into the bushes . . ."

Staring at John Eustace, Jeb fought the waves of sick-ness. "'Truth,'" he said softly, quoting his favorite Shake-

speare, "'will come to light; murder cannot be hid long.'"
With the words, he saw the gun rising. "Susannah. Step
away from him. Now!"

As if paralyzed, she didn't move. John Eustace's hand
tightened until it seemed he would crush the gun itself. He
looked straight into Jeb's eyes as if memorizing the sense of
betrayal he would see there. "I didn't mean to kill her, even
to hurt her. If I had it to do over again, I wouldn't—
because you loved her, even knowing what she was." His
eyes filled. "I love you, Jeb. More than my own life."

"Then, Christ, don't make another mistake." The seconds seemed to have slowed, to be standing still. Jeb
swallowed, afraid to lunge at John Eustace. But he
would take the bullet himself before he let his grandfather use Susannah as a shield, before he risked the
woman he loved, and their child.

Susannah found her voice. "Put the gun down, John
Eustace."

Terror gripped her as tightly as his hold on the pistol.
If he raised it another few inches, took aim, and
squeezed the trigger . . . Jeb was more in the line of fire
than she, yet he had ordered her to move away. She
could not imagine life without him, and if, at such close
range, with such skill, John Eustace fired . . .

"Forgive me, Jeb," he whispered.

She watched the barrel rise, saw the glint of metal in
the lamplight, saw John Eustace's finger jerk ever so
faintly on the trigger. Then in the split second before
she moved, she saw that he wasn't aiming at Jeb, or at
her; he wouldn't harm either of them, or the baby she
carried. He meant to kill himself. If he did, how would
Jeb deal with that?

In that fraction of time, Susannah threw herself at
John Eustace.

The gun went off. The sound shattered the silence in the room. Shards of plaster flew, then she felt a warm gush and saw crimson begin to drip onto her breast, onto the cloth-covered mound of her belly, onto the floor.

In horror she felt herself crumple.

"Susannah!" she heard Jeb cry.

Then she saw nothing. Only blackness.

22

Susannah surveyed her San Francisco living room. Pillows plumped, tables polished, candles in crystal holders lighted, and in the far corner between the marble fireplace and the front windows, the Christmas tree.

Nine feet tall, its gossamer angel brushing the ceiling, the noble Douglas fir had been hung with every delicate ornament that caught her eye, and Jeb had draped it with silver icicles. Susannah cast a critical gaze at his handiwork. She and Jeb had quarreled, good naturedly, over the proper method—hers artfully arranged on each branch, his flung in gobs.

"This is our first Christmas," she'd said. "I want it to be perfect."

"Just being together makes it perfect," he'd answered, cradling her close.

In the nearly three months since that horrible night in

Elvira when they'd nearly lost each other, she and Jeb had truly become a couple, but if she sometimes still saw shadows in his eyes when he mentioned John Eustace, she supposed he glimpsed the same in hers, about Drake and Leslie.

As she dimmed the lights, Susannah noticed Studley dancing in front of the tree, grabbing mouthfuls of tinsel, which she took from his mouth with a distracted air. Her parents would show up any minute, with suitcases in hand. Leslie had just been released from the Ford center with a clean bill of health, and Susannah had invited her to spend Christmas with her and Jeb. She didn't know what would happen when Drake also arrived.

"Ready for the fireworks?" Jeb said, coming into the room.

In a white shirt with the sleeves rolled back, stone-washed jeans and boots, he made her mouth water, but his smile made her grin.

She didn't know whether he meant her parents—or their baby, which she was trying not to think of as being late. Susannah's actual due date had barely passed, but she'd hoped to deliver on time if not early, as painlessly as possible, and be home with their son or daughter for Christmas. Jeb claimed babies made their appearance when ready and not before; two or three days meant nothing at all. Susannah wondered if he was really that calm, or accepting. She certainly wasn't—about her parents either.

"As ready as I'll ever be." She patted her abdomen. "For this baby too."

Pregnant or not, Susannah had been happy not to spend Christmas on the road, and several weeks before the tour broke for the holidays, Jeb had sent her on to California, deferring to her complaints that she couldn't pass a bathroom without having to stop. Her nerves at the moment didn't help the problem.

"We've read all the books, watched that video a thousand times. The doctor says you're fine." But he frowned as the memory of *So You're Having Your Baby by Lamaze* flashed through Susannah's mind too. Jeb had more experience at childbirth than she did, not all of it good. "Besides," he added, "it's not enough that you invited Drake and Leslie, who'll probably go at each other's throats before we serve the turkey. John Eustace will be released from the hospital today too. No telling what might happen."

"It's all right that I asked him to stay with us, isn't it?" she asked.

Jeb didn't quite meet her gaze. "Sure. Why not? It's Christmas and holidays are for family. I'm glad you're learnin' that." He slipped his arms around her. "Lord, I used to be able to span your waist. Now it's like huggin' a hot air balloon."

Susannah kissed his bared throat. "Thank you very much."

"Think I'll keep you lookin' like this every year."

She groaned in mock distress. "I can hardly wait."

"Wait until you see what Santa brought," he said, then kissed her cheek right where the bullet from John Eustace's gun had creased it, where the thin scar still showed, which her plastic surgeon had assured her would fade over time. Jeb left her standing in the entryway, peering out the front door for the next cab that might stop at the curb.

"It's John Eustace," she said when a limousine pulled up instead. Susannah whirled—as best she could—checking the house once more. The scent of roasting turkey wafted through the foyer, permeating even the pine ropes tied around the stairway with red velvet ribbon.

Jeb didn't reappear. He seemed to be making a project of changing one soft white bulb in a string on the Christmas tree.

Hearing the car, Studley raced from the other room, more icicles trailing, flinging himself at the closed door and barking. Susannah opened the front door, shaking the huge wreath and its pinecones, setting its red and gold ribbons quivering. Jeb's driver helped John Eustace from the long black car, carrying his overnight bag and cane up the walk.

"Jeb?" she called.

John Eustace came into the house on a drift of damp bay air, his gaze directed just to the right of Susannah's cheek, his watery blue eyes looking more moist than usual.

"Merry Christmas, PawPaw." Susannah gingerly put her arms around him.

"I'm not a china doll. I won't break." He finally looked at her, his gaze telling her that he hadn't known what reception to expect. "Come give me a proper embrace, Miss Susannah. You were standin' under that mistletoe above the door and I aim to have a Christmas kiss from a pretty girl."

Kissing him, Susannah tried not to look toward the living room.

"Give him space." John Eustace touched his side. "I'm having to adjust to this brand-new hip of mine, and Jeb's having to get used to the notion of having another felon in the family. Both sides now."

After John Eustace's extradition to New York State, Jeb had posted his grandfather's bond. But he had yet to speak with him, and Susannah sensed that Jeb hadn't come to terms with his feelings.

"Come into the living room," she urged, an arm around John Eustace's waist. "You must want something to drink and maybe a snack before dinner."

His back to them, Jeb knelt under the tree, arranging brightly colored packages.

"Make mine bourbon, if you please," he and John Eustace said at the same time.

The doorbell rang and Susannah excused herself, not sure whether she wanted to answer and find her parents there, arguing already, or whether she wanted to stay to ease things between Jeb and John Eustace.

"Susannah. You look radiant." Sleek and trim, reeking of some new perfume that quarreled with the scents of pine and roasting turkey, Leslie swept into the house.

"Mother. You look . . . healthy."

"I feel marvelous. I've been playing tennis"—she slid a sable bomber jacket off her shoulders, handing it to Susannah—"and keeping up with my self-defense classes. Learning French. And I met the most intriguing man."

Drake came up the steps, pushing into the house as if he owned it. "Susie." He bussed her cheek, the scar, then looked her over from cream silk shirt to green velvet jumper. "Carrying lower, I see. Can't be long now. Where's the new father-to-be?"

He and Jeb must have reached some rapprochement. They'd been civil to each other since Drake had sent the journals, and her father sounded nearly happy about the baby. Drake, she thought, who was the least paternal person she knew.

"Jeb's chewing his nails." She took her parents, one on each arm. "We'll be ready to eat soon, but I think he wants to open presents first."

She found Jeb and John Eustace sitting on opposite sides of the room, Jeb on a footstool near the tree, gaz-

ing into the presents, John Eustace on the sofa with his
left leg propped on the cushions.

Over drinks and hors d'oeuvres, they tore wrappings
from the myriad gifts under the tree. Sweaters and ties,
jewelry for Leslie, a popular new scent, compact discs,
and for Drake and John Eustace each, copies of the latest medical thriller. When Susannah opened her last
present from Jeb, she frowned.

Inside the box she found only an envelope with her
name on it.

Casting a puzzled look at him, she opened it, read the
thick vellum note inside written in his bold hand, and
felt tears spring to her eyes.

"Jeb, nothing could have been more welcome. Thank
you."

The note informed her that he had offered Miranda's
father a job on his road crew, that Steve Colby had
accepted and would begin work when Jeb's tour continued through the West, then on to the Northeast starting in
January. Miranda and her mother would travel with him
when possible; when it wasn't, they would keep Studley
company at home in San Francisco. In Susannah's house,
as resident caretakers.

"There's nothing I needed more," she said, blinking.

Jeb put an arm around her shoulders, squeezing
lightly. "Merry Christmas, Miss Susannah. Many more."

Susannah's gift to Jeb—one of them—kept her grinning
with anticipation as he opened the box. She'd received the
contents only the day before by Federal Express, just in
time for wrapping in blue and gold and silver.

When Jeb pulled out the platinum disc encased in
plexiglass with its gold plaque at the bottom, his face
went comically blank. "Where did you get this?"

"From Breeze."

"Platinum," he said. "Really?"

"A million copies of the new album. Since September, Mr. Cody."

"I'll be damned. Double gold, platinum damned."

Susannah said, "Keep digging."

The next cloud of tissue paper covered another blue-wrapped plastic frame with gold plaque—and four discs in an arched row.

His shocked gaze met hers. "Quadruple?"

"For *Jeb Stuart Cody*," his first album.

"Well, I'll be damned."

Despite the occasional boos and hollers at his concerts, Jeb's career had taken a dramatic upturn after John Eustace's arraignment. Absolved of any blame in Clary's death, Jeb was beginning to enjoy his work again, and any day now, Susannah thought, he just might write another song, another hit single like "Little Rich Girl," which currently occupied first and second places on the country music and Billboard charts. Traditional and mainstream. Life seemed almost perfect. Once he overcame his awkwardness with John Eustace, once the baby arrived safely . . .

During dinner Susannah felt the first twinge of pain. Centered low in her back, it ground her against the chair and she bit her lip to keep from showing how much it hurt. It was nothing, she told herself. She'd been having pains, back and front, for weeks. Braxton-Hicks contractions, her obstetrician said, just nature practicing.

"You okay?" Jeb's turkey-loaded fork suspended in midair.

"Great." The pain ebbed, and Susannah looked down at her plate, suddenly not hungry for the whipped sweet potatoes, herbed stuffing, and cranberry sauce pooled there.

By ten o'clock, the pains had definitely grown worse, more frequent, and although frightened at the coming ordeal of greater magnitude they promised, she would have told Jeb, but he was finally talking, in stiff, short sentences, with John Eustace, his eyes averted. So she said nothing. Surely it was too soon.

At eleven o'clock the contractions abandoned her lower spine, shifting around to her distended abdomen. Leading Leslie and Drake up the stairs, she concentrated on settling them in for the night—the first time Drake had ever stayed with her instead of at a hotel, the first, family Christmas in her home with Jeb. To her surprise her parents hadn't exchanged a hostile word all day or evening. When Susannah said as much, her father answered with a smile.

"We agreed to be on our best behavior."

They'd even played Scrabble around the cleared dining room table after dessert. And Drake, reaching for a cigarette, put it back without lighting it. Because of the baby, he'd told Susannah.

"Les, I've given you the front room," she said, muffling a small groan as another pain streaked across her abdomen. The stair climb had made her gasp, that was all, made her thighs ache. "And Drake, the room across from Jeb's and mine on the third floor." John Eustace had made his way upstairs with Jeb's help moments before, and she could hear the two of them talking, with long silences between, from the room nearest to her mother's.

Leslie kissed her good night, showing Susannah more affection than she had in years. Her eyes looked clear, her skin too. "It's been a lovely day, Susie. I wouldn't have missed it for the world."

Drake touched Susannah's shoulder. "It's probably

the first Christmas I haven't missed because of some patient's complication. Thanks, sweetheart."

Feeling slightly dazed—from her parents' acceptance or the intermittent pains, she couldn't have said—Susannah left them and, with a last glance toward John Eustace's door, went upstairs.

She had a growing feeling that at least one problem would permanently resolve itself tonight. Presuming she could make it through. . . . She only hoped Jeb could too.

"By the way." Jeb leaned against the doorframe of John Eustace's room. "I spoke to your lawyer yesterday. He expects they'll let you off, in time, with a stern lecture and probation. . . . He's not hazarding a guess as to how much."

The old man shuffled around the room, putting his favorite books on the nightstand, shaking out his flannel sleep shirt, grunting as he leaned on his cane to drop his carpet slippers by the bed. "I'm grateful to you."

"I don't want your gratitude. Thank your lawyer. I'd have done the same," he said, "for Clary, you know."

Without looking his way, John Eustace shrugged off his suit jacket, then pulled off his tie, and with fingers that faintly trembled, unbuttoned his shirt. Jeb felt a wave of sadness at the wrinkled throat revealed in its opening, the slack chest muscles that presented themselves when his grandfather slipped out of the shirt. He nearly smiled, though, at the old-fashioned sleeveless underwear, the baggy boxer shorts.

"You ought to buy yourself some clothes," he said, with a glance toward the hallway behind him. He could have sworn he heard Susannah groaning.

"Didn't know you'd hang around to watch me strip."

"A sorrowful sight all right." Jeb gave in to the smile. He'd gone over that night in Elvira a hundred times, on a score of sleepless nights since, and he could still hear that gun exploding, see the plaster flying, feel his own horror at the blood on Susannah's cheek, at the sight of her sliding to the floor. John Eustace, standing there, white and shocked.

Hearing another muffled sound from the third floor, he edged backward into the hall. "I'll leave you to rest now. I imagine you're glad to be out of that hospital."

"Out of jail," John Eustace murmured, climbing into bed with a moan.

Jeb paused. "If you need anything . . ."

"I'm fine." He rolled onto his good side. "Thanks to you and Susannah's badgering, half of me's plastic now. Should last for another three quarters of a century. No need to worry about me."

"PawPaw?" Jeb lingered just outside the room. When no response was forthcoming, he said, "I'm sorry, I know today was difficult for you. But I can't condone what you did to Clary. I know there were extenuating circumstances, that her death was accidental—"

"Come here, boy."

The whispered words drew him to the bed. John Eustace turned onto his back, gazing up at him with those watery blue eyes, his shock of white hair stark against Susannah's new mulberry-colored guest room sheets. "I love you, Jeb. Maybe too much."

"I still can't accept what you almost did to yourself, either. I don't know how."

"Give us time, then. I haven't accepted it myself."

He caught Jeb's hand, his gnarled fingers squeezing Jeb's younger, stronger ones, as he had held on to him through the years, through sorrow and laughter, love and loss. "Time," Jeb agreed, his tone hoarse.

Slowly, by degrees, John Eustace released him. Then he whispered, "Merry Christmas, son. Now go on upstairs to that pretty woman of yours. She's waitin' for you."

Son, Jeb thought. John Eustace had always been more a father to him than his own. He had reached the hall again before he could say the words, and still, he had to qualify them. "I didn't want to keep on, but I can't seem to help myself. No matter what's happened, John Eustace, I love you too."

"Then we'll get by sooner or later. Won't we?"

"I'd guess we will."

Climbing the stairs, Jeb kept clearing his throat past the lump that had settled in it. His grandfather was aging. The time in the hospital for his hip surgery had taken its toll, and perhaps the best thing would be a trip, somewhere warm and sunny, at the next break in Jeb's tour. He and Susannah, John Eustace and the baby.

He found Susannah in the new nursery on the third floor across from their room. She hadn't turned the lights on, except for the small circus lamp on the white dresser, but stood over the matching crib, tucking in raspberry-colored sheets and fluffing the snowy white comforter.

"Is John Eustace tucked in?" she asked, not turning around.

"I think his hip is achin' him some but he wouldn't say so." Jeb sauntered into the room, which always made him smile. Its upper half had a wallpaper pattern of small, navy-blue bear pawprints with larger ones tracking across the white, angled ceiling and over the window frames. Red-and-white vertically striped paper decorated the bottom half of the walls, matching the puffy valances at the windows. Its whimsy pleased him. He wished his mama could have seen it. He said, "What about your parents?"

Susannah floated over to the dresser, pulling open drawers and rifling through the contents as if taking inventory: neat stacks of sleepers, tiny underwear, receiving blankets. He'd married one of the world's great organizers.

"Can you believe they haven't said a cross word to each other?" she finally said, then paused halfway through a pile of pristine diapers no bigger than Jeb's hand. He watched her breathe for a moment before she relaxed and went back to counting the diapers aloud. "Eighteen, twenty . . . I actually heard my mother ask him about the woman he's been seeing back in Greenwich. A wealthy widow, not more than five years younger than he is."

Jeb frowned a little. "I heard him ask Leslie about that 'intriguing man' she met."

"He's a recovering alcoholic."

"So is she." He walked closer. "Do I hear condemnation, Miss Susannah?"

"No. Of course not. I just don't want her to make a mistake . . . get involved too quickly just when she's doing so well."

"I think I hear a worried mother in the making," he said, slipping his arms around her from behind. "Having practically been one myself, I recognize the signs." He laid his chin on her shoulder. "Leslie's doin' all right. So is Drake. So is John Eustace, for that matter. I have a feeling that, whatever their shortcomings, they can all find their way. I suggest we let 'em be. And tend to our own."

"And Breeze?" Susannah murmured, shutting the diaper drawer.

"What about her?" To Jeb's delight, she'd been seeing Michael Alsop.

"When you two start touring together next fall, you won't feel it's your responsibility to keep an eye on her? Prevent her from making any mistakes herself?"

"No, ma'am." But he looked forward to the new tour, the next album, on which he and Breeze would sing their duet of "Do You Love Me?" in the hope it would fly to the top of the charts, both country and pop. After the first rehearsals of what promised to be a powerful, poignant, vocal duel between their two strong voices, he had few doubts.

"Susannah?" he said.

"What?" To his surprise she stiffened when he tightened his embrace.

"I've been thinkin'. About John Eustace and Clary." With a slight nudge in his ribs, Susannah suddenly slipped away, darting across the room to the closet. Jeb began to feel uneasy. "I mean, that message she left on your machine. 'Help him,'" he said, then had to swallow before he could say the rest. "Maybe she didn't mean me at all. Maybe she meant help John Eustace."

"But I didn't know him then—" Turning, she broke off, her eyes bright as they met his. "Maybe you're right," she said. "Maybe she did mean that."

On her way back to the crib with a small stuffed bear, she stopped.

"This has been the best Christmas I've ever had." She raised her mouth to his, approaching him from the side because her stomach kept getting in the way. "I love you. And don't you forget it. I won't let you," she said, "not for the rest of your life."

She was gone again before Jeb could reciprocate. He watched Susannah fluff the comforter once more, rearrange the bearpaw-printed bumper pads that lined the crib.

"Is that why you're flyin' around this nursery like Peter Pan? Showin' me what a fine wife and mother-to-be you are? You've already straightened those sheets once." Jeb's smile turned into a frown. Her behavior was all too familiar. "Come on to bed now. Or have you got an urge to clean this whole house tonight? Next thing, you'll be on your hands and knees, scrubbin' the bathroom floor . . . just like my mama used to do every time she was about to—"

His own words froze him in place, and he knew what was happening. Susannah's fingers were white on the crib rails, and she was breathing through her mouth. As soon as she started to relax, he spun her around.

"How the hell long have you been havin' these pains?"

"A while."

Jeb caught her shoulders. "Since when?"

"Dinnertime," she managed, then all the tension seemed to flow from her body. Her eyes, meeting his, showed the strain of the recurrent pain she'd been trying to hide, but she lifted her chin defiantly. "They weren't bad at first."

"Of course they weren't."

They'd started in her lower back, she said. No surprise to him. More false labor, she'd assumed. But Jeb knew better.

"How frequent?"

"I . . . can't say for sure. Sometimes six minutes or so, then almost right away. Then longer."

Jeb released her and ran into the hall. Leaning over the railing, he shouted: "Drake! John Eustace! Somebody get up here!"

Drake, who'd gone down for a nightcap, pounded up the stairs with John Eustace lumbering behind him, Leslie bringing up the rear, her hair in corkscrew curlers around her face, her eyes devoid of makeup, her spare body swathed in an old terrycloth robe.

"What's happening? What's wrong?" they all said. "Susannah?"

He turned stark eyes on his grandfather, who'd been the family physician all his life. "She's havin' the baby."

The old man clapped his shoulder, his grip surprisingly strong, and John Eustace's eyes cleared of his own pain. But then he'd never loved anything more than a medical crisis, with which he could deal.

"How far apart are her contractions?"

"She doesn't know. She just had a big one."

"I'm right here, Jeb," Susannah said, coming up behind him in the nursery doorway, sounding normal now. "Don't talk about me—or take care of me—as if I weren't."

Drake and John Eustace took charge, issuing orders in turn.

"Help her dress, boy."

"Leslie, get her overnight bag."

"Jeb, where's that doctor's name and number?"

"Susie, let me know when the next pain hits. We have to time them."

"Has your water broke?" John Eustace asked.

"Drake," Leslie trilled. "We're going to be grandparents!"

Jeb would have broken up laughing, but terror held him, as John Eustace had held Clary's life in his hands.

Susannah sagged against the hall railing. "Ohmygod . . ."

"Five minutes," Drake announced, establishing the pain interval with swift efficiency and calling the news to John Eustace, who by then was on the phone on the second-floor landing. Drake turned. "Jeb, where's the car?"

"It'll be around as soon as I call. PawPaw, get off the damn phone!"

"There you go," Susannah tried to joke, "with your favorite adjective."

His heart lodged in his throat. "*Damn*, where is my *damn* coat?"

"Take it easy, boy. This is the real world here. Women have babies every day."

Susannah had been born and bred to the social niceties, raised with them. She'd never screamed aloud in her life and promised herself she wouldn't start just because she was having a baby. She'd concentrate on easing Jeb's mind, she decided. She'd soothe his fears and erase his memories of Rachel and their son.

Jeb did his part and she would never forget his gentle back rubs on her spine, his hands kneading her shoulders. His trembling hands.

His reminders to breathe, to stay on top of the pains.

The chips of ice he fed her.

The comforting words he whispered in her ear.

The encouragement he offered when she faltered, his gaze linked with hers when she knew he wanted to turn away, not to let her see his worried eyes.

The private birthing room didn't resemble any hospital room she'd ever seen. Weeks before her due date, Jeb had arranged for her furniture to be delivered, set up and made to resemble, as closely as possible, a bedroom in her own home. It was common practice, he'd said, among the wealthy, like Leslie's friends, and with royalty. Susannah had felt like a princess, and greatly cherished. If only she wasn't in such pain now, with no way out but one, she would have enjoyed his efforts. But soon even the soft, classical Montoya guitar music from the stereo didn't soothe her.

Maybe she wasn't brave enough herself, strong enough.

"*Jeb!*" she yelled, plucking at the Indian star quilt he'd lent her for the occasion, feeling a gush of fluid between her legs, and then, "Oh God, I hate you for doing this to me!" Staring into her eyes, he flinched, and Susannah immediately added, "I'm sorry. I'm sorry. I didn't mean it."

"Yes, you did, sugar." His voice as tender as lovemaking, he used his endearment for her, a term Susannah had long ago accepted as more intimate between them than with any of his fans. "I don't blame you a bit. If I were in your place, I'd hate me too just now." Then, "Let me call a nurse before you float away. I think your water just broke. You're lyin' in a puddle."

The hours ticked past in increments of pain. In the lucid intervals, which grew shorter and less frequent, she talked with Jeb, at one point about Clary and the complex woman she had been.

"Neither of us ever knew who she really was," Jeb said at three in the morning, his eyes bleary, his jaw beard-shadowed. "Maybe like most of us, Clary was part good and part bad. And John Eustace simply saw her worst side. He can put blinders on when it pleases him. Look how he sees me . . . and I'm only human too."

He'd made his peace, Susannah knew. Earlier in the nursery he had chosen to believe that Clary meant her message for John Eustace, not for Jeb. And loving him, Susannah hadn't shattered his belief.

"I think your grandfather sees you pretty clearly." She paused, feeling the pain build again. "You needn't stop loving him, Jeb. Or Clary."

"You either," he said. The contraction peaked, and

this time her voice rose to a shriek, mortifying, essential. Sweating, weak, faint of heart, she hung on for Jeb's sake, her gaze fixed on his, their hands linked. If she lost it, if she left him, he'd be alone again. Remembering Rachel, remembering her. "I'm okay," he said, as if sensing her thoughts.

"How am I doing?" Susannah asked, prompting him to lean down and kiss her softly on the mouth.

"You're doin' fine."

The words—the reverse of his onstage greeting to his fans—made her smile at a moment when she couldn't have imagined smiling. Tears gathered in her eyes.

"All right, then," she whispered.

And the very air around her seemed to change. Susannah felt a new sense of purpose, of strength. She felt the need to push, in those next moments working harder than she'd ever worked at anything before. She pushed, then pushed some more, no longer hearing Jeb's encouragement beyond the deep, soft drone of his voice, feeling nothing but his enduring love and her own urge to bring forth the new life within her body.

When the baby at last slid free, into the doctor's waiting hands with her husband looking on, she felt another rush—of pure love. And joy.

"Jeb?"

His voice was filled with awe. "It's a girl."

Then he bent to kiss her.

He had stayed with her, cared for her, despite his fears. Despite her own, she had cared for him. They had taken care of each other. Susannah, feeling suddenly drained but entirely loved, promised herself they always would.

*　　*　　*

Rosy dawn light was already filtering through the drawn curtains an hour later when Susannah, freshly gowned and in a clean bed, placed their newborn daughter in Jeb's arms, trying not to notice that his hands were shaking. Badly, so that for an instant she feared he might drop her. As if by instinct, he tightened his arms around the baby and held on, and his gaze locked with Susannah's.

"She's beautiful, isn't she?" she whispered.

"So are you," Jeb said.

"I never knew life could be this peaceful, this happy." She watched the morning light slide over his hair, dip and glide into its rich color. Susannah cleared her throat. "I may not have acted like the lady my mother raised me to be awhile ago."

She'd even said she hated him once.

"Tell me now," he said, "how you really feel."

"I love you, Jeb. With all my heart."

"Same here." She could see it in his eyes. "I love you too." He leaned closer, taking care not to push against the baby in his arms, and kissed her mouth. Softly, warmly, gently. Then he sat back in the chair by her bed, gazing down at their daughter in a loving assessment that made Susannah's eyes burn.

"I think," he said after a moment, "we should name her—"

"Clary." She whispered it.

Jeb's eyes lifted to hers. "You think so too?"

"Clarice Cody."

"She may not have intended for us to get together, but she was the one who brought us to each other. Maybe that was her way of making things right. I think the name should have a second chance. Clarice Whittaker Cody," Jeb amended.

Her fingers, plucking at the sheet, went still.

"You and your family names," she murmured.

"It's okay?"

"It's perfect." *And oh, Jeb, so are you.*

The baby shifted, a series of minuscule, sinuous movements of limbs and then a wide yawn, drawing Jeb's gaze from Susannah. But not before she had seen in those bedroom eyes everything she needed to know, everything she'd ever wanted.

Jeb cradled their daughter closer and looked down at the now-sleeping baby in his steady arms; her hair, so like his own, dark silk against his forearm; her drowsy mouth pursed and suckling at empty air. In the otherwise silent room, the elemental nursing noises sounded loud, making him laugh a little.

"You're not gettin' any help from me, little girl," he said, his voice a throaty purr that soothed her instantly, as it alternately soothed and roused women everywhere. . . . Susannah, most of all, who knew that her child would never lack a father's love.

As he handed the baby to her, they brushed fingers and both looked down at the small, hour-old person between them. For a moment Jeb glanced away, as if overcome. Then he looked up again, a fraction of a second before his grin overtook the tears in his eyes.

"Oh, Susannah," he whispered. "I think I'm writin' a song."

Putting their baby to her breast, Susannah could already hear it.

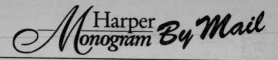

LORD OF THE NIGHT
by Susan Wiggs
A Venetian lord dedicated to justice suspects a lucious beauty of being involved in a scandalous plot.

ORCHIDS IN MOONLIGHT
by Patricia Hagan
Caught in a web of intrigue in the dangerous West, a man and a woman fight to regain their overpowering dream of love.

A SEASON OF ANGELS
by Debbie Macomber
Three willing but wacky angels must teach their charges a lesson before granting a Christmas wish.
National Bestseller

Desert Song by Constance O'Banyon

The enthralling conclusion of the passionate DeWinter legacy. As Lady Mallory Stanhope set sail for Egypt she was drawn to the strikingly handsome Lord Michael DeWinter, who was on a dangerous mission. From fashionable London to the mysterious streets of Cairo, together they risked everything to rescue his father, the Duke of Ravenworth, from treacherous captors.

A Child's Promise by Deborah Bedford

The story of a love that transcends broken dreams. When Johnny asks Lisa to marry him she knows it's the only way to make a new life for herself and her daughter. But what will happen when Johnny finds out she's lied to him? "A tender, uplifting story of family and love...You won't want to miss this one."—Debbie Macomber, bestselling author of *A Season of Angels*.

Desert Dreams by Deborah Cox

Alone and destitute after the death of her gambling father, Anne Cameron set out on a quest for buried treasure and met up with handsome and mysterious Rafe Montalvo, an embittered gunfighter. They needed each other in order to survive their journey, but could newfound passion triumph over their pasts?

One Bright Morning by Alice Duncan

Young widow Maggie Bright had her hands full raising a baby and running a farm on her own. The last thing she needed was a half-dead stranger riding into her front yard and into her life. As she nursed him back to health, she found herself doing the impossible—falling in love with the magnetic but difficult Jubal Green.

Meadowlark by Carol Lampman

Garrick "Swede" Swensen rescued a beautiful young woman from drowning only to find her alone, penniless, and pregnant. He offered Becky his name with no strings attached, but neither of them dreamed that their marriage of convenience would ever develop into something far more. When Swede's troubled past caught up with him, he was forced to make the decision of a lifetime.

Oh, Susannah by Leigh Riker

Socialite Susannah Whittaker is devastated by the death of her best friend, Clary, the sister of country music sensation Jeb Stuart Cody. An unlikely pair, Jeb and Susannah grow closer as they work together to unveil the truth behind Clary's untimely death, along the way discovering a passion neither knew could exist.